Praise for Lars Kepler's

LAZARUS

"Kepler treats us readers to a nonstop roller coaster of suspense, taking us deep into the hearts and minds of perfectly realized characters. And, oh, what a villain!" —Jeffery Deaver, *New York Times* bestselling author of *The Goodbye Man*

"Fast and furiously paced. . . . Intense, cinematic."
—*Evening Standard* (London)

"The Kepler duo are unmatched in their ability to crank up the tension, murder by murder, to an almost unbearable degree."
—*Air Mail*

"*Lazarus* is a thriller par excellence, though it's advisable to read it in small increments, for the accumulation of too much horror at one time will definitely lead to sleepless nights, continuous checking of locks, and an increase in one's lighting bill."
—*New York Journal of Books*

"The plot unfolds at an exhilarating pace as the Kepler duo keeps a tight grip on the cat-and-mouse action, a dynamic that reveals itself to be all the more disturbing as the novel progresses."
—*CrimeReads*

"Pulse-pounding. . . . Truly terrifying. . . . *Lazarus* is not for the faint of heart. . . . If you know you love dark and twisted, some-times painful, and sometimes disturbing crime fiction, this book will hold you hostage. . . . For fans of Kepler, this is a ride you will not forget."
—The Nerd Daily

"Creepy, thrilling.... Kepler's books are known for being action-packed, dark, and gory, and in *Lazarus*, they up the ante.... Fans of Kepler's superb serial killer thriller *The Sandman* will fall instantly in love.... *Lazarus* is a bloody, page-turning, action-packed serial killer thriller perfect for a weekend binge-read."
—*Crime by the Book*

"Kepler maintains an almost unbearable level of tension throughout and does an outstanding job of making readers fear that anyone could die a horrible death at any time. Fans of serial killer fiction won't want to miss this one."
—*Publishers Weekly* (starred review)

"Kepler combines explosive action with masterfully developed tension. Readers already onboard with this standout series will find a bar-raising entry here, and reassurance that the door is open for Joona's return. Strongly recommended for fans of Nicci French, Stieg Larsson, and Jussi Adler-Olsen."
—*Booklist* (starred review)

LARS KEPLER

LAZARUS

Lars Kepler is the pseudonym of the critically acclaimed husband-and-wife team Alexandra Coelho Ahndoril and Alexander Ahndoril. Their novels have sold more than fifteen million copies in forty languages. The Ahndorils were both established writers before they adopted the pen name Lars Kepler and have each published several acclaimed novels. They live in Stockholm, Sweden.

www.larskepler.com

ALSO BY LARS KEPLER

THE KILLER INSTINCT SERIES

The Hypnotist

The Nightmare

The Fire Witness

The Sandman

Stalker

The Rabbit Hunter

LAZARUS

A Killer Instinct Novel

LARS KEPLER

Translated from the Swedish by
NEIL SMITH

VINTAGE CRIME/BLACK LIZARD
Vintage Books
A Division of Penguin Random House LLC
New York

FIRST VINTAGE CRIME/BLACK LIZARD EDITION, NOVEMBER 2021

Copyright © 2018 by Neil Smith

All rights reserved. Published in the United States by Vintage Books, a division of Penguin Random House LLC, New York. Originally published in Sweden as *Lazarus* by Albert Bonniers Förlag, Stockholm, in 2018. Copyright © 2018 by Lars Kepler. Published in agreement with the Salomonsson Agency. This translation was originally published in hardcover in slightly different form in Great Britain by HarperCollins*Publishers* UK, London, and subsequently published in hardcover in the United States by Alfred A. Knopf, a division of Penguin Random House LLC, New York, in 2020.

Vintage is a registered trademark and Vintage Crime/Black Lizard and colophon are trademarks of Penguin Random House LLC.

The Library of Congress has cataloged the Knopf edition as follows:
Names: Kepler, Lars, author. | Smith, Neil (Neil Andrew), translator.
Title: Lazarus / Lars Kepler ; translated from the Swedish by Neil Smith.
Other titles: Lazarus. English.
Description: First edition. | New York : Alfred A. Knopf, 2020. | Series: Killer instinct.
Identifiers: LCCN 2020011629 (print) | LCCN 2020011630 (ebook)
Subjects: GSAFD: Mystery fiction.
Classification: LCC PT9877.21.E65 L3913 2020 (print) | LCC PT9877.21.E65 (ebook) |
    DDC 839.73/8—dc23
LC record available at https://lccn.loc.gov/2020011629
LC ebook record available at https://lccn.loc.gov/2020011630

Vintage Crime/Black Lizard Trade Paperback ISBN: 978-0-593-31083-0
eBook ISBN: 978-0-593-31784-6

Book design by Betty Lew

www.blacklizardcrime.com

Printed in the United States of America
10 9 8 7 6 5 4 3 2 1

LAZARUS

PROLOGUE

THE LIGHT OF THE WHITE SKY REVEALS THE WORLD IN ALL ITS cruelty, the way it must have appeared to Lazarus outside the tomb.

The ribbed metal floor is vibrating beneath the priest's feet. He clings to the railing with one hand and tries to maintain his balance with his walking stick in the other.

The gray sea is billowing like a tent canvas.

The ferry is being drawn along the two steel cables stretched between the islands. They rise, dripping out of the water in front of the boat, and sink back down behind it.

The ferry master brakes as foaming waves swell up and the gangplank extends with a clatter to the concrete jetty.

The priest stumbles slightly when the prow bumps the jetty. The jolt reverberates through the hull.

He's here to visit the retired churchwarden Erland Lind, who didn't show up for the Advent service in Länna Church as he usually does.

Erland lives in the parish's cottage behind Högmarsö Chapel. He suffers from dementia, but still gets paid to cut the grass and salt the driveway in icy weather.

The priest walks along the winding gravel path, his face turning numb in the cold air. There's no one in sight, but just before he reaches the chapel he hears the shriek of a lathe from the dry dock down in the boatyard.

He can no longer remember the Bible quote he tweeted that morning. He had been thinking of repeating it to Erland.

Against the backdrop of flat farmland and the strip of forest, the white chapel almost looks as if it's made of snow.

Because the church is shut for the winter, the priest walks directly to the small cottage and knocks on the door with his stick, waits, then goes inside.

"Erland?"

There's no one home. He stamps his shoes and looks around. The kitchen is a mess. The priest gets out the bag of cinnamon buns he brought and puts it down on the table, next to a foil tray with leftover mashed potatoes, dried-up gravy, and two gray meatballs.

The lathe down by the shore falls silent.

The priest goes outside, tries the door to the chapel, then looks into the unlocked garage.

There's a muddy shovel and a black plastic bucket full of rusting rattraps on the floor.

He uses his stick to lift the plastic covering a snowblower, but stops when he hears a distant moaning sound.

He goes back outside and walks over to the ruins of the old crematorium on the edge of the forest. The oven and the sooty stump of its chimney stick up from the tall weeds.

The priest walks around a stack of wooden pallets. He can't help looking over his shoulder.

He's had an ominous feeling ever since he boarded the ferry.

There's nothing reassuring about the light today.

He hears the odd moaning again, closer. It sounds like a calf trapped in a box.

He stops and stands still.

Everything is quiet. His breath steams from his mouth.

Behind the compost heap there's a patch of muddy, trodden ground. A bag of mulch leans against a tree.

The priest walks toward it but stops when he reaches a half-meter-long metal pipe sticking out of the ground. Perhaps it marks the property's boundary.

Leaning on his stick, he looks up at the forest and sees a path covered with pine needles and cones.

The wind is whistling through the treetops, and a solitary crow caws in the distance.

The priest turns around, and hears the strange moaning sound behind him. He picks up his pace. He passes the crematorium and cottage, and glances over his shoulder. All he wants right now is to get back to his vicarage and sit down in front of the fire with a glass of whiskey.

1

A DIRTY POLICE CAR DRIVES AWAY FROM CENTRAL OSLO. THE nettles beside the road tremble in the wind and an air-filled plastic bag rolls around in the ditch. Karen Stange and Mats Lystad are responding to the call even though it's late.

It's time for them to call it a day, but instead they're on their way to Tveita.

Residents in an apartment building have been complaining about a terrible smell. The maintenance company sent someone to check the garbage cans, but the smell turned out to be coming from an apartment on the eleventh floor. The neighbors could hear quiet singing inside, but the tenant, Vidar Hovland, wasn't answering the door.

Karen and Mats drive past an industrial park.

Behind the barbed-wire fence sit dumpsters, trucks, and piles of salt, ready for winter.

The apartment building on Nåkkves Road looks like a huge concrete staircase on its side split into three parts.

A man in gray overalls is waving to them. He's standing in front of a van with "Morten's Lock Service Ltd" printed on its side. Their headlights sweep over him, and the shadow of his raised hand reaches several stories up the building behind him.

Karen pulls over to the curb and stops gently. She and Mats get out of the car.

The sun has already set, and the air is cold. It feels like it might snow.

The two police officers shake hands with the locksmith. He's clean-shaven, and his cheeks are gray. His chest seems shrunken, and he moves in a twitchy, nervous way.

"Have you heard the one about the Swedish police being called to a cemetery? They've already found almost three hundred buried bodies," he jokes almost breathlessly. He looks down at the ground as he laughs.

The heavyset man from the building maintenance company is sitting in his pickup, smoking.

"The old guy probably left a trash bag full of fish in the hall," he mutters, then shoves the truck's door open.

"Let's hope so," Karen replies.

"I banged on the door and shouted through the mail slot. I said that I was going to call the police," he says, flicking the cigarette butt away.

"You did the right thing," Mats replies.

Dead bodies have been found here twice in the past forty years, one in the parking garage and the other inside one of the apartments.

The two officers and the locksmith follow the maintenance guy through the door and are immediately hit by the nauseating smell.

They all try to avoid breathing through their noses as they get into the elevator.

"The eleventh floor's a favorite," the maintenance guy says. "We had a difficult eviction there last year, and in 2013 one of the apartments was completely gutted by a fire."

"On Swedish fire extinguishers it says they have to be tested three days before any fire," the locksmith says.

The smell when the elevator opens is awful. The locksmith covers his nose and mouth with his hand, and Karen struggles to stop herself from retching. The maintenance man pulls his sweatshirt over his nose and points to the apartment with his other hand.

Karen walks over, puts her ear to the door, and listens. There's no sound from within. She rings the doorbell, and a subdued melody rings out.

Suddenly she hears a weak voice from inside the flat. A man's voice, singing or reciting something.

Karen bangs on the door, and the man falls silent, then starts again, very quietly.

"Let's go in," Mats says.

The locksmith walks over to the door, puts his heavy bag down on the floor, and unzips it.

"Can you hear that?" he asks.

"Yes," Karen replies.

Another apartment's door opens, and a small girl with tousled fair hair and dark rings under her eyes looks out.

"Go back inside," Karen says.

"I want to watch." The girl smiles.

"Are your mom and dad home?"

"I don't know," she says, and quickly shuts the door.

Rather than use a lock-pick gun, the locksmith drills the entire lock out. Shiny spirals of metal fly off and fall to the floor. He picks up the hot sections of the cylinder and puts them in his bag, pulls the bolt out, and then backs away.

"Wait here," Mats tells the maintenance guy and locksmith.

Karen draws her pistol as Mats pushes the door open and calls into the apartment.

"This is the police! We're coming in!"

Karen looks at the pistol in her pale hand. For a few moments, the black metal object looks completely alien.

"Karen?"

She looks up and meets Mats's eye, then raises the pistol, turns toward the apartment, and goes inside with her other hand over her mouth.

She doesn't see any trash bags in the hall. The stench must be coming from the bathroom or the kitchen.

The only sounds are her boots on the vinyl floor and her own breathing.

She walks past a narrow hall mirror and into the living room, quickly securing the corners and glancing around at the chaos. The television has been tipped over, potted ferns have been smashed. The sofa bed is standing askew, one of its cushions torn open, and the floor lamp is lying on its side.

She aims her pistol toward the hallway leading to the bathroom and kitchen, lets Mats move past her, and then follows him.

Their boots crunch on broken glass.

One wall lamp is lit, small dust particles hovering in its light.

She stops and listens.

Mats opens the bathroom door, then lowers his weapon. Karen tries to look in, but the door is blocking the light. All she can make out is a dirty shower curtain. She takes a step closer, leans forward, and nudges the door. Light reaches across the tiles.

The sink is smeared with blood.

Karen shudders. Then she suddenly hears a voice behind them. An old man, talking quietly. She's so startled that she lets out a yelp as she swings around and aims her pistol along the hallway.

No one is there.

She returns to the living room, hears a laugh, and points her gun at the sofa, her body full of adrenaline.

There could easily be someone hiding behind it.

Karen hears Mats trying to say something to her, but doesn't catch what.

Her pulse is throbbing in her head.

She moves forward slowly, her finger resting on the trigger, then notices she's shaking and steadies herself with her other hand.

The next moment, as the old man starts to sing again, she realizes that the voice is coming from the stereo.

Karen continues around the sofa, then lowers her weapon and stares at the dusty cables and empty bags of potato chips.

"Okay," she whispers to herself.

On top of the stereo is a CD case from the Institute for Language and Folklore. The same track is playing on a loop, over and over again. An old man says something in heavy dialect, laughs, then starts to sing—"There's a wedding here at our farm, with empty plates and cracked dishes"—before falling silent.

Mats is standing in the doorway, gesturing for her to move on, eager to get to the kitchen.

It's almost dark outside now. The curtains are quivering gently in the heat from the radiators.

Karen follows her partner into the hall. The air is thick with the smell of excrement and cadaver, strong enough to make their eyes water. She sways slightly and reaches out to the wall for support with the hand holding the pistol.

She can hear Mats taking short, shallow breaths, and focuses on not letting her nausea overwhelm her.

She follows him into the kitchen and stops.

On the linoleum floor lies a naked person with a bulging stomach and a swollen head.

A pregnant woman with a distended, gray-blue penis.

The floor lurches beneath her, and her vision contracts.

Mats is leaning against the chest freezer, moaning gently.

Karen tries to tell herself that she's in shock. She can see that the dead body is a man's, but the swollen stomach and spread thighs make her think of a woman giving birth.

She can feel her hands trembling as she puts her pistol back in its holster.

The body is in an advanced stage of decomposition. Large parts of it look slack and wet.

Mats crosses the floor and throws up so hard in the sink that the vomit splashes the coffeemaker on the counter.

The dead man's head looks like a blackened pumpkin. His jaw is broken, and the gullet and Adam's apple have been pushed out through the deformed mouth by the gases that have built up inside.

There was a fight, Karen thinks. He got injured, broke his jaw, hit his head on the floor, and died.

Mats vomits again, then spits out the bile.

Karen looks back to the man's stomach, parted legs, and groin.

Mats is sweating badly and his face is white. Just as she's about to go over and help him, someone grabs hold of her leg. She lets out a shriek. She fumbles for her pistol, then realizes it's the girl from the apartment next door.

"You're not allowed in here," she gasps.

"It's fun," the girl says, looking at her with dark eyes.

Karen's legs are shaking as she leads the child back through the apartment and out onto the landing.

"No one's allowed in," she says to the man from the maintenance company.

"I was just opening the window," he replies.

Karen really doesn't want to go back into the apartment. She knows she's going to end up having dreams about this, waking in the middle of the night with the man's spread legs etched on her retina.

When she enters the kitchen, Mats is shutting off the faucet in the sink. He looks at her with wet eyes.

"Are we done here?" she asks.

"Yes, I just want to look in the freezer," he says, pointing to the bloody fingerprints around the handle.

He wipes his mouth, opens the lid, and leans forward.

Karen watches as his head jerks back and his mouth opens without a sound.

He staggers backward, and the freezer slams shut so hard that it makes a coffee cup on the table jump.

"What is it?" she asks, walking closer.

Mats is clutching the edge of the sink. He knocks over a plastic bottle. His pupils have shrunk to the size of a drop of ink, and his face is unnaturally white.

"Don't look," he whispers.

"I need to know what's in the freezer," she says. She can hear the fear in her own voice.

"For the love of God, don't look. . . ."

2

DUSK IS FALLING SLOWLY. THE DARKNESS ONLY BECOMES apparent when the three greenhouses start to glow like rice-paper lanterns.

Valeria de Castro's curly hair is pulled into a ponytail. Her boots are caked with mud, and her padded red jacket is dirty. It fits tightly across her shoulders.

Her breath forms clouds in the crisp, frosty air.

She's done for the day. She pulls her gloves off as she heads up toward the house.

She goes upstairs, runs a bath, and puts her dirty clothes in the laundry basket.

When she turns toward the mirror, she notices some dirt is smeared on her forehead and her cheek is scratched from the bramble patch.

She needs to do something about her hair, she thinks. She smiles wryly at herself. She looks so happy.

She pulls the shower curtain back, leans one hand on the tiled wall, and steps into the bathtub. The water is hot, so she waits a second before lowering herself in.

She leans her head back against the edge of the bath, closes her eyes, and listens to the drops falling from the tap.

Joona is coming over this evening.

They had a fight. It was so stupid. She felt hurt, but it was all just a misunderstanding.

She opens her eyes and sees the reflections of the water on the ceiling. Rings from each droplet spread out across the surface.

The shower curtain has slipped along the rail, so she can no longer see the bathroom door and lock.

The water laps softly as she puts one foot up on the edge of the bath.

She shuts her eyes again and continues thinking about Joona, then realizes she's falling asleep and sits up.

Valeria is too hot now. She has to get out of the bath. She stands up and lets the water run off her body, then tries to look at the door in the mirror, but the glass has fogged up.

She carefully steps out of the bath onto the slippery floor, grabs a towel, and starts to dry herself.

She nudges the bathroom door open, waits a moment, then looks out onto the landing.

The shadows on the wallpaper are still.

Everything's silent.

She doesn't scare easily, but her time in prison has left her wary about certain situations.

She leaves the bathroom and walks across the cool landing and into the bedroom. Her body is steaming. It isn't completely dark yet—there are still some translucent clouds cutting across the sky.

She gets a clean pair of underwear from the chest of drawers and pulls them on, takes her yellow dress out of the closet, and lays it on the bed.

There's a noise downstairs.

Valeria freezes instantly.

She holds her breath, listening.

What could it have been?

She isn't expecting Joona for another hour or so, but she's already made a spicy lamb stew with fresh cilantro.

Valeria takes a step toward the window and has started to lower the blinds when she catches sight of someone standing next to one of the greenhouses.

She jerks back and loses her grip on the cord, and the blinds fly up with a bang.

There's a rattling sound as the cord gets tangled up in the blinds.

She quickly turns off the bedside lamp and goes back to the window.

No one is there.

She's almost certain she saw a man standing perfectly still at the edge of the forest.

He was as thin as a skeleton and was looking up at her.

The glass in the greenhouses is glinting with condensation. There's no one out there. She can't let herself be afraid of the dark.

Valeria tells herself that it's just a customer or supplier who disappeared when he saw her naked in the window. She often gets visitors after the nursery has closed for the day.

She reaches for her cell phone, but it's dead.

She quickly pulls on her long red bathrobe and starts to go downstairs. After just a few steps, she feels a cold breeze around her ankles. As she descends, she sees that the front door is wide open.

"Hello?" she calls quietly.

There are fallen leaves on the doormat. They've blown in across the wooden floor. Valeria slips her wet feet into her Wellington boots, grabs the large flashlight from the coatrack, and goes outside.

She follows the path down to the greenhouses, checks the doors, and shines the light between the rows of plants.

The dark leaves come into focus as shadows and reflections play across the glass walls behind them.

Valeria walks around the farthest greenhouse. The edge of the forest is black. The cold grass crunches beneath her feet as she walks.

"Can I help you with something?" she says loudly, pointing the light toward the trees.

The tree trunks look pale and gray in the light, but deeper in the woods there is nothing but darkness. Valeria walks past her old wheelbarrow. She can smell the rust on it. She carefully moves the beam from tree to tree.

The long grass looks untouched. In among the trunks she catches sight of something on the ground. It looks like a gray blanket covering a log.

The flashlight is getting weaker. She shakes it, and its strength improves. She moves closer.

As she holds a branch out of the way, she feels her heart start to beat faster, and the flashlight trembles in her hand.

It looks almost like there's a body under the blanket, someone hunched up, maybe missing one or both arms.

She has to pull the blanket off and look.

The forest is completely silent.

A dry branch snaps beneath her boot, and suddenly the whole edge of the forest is bathed in white light. It's coming from behind her, and when it moves, several long, thin shadows merge with hers as they slip across the ground.

3

JOONA LINNA LETS HIS CAR ROLL SLOWLY TOWARD THE FAR-
thest greenhouse. The narrow, cracked asphalt drive is lined with
tall grass and tangled forest.

He has one hand resting on the steering wheel.

There's a lonely look in his eyes, which are as gray as sea ice.

Joona keeps his hair cut short, because it sticks out in all directions if he lets it grow too long.

He's tall and muscular—a result of decades of hard exercise.

He's wearing a dark-gray jacket and a white dress shirt with the
top few buttons undone.

A bouquet of red roses is lying on the passenger seat beside him.

Before Joona Linna joined the Police Academy, he was in the
military, part of the Special Operations Group, where he qualified
for a cutting-edge course in the Netherlands on unconventional
close combat and urban guerrilla warfare.

Since Joona became a superintendent with the National Crime
Unit, he has solved more complex murder cases than anyone else
in Scandinavia.

Last autumn, Joona's prison sentence was reduced to community service as a neighborhood officer in Norrmalm in Stockholm.
He's been staying in one of the police service's apartments on Rörstrands Street, opposite the Philadelphia Church. In just a few
weeks' time, his dues will be paid and he will return to duty as a
superintendent, and get his office in police headquarters back.

Joona gets out and stands in the cool air.

The lights are on in Valeria's little house, and the front door is wide open.

The light from the kitchen window is spreading out through the bare branches of the weeping birch and across the frost-covered grass.

He hears a snapping sound from the forest and turns around. A weak light is moving among the trees. Leaves rustle as footsteps approach.

Joona carefully unfastens his holster with one hand.

He steps aside when he sees Valeria emerge from the forest with a flashlight in her hand. She's wearing a red bathrobe and Wellington boots. Her cheeks are pale and her hair is wet.

"What are you doing in the forest?" he asks.

She's looking at him oddly, as if her thoughts were a long way away.

"I was just checking the greenhouses," she says.

"In your bathrobe?"

"You're early," she points out.

"I know, it's very rude. I tried to drive slower," he says, fetching the bunch of roses.

She thanks him, looks at him with her big brown eyes, and invites him up to the house.

The kitchen smells like cumin and bay. Joona starts to say something about how hungry he is, then changes his mind and explains that he knows he's early and isn't in any rush to eat.

"It'll be ready in half an hour." She smiles.

"Perfect."

Valeria puts the flowers down on the table and goes over to the stove. She lifts the lid of the pan and stirs it, then puts her reading glasses on and checks the cookbook before adding chopped parsley and cilantro from the cutting board.

"You're staying the night, aren't you?" she asks.

"If that's okay."

"I mean, so you can have some wine," she explains with a blush.

"I guessed as much."

"You guessed as much," she says, imitating his Finnish accent with a wry smile.

"Yes."

She takes two glasses from one of the top cupboards, opens a bottle of wine, and pours it.

"I've made the bed in the spare room and left a towel and a toothbrush."

"Thanks," Joona says, taking the glass.

They drink a silent toast, tasting the wine and looking at each other.

"I didn't get to do this in prison," he says.

Valeria puts the roses in a vase on the table, then turns serious.

"I'm going to say it straight out," she begins, pulling at the belt of her old bathrobe. "I'm sorry I reacted the way I did."

"You've already apologized," Joona replies.

"I wanted to say it face-to-face. . . . I behaved stupidly and immaturely when I found out you were still a police officer."

"I know you thought I lied, but I—"

"It wasn't just that," she interrupts, and blushes again.

"Everyone likes a police officer, don't they?"

"Yes," she replies, trying so hard not to smile that the tip of her chin wrinkles.

She stirs the pot again, puts the lid back on, and lowers the heat slightly.

"Let me know if there's anything I can do."

"No, it's just . . . I was planning to do my hair and makeup before you came, so I'll just run up and do that now," she says.

"Okay."

"Do you want to wait here or keep me company?"

"I'll keep you company." Joona smiles.

They take their wineglasses upstairs and go into the bedroom. The yellow dress is still lying on the neatly made bed.

"You can sit in the armchair," Valeria mumbles.

"Thanks," he says.

"You don't have to watch."

He looks away as she takes the bathrobe off, pulls on the yellow dress, and starts to fasten the small buttons that run up from the waist.

"I don't usually wear dresses, just on the occasional summer day when I go into the city," she says, looking at her reflection in the mirror.

"Really beautiful."

"Stop looking," she says, smiling, as she fastens the last of the buttons over her breasts.

"I can't," he replies.

She moves closer to the mirror and starts to pin up her damp hair. Joona looks at her slender neck as she leans forward to put lipstick on. She sits down on the bed and picks up one of her earrings from the bedside table, then stops and meets his gaze.

"I think my reaction was because of that time in Mörby Centrum. . . . I'm still ashamed of that," she says quietly. "I don't even want to think about what you must have thought of me."

"That was one of my first operations with the Rapid Response Unit," he replies, looking down at the floor.

"I was an addict, a junkie."

"People take different paths, that's just how it is," he replies, looking her in the eye.

"But it upset you," she says. "I could tell . . . and I remember trying to counter my shame with a kind of hatred."

"You know, I could only ever picture you the way you were in high school. . . . You never answered any of my letters. I did my military service after that and ended up abroad."

"And I ended up in Hinseberg Prison."

"Valeria . . ."

"No, it was just so pointless, so fucking immature—I made every bad decision I possibly could. . . . And then I came close to ruining things for us again."

"You just weren't expecting me to go back to my job as a police officer," he says softly.

"Do you even know why I was in prison?"

"I've read the file. It's no worse than anything I've done."

"Okay, as long as you know that I'm no angel."

"Of course you are," he retorts.

Valeria looks at him, as if there's more to see, as if there's something hidden that might soon become apparent.

"Joona," she says seriously, "I know you're convinced that it's dangerous to spend time with you, that you expose the people you care about to danger."

"No," he whispers.

"You've been through some terrible things, for a very long time, but it doesn't always have to be that way. It's not written in the stars."

4

JOONA AND VALERIA ARE SITTING AT THE KITCHEN TABLE. The vase of roses has been moved to the counter so they can see each other. Joona is eating one last helping even though he's already full, and Valeria is wiping her plate with a piece of bread.

"Do you remember when we went on that canoe trip together?" Valeria asks, emptying the last of the wine into Joona's glass.

"I think about that summer a lot."

The two of them had decided to spend the night on a small island they had spotted. It lay in an inlet, and was barely bigger than a double bed, with soft grass, a few bare rocks, and five trees.

Valeria wipes the lipstick from the rim of her glass.

"Who knows how differently our lives might have turned out if that storm hadn't blown in," she says without looking at him.

"I was so in love with you in high school," he says, the same feelings washing over him again.

"I don't think it ever really stopped for me," she says.

He puts his hand on hers, and she looks at him with shimmering eyes before picking up another piece of bread.

Joona wipes his mouth on his napkin and leans back, making his chair creak.

"How's Lumi?" Valeria asks. "Is she doing okay in Paris?"

"I spoke to her on Saturday. She sounded happy; she was going to a party at Perrotin, which apparently is a gallery I should know about . . . and I asked if she was going to be out late and how she was going to get home."

"The worried dad," Valeria says with amusement.

"She said she'd probably get a taxi, and then I might have gotten a little annoying. I told her to make sure she sits behind the driver and puts the seat belt on."

"Okay." Valeria smiles.

"I realized she wanted to end the call, but I couldn't help telling her to take a photograph of the taxi driver's license and send it to me, and so on."

"She didn't send the picture, did she?"

"No," he says, laughing.

"Young people want us to care, but not too much. They want us to have faith in them."

"I know, but it just comes out—I have trouble not thinking like a police officer."

They remain seated at the table, drinking the last of the wine. They talk about the nursery and Valeria's two sons.

The darkness outside is thick now. Joona thanks her for the meal and starts to clear the table.

"Would you like me to show you the guest bedroom?" she says shyly.

When they stand up, Joona hits his head on the light, which makes a metal clanging sound. They go up the creaking staircase together to a narrow room with a deep window-alcove.

"Nice," he says, stopping right behind her.

She turns around and finds herself unexpectedly close to him, moves backward, and gestures slightly awkwardly toward the wardrobe.

"There are extra pillows in there . . . and blankets, if you're cold."

"Thanks."

"Or you could sleep in my bed, of course, if you like," she whispers, taking his hand and leading him with her.

She turns to face him in the doorway to her bedroom, stands on tiptoe, and kisses him. He kisses her back, puts his arms around her, and almost picks her up off the floor.

"Shall we make the sheets into a tent?" he whispers.

"That's what we always used to do." She smiles, and feels her heart beat faster.

She unbuttons his shirt and pushes it down over his shoulders, grabs his biceps and looks at him.

"It's funny. I remember your body, but you were just a tall boy back then. You didn't have all these muscles and scars."

He unbuttons her dress, kisses her on the lips and the side of her neck, then looks at her again.

She's slim, with small breasts. He remembers her dark nipples. Now she has tattoos on her shoulders, and her arms are muscular and covered with scratches from thorny shrubs.

"Valeria . . . how can you be so beautiful?" he says.

She pulls down her underpants and lets them fall to the floor, then steps out of them. Her pubic hair is black and tightly curled.

With trembling hands she starts to unbutton his pants, but can't quite figure out how the catch on his belt works and only succeeds in pulling it tighter.

"Sorry," Valeria says, giggling.

She blushes and forces herself not to stare too intently as he takes his pants off.

They pull the large duvet over themselves, then sit down beneath it on the bed, laughing and looking at each other in the soft light, before starting to kiss again.

They roll to one side, and push the duvet off. They feel like teenagers again, almost strangers, yet oddly familiar.

She sighs as he kisses her neck and lips. She sinks back onto the bed and looks into his intense gray eyes, feeling giddy, as if her heart is bursting with joy.

He kisses her breasts and carefully sucks one of her nipples. She pulls his head toward her face, and he feels her heart racing.

"Come here," she whispers, parting her legs as he lies on top of her.

Joona can't stop looking at her, her serious eyes, her half-open lips, her neck, the shadow of her collarbone.

Valeria pulls him closer and feels how hard he is as he slips inside her.

His weight presses her into the mattress, and the muscles in her thighs strain as her legs are pushed apart.

He feels her squeezing, moist warmth, then lets out a gasp as he changes rhythm.

She opens her eyes and sees the tenderness in his, and the lust.

She responds to his movements, and the soft light runs across her breasts, stomach, hips.

Her breathing speeds up, and she raises her hips, leans her head back, and closes her eyes.

The duvet slides to the floor.

The water in the glass on the bedside table is swaying, casting reflections that move in an elliptical pattern across the ceiling.

5

IT'S SUNDAY, AND THE EARLY-WINTER DAY IS SO DARK THAT it feels like it's already evening. Joona has spent the past two nights at Valeria's, but is going back to work tomorrow.

Valeria is sitting at the desk up in her bedroom, going through some business on her laptop, when she hears a car.

She looks out of the window and sees Joona put his shovel in the wheelbarrow and wave toward a white Jaguar that's approaching along the gravel driveway.

Joona tries to get The Needle to stop, but he drives straight over the row of potted hyacinths. There's a cracking sound as the pots break and damp compost sprays up around the tires. The car comes to a stop with one wheel perched on the tall edging stone.

Valeria stands in the window and watches as a tall man in aviator glasses gets out of the precariously balanced car. He's wearing a white lab coat under his unzipped parka. His thin nose is crooked and his cropped hair is gray. The Needle is a professor of forensic medicine at the Karolinska Institute and one of the leading experts in his field in Europe.

JOONA SHAKES HANDS WITH HIS OLD FRIEND AND SAYS HE looks paler than usual.

"You should be wearing a scarf," Joona says, trying to fasten The Needle's collar.

"Anja gave me this address," he says without returning Joona's smile. "I need to—"

He breaks off abruptly when he sees Valeria coming down the steps.

"What happened?" Joona asks.

Nils Åhlén's thin lips are colorless, and he has a hunted look in his eyes.

"I need to talk to you in private."

Valeria walks over to them and holds her hand out to the tall man.

"This is Valeria," Joona says.

"Professor Nils Åhlén," The Needle replies formally.

"Nice to meet you." Valeria smiles.

"I need to have a word with Nils," Joona says. "Is it okay if we go into the kitchen?"

"Of course," she says, and leads them up to the house.

"I'm sorry to have to disturb you on a Sunday," The Needle says.

"Don't worry, I was doing some work upstairs anyway," Valeria says, and heads for the stairs.

"Don't come down—I'll let you know when we're done," Joona calls after her.

"Okay."

Joona shows The Needle into the kitchen and invites him to sit down. The fire in the stove crackles.

"Would you like coffee?"

"No thanks . . . I won't . . ."

He trails off and sinks onto a chair.

"So how are you really doing?"

"This isn't about me," The Needle replies, sounding troubled.

"So what happened?"

Nils doesn't meet his gaze, just brushes the tabletop with one hand.

"I have a lot of dealings with my colleagues in Norway," he begins tentatively. "And I just got a call from the Norwegian Institute of Public Health. . . . That's where their Forensic Medicine and Pathology departments are based these days."

"I know."

The Needle swallows hard, takes his glasses off, makes a half-hearted attempt to polish them, and then puts them back on.

"Joona, I'm sitting here, but I still don't know how on earth to tell . . . I mean, not without you . . ."

"Just tell me what happened."

Joona pours a glass of water and puts it down in front of The Needle.

"As I understand it, the Norwegian Criminal Police have taken over the preliminary investigation into a suspected murder from the Oslo Police. . . . They found a dead man in an apartment. All the evidence suggested a run-of-the-mill drunken fight at first, but when they looked in the victim's freezer they found body parts belonging to a large number of different people, frozen at various stages of decomposition. . . . They're working on the theory that the dead man was a previously unknown grave robber; he may also have been involved in necrophilia and cannibalism. . . . He used to travel around to fairs and auctions as an antiques dealer, and took the opportunity to raid local graves and help himself to souvenirs."

Nils Åhlén takes a sip of water, then wipes his top lip with a trembling finger.

"What does this have to do with us?"

Nils meets Joona's gaze for the first time. "He had Summa's skull in his freezer."

"My Summa?"

Joona reaches out for the counter and knocks over the empty wine bottle, but he doesn't appear to notice as it clatters into the sink with the glasses and plates.

"Are you sure?" he whispers, looking out of the window at the greenhouses.

The Needle pushes his glasses farther up his nose and explains that the Norwegian police have tried to find matches for DNA from the body parts found in the freezer in police databases.

"They found Summa's dental records. And, because I signed her death certificate, they called me."

"I see," Joona says, and sits down opposite his friend.

"They found all his travel documents in his apartment. In the middle of November, he was at an estate sale in Gällivare. That's not far from where Summa is buried."

"Are you sure about this?" Joona repeats.

"Yes."

"Can I see the pictures?"

"No," The Needle whispers.

"You don't have to worry," Joona says, looking him in the eye.

"Don't do it."

But Joona has already opened his case and taken out the file from the Norwegian Criminal Police. He lays down one photograph after another on the kitchen table.

The first one shows the open freezer from above. A child's gray foot is sticking out of a frosted lump of white ice. A skeletal spine is nestled next to a bearded face and a bloody tongue.

Joona leafs through photographs of the thawing body parts on a stainless-steel counter. A human heart in an advanced state of decay, a leg cut off at the knee, an entire baby's body, three fleshless craniums, some teeth, and a torso complete with breasts and arms.

Suddenly Valeria walks into the kitchen and puts two used coffee cups on the drying rack.

"For God's sake!" Joona snaps, trying to cover the pictures, even though he knows she's already seen them.

"Sorry," she mumbles and hurries out.

He gets to his feet, leans one hand against the wall, and stares out at the greenhouses, then turns again to the pictures.

Summa's skull.

It's just a coincidence, he tells himself. The grave robber didn't know who she was. There's no indication on the gravestone, and nothing in any of the public registers.

"What do we know about the assailant?" he asks after he hears Valeria go back upstairs.

"Nothing; they have no leads at all."

"And the victim?"

"All the evidence suggests a fight in the apartment. He had a lot of alcohol in his blood when he died."

"Isn't it a bit strange that the police don't have any leads on the other person?"

"What are you thinking, Joona?" Nils Åhlén asks apprehensively.

6

VALERIA IS SITTING UPSTAIRS AT HER COMPUTER WHEN Joona comes up and knocks on the door.

As she turns toward him, the pale light through the leaded window gives her hair a chestnut-red shimmer.

"Nils is gone," Joona says in a subdued voice. "Sorry I was angry, I just didn't want you to have to see that."

"I'm not so fragile," she replies. "You know, I've seen dead bodies plenty of times."

"For me, this is personal," Joona says, then falls silent.

There's a family grave in Stockholm with the names Summa Linna and Lumi Linna on the headstone, but the urns under the ground don't contain their ashes. The deaths of Joona's wife and daughter were fabricated, and they lived on for many years in a secret location with new names.

"Let's go down to the kitchen and heat that soup up," Valeria says after a while.

"What?"

She gives him a hug, and he wraps his arms around her and rests his cheek against her head.

"Let's go and eat," she repeats quietly.

They go down to the kitchen, and she takes the soup out of the fridge. She puts the pan on the stove and turns the burner on, but when she switches on the light in the exhaust fan, Joona walks over and turns it off.

"So—what happened?" Valeria asks.

"Summa's grave has been vandalized and . . ."

Joona stops speaking and turns his face away. She sees him wipe tears from his cheeks.

"You're allowed to cry, you know," she says gently.

"I honestly don't know why this upsets me so much. . . . Someone has dug up her grave and taken her skull back to Oslo with him."

"God," she whispers.

He goes and stands by the window and looks out at the greenhouses and forest. Valeria can see that he's closed the curtains in the living room, and there's a knife lying on the old dresser.

"You know Jurek Walter's dead," she says in a serious voice.

"Yes," Joona whispers, closing the curtains at the kitchen window.

"Do you want to talk about him?"

"I don't think I can," he says simply, and turns toward her.

"Okay," she replies in a composed voice. "But you don't have to keep anything from me; I can handle it, I promise. . . . I know what you did to save Summa and Lumi, and I understand that he's a monster."

"He's worse than anything anyone could ever imagine. He digs his way inside of you . . . and leaves you hollowed out."

"But it's over now," Valeria whispers, and reaches out toward him. "You're safe now, he's dead."

Joona nods. "This has dredged it all up again. . . . It's like I could feel his breath on the back of my neck when I heard what had happened to Summa's grave."

Joona goes to the window again and peers out between the curtains. Valeria looks at his back in the gloom of the kitchen.

They sit down at the kitchen table, and she asks him to tell her more about Jurek. Joona puts his hands on the table to stop them from shaking and says in a low voice: "He was diagnosed with nonspecific schizophrenia, chaotic thinking, and acute psychosis characterized by bizarre and extremely violent behavior, but that doesn't mean a thing. He was never schizophrenic—the only thing that the diagnosis shows is how terrified the psychiatrist who conducted the evaluation was."

"Was he a grave robber?"

"No," Joona says.

"There you are, then," she says, and tries to smile.

"Jurek Walter would never bother with trophies," he says heavily. "He wasn't a pervert . . . but he had a passion for ruining people's lives. Not killing them, not torturing them . . . not that he would have hesitated to do either in an instant, but to understand him you have to realize that he wanted to destroy his victims' souls, extinguish the spark inside them. . . ."

Jurek wanted to take everything away from his victims, then watch as they struggled through life—going to work, eating, watching television—until the terrible moment when they realized that they were already dead.

They sit in near-darkness as Joona talks to Valeria. Jurek is the worst serial killer in Nordic history, but the public doesn't even know who he is, because all information about him has been classified.

Joona explains how he and his partner, Samuel Mendel, began to close in on him. They took turns keeping watch outside one particular woman's home. Her two children had gone missing in circumstances that were reminiscent of a number of other cases.

It was as if they'd been swallowed up by the earth.

A very high percentage of missing people in recent years came from families in which someone else had already gone missing.

Joona falls silent, and Valeria watches as he knits his hands together in an attempt to hold them still. She gets up to make some tea, and fills two mugs before sitting down again and waiting for him to go on.

"The weather had been mild for two weeks. It was beginning to thaw, but that day it started to snow again," he says. "So now there was fresh snow on top of what was already there. . . ."

Joona has never spoken about those last hours, when Samuel arrived to relieve him.

A thin man had been standing at the edge of the forest, staring up at the window where the woman whose children had gone missing was lying asleep.

The man's face, so thin and wrinkled, was completely impassive.

Joona started thinking that the very sight of the building seemed to give the man a feeling of contentment, as if he were already dragging his victim off into the forest.

The thin figure watched for a while before turning back and vanishing.

"You're thinking back to the first time you saw him," Valeria says, putting her hand over his.

Joona looks up and realizes that he's stopped talking, and nods before telling her that he and Samuel had followed the fresh trail of footprints.

"We ran along an old railroad track, into Lill-Jans Forest. . . ."

But in the darkness among the trees they lost the man's trail. Suddenly there was nothing to go on, and they started to head back.

As they were walking back along the railroad track, they saw that the man had left the rails and set off into the forest instead.

Because the ground beneath the fresh snow was wet, his shoes had left dark prints. Half an hour before, they had been white, impossible to see in the weak light, but now they were as dark as cast iron, unmistakable.

In the forest, they heard a whimpering, moaning sound.

It sounded like someone crying from the very depths of hell.

Between the tree trunks, they spotted the man they had been pursuing. The ground was dark with freshly dug soil around a shallow grave. A filthy, emaciated woman was trying to get out of a coffin. She was sobbing as she struggled, but every time she was close to climbing out, the man shoved her back down.

They drew their pistols and rushed in. They pinned the man on the ground, and cuffed his hands and ankles.

Samuel was sobbing as he called the ambulance.

Joona helped the woman out of the coffin and put his coat around her. He held her and told her that help was on its way; then he saw a flash of movement between the trees. Some of the branches had been disturbed—the snow on them was falling softly to the ground.

"Someone had been standing there watching us," he says quietly.

The fifty-year-old woman survived, even though she had been in the coffin for almost two years. Jurek Walter had appeared from time to time, opening the coffin and giving her water and food. She had gone blind, was badly emaciated, and had lost her teeth. Her muscles had withered away, and she was crippled by sores. Her hands and feet were both badly frostbitten. At first she was thought to be merely traumatized, but it turned out she had suffered severe brain damage.

Large parts of the forest were cordoned off that same night. The following morning, a police dog identified something suspicious just two hundred meters from where the woman had been buried. Excavations uncovered the remains of a man and a boy, buried in a blue plastic barrel. It was later confirmed that they had been buried alive four years before, but hadn't survived for long, even though a tube supplied the barrel with air.

Joona can see that Valeria is shaken. All the color has drained from her face, and she has one hand clasped over her mouth.

She's thinking back to Joona's description of the first time he saw Jurek, standing in the snow beneath the window of his next victim. It reminds her of the man she saw on Friday, at the edge of the forest next to the greenhouse. She should probably tell Joona about that, but doesn't want to give him any reason to think that Jurek is still alive.

7

A PROSECUTOR TOOK OVER THE INVESTIGATION AFTER Jurek was arrested, but Joona and Samuel conducted the interviews.

"It's hard to understand, but somehow Jurek Walter got inside the head of anyone who got close to him," Joona says, meeting Valeria's gaze. "Despite the way it seems, there's nothing supernatural about it—he just had a cold awareness of human weakness. He would pick up on something fundamental and then use it to immobilize you. You completely lost the ability to defend yourself.

"Jurek Walter didn't confess to anything while in custody. He didn't claim to be innocent, either. He spent most of his time taking us through a philosophical deconstruction of the concepts of crime and punishment.

"I didn't realize until the closing arguments that Jurek's plan was to get me or Samuel to say that there was a possibility that he was innocent ... that he had merely stumbled upon the grave and was trying to help the woman out when we arrested him."

One evening when Joona and Samuel were running together, Samuel raised the hypothetical question of what would have happened if anyone other than Jurek had been beside the grave when they arrived.

"I can't help thinking about it," Samuel said, "that anyone who had been standing by the grave at that moment would have been prosecuted."

It was true that there wasn't any concrete evidence. It was mostly the circumstances of the arrest and the lack of any adequate alternative explanation that had supported the prosecution.

Joona knew Jurek was dangerous, but at the time he had no idea just what level of danger they were dealing with.

Samuel Mendel became more withdrawn. He couldn't handle it. He couldn't take being in Jurek's vicinity. He felt dirty, like his soul was being poisoned.

"Even though I don't want to, I find myself saying things that suggest he could be innocent," Samuel said.

"He's guilty ... but I think he's got an accomplice," Joona replied.

"Everything points to a lone madman."

"He wasn't alone at the grave when we got there," Joona interrupted.

"Yes, he was. You just think he wasn't because he's been manipulating us, making you think that you saw the real perpetrator fleeing into the forest."

Joona has thought about the last conversation he had with Jurek before the trial's closing arguments many times.

Jurek was sitting on a chair in the heavily guarded interview room, his lined face staring down at the floor.

"It's completely irrelevant to me if I'm found guilty, even though I'm innocent," he said. "I'm not afraid of anything, not pain, not loneliness, not boredom. The court's going to go along with the prosecutor . . . and they're going to say my guilt has been proved beyond reasonable doubt."

"You're refusing to defend yourself," Joona says.

"I refuse to engage with technicalities. Digging a grave and filling it in are basically the same thing."

Joona knew he was being manipulated. Jurek needed him on his side in order to be released. That was why he was trying to sow seeds of doubt. Joona knew what Jurek was up to, but, still, he couldn't ignore the fact that there was a crack in the case.

"He thought he'd won you over," Valeria says in a frightened voice.

"I know that he thought we had an agreement."

During the trial, Joona was called as a witness to talk about the arrest.

"Is it possible that Jurek Walter was in fact trying to rescue the woman from the grave?" the defense lawyer asked.

An internal compulsion was nudging Joona toward the edge, pushing him to agree that this was within the bounds of plausibility. Joona began to nod in response, but stopped and forced himself to go back to his exact memory of the appalling scene in the forest clearing, where Jurek Walter was unquestionably shoving the woman back into the grave every time she tried to crawl out.

"No . . . he was the person keeping her captive in the grave. He's the one who killed them all," Joona replied.

After due consideration, the Chair of the Court declared that Jurek Walter was being sentenced to secure psychiatric treatment. There would be specific restrictions on any eventual parole proceeding.

Before he was taken out of the court, Jurek turned toward Joona. His face was covered with tiny wrinkles, and his pale eyes looked strangely empty.

"Now Samuel Mendel's sons are going to disappear," Jurek said calmly. "And Samuel's wife, Rebecka, will disappear. But . . . No, listen to me, Joona Linna. The police will look for them, and when the police give up, Samuel will keep looking, but when he eventually realizes that he'll never see his family again, he'll kill himself. . . ."

Light was playing through the leaves in the park outside, casting quivering, transparent shadows across his thin figure.

"And your little daughter," Jurek went on, looking down at his fingernails.

"Be careful," Joona said.

"Lumi will disappear," Jurek whispered. "And Summa will disappear. And when you realize that you're never going to find them . . . you're going to hang yourself."

He looked up and stared directly into Joona's eyes. His face was quite calm, as if things had already been settled.

"I'm going to grind you into the dirt," Jurek said quietly.

Joona goes over to the curtains and looks out at the darkness, where the branches of the birch trees are blowing in the wind.

"You haven't told me much about your friend Samuel," Valeria says.

"I've tried, but . . ."

"It wasn't your fault that his family went missing."

Joona sits down again.

"I was sitting at home, at the kitchen table, with Summa and Lumi. . . . She'd just made spaghetti and meatballs when Samuel phoned. . . . He was so upset that it took a while for me to realize that Rebecka and the boys had left for the house on Dalarö several hours earlier but never arrived. He'd already been in touch with the hospitals and the police. . . . He tried to pull himself together, tried to take deep breaths, but his voice still broke when he asked me to check and make sure that Jurek hadn't escaped."

"Which he hadn't," Valeria said.

"No, he was still in his cell."

All traces of Rebecka and the boys disappeared on the gravel road just five meters in front of their abandoned car. The police dogs couldn't pick up any scent. A thorough search of the forests, roads, buildings, and nearby bodies of water was conducted for two months. When the police and volunteers had given up, Samuel and Joona continued looking on their own, without ever talking about what they feared most.

"Jurek Walter had an accomplice, and he took Samuel's family," Valeria says.

"Yes."

"And then it was your turn."

Throughout this period, Joona kept watch over his family, went with them everywhere, but he realized that this wasn't going to be enough, not in the long term.

Samuel stopped looking, and returned to work a year or so after his family went missing, but he lasted only three weeks before finally giving up hope. He drove to his summer house, went down to the beach where his sons used to swim, and shot himself in the head with his service weapon.

Joona tried talking to Summa about moving, about starting a new life, but she didn't appreciate just how dangerous Jurek Walter was.

At first he tried to find a way all of them could get out together: perhaps they could get new identities and live quietly in some distant country.

Still, deep down he knew that wouldn't be enough. New, secret identities wouldn't be 100 percent secure. They would merely offer a grace period.

"But why didn't you just take off together?" Valeria whispers.

"I would have given anything to do that, but ..."

When Joona realized what had to be done, it became an obsession. He started to work on a plan that could save all three of them.

There was one thing more important to him than being with Summa and Lumi.

Their lives.

If he took off or disappeared with them, it would be a direct challenge to Jurek's accomplice. And if you look for people who are trying to hide, you always find them sooner or later. So you can't give them any reason to look, he thought.

There was only one solution: Jurek and his shadow needed to believe that Summa and Lumi were dead. Joona was going to arrange a car accident and make it look like they were both killed.

"But why not all three of you?" Valeria exclaimed. "You could have pretended that you were in the car as well—that's what I would have done."

"Jurek would never have believed that. My solitude was what tricked him, the fact that I lived alone year after year. He assumed that no one would be able to sustain that, not without eventually being lulled into a false sense of security and giving in to the temptation to see their family."

"So you thought you were being watched by his shadow the whole time."

"I was," Joona says in a hollow voice.

"We know that now, but did you ever see anyone?"

"No."

Several years later, Joona knows he did the right thing. They all paid a high price, but it saved Summa's and Lumi's lives.

"Jurek's twin brother, Igor, was helping him the whole time," Joona says. "It was appalling. . . . He had no life of his own. He was mentally traumatized. His only purpose in life was to execute Jurek's will."

Joona falls silent and thinks of the scars on Igor's back, evidence of a lifetime of abuse from a razor strap.

When Jurek escaped after fourteen years in isolation, he carried out his plan like nothing had happened. A lot of people lost their lives in the terrible days Jurek Walter was free.

"But both Jurek and his brother are dead now," Valeria points out.

"Yes."

Joona thinks of how he shot the brother three times in the heart from close range. The bullets went right through his body, and Igor was thrown backward into a gravel pit. Even though Joona knew Jurek's twin brother had to be dead, he still shuffled down the steep slope to make absolutely sure.

Saga Bauer shot Jurek and saw his body get carried away by a river and washed out to sea.

By the time Joona was finally reunited with his wife, Summa, she was dying of cancer. He took her and Lumi to a house in Nattavaara, in the far north of Sweden. The little family had six months together. When Summa died, they buried her where her grandmother grew up, in Purnu in Finland.

It wasn't until a year later that Joona finally dared to believe it was really over, when Saga found the remains of Jurek's body, and the fingerprints and DNA analysis confirmed that it was definitely him.

Joona felt he could finally breathe again.

The grief and psychic wounds from Joona's time chasing Jurek will always be there, and Saga Bauer hasn't been the same since she went undercover to infiltrate the secure facility where he was imprisoned. She's become darker, and sometimes Joona can't help thinking that she's trying to run away from her fate.

8

SAGA BAUER IS RUNNING ACROSS THE OLD SKANS BRIDGE. She sprints through the damp shadows of the newer bridges up above. Heavy traffic is thundering past her.

She lengthens her stride as she approaches the other side. Her T-shirt across her chest is dark with sweat.

She runs all the way to the district of Gamla Enskede after work almost every day to pick up her half-sister, Pellerina, from school.

Saga has reconnected with her father after being estranged from him since she was a teenager. Even though they've worked through the worst of the misunderstandings, Saga is finding it hard to slip back into being someone's daughter. Maybe they'll never be able to fix their relationship completely.

Saga speeds up as she passes beneath the echoing viaduct that carries Nynäs Street and the railroad tracks.

She's muscular, like a ballet dancer, and strikingly beautiful. Her long blond hair is braided with colorful ribbons, and her eyes are a piercing blue.

Saga is an officer with the Swedish Security Police, but this fall her boss kept her off active duty. She had to write reports and take part in turgid meetings about cooperation between the police in Sweden and the United States. In order to avoid open disagreement and internal criticism, the collaboration has been declared a great success. Among other things, it forced Saga and Special Agent Lopez of the FBI to become friends on Facebook.

Saga passes the dismal-looking rec center and heads into the suburbs, then sprints the last stretch before she gets to Enskede School.

Dust is flying up from the soccer field, drifting through the tall chain-link fence.

Pellerina is twelve now but isn't allowed to go home on her own when school lets out. She stays behind to participate in after-school activities until she's picked up.

Pellerina has Down syndrome and was born with Fallot's tetralogy, a combination of four different heart defects that prevented blood from getting to her lungs. She had a stent installed when she was four weeks old and had to undergo serious heart surgery before her first birthday. She has learning difficulties but is able to attend a regular school with the help of specially trained assistants.

Saga's pulse and breathing calm down as she walks around the school and approaches the door to after-school care. She can see her little sister through the window. Pellerina looks happy. She's jumping around and laughing with two other girls.

Saga enters through the coat room and takes her shoes off beside the line of tape on the floor. She can hear music from the dance-and-yoga room and stops in the doorway.

A pink shawl has been draped over a lamp. The bass of the music is making one of the windows rattle, and the paper snowflakes stuck to it seem to dance.

Saga recognizes Anna and Fredrika from her sister's class, both a head taller than Pellerina.

They're all barefoot. Their socks are lying in the dust beneath one of the chairs. They're standing in a row in the middle of the floor, counting off the music, then wiggling their hips, taking a step forward, clapping their hands, and spinning round.

Pellerina is smiling widely as she dances. Saga can see that she's doing the routine well—she's learned all the moves—but she's a bit too enthusiastic, jutting her hips out more than the other two girls.

Anna turns the music off. Out of breath, she tucks a lock of hair behind her ear and claps her hands.

From her vantage point over by the door, Saga sees the two

girls exchange a look above Pellerina's head, and Fredrika makes a mocking face, which makes Anna laugh.

"Why are you laughing?" Pellerina asks, still panting as she puts her thick glasses back on.

"We're laughing because you're so clever and pretty," Fredrika says, stifling a giggle.

"You're both clever and pretty, too," Pellerina says with a smile.

"But not as pretty as you," Anna says.

"Yes, you are." Pellerina laughs.

"You should think about going solo," Fredrika says.

"What does that mean?" Pellerina asks, pushing her glasses farther up her nose.

"That it might be better if we filmed you dancing on your own . . ."

Fredrika stops abruptly when Saga walks into the room. Pellerina runs over and hugs her.

"Are you having fun?" Saga asks calmly.

"We're practicing our dance," Pellerina replies.

"Is it going well?"

"Really well!"

"Anna?" Saga says, looking at the girl. "Is it going well?"

"Yes," she says, and glances at Fredrika.

"Fredrika?"

"Yes."

"I know you're both nice girls," she says. "Let's keep it that way."

Saga waits in the coat room as Pellerina hugs her teaching aide several times, pulls on her winter overalls, and puts her drawings in a bag.

"They're the coolest girls in the class," Pellerina explains as they walk across the schoolyard, hand in hand.

"But if they tell you to do funny things, you should say no," Saga says as they walk home.

"I'm a big girl."

"You know I'm a worrier," Saga explains, feeling a lump in her throat.

She squeezes Pellerina's hand and thinks about the girls making faces over her head. It sounded like they were thinking of filming Pellerina to send around online and mock her.

Afterward, people always claim these things are just innocent games that get out of hand. But really, there is never any doubt about its simple cruelty.

9

PELLERINA LIVES WITH HER DAD IN A BRIGHT-RED HOUSE with a red-tiled roof on Björk Street in Gamla Enskede. The old apple trees and the grassy lawn are sparkling with tiny ice crystals.

As Saga closes the gate, Pellerina runs to the door and rings the bell.

Lars-Erik Bauer is wearing cords and a crumpled white dress shirt that's open at the neck. He's due for a haircut, but his gray, unkempt hair makes him look appealingly eccentric. Every time Saga sees her father, she's struck by how old he is now.

"Come in," he says, and helps Pellerina out of her overalls. "You're welcome to stay for dinner, Saga."

"I don't have time," Saga replies automatically.

Pellerina's thick glasses have steamed up. She takes them off and clambers up the stairs to her room.

"I'm making macaroni and cheese; I know that's one of your favorites."

"When I was little."

"Just let me know what you'd like—I can go to the store," her dad says.

"Stop it," she says with a smile. "It doesn't matter, I'll eat anything. Macaroni and cheese will do just fine."

Lars-Erik looks genuinely delighted that she will stay for a while. He takes her coat, hangs it up, and tells her to make herself at home.

"I'm worried that a couple of the girls at that after-school club aren't being very nice," Saga says.

"In what way?" her dad asks.

"I don't know, just a feeling—they were making faces."

"Pellerina usually handles things well on her own, but I'll talk about it with her," he says before they head upstairs to her sister's room.

Lars-Erik is a cardiologist, and has bought an EKG machine so he can monitor Pellerina's heart, since she could suffer a recurrence of her earlier problems.

Saga looks at her sister's latest drawings while their dad connects the electrodes to her chest. The pale scar from her operations runs vertically down her breastbone.

"I'm going to start dinner," Lars-Erik says, and leaves.

"I've got a silly heart," Pellerina sighs, putting her glasses back on.

"You've got the best heart in the world," Saga says.

"Daddy says I'm all heart." She smiles.

"He's right—and you're the best little sister in the universe."

"You're the best. You look just like Elsa," Pellerina whispers, reaching out for Saga's long hair.

Usually it annoys Saga when anyone compares her to a Disney princess, but she likes the fact that Pellerina sees herself and Saga as the two sisters in *Frozen*.

"Saga?" Lars-Erik calls from the bottom of the stairs. "Can you come down here for a moment?"

"I'll be back soon, Anna," she says, patting her sister's cheek.

"Okay, Elsa."

Lars-Erik is chopping leeks when Saga walks in. There's a package on the kitchen table. It's wrapped in aluminum foil and has a paper heart stuck on top, with the words "To my darling daughter, Saga."

"I ran out of wrapping paper," he says apologetically.

"I don't want presents, Dad."

"It's nothing, just a little token."

Saga tears the foil off, crumples it into a shiny ball. Inside is a flowery cardboard box.

"Open it," Lars-Erik says with a wide smile.

The box contains an old-fashioned porcelain Christmas elf,

carefully packed in shredded paper. He's wearing a tree-green outfit, has piercing eyes, pink cheeks, and a cheerful little mouth. He's holding a large bowl in his arms.

Her Christmas elf, which used to get brought out every Christmas and filled with pink and yellow toffees.

"I've been looking for one . . . well, for ages, really," Lars-Erik says. "And today I just happened to wander into an antique shop in Solna, and there he was."

Saga remembers that her mom threw the elf on the floor once when she was angry with her dad, smashing it to pieces.

"Thanks, Dad," she says, and puts the box down on the table.

When she goes back up to see Pellerina, she notices that her heart rate has increased, as though she has been running. Pellerina is staring at her phone open-mouthed, with a look of horror on her face.

"What happened?" Saga asks in a concerned voice.

"No one can see, no one can see," her sister says, pressing the phone to her chest.

"Dad!" Saga calls.

"It's not allowed!"

"Don't worry, sweetheart," Saga says. "Just tell me what you were looking at."

"No."

Lars-Erik hurries up the stairs and comes into the bedroom.

"Tell Daddy," Saga says.

"No!" Pellerina cries.

"What is it, Pellerina? I'm in the middle of cooking," he says, to encourage her to speak.

"It's something on her phone," Saga explains.

"Show me," Lars-Erik says, and holds out his hand.

"It's not allowed," Pellerina says, sobbing.

"Says who?" he asks.

"The e-mail."

"I'm your dad, so I'm allowed to see."

She hands him the phone, and he reads it with a frown.

"Oh, sweetheart," he says with a smile, putting the phone down. "It isn't real—you know that, don't you?"

"I have to forward it, otherwise . . ."

"No, you don't have to; we don't send silly e-mails in this family," Lars-Erik says firmly.

"One of those chain e-mails?" Saga asks.

"Yes, a really silly one," he replies, then turns back to Pellerina. "I'll get rid of it."

"No, please!" she pleads, but Lars-Erik has already deleted it.

"It's all gone now," he says, and hands the phone back to her. "We can forget all about it."

"I get chain e-mails, too," Saga says.

"But do they come to see you, too?"

"Who?"

"The clown girls," Pellerina whispers, pushing her glasses farther up her nose.

"It isn't real, it's just made up," her dad says. "Some little kid made it all up to scare people."

After Lars-Erik removes the electrodes and switches the EKG monitor off, Saga takes her little sister downstairs and puts her on the sofa in front of the television. She wraps her up in a blanket, and puts Frozen on. It's her evening routine.

It's dark outside now. Saga goes into the kitchen to help her dad with the cooking. He's just poured the cream, eggs, and grated cheese onto the macaroni. She picks up a pair of sticky oven-mitts and puts the dish in the oven.

"What did the e-mail say?" she asks quietly.

"That you have to send the e-mail to three other people to escape the curse," he says, sighing. "Otherwise, the clown girls will come when you're asleep. They'll paint a laughing mouth on your face and poke your eyes out—that sort of thing."

"I can see why she'd be scared," Saga says.

She goes and checks on Pellerina, who's fallen asleep. Saga takes her glasses off and puts them down on the coffee table.

"She's sleeping," Saga says, back in the kitchen.

"I'll wake her when it's time to eat. This always happens—school wears her out."

"I should go," she says.

"Don't you have time to eat first?" he asks.

"No."

He goes into the hall with her and hands her her coat.

"Don't forget your elf," he reminds her.

"He can stay here," Saga says as she opens the door.

Lars-Erik stands in the doorway. The light plays on his lined face and unkempt hair.

"I thought you'd like it," he says quietly.

"We're just not there yet," she says, and walks away.

10

IT'S THREE O'CLOCK, AND THE WHITE SKY IS ALREADY GROW-
ing dark.

Joona never objects to being on patrol, but after Nils Åhlén's
visit it feels like the world has become a more dangerous place.

As he walks past the wrought-iron railings outside Adolf
Fredrik's Church, he sees a black-clad group standing around an
open grave. The surrounding gravestones have been vandalized
and are covered with swastikas.

HE HEADS TOWARD HÖTORGET, WHERE THE FARMER'S MAR-
ket is selling fruit and vegetables. His mind keeps wandering to the
grave robber in Oslo. As soon as he gets Summa's skull back from
Norway, he's planning to rebury it with the rest of her remains. He
hasn't decided yet whether to tell Lumi about what happened. It
would really upset her.

Joona has just passed the Stockholm Concert Hall when he
hears someone yelling in an aggressive, drunken voice. He hears a
glass bottle breaking, and when he spins around he sees shards of
green glass on the road.

People are keeping their distance from a man who's clearly under the influence of narcotics. He's unshaven, and his blond hair
is gathered in a messy tangle at the back of his head. He's wearing
a battered leather jacket, and jeans that are wet with urine around
the crotch and one leg.

The man has no shoes or socks, and one foot is bleeding.

He's swearing at a woman who's hurrying away. Then he stands still with an imperious expression and points a finger at the people around him, as if he were about to say something incredibly important.

"One, two, three, four ... five, six, seven ..."

Joona walks closer and sees that there's a young girl standing behind him. Her face is dirty, and she looks like she's about to burst into tears. A pink tracksuit jacket is her only protection from the cold.

"Can we go home now?" she asks, tugging tentatively at the man's jacket.

"One ... two ... three ..."

He loses his train of thought and reaches out for the streetlight to stop himself from falling. His eyes look drugged—his pupils have shrunk to pinpricks—and snot is streaming from his thin nose.

"Do you need any help?" Joona asks.

"Yes, please," the man mutters.

"What can I do?"

"Shoot the ones I point at."

"Are you armed?"

"I'm just pointing at all the ones who—"

"Stop that," Joona interrupts calmly.

"Okay, okay," the man mutters.

"Are you armed?"

The man points at a man who's stopped to look, then at a woman walking past with a stroller.

"Daddy," the girl pleads.

"Don't be scared," Joona says to her. "I need to find out if your dad has a weapon on him."

"He just needs some rest," she whispers.

Joona tells the man to put his hands behind his head, and he does. But when he lets go of the streetlight he loses his balance and stumbles backward into the shadow of the concert hall's blue wall.

"What are you on?"

"Just a little K, and some speed."

Joona crouches down next to the girl. Her father has started to point his finger discreetly at different people again.

"How old are you?"

"Six and a half."

"Do you think you could take care of a teddy bear?"

"What?"

Joona opens his bag and pulls out the stuffed toy. In the period before Christmas, the police have been provided with teddy bears to offer to any child who's in trouble or who's witnessed anything violent. Often it's the only present they'll get.

The girl stares at the little bear, which has a striped shirt and a big red heart on its chest.

"Would you like to look after it?" Joona smiles.

"No," she whispers, and glances up at him shyly.

"You can have it if you want," Joona explains.

"Really?"

"But it needs a name," Joona says, handing the stuffed toy over to her.

"Sonja," the girl says, pressing the bear to her neck.

"That's a lovely name."

"It was my mommy's name," she tells him.

"We need to take your dad to the hospital—is there anyone you can stay with in the meantime?"

The child nods and whispers something in the teddy bear's ear.

"Grandma."

Joona calls an ambulance, then contacts an acquaintance at Social Services and asks her to pick the girl up and take her to the address they've looked up.

He's just explained everything to the girl when a police car arrives at the scene. Its blue lights flash across the asphalt.

Two uniformed colleagues get out of the car and nod to Joona.

"Joona Linna? Your boss contacted me over the radio," one of them says.

"Carlos?"

"He wants you to answer your phone."

Joona takes his phone out and sees that Carlos Eliasson—head of the National Operations Unit—is calling him. His phone has been on silent. "Joona," he says as he answers.

"Sorry to disturb you while you're working, but this is top priority," Carlos says. "A superintendent with the German police, Clara Fischer at the BKA, is trying to get in touch with you as soon as possible."

"What for?"

"I've agreed to let you help them with a preliminary investigation. The police in Rostock are looking into a death at a campsite, probably murder. . . . Victim's name is Fabian Dissinger—a serial rapist who was recently released from a secure psychiatric unit in Cologne."

"I'm still on probation, I'm on patrol duty until—"

"She asked for you specifically," Carlos interrupts.

11

JOONA IS DRIVING PAST PALE-GREEN FIELDS AND LARGE stone houses in a rented BMW.

He still doesn't know why Superintendent Clara Fischer has requested assistance from him specifically. They've never been in contact before, and the man who was found dead at the campsite has never cropped up in any of Joona's cases.

Superintendent Fischer didn't specify exactly what she thought Joona would be able to contribute, but because the German and Swedish police forces have a long history of cooperation, Carlos gave the go-ahead.

During the flight, Joona had time to read three of the case files he had been sent by the Bundeskriminalamt. They relate to a murder victim, Fabian Dissinger, who was convicted of twenty-three violent rapes of both men and women in Germany, Poland, and Italy. According to one psychiatric report, he had antisocial personality disorder with sadistic tendencies and elements of psychopathy.

Joona makes a sharp left and drives through a patch of woodland. He sees a muddy motocross course in a clearing on his right, and then nothing but trees until he reaches the campsite, Ostseecamp Rostocker Heide.

Joona parks just outside the police cordon and walks over to the group of German police officers waiting for him.

The winter sun is glinting off the cables and satellite dishes on the roofs of the RVs.

Superintendent Clara Fischer is a tall woman with a proud bearing, who looks like she might be quick to take offense. Her dark-brown eyes seem to grow sharper as she watches Joona approach. Her short curly hair is graying at the temples. She's wearing a black leather jacket that hits below her hips, and black leather boots with low heels that are now completely gray with mud from the wet ground.

Clara studies Joona carefully, as if the slightest shift in his expression is of great significance.

"Thanks for coming on such short notice," she says, not breaking eye contact as she shakes his hand.

"I like campsites—"

"Great."

"—but I'm wondering why I'm here," he concludes.

"Certainly not because Fabian Dissinger's death is a great loss to Germany," Clara replies, pointing toward a plot.

They set off along one of the paved paths that span the campsite. The winter air is cold, and white rays of sunlight shine through the bare treetops.

"I'm not saying he got what he deserved, but if I had my way he'd have spent the rest of his life in a secure psychiatric unit," she says calmly.

"Not an unreasonable opinion, given what I read in the files."

They pass the shower building and a small shop. A few campers are standing outside the cordon, taking pictures of the crime scene on their phones. The red-and-white plastic tape is rippling in the wind.

"Not an unreasonable opinion," Clara repeats, and glances at him. "I know that some of our colleagues in Berlin refused to work on a case last week: a known pedophile had drowned in a ditch near a school. They didn't want to be working on that when they don't even have the resources to investigate the mugging and murder of a young woman in Spandau."

An empty beer can rolls across a patch of sand surrounding a cluster of recycling bins. There's a bundle of Bubble Wrap wedged between two of the containers. Some broken glass sparkles in the sunshine.

Joona and Clara walk in silence through a group of older camp-ers that have been shut up for the winter. Two uniformed officers are guarding the inner cordon. They greet Clara with respectful salutes.

"A Cabby 58 from 2005," she says, nodding toward the camper. "Dissinger had been renting it for the past two months and four days."

Joona looks at the boxy camper, perched on concrete blocks. Trickles of red-brown rust have run down the side from a crooked aerial on the roof.

Two forensics officers in white overalls are examining the area. There's a sooty aluminum saucepan full of rainwater and dead flies near a picnic table on the gravel outside the RV. There are num-bered stakes stuck in the ground to mark any finds.

"I presume you haven't had time to look at the reports we sent yet."

"Not all of them, no."

She smiles bleakly. "Not all of them," she repeats. "We found a huge quantity of violent porn on his computer . . . so I think it's fair to say that eleven years of psychiatric treatment didn't sort out all his problems. He was locked up, medicated, and waiting for a chance to pick up where he left off."

"Some people are like that," Joona replies simply.

A tall officer in protective white overalls leaves the camper to make space for them, and says something to Clara that Joona doesn't hear.

They walk up the stairs in front of the open door.

The whole time, Clara openly stares at him without embar-rassment. It's as if she's on the verge of asking a question but keeps stopping herself.

Translucent plastic has been laid out to protect the cork floor-ing. It creaks under their weight.

There's a brown jacket with threadbare lapels and bloodstained sleeves lying on the sun-bleached pale-blue fitted benches.

"Someone should have heard the fight," Clara says quietly.

The glass top covering the small sink and gas stove is laden with test tubes of biological samples and plastic bags containing seized items—coffee cups, beer glasses, cutlery, toothbrushes, and cigarette butts.

"Dissinger received a visitor. He was probably planning his usual attack, but time had gotten the better of him. He was weaker, older. . . . The tables turned, and he was assaulted and killed by the person he was planning to rape."

Sunlight is streaming in through the grimy windows and stained cream curtains. The remains of broken spiderwebs are trembling in the draft from the open door.

"He was found by two teenagers. . . . A few days ago, he apparently told one of them he'd be happy to offer them a drink."

"I'd like to talk to them," Joona says, looking at the blood on the rounded corner of one of the cupboards.

"They're pretty shaken, but if they hadn't arrived too late for that drink they'd probably be in a considerably worse state."

The double bed is stained with blood, and one of the reading lights set into the headboard has been pulled out and is hanging by its wires. Someone has dragged the bare mattress off the bed, then shoved it back.

"His relatives aren't exactly lining up to organize his funeral, so I left him hanging in there until you got here," Clara concludes, and gestures toward the closed door to the bathroom.

12

JOONA OPENS THE SLIDING DOOR TO THE BATHROOM. A large man, bare-chested, is hanging from a medicine cabinet between the toilet and the sink. His feet reach the floor, but both his legs have been broken at the knees and were unable to support his weight.

He has a length of steel wire around his neck. It's cut into the skin below his Adam's apple by at least five centimeters.

Blood has run down his hairy chest and bulging stomach to his jeans.

"You're certain about the ID?"

"One hundred percent," Clara says, looking intently at Joona again.

The man's face has been smashed in. There isn't much left of his features.

The hands hanging by his sides are black with pooled blood.

"He must have had plenty of enemies after the trial," Joona says thoughtfully. "Have you—"

"Statistically speaking, revenge is an unusual motive," Clara says, cutting him off.

Joona looks at the wall behind the body. The dead man evidently struggled for a long time before he asphyxiated. In his efforts to loosen the wire by swinging back and forth, he managed to break the sink. Joona is certain they're going to find fractures to the hyoid bone and at the top of the thyroid cartilage.

"I'm working on the hypothesis that he lured a young guy whose life had gone off the rails—juvenile detention, petty crime, prostitution, steroids, Rohypnol," Clara says, pulling on a pair of white latex gloves.

"There wasn't a fight," Joona says.

"No?"

"He should have been able to put up a decent fight, but his knuckles aren't damaged at all."

"We'll get the body to the lab now that you've seen it," she mutters.

"He doesn't have any other defensive injuries, either," Joona goes on.

"He must have," she says, looking at the dead man's arms.

"He didn't defend himself," Joona says calmly.

Clara Fischer sighs, lets go of the arms, and stares intently at Joona.

"How can you know so much?"

"What am I doing here?" Joona asks.

"That's what I was thinking of asking you," Clara says, taking a plastic sleeve from her bag and showing him an old flip phone.

"A phone," he says.

"A phone that we found between the cushions on the sofa . . . It belonged to Fabian Dissinger," she says, switching it on inside the plastic. "Two days ago, he called this number—do you recognize it?"

"That's my number," Joona says.

"One of the last calls he made was to your personal phone."

Joona takes out his cell phone and sees that he missed the call.

"Tell me what you know," Clara says.

"Well, now I know why you wanted me here."

"You need to tell me why he called you," she says impatiently.

Joona shakes his head. "Fabian Dissinger hasn't ever featured in any of my investigations."

"Just tell me the truth," Clara says irritably.

"I have no idea."

She blows a strand of hair away from her mouth. "You have no idea. There must be a connection, though," she persists.

"Yes." Joona nods, taking a step closer to the hanged man and looking at his eyes.

One of them is hidden by blue-gray swelling and pulpy red flesh, but the other is open, and the mucous membrane is dotted with small specks of blood.

He realizes that Clara withheld the information about the phone to see if his reaction to the crime scene revealed anything.

"Give me something," she says, staring at him. In spite of the cold air in the RV, she has tiny beads of sweat on her top lip.

"I'd like to be present for the postmortem," Joona replies.

"You said there wasn't a fight."

"The violence was one-sided. . . . It's an almost uncontrolled explosion of aggression, and yet there is also evidence to suggest the perpetrator was trained in military techniques."

"You were in the military, the Special Operations Group, before you joined the police."

They move away from the bathroom to let two forensics officers lay a body bag on the floor, then fasten plastic bags around the victim's hands, cut the wire, and lift the big, rigid body down.

The dead man's weight makes the officers groan, and they give each other instructions as they carry him feetfirst out through the narrow doorway. Joona gets a glimpse of Fabian Dissinger's broad back and hairy shoulders as they lower him down on the bag.

"Hang on, turn him over," Joona says, moving closer.

"*Könnten Sie bitte die Leiche auf den Bauch wenden,*" Clara says in a neutral voice.

The forensics officers stare at them, but open the bag again, turn the body over, and make room for Joona and Clara.

Joona feels his heartbeat accelerate as he looks at the lower part of the victim's back: the skin from the bottom of his shoulder blades down to his buttocks is unnaturally striped, as if he'd been lying on a reed mat.

"What's happened to his back?" Clara whispers.

Without bothering to put on protective gloves, Joona crouches down and carefully feels the horizontal scars with his fingertips— hundreds of parallel stripes made by scars that have bled and healed over and over again.

"I know you've got a legendary reputation as a detective," Clara says slowly. "But you've also got a criminal conviction, you're on probation, and I'm going to arrest you and take you in for questioning unless you can explain how—"

Joona stands up, pushes past her, and accidentally knocks over some evidence bags containing glasses and ashtrays when he reaches out to the stove for support. He goes through the door and out into the sunshine.

"You're involved, Joona, aren't you?" Clara says, hurrying after him.

He doesn't reply, just walks across the gravel, pushing a forensics officer who's looking at his phone out of the way as he heads for the gate.

"Stop!" Clara says behind him, but without any great urgency.

Joona passes two uniformed officers. He knows that if someone tries to stop him he'll hurt them.

They obviously recognize the determination in his face and back cautiously away from him.

The dead man in the camper shows signs of having been beaten.

Jurek Walter's twin brother had similar scars on his back. He had been whipped for years with a shaving strap, a length of coarse leather used to sharpen razor blades.

Joona isn't quite sure what these similarities mean, but there's no doubt that they're a message for him.

He starts to run toward the parking lot, and jumps into his car. He turns the wheel hard and stomps on the accelerator, sending mud flying up over the sides.

As he drives away from the campsite, he calls the Norwegian Criminal Police. He needs to know if there were any injuries on the back of the grave robber who was found dead in Oslo, the man who had Summa's skull in his freezer.

13

JOONA TAKES A TAXI STRAIGHT FROM THE AIRPORT TO THE Karolinska Institute's Department of Forensic Medicine, on the outskirts of Stockholm.

There are electric Advent lights in the windows of the redbrick building. Outside, the black rosehips on the bare bushes are covered in frost.

Joona didn't take his migraine medication today, because it makes him feel less sharp.

He enters through the glass doors and turns left into the hallway, where he bumps into the elderly janitor with his cart.

"How's Cindy doing?" Joona asks.

"She's much better now, thanks," the man says with a smile.

Joona can't count the number of times he's stood in this hallway during his years with the police, waiting to hear what Nils Åhlén had discovered. Today is different though, since they only have photographs of the bodies to work with.

The grave robber in Oslo didn't have the same scars from past beatings on his back that the sex offender in Rostock did. But just before his death he received five hard blows from either a belt or a strap.

Fabian Dissinger had been abused over a long period of time, had lain on his stomach while someone beat him from the side.

The wounds healed, were reopened by fresh blows, then healed again.

The lights are on in the main postmortem lab.

Saga is crouching down with her back against the tiled wall, and Nils is standing, wearing his medical coat, rubbing his thin hands.

"The Norwegians have sent the pictures. I forwarded them to you," Joona explains.

"Thanks," Nils says.

"Don't I get a hug?" Saga says, getting to her feet.

Her blond hair is in braids, and as usual she's wearing faded jeans and a jacket from her boxing club.

"You look happy," he says, walking over and giving her a hug.

"I guess I am," she replies.

He takes a step back and looks her in the eye. She keeps holding his arm with one hand for a few moments.

"Even though you're dating a police detective."

"Randy." She smiles.

Nils Åhlén opens his e-mail and clicks on the attachments. The three of them gather in front of the screen as Nils brings up the images from the two crime scenes.

"What's this all about?" Saga eventually says. "Both men were assaulted and killed, with extreme force, excessive brutality ... neither of them made much of an effort to defend himself . . . and both have been whipped across the back."

"The same way Jurek's brother was," Joona says.

"That's debatable," she says.

"Fabian Dissinger has exactly the same sort of scars as Jurek's twin brother ... although the brother's were much worse, of course, a lot older, and . . ."

"In which case they're not the same," she points out.

"Both victims had a direct connection to me," Joona says.

"Yes," she replies.

"We know everyone says Jurek is dead," Joona says after a pause. "But I've been thinking that ... well, maybe he isn't."

"Stop it," Saga says in a tense voice.

"Joona," Nils Åhlén says, nudging at his glasses nervously. "We've got a body, we've got a hundred-percent DNA match—"

"I just want to go through the evidence again," Joona says, cutting him off. "I need to know if there's even a theoretical possibility that he could still be alive, and—"

"There isn't," Nils interrupts.

Saga shakes her head and heads toward the door.

"Wait, this affects you, too," Joona says to her back.

"I'll get the file," Nils Åhlén says. "We'll do it your way."

"You're both crazy," Saga mutters as she turns and walks back to them.

Nils unlocks his filing cabinet and pulls out Jurek's file. He goes to the medical fridge and takes out a sealed jar containing a finger preserved in formalin. The glass enlarges it slightly. Small white particles are swirling around the swollen finger, which is pale as ice.

"The only evidence we have that Jurek is dead is one finger," Joona says.

"There was an entire damn torso," Saga says, raising her voice. "Heart, lungs, liver, kidneys, intestines . . ."

"Saga, listen," Joona says. "I just want us to do this, I want us to go through what we know together. Because it will either help us relax, or . . ."

"I shot him, I killed him," Saga says. "He could have killed me, I don't know why he hesitated, but I shot him in the neck, the arm, the chest. . . ."

"Calm down," Nils says, pulling an office chair over for her.

Saga sits down, puts her face in her hands for a few moments, then lowers her hands and takes a deep breath.

"Jurek Walter died that night," she goes on, her voice breaking. "I don't know how many times I've been through it all in my head . . . how hard it was running through the deep snow, the way the flare reflected off the tiny crystals. . . . I had a clear view of him, and I shot him. The first shot hit him in the neck, the second in his arm. . . . I walked toward him and shot him again—three shots to the chest. Every single damn shot hit him, and I saw the blood spray from the exit wounds onto the snow behind him."

"I know, but . . ."

"It's not my fault that he fell into the damn rapids, but I fired into the water and saw a cloud of blood billow out around him, and I followed him downstream, firing and firing, until the body was swept away by the current."

"Everyone did what they had to, and more," Nils Åhlén says slowly. "The police sent divers down that same night, and the following morning they searched the banks with sniffer dogs for more than ten kilometers downstream."

"They should have found the body," Joona says in a subdued voice.

He knows that Saga searched on her own. It formed part of her long road back to normal life, a way for her to work privately through what had happened. She's told him about how she followed the river all the way to the sea near Hysingsvik, then marked out an area on the map and systematically searched the archipelago by dividing it into squares. She studied the sea currents and went out to every single island and skerry along a sixty-mile length of coast, spoke to residents and summer visitors, fishermen, people who worked the ferries, oceanographers.

"I found him," Saga whispers, looking at Joona with bloodshot eyes. "Damn it, Joona, I found him."

He's heard her explanation of how, after more than a year of looking, she bumped into a man on the rugged north coast of Högmarsö. He was a retired churchwarden, collecting driftwood from the beach. She spoke to him and discovered that he had found a man's corpse at the water's edge five months earlier.

Saga had gone with him to the inhabited part of the island. The churchwarden's cottage and an old crematorium were tucked behind a sugar-white chapel.

"Jurek's body had been carried by the current and washed ashore during the storms we had at the end of that winter," Saga says, without taking her eyes off Joona.

"That all checks out," Nils says. "Do you see it, Joona? It all makes sense. He's dead."

"All that was left of Jurek were his torso and one arm," Saga goes on. "The churchwarden told me he carried the swollen body through the forest in his wheelbarrow, and left it on the floor of the toolshed behind the chapel. But the smell drove his dog crazy, so he ended up having to move it to the old crematorium."

"Why didn't he call the police?" Joona asks.

"I don't know. He made his own hooch and was messing with his benefits," she says. "Maybe he'd already started to go senile. . . . But he took pictures of the body on his phone in case the police did show up asking questions . . . and he kept one of the fingers at the back of his freezer."

Nils Åhlén pulls a printed picture from the file and passes it to Joona. He takes the photograph and angles it so the reflection of the lab's fluorescent lights doesn't obscure it.

On a cement floor, beside a red lawn mower, lies a bloated body with no head. A pool of water has spread out around it. The white skin has slid off the chest, and three jagged entry wounds gape like craters.

Saga moves to stand next to him so she can see the picture.

"That's Jurek. That's where I hit him."

14

THE NEEDLE LAYS OUT COPIES OF THE SCANNED FINGER-prints, Jurek Walter's DNA profile, and the lab results.

"The match is exact. We've got both DNA and fingerprints—not even identical twins share the same fingerprints," he explains.

"I don't doubt that that's Jurek's finger," Joona says quietly.

"It was cut off a dead body," The Needle says emphatically.

"Joona, he's dead—aren't you listening?" Saga asks.

"All he needed was to have one dead body part," Joona replies. "The finger could have been cut from an amputated hand that had been lying in brackish water for the same length of time as the body."

"Oh, for God's sake," she groans.

"Purely theoretically," Joona persists.

"Nils, tell him that's just not possible."

The Needle pushes his glasses up his nose again and looks at Joona. "You're suggesting he might have cut his own hand off in order to . . ."

He trails off and meets Joona's gaze.

"Let's say Jurek was incredibly lucky and somehow survived being shot. Let's say he swam with the current, made it to land, and survived that too," Joona says seriously.

"Those shots were fatal," Saga protests.

"Jurek used to be a child soldier," Joona says. "Pain is nothing to him; he would have cauterized the wounds himself and amputated his own arm if that's what it took."

"Joona, you do realize that this is impossible," The Needle says wearily.

"It's only impossible if it genuinely can't be done."

"Okay, we're listening," Saga says, sinking back onto her chair.

Joona's face is pale and impassive. "Jurek finds a man with roughly the same build as him, the same age," he says. "He shoots him the same way you shot him. . . . Then he removes the dead man's head and leaves the rest of the body to soak somewhere along the coast . . . in some sort of cage or crate."

"Along with his own hand," The Needle says quietly.

"It wouldn't even be that bizarre for him—he used to keep people buried alive in coffins."

"To do that, he would have needed the cooperation of the churchwarden Saga met."

"Jurek has ways of making people do his bidding."

Joona looks at The Needle and Saga. His pale-gray eyes look almost black now, and his face is beaded with sweat. "Am I right? Is there at least a theoretical possibility that Jurek is still alive?" he asks in a whisper.

"Joona," The Needle pleads, but then he nods in response.

"That's just nonsense. This is nothing, for God's sake!" Saga exclaims, sweeping the reports and photographs onto the floor.

"I'm not saying I believe that he's alive," Joona says tentatively.

"Good, Joona, because that would have felt kind of weird," she blurts out. "Considering that I shot him and then found his body."

"It was actually only a finger."

"In theory, Joona's right," Nils says.

"Okay, what the hell," Saga says. "Let's say you're right in theory. Even so, no matter how you look at it, there's no logic to your suspicions. Why the fuck would Jurek want to whip and kill two perverted ex-cons in Norway and Germany?"

"That doesn't sound like his MO," Nils Åhlén concedes.

Joona closes his eyes, and his eyelids flicker as he tries to compose himself enough to pursue his line of reasoning.

"Jurek had three types of victim," he begins, opening his eyes.

"The true victims, his primary targets, were the ones he didn't kill himself, like Samuel Mendel."

"Which is why it was so hard to establish a pattern," Nils says.

"The second category included the people he took from his prime targets, the people who made their lives worth living."

"Children, wives, siblings, parents, friends," Nils said.

"Jurek didn't actively want to kill them, either. As individuals, they had no significance to him."

"Which is why he kept them locked up or buried in coffins and drums," Nils says, nodding in agreement.

"The third category were people who just happened to get in his way. . . . He didn't really want to kill them, either, but he did so for practical reasons, to remove them as obstacles."

"So he never really set out to kill anyone?" Saga says.

"He didn't get anything out of the act of killing itself. There was no sexual motive. It wasn't even about domination, just his own personal sense of justice—he wanted to break down the primary victims and eventually make them choose death over life."

He looks down at the photographs of the decayed torso, whipped backs, and lab reports.

"Now we have two victims with no apparent connection to each other, with injuries inflicted in a way that is reminiscent of what happened to Jurek's brother. One victim had Summa's skull in his freezer, and the other tried to contact me."

"That can't be a coincidence," Saga concedes. "But these murders don't fit Jurek's persona."

"I agree. I completely agree. I don't think it's Jurek, either, but maybe someone's trying to tell me something, and maybe that person has some sort of connection to him," Joona says.

"What if there are other victims?" Saga asks, looking him dead in the eye.

15

STELLAN RAGNARSON IS A LANKY MAN WITH KIND EYES AND
a somewhat anxious smile. He started cutting his hair very short
after it got too thin to look boyish.

This evening, he's wearing shiny black sweatpants and a washed-
out gray New York Rangers hoodie.

He takes half a kilo of steak from the fridge, tears off the plastic,
and drops the meat into a large stainless-steel bowl.

Marika is sitting at the drop-leaf table with her phone and a
bar of chocolate.

She's five years younger than him, and works at the gas station
on the E65, opposite the ICA Kvantum supermarket.

"You spoil him," she says, breaking off three chunks of chocolate.

"I can afford it," he replies, and puts the bowl down on the floor
below the kitchen window.

"Today, maybe."

Stellan smiles as the big dog devours the meat with a snap of
its jaw. Rollof is an impressive-looking Rottweiler, self-assured and
calm. His tail was docked when he was a puppy because it was
coiled up over his back.

Stellan is unemployed, but he won some money on the horses
yesterday and surprised Marika by buying her a rose.

They go and sit on the sofa, eat toasted ham-and-mustard sand-
wiches, and watch *Stranger Things*.

Marika's phone rings just as they're finishing. She looks at the
screen and says it's her sister again.

"Take it," he says, standing up. "I'll go up and play for a bit before I take Rollof out."

"Hi, sis," Marika answers with a smile, and plumps the cushion up behind her back.

Stellan gets a can of beer from the fridge and goes upstairs to his computer.

Six months ago, he began to explore the dark web, an untraceable part of the Internet that's said to be five thousand times the size of the ordinary Internet.

Most people are aware that every computer and phone has its own IP address, a combination of letters and numbers that can be used to identify users and locate them geographically.

Stellan was attracted to Darknet, a part of the dark web that employs servers without IP addresses. That's where most of the really dangerous deals and developments are happening: guns, drugs, rape, contract killings, slave trading, and organ theft.

But after what happened eleven days ago, he stopped looking at the dark web altogether. He cut off all contact and tried to get rid of the software, without success.

It doesn't matter, he tells himself.

He's not using the dark web anymore. He just sticks to online gaming.

He's started to get caught up in the game Battlefield. It's intense, but it's still just a game. You put together a team to carry out a military operation. You spend most of your time talking about the mission, but it's still fun getting to know new people from all around the world.

Stellan puts his beer down on the desk and sticks a Band-Aid over the little camera lens on the computer before putting on his headphones and microphone.

Their task in the game is to eliminate a terrorist leader in a run-down building in Damascus. They've been given satellite pictures of the building, and have been flown in from their base by helicopter.

Stellan takes one hand off the handset to open the can, but doesn't have time to drink before he has to get back to the game.

They force entry through a back door and enter the building in two pairs. Stellan and his backup, who goes by the name Straw, run through a pillared walkway along the side of a courtyard filled with cracked marble tiles and rusting military equipment strewn among desiccated palm trees.

"Take it nice and slow, now," Stellan says over the voice chat.

"I can take the lead if you're getting cold feet," Straw says, then lets out a belch.

"You haven't even seen the guards, have you?" Stellan says quietly.

The guards' cigarettes are just visible in a dark corner. When they inhale, the light of the burning tobacco flares momentarily.

Straw sighs in Stellan's headphones, then walks straight out and shoots the guards. The heavy fire echoes through the walkway and off the walls.

"Fuck, you can't do that before we've checked the courtyard," Stellan says, reaching for the beer again.

He tries to pop the tab as Straw's avatar saunters into the courtyard with his gun hanging from his hip.

"Do you need help with that can?" he asks.

Stellan pulls off his headphones and stands up so fast that his chair topples over behind him. He stares at the screen, looks at the Band-Aid covering the lens, then hears a voice from the headphones, now lying on the desk next to the controller.

"Sit back down," Straw calls.

Stellan pulls out the headphones and shuts the computer down. He unplugs it and carries the laptop to the closet to stuff it inside. He tries to figure out how anyone could see him.

He goes over to the window and looks out at the dark street. There's a parked car with misted-up windows outside. Stellan lets the blinds fall with a clatter, picks the chair up from the floor, and sits down, his heart racing.

"What's going on?" he whispers to himself.

He tucks the handset and headphones into one of the desk drawers with trembling hands.

It must have something to do with what happened eleven days ago.

"Fuck, fuck, fuck . . ."

He now realizes how stupid it was to investigate Darknet. Even after two years studying IT in prison, he was in over his head. There's no real anonymity on Darknet. There's always someone who can outsmart the system.

But until eleven days ago he had been obsessed with it, unable to resist the temptation.

He went way too far before realizing that he was in a league beyond anything he could have imagined. Some of the people on Darknet were deadly. They knew no boundaries at all. He had watched two men shoot a boy sitting in front of his computer in real time. Blood sprayed across the *Star Wars* posters and a sagging Trump mask that was lying on the floor.

Stellan read up on the risks and found out that anyone who used the Vidalia browser was considered an accomplice to all activity on the dark web. But Tor software is supposed to protect users, making them impossible to trace.

It's all a matter of mix cascades, a relay system that means that your signals are sent through a random sequence of proxy servers around the world.

Stellan doesn't understand it completely but thought that the software would give him access to the darkest parts of the Internet without anyone's being able to identify or trace him.

16

STELLAN GETS UP ON SHAKY LEGS, NUDGES THE BLINDS aside, and looks out at the street again. The car is gone. He goes downstairs and pulls out the router cable in the living room. Marika is sitting on the sofa in front of the television, and pats the seat beside her when she sees him.

"I have to take Rollof out," he says in a toneless voice.

She pouts exaggeratedly. "You always put the dog first."

"He needs exercise, he's a big dog."

"What's the matter? You don't look great," she says.

"It's just . . . we can't use the Internet anymore."

"Why not?"

"We need to switch networks. We've got a virus that will destroy everything if we try to get online."

"But I need to go online."

"Now?"

"Yes, I've got to pay the bills, and—"

"Go to your sister's and use her computer," he says, cutting her off.

Marika shakes her head. "This is crazy."

"I'll call tech support after I take Rollof out."

"This shouldn't be allowed to happen," Marika mutters.

Stellan goes out into the hall, and the moment he takes the leash down and the silvery links rattle, Rollof comes rushing over.

It's a quiet, rainy winter's evening in southern Sweden. The fields are brown and bare.

Stellan and Rollof walk along the side of the E65, as usual. Heavy trucks thunder past occasionally. Stellan can't help looking over his shoulder at regular intervals, but they're alone.

Thin mist is hanging over the empty lots on the other side of the wide road. Rollof sticks close to him, breathing calmly.

It's a raw night, dark and cold. They turn right onto Aulin Street and walk along the yellowed grass, with the big industrial park on their left. The huge parking lots are deserted at this time of night.

Stellan knows that he isn't thinking very clearly, that he might be behaving irrationally, but he's decided to burn down the workshop. If he burns it down, he'll be able to collect insurance, move away from Ystad, change his Internet supplier, and get new computer equipment.

There's a light on in one of the old greenhouses up ahead. Rollof stops, then barks and growls at the dense bushes in one of the deserted plots.

"What is it?" Stellan asks in a low voice.

The collar is straining around the dog's thick neck, making his breathing sound strained. Rollof is dependable, but he can be a real handful when he encounters other male dogs.

"No fighting, now," Stellan warns, pulling him away.

The other dog doesn't bark back, but some of the branches in front of the greenhouse start to sway.

Stellan feels a shiver run down his spine. For a moment, he thought there was someone standing over there.

He heads into the big industrial park. The streets are empty, and between the streetlamps everything is pitch-black. His shadow grows longer, then disappears altogether before he reaches the next circle of light. His footsteps echo off the brick and the corrugated metal walls.

It isn't easy to get a job in Sweden when you have a criminal record. Stellan was convicted of a double murder when he was twenty years old. Since he was released, he's had a number of temporary jobs, taken courses, tried to get better qualifications, but mostly he's been living off of social security.

His restless search of the dark web, his voyeuristic observation of what other people were doing, all stemmed from an old fantasy that he had talked about in prison. He would kidnap some girls and make them earn money for him. He had read about it, mulled it over, considered the risks, and decided to figure out the best way to succeed.

That was what he had in mind. He advertised in a couple of forums that he wanted to buy three girls, but hadn't gotten any responses. Then he made the advertisements more specific and explained that he wanted to keep the girls in cages and exploit them sexually, and he suddenly started to get responses. Many of them were provocative, and some tried to frighten him off. Others seemed like serious offers, but he worried they were connected to organized crime.

Stellan doesn't know why he can't stop thinking about the idea, about keeping young women in cages. Maybe it's the idea that it might actually be achievable.

Ten years ago, he inherited an old industrial unit that he tried to rent out. While he was waiting for more responses on the dark-web marketplaces, he built a sturdy inner wall toward the back of the long, narrow building. Without measuring the walls inside and out, it was impossible to tell that there was a hidden room, even though it contained five cages with beds, a shower, a toilet, and a small kitchen area with a fridge.

Stellan had almost finished it when he was contacted by Andersson.

He didn't know how dangerous Andersson was.

Andersson showed an interest in his plans and was prepared to deliver five young girls from Romania. The offer was perfect in every detail. But at the same time, Andersson radiated a compressed power that made Stellan shiver with fear.

He did more research into the Tor network.

If he was careful, he couldn't be traced, because his information was relayed via countless nodes and was encrypted until it reached its recipient.

The deal was a little too big for him. But if he built up a client base, he could earn a fortune.

Stellan couldn't stop thinking about the imprisoned girls, though he didn't actually know what he was going to do with them. He didn't want to rape them, he didn't want to beat them. He fantasized about their becoming so demoralized that they would consent to anything without resistance.

Andersson got him to talk about his background and asked complicated questions about loyalty. This annoyed him, so he created a sort of Trojan horse in the form of an innocuous-seeming file that would give him the upper hand.

When the attachment was opened, Andersson revealed his exact location.

And now Andersson knew that he knew.

Stellan had his address.

Don't fuck with me—that had been his thought.

Andersson's response had been as rapid as it was unexpected.

"You shouldn't have done that," he wrote. "You have to regain my trust. And the only way is by filming yourself slicing your Achilles tendons."

That was eleven days ago.

Stellan pretended to think it was all a joke, but deep down he knew Andersson was deranged. Without making a big deal of it, he tried to pull out of the arrangement, explaining that he'd run into difficulties and was going to have to put the whole thing on ice.

"It's too late for that," Andersson replied.

"What do you mean?"

"I'll be paying you a visit soon."

"Andersson, I'm very sorry," Stellan wrote. "I didn't mean to—"

He stopped when the fan on his computer started to whir wildly.

"I own you," Andersson replied.

The next moment, Stellan's screen went black. The room went dark. The computer restarted, the hard drive rattled, the screen flickered. Then the connection came back up, and suddenly Stellan saw himself on the screen.

Andersson was controlling his laptop remotely, and had activated the camera and seen him sitting at his desk without a shirt on, a coffee mug next to the keyboard.

With his heart pounding, Stellan left the dark web, went into his system settings, shut off the Internet connection, and tried to remove the Tor browser from his computer.

Since then, Stellan hasn't ventured onto Darknet. The suffocating feeling of being watched and observed has gotten worse with each day.

The gates of 18 Herrestadsgatan are still open. Rollof raises his leg and pisses on the post, as usual. They pass Jeppsson Engineering and a blue canvas covering an old bus.

Stellan and the dog leave the gravel drive and walk across the wet grass, past a big silver-colored building, toward a long, narrow yellow-brick warehouse with a flight of metal steps in front.

The sign announcing Ystad Tire and Mechanical Workshop is still there, even though the business is long gone.

Stellan ties the leash to a concrete block meant to hold roadwork signs. He ruffles the loose skin on the back of Rollof's neck and tells him that he'll be back soon.

Stellan switches the lights on, and the fluorescent strip lights flicker and buzz into life, spreading their harsh glare across dirty benches and heavy mountings. The cement floor is covered with oil stains and drill holes where machinery once stood. There's evidence of the defunct workshop everywhere. Anything that could be sold at the auction that followed the bankruptcy was taken away.

Just before he reaches the false wall, he hears Rollof start to growl outside. Stellan unlocks the door of the cleaning closet, pulls out the industrial vacuum cleaner, takes down the topless calendar, inserts a long key into the lock, and pushes the hidden door open.

Inside the secret room, he has constructed cages out of heavy-duty wire mesh, firmly fixed to the concrete floor. All that they contain at the moment are plain, unmade beds from Ikea and plastic bedpans.

The ceiling lamp is casting checkered shadows across the mattresses.

The little kitchen consists of an all-in-one unit containing a sink, a hot plate, a handheld shower to fit on the tap, a microwave oven, and a small fridge.

He knows that the sensible thing to do would be to dismantle the cages before he sets fire to the workshop. Stellan walks over to the farthest cage, inserts the crowbar between the brick wall and the mesh frame, and pushes.

He's planning on siphoning off the diesel from the bus outside Jeppsson's once he's destroyed the cages, drenching everything, then starting the fire in here, in one of the radiators. The workshop isn't insured for its full value, but he can hardly call and ask to change the terms now.

Stellan wrenches out one side of the frame, pushing it away from him as it falls. His phone buzzes, and he hooks the crowbar onto the mesh as he takes the phone out and looks at the screen. He's received a text message from a number he doesn't recognize: "Pour gas over yourself and—"

Stellan doesn't finish reading the text, just throws his phone at the wall, unable to figure out how Andersson could have gotten his phone number.

"What's going on?" he says, stamping on the phone until it shatters.

He decides not to bother dismantling the cages. They'll probably burn along with everything else, so he won't be found out.

Suddenly the lights go out. The fuse must have blown. Stellan feels his way out, stumbling over a paper bag containing screws, angle irons, and a random assortment of other spare parts. He pulls open the heavy security door, goes out through the cleaning closet into the workshop. All the lights have gone out. Weak gray light is coming in through the windows that haven't been covered with plywood. Stellan can see that the door to the fuse box, with its old enamel fuses, is already open.

Outside the door, Rollof starts barking. The dog is clearly agitated. He's pulling at his leash, then starts growling and barking again.

A shadow passes one of the windows. Someone's creeping around the building.

Stellan's heart is beating so hard that his throat hurts.

He looks at the door in front of him, unsure of what to do.

The chain from the broken winch is swinging behind him.

Stellan spins around but can't see anyone.

He heads toward the door, and has just heard quick footsteps behind him when he feels an excruciating pain in his temple.

He staggers sideways. His legs buckle, and he collapses to the floor. He hears himself making guttural moaning sounds.

His back arches in a cramp; then his body starts to jerk uncontrollably. Someone grabs him by one leg and is dragging him across the floor.

"I'm sorry," he gasps, blinking the blood from his eyes.

The man shrieks something, then stomps on his mouth. Stellan feels the stomping until he loses consciousness altogether.

When he comes to, his face feels wet and warm.

He's lying on his side. He tries to raise his head as he sees the man overturn the old desk, then come back with a rusty saw in one hand and kick him in the stomach.

Stellan's breathing rattles off the concrete floor.

He needs to crawl out and release Rollof.

The man stomps on the base of his spine several times, then walks around him.

Stellan feels the man grab the back of his head, put the jagged blade to his neck, and start to saw.

He just has time to think that the pain is utterly unbearable before everything fades away.

17

JOONA AND NILS ÅHLÉN ARE STANDING IN THE ELEVATOR IN silence, not looking at each other. The floor is wet with melted snow. The only sound is the swishing of the cables in the shaft as they head up to the conference room on the eighth floor.

Nathan Pollock from the National Homicide Commission has already called a first meeting. He's the person in the National Operations Unit responsible for finding victims who might fit the pattern of the two known cases.

Joona looks like he's concentrating intensely. The collar of his coat is uneven, half up, half down.

Since they agree that it's theoretically possible that Jurek Walter survived Saga's gunshots, Joona has to follow his suspicions to the end of the road. He can't fend off a feeling of impending disaster.

Neither the choice of victim nor the method makes sense. Neither fits with Jurek's sense of balance.

Jurek isn't interested in excessive violence; he just does whatever is necessary to achieve the result he's after.

The dead men in Germany and Norway both have a link to Joona, but there's nothing to indicate any clear connection to Jurek.

The fact that the victim at the campsite in Rostock was whipped doesn't necessarily mean anything. He could have been a masochist— he could have harmed himself—or been assaulted by the other patients in the secure psychiatric unit.

It hasn't even been established beyond reasonable doubt that he was beaten using a razor strap. Maybe Joona's imagination is just running wild.

And the man in Oslo only had a few abrasions on his back. They could have been a part of the assault that resulted in his death.

Joona forces himself to pay attention as Nils tells him that his assistant, Frippe, has started playing golf with his wife.

Joona tries to smile, and reminds himself that he's probably overreacting.

Jurek is dead.

The man in Oslo and the man at the campsite must have been killed by the same person, but just because there was a definite connection to him in both cases doesn't mean that connection has to be Jurek.

Joona has been trying to figure out how the murdered sex offender could have his private phone number and why he called. Fabian Dissinger hasn't cropped up in any Swedish investigation, at least not since Joona started working in the police department.

Same thing with the grave robber in Oslo.

The elevator doors slide open.

Anja is waiting for them. Without saying a word, she hugs Joona tightly, then takes a step back.

She shows them into the conference room with a satisfied smile. An Advent candelabra with a dusty cable is poking out of the trash can. Three smaller tables have been pushed together. On one of them there's a closed laptop and two bundles of paper and folders.

The inner courtyard is visible through the low windows. Joona can see the flat roofs covered with masts and satellite dishes, the exercise yard of the jail holding cells, and the spire of the old police headquarters.

"You were quick," Nathan says behind them.

As usual, his gray hair is tied in a ponytail, and he's wearing a black jacket, slim-fitting pants, and shoes with Cuban heels.

"How are things?" Joona asks, shaking his old friend's hand.

"Shit, thanks," Nathan replies.

He walks over to the wall and pulls down a Christmas picture and a poster telling police officers to keep an eye on their teenage children.

"Nathan thinks Christmas is bad for the room's feng shui," Anja says.

"What did you find?" Joona says, sitting down on one of the chairs.

Nathan jerks his head slightly to get his ponytail in the right place, then opens the laptop and starts to tell them about his dealings with Europol.

"We asked about murder victims in the past six months who were serious criminals or mentally ill . . . violent assaults, sexual offenses."

"With particular emphasis on signs of beatings and whipping," Anja adds.

"We asked them to discount terrorism, organized crime, the drug trade, and financial crimes," Nathan goes on.

"Their response was that there haven't been any murders that fulfill those criteria," Anja says, filling four glasses from the carafe of water.

"But there must be some, just statistically," Nathan continues. "So we contacted the national police authorities, then moved on to separate districts and departments."

"I don't want to say it's been tough, but there are forty-five different nation-states in Europe, so that means an awful lot of department heads," Anja explains. "Some of them are suspicious and don't want to reveal details, but the biggest problem is probably . . ."

She trails off and sighs.

"This all gets a bit messy," she goes on. "But, in general, the police don't put a huge amount of effort into cases where one criminal has killed another. And if any of their worst offenders dies, they're usually relieved. That isn't the official attitude, of course, but it's inevitable. . . . No one gets personally motivated by a pedophile's death; you don't spend a lot of time calling other districts, other countries."

"I spoke to a Hungarian officer who said he didn't want to sound like Duterte, but even though they can hardly encourage murder, they really don't have any objection to having society cleaned up," Nathan says.

"And I spoke to an English superintendent who said he'd put our murderer on the payroll if he moved to Tottenham."

Joona raises his glass, looks at the surface of the water and the round, translucent shadow on the table, and feels a degree of relief for the first time.

Jurek isn't trying to make the world a better place. He would never feel any obligation to punish offenders—that isn't how he works.

"But I want to stress that we're far from finished with our inquiries," Nathan says, taking an apple from the bowl in the middle of the table. "We just thought you'd want to see the three responses we've received so far that match the criteria."

A roaring sound fills Joona's head.

"Match?" he repeats, putting his fingertips to his left temple.

"Let's see," Nathan says, opening a file on the laptop. "This one took a lot of persuasion. . . . At first they said they didn't have any murders at all; then I was eventually put through to a superintendent in Gdańsk, and without any hesitation he told me that they'd just found a middle-aged man in the abandoned branch of the Vistula River known as 'the Dead Vistula.' . . . The man hadn't drowned. He'd been beaten to death. His face had been bitten, and his head was almost severed from his body."

"He'd been in prison for three murders and desecration of a corpse," Anja says.

"What else?" Joona asks, his mouth suddenly dry.

"I spoke to Salvatore Giani this morning; he sends his regards," Nathan says, and takes a bite of the apple.

"Thanks," Joona whispers.

"Salvatore had a murder in Segrate, on the outskirts of Milan. . . . Last Thursday a woman by the name of Patrizia Tuttino was found with her neck broken in the trunk of her own car, outside the Department of Reconstructive Surgery at the San Raffaele Hospital. . . . During the search of her house, they discovered that she had carried out at least five contract killings before she embarked upon her gender reassignment."

Nathan frowns as he taps at the laptop, then turns it toward Joona to show him a picture.

The shadow of the hospital building's cupola reaches across the pavement to a red Fiat Panda with a damaged front bumper. There's a dead body lying in the open trunk. The inside of the plastic bag over her head is smeared with lipstick. Her dress and fur coat are black with mud.

"And the third victim?" Joona asks.

Nathan rubs his forehead.

"There's a popular national park outside Brest-Litovsk in Belarus, the Białowieża Forest. Last week, a man's body was found in the undergrowth behind a dumpster at the new tourist attraction based around Ded Moroz, who's a sort of Slavic Santa Claus. . . . The victim was a man who worked as a guard in the park. He'd been brutally assaulted. Both his arms were broken, and he'd been shot in the back of the neck. His name was Maksim Rios."

"I see," Joona says.

"Our Belarusian colleague said the man had been whipped during the past year, like some poor kid in an orphanage, as he put it."

"I need to think," Joona says.

"We're still waiting for pictures, as well as responses from many more countries. . . . As Anja says, the problem is that most of them don't have any objection to having their offenders disappear."

Joona sits with his hands over his face as he listens to Nathan relate the sarcastic response from the police in Marseille.

Serial killers like this don't exist, Joona is thinking.

Occasionally, a serial killer will try to excuse his need to kill with the idea that society needs to be cleansed, but on those occasions the victims are usually homosexuals, prostitutes, or specific ethnic or religious groups.

It can't be Jurek. He would never kill anyone for demonstrating a lack of morality. That is of no interest whatsoever to him.

Unless there's some advantage to it, Joona suddenly thinks, and gets up from his chair.

The murders have nothing to do with cleansing society.

It's a competition, a contest—they're eliminating the losers.

"He's alive," Joona whispers, pushing his chair out from under the table.

Jurek Walter is alive. He's been recruiting a new accomplice and testing candidates to see who would be most suitable. He's restricted his search to people with no moral boundaries.

Jurek needs someone to take his brother's place, someone who's utterly loyal, who's prepared to accept punishment for the slightest mistake.

Jurek didn't plan for the man in Oslo to take Summa's skull, he didn't want the man at the campsite to call me—they were unintended results of his indoctrination.

The accumulation of dead bodies means that the selection is complete. The victims that have been found so far are the ones who didn't get through to the next round.

That's the motive.

The motive they haven't been able to identify.

Joona is aware that Nathan is saying something to him, but he can't hear him. He can't take anything in.

"Joona? What is it?"

Joona turns away, walks unsteadily toward the door, and opens it. He makes sure he's got his pistol in the holster under his arm, and heads for the elevator bank as he pulls out his phone and looks up Lumi's number.

Anja catches up with him in the corridor.

"What's going on?" she asks anxiously.

"I have to go," he says, reaching out for the wall with one hand.

"We've just received an e-mail from Ystad that you should see. The police there have found a man's body in an industrial park—his head, face, and chest have been completely smashed in. . . ."

Joona accidentally pulls down a poster for a women's indoor hockey tournament as he makes his way to the elevators.

"It fits the pattern," Anja calls after him. "The victim's name is Stellan Ragnarson. He served time for cutting the throats of his girlfriend and her mother."

Joona quickens his pace and puts the phone to his ear as the call goes through. He presses the button for the elevator, but when it doesn't come he starts to run down the stairs.

"Lumi," she answers in a subdued voice.

"It's Dad," he says, and stops moving.

"Hi, Dad. . . . I'm in a lecture, I can't—"

"Lumi," he interrupts, trying to suppress the panic that's building up inside him, "listen to me. . . . I was wondering, do you remember the solar eclipse in Helsinki?"

For a few moments she says nothing. Anxious beads of sweat have broken out on Joona's forehead and neck.

"Yes," she eventually replies, and swallows hard.

"I was just thinking about that day, but we can talk about it later. . . . I love you."

"I love you, Dad."

18

LUMI DROPS HER IPHONE INTO HER BACKPACK AND CLOSES her notebook with trembling hands. If Professor Jean-Baptiste Blom hadn't interrupted his lecture because of a problem with his laptop, she'd never have taken the call.

She can't believe this is really happening, that her dad has called to ask her about the solar eclipse.

It was never supposed to happen.

Winter light is flooding into the lecture hall through the large windows. The paint is faded in patches; the floor is shabby.

The art history students are still sitting in their places, talking quietly or checking their phones, while the professor tries to get his laptop to work.

"I have to go," Lumi whispers to Laurent, who's moved to sit closer to her.

"Who was that?" he asks as his warm hand slides down her back.

Lumi puts her notebook and pens in her bag, stands up, removes her boyfriend's hand from her butt, and starts to make her way along the row.

"Lumi?"

She doesn't answer, pretends not to hear, but realizes that he's gathering his things and is coming after her.

Lumi reaches the aisle and sees the professor smile through distinctly uneven teeth when the first picture appears on the large screen. It's Robert Doisneau's photograph of a man swimming with a floating cello.

She walks quietly toward the door as the professor resumes his argument about the dramaturgy of the moment.

She puts her jacket on when she gets out into the hallway. She glances toward the bathrooms, feeling she's about to throw up, but heads for the exit.

"Lumi?"

Laurent catches up with her and takes hold of her arm. She spins around, adrenaline pumping through her body.

"What's going on?" he asks.

She looks at his concerned face, his stubble, and his long, boyish hair, messy and charming, as if he just got out of bed.

"I just need to sort something out," she says quickly.

"Who was that?"

"A friend," she says, backing away.

"From Sweden."

"I've got to go."

"Is he here in Paris? Does he want to see you?"

"Laurent . . ." she pleads.

"You're really weird, you know that, right?"

"It's just something private, nothing to do with—"

"You do know I just moved in with you?" he interrupts with a smile. "And you remember what we did last night, and again this morning . . . and what we're going to do again tonight?"

"Stop it," she says; she feels she might burst into tears any second.

He sees the look on her face and turns serious.

"Okay," he says.

The second hand on the big wall-clock is slowly ticking. A police car drives past outside. She lets him hold her hand in both of his, but can't bring herself to look him in the eye.

"But you're still coming to the party later, aren't you?" he asks.

"I don't know."

"You don't know," he repeats quietly.

Lumi pulls away and hurries for the exit, passes through the glass doors, and crosses the Rue Fénelon.

She stops in front of the broad flight of steps leading up to the church, removes a peace button from her jacket, and uses its pin to remove the SIM card from her cell phone.

She drops it on the ground, stamps on it to destroy it, then hurries on.

On the other side of the Boulevard de Magenta she tosses her cell phone in a bin, then walks to the Gare du Nord, where she takes the métro to the huge railroad terminus of the Gare de Lyon.

She feels her throat ache as anxiety wells up. She's having trouble breathing, pushing her way through a group of tourists.

The concourse is full of the noise of excited travelers, baggage carts, braking trains, and echoing public announcements. The throng of people is reflected in the great glass roof, like some huge single organism.

Lumi hurries past the flower stalls, newsagents, and fast-food joints, takes the escalator to below the main station passageway, and passes security to reach the storage lockers.

She's still breathing hard as she stops in front of one of the small lockers, taps in a code, and removes a bag, then goes into the women's bathroom, locks herself into the last stall, takes her jacket off, and hangs it up on the hook. She opens the bag, takes out a small Swiss Army knife, unfolds the screwdriver tool, crouches under the sink, and runs her hand carefully over the wall. Just above the overflow pipe, a few centimeters off the floor, she finds the painted-over screws. She fits the screwdriver into the heads and removes the panel concealing the valves in the pipes. She reaches in and pulls out the package, screws the hatch back in place, stands up, and looks at herself in the mirror.

Her lips are white and her eyes look glassy.

Lumi tries to concentrate on what she's about to do, even though she can't really believe it's happening.

She loosens the string, and is just about to remove the paper wrapping from the package when she hears someone come into the bathroom.

She hears a woman talking, complaining in a slurred voice about escorts. The woman walks along the stalls, hitting each door with the palm of her hand as she goes.

Without making a sound, Lumi removes the wrapping from the pistol, a small Glock 26 with a night sight.

She inserts one of the magazines and tucks the gun into her bag.

The woman outside is still ranting to herself.

With very deliberate movements, Lumi takes an envelope of cash out of the bag, divides the bundle of notes into two stacks, puts one in her purse, and places the other back in the bag. She picks out one of the passports, checks the name, mouths it to herself, then takes one of the cell phones out of the bag.

The woman is quiet now, but Lumi can hear her heavy breathing.

Something falls to the floor with a clatter.

Lumi switches the phone on and taps in the PIN.

She's worried that something bad has happened to her dad—that's her main concern. Lumi didn't ask any questions, but she can't help hoping that he's wrong. Part of her is wondering if he's been expecting disaster to strike for so long that he is beginning to see ghosts.

But now he's called her and asked if she remembers the solar eclipse in Helsinki.

That means just one thing: that their disaster plan has been activated.

Lumi wipes the tears from her cheeks, and tries to breathe calmly. She puts on her new jacket, tucks the old one into her bag, pulls the hood up over her head, flushes the toilet, and leaves the stall.

A large woman is standing in front of the mirror at one of the sinks. The floor below her is soaking wet.

Lumi hurries out and goes to one of the counters in the departure hall and takes a numbered ticket; when it's her turn, she buys a seat on the next train to Marseille. She pays cash, then makes her way to the platform.

The heavy smell of the train brakes hangs in the air.

Lumi waits with her head lowered, her bag between her feet. The sign on the platform says the train won't be there for another twenty minutes or so.

She thinks back to those months in Nattavaara. The last time she spent with her mom was also the first she spent with her dad.

She didn't really know him before then, just had a few random memories and stories to go on. But she loved being close to him, those evenings at the dinner table, the early mornings.

She loved the fact that he had trained her, patiently and tirelessly. They grew close through their preparations for this moment.

Lumi lifts her chin and listens. The PA system is announcing delays. There's the sound of train whistles in the distance.

A thin man in a lead-colored coat is walking along the opposite platform, making his way among the waiting passengers, but then he suddenly runs for the stairs.

Lumi lowers her gaze and thinks back to when Saga Bauer came to see them, to tell them that Jurek Walter's body had been found. It felt like throwing open the doors to the garden on a summer morning. She could walk out into a new world, she could move to Paris.

A train is approaching, rattling as it passes before pulling up at Platform 18 with a hiss. Lumi picks up her bag, climbs on board, and finds her seat. She sits with her bag in her lap, and is looking out of the window when she sees the man in the gray coat outside the train.

She quickly sinks down onto the floor, pretending to look for something in her bag, and checks the time.

They should have left by now.

She doesn't answer when the woman next to her asks if she can help with anything.

A whistle blows on the platform, and the train starts to move. She waits for a long while before sitting back up in her seat and apologizing to the woman.

Lumi closes her eyes tightly to stop herself from crying.

She finds herself thinking back to the end of her first term, when she accidentally insulted another student by suggesting that his photographs might be sexist. At the exhibition later that month he had scrawled "Five Sexist Pictures by a Sexist" across the photos.

They ended up going out with each other, and this summer he moved in with her, to see if they could make it work.

She opens her eyes but can still see him in front of her. Laurent, with his untidy hair and pilled sweaters. Those intense brown eyes. Laurent, with his beautiful smile, southern French accent, and pouting lips.

Paris and its sprawling suburbs are already long gone.

Lumi thinks of how she pulled away from Laurent and ran from him.

When the train pulls into Lyon two hours later, she gets to her feet, pulls the hood of her sweatshirt over her head, and steps out onto the platform. The wind is warmer here.

Lumi never had any intention of traveling all the way to Marseille.

She joins the stream of people moving through the huge station, takes the escalator to the lower floor, and walks along a tiled passageway to the Hertz rental-car desk. She takes out her fake passport, fills in all the forms, pays cash, and is given the key to a red Toyota.

She can be in Switzerland in just two hours.

19

JOONA IS DRIVING AS FAST AS HE CAN ALONG JÄRLASJÖN. The heavy snowfall vanishes without a trace the instant it hits the dark surface of the lake. He tries calling Valeria again, but there's still no answer.

Panic flashes through his mind. It's as if Jurek were sitting in the darkness of the back seat of the car, leaning forward to whisper to him:

"I'm going to grind you into the dirt."

Joona is cursing himself for being so slow, for not spotting what Jurek was doing earlier.

Valeria isn't answering her phone.

If he meets a vehicle coming the other way, he's going to have to assume that it's Jurek or one of his accomplices. He'll have to block the road with the car and try to take the other driver out.

He's able to drive even faster when he reaches the narrow road past Hästhagen. The swirling snow behind the car glows red in the glare of the taillights. The forest opens up, and the dark soil of the fields is covered by a layer of freshly fallen snow.

The falling snowflakes are smaller now, and fly up into the air as he turns into the drive that leads to Valeria's nursery.

There are fresh tire tracks from a heavy vehicle on the drive. They weren't made by Valeria's car, which is parked in its usual place, a thin layer of snow covering it.

The lights are on in the greenhouses, but he can't see anyone inside.

Joona turns the wheel sharply to the left, heading toward the deep ditch, then reverses and stops, so the car is blocking the road for any other vehicles. He takes his bag from the passenger seat and gets out of the car, then puts his hand under his jacket and draws his Colt Combat.

The windows of Valeria's house are dark. There's no sound. The snow is slowly drifting down, white against the sky.

As he approaches the first greenhouse, he sees signs of recent movement on the ground. A bucket full of fertilizer has been overturned.

Joona walks along the glass walls, peering in. There are green leaves pressed up against the glass, which is foggy with condensation.

He hears the sound of a dog barking in the distance.

When he reaches the farthest greenhouse, he sees Valeria's red padded jacket lying on the floor next to one of the benches. He cautiously nudges the door open, walks into the humid air, stops to listen, then continues between the benches with his pistol aimed at the floor. He moves through the steaming vegetation, a striking contrast to the world outside, which has gone into hibernation for winter.

He hears a clatter, possibly a pair of scissors landing on the cement floor.

Joona moves his finger to the trigger and crouches beneath the branches of a row of cherry trees. There's someone moving around inside the greenhouse. He can see rapid movements through the damp foliage.

Valeria.

She has her back to him, and is holding a knife in her hand.

Walking slowly, Joona puts his pistol back in its holster and holds a protruding branch aside.

"Valeria?"

She turns around with a surprised smile. She's dressed in a dirty Greenpeace T-shirt, and her curly hair is pulled up into a thick ponytail. There's a streak of compost across her left cheek.

She puts the knife down on a stool and pulls off her gloves.

He sees that she's been grafting new branches onto apple-tree rootstock, binding the grafts with twine to hold them in place, then painting them with wax to seal them.

"Careful, I'm a bit dirty," she says, stifling a smile in a way that makes the tip of her chin wrinkle.

She leans forward and kisses him on the lips without touching him.

"I've been trying to call you," Joona says.

Valeria feels the back pockets of her jeans.

"Must have left my phone in my jacket."

Joona glances out at a dark branch when a gust of wind passes through the trees.

"I thought we were going to meet at Farang?"

"We need to talk; things are happening that . . ."

He falls silent and takes a deep breath.

"You think he's alive," she whispers. "But they found the body. It was his, wasn't it?"

"I've been through it all with Nils, but it isn't enough. . . . Jurek Walter's alive. I didn't think he was, but he's alive."

"No," she says, quietly but firmly.

Joona looks over his shoulder, but he can't see the door of the greenhouse. There are too many plants in the way.

"You need to trust me," he says. "I'm going to get Lumi to a safe place abroad to protect her, and—well, I'm asking you to come with me."

Valeria's face has turned gray, as it does when she's worried. The wrinkles around her mouth become more defined, and her face hardens.

"You know I can't do that," she says quietly.

"This is a difficult decision."

"Is it? Because I'm almost starting to wonder what this is all about. . . . I don't want to exaggerate my own significance, but this has come right when we're starting to get serious. . . . I've always wanted you to know you weren't under any sort of pressure. I'm not trying to compete with Summa, because I can't, I know that."

Joona takes a step to one side so he can get a better view of the greenhouse behind her.

"I hear what you're saying, but . . ."

"Sorry, I didn't mean . . . That was a silly thing to say."

"I do understand," he says. "We can discuss everything, but Jurek's alive . . . and he's killed at least five people in the past month."

Valeria rubs her forehead with her dirty fingers, leaving two black streaks above her right eyebrow.

"Why haven't I read anything about that in the papers?" she counters.

"Because the victims are spread across Europe, and they're criminals as well, murderers and sex offenders. . . . Jurek's looking for someone he can work with. He's been testing various candidates and killing the ones who don't make the grade."

He looks at his watch, then glances up toward the dark house.

"Do you genuinely think it's dangerous for the two of us to stay here?"

"Yes," he says, looking her in the eye. "There's a good chance you're already being monitored. He'll have been watching you, getting to know you, your routines."

"It just sounds so over-the-top."

"You have to trust me. Come with me," Joona pleads.

"When are you thinking of leaving?" she says after a pause.

"Now."

She looks at him in astonishment and moistens her lips.

"Can I join you later?"

"No."

"You're saying I just have to pack a bag and leave?"

"There's no time to pack."

"How long are we going to be in hiding?"

"Two weeks, two years . . . as long as it takes."

"All this would be ruined, everything I've worked so hard to achieve," she says in a toneless voice.

"Valeria, you can always start again. I'll help you."

She stands there silently, her eyes lowered.

"Joona," she says, and looks up, "you've done what you could. I appreciate that this could be serious, but I don't have a choice. I can't leave. I've got my greenhouses, my client base. . . . This is my home . . . and I'm going to celebrate Christmas with my boys for the first time. . . . You know how much that means to me."

"You could be back in time for Christmas," Joona says, feeling desperation rising. "Listen, Valeria. When Jurek escaped, I was seeing a woman, Disa. . . . I thought I'd never dare do that again."

"Disa? Why haven't you ever mentioned her?"

"I didn't want to frighten you," he says.

She shuts her eyes when she realizes what he means. "He killed her."

"Yes."

She wipes her mouth with the back of her hand.

"That doesn't mean he's going to kill me," she says in a shaky voice.

"Valeria, you need to take this seriously—come with me," Joona begs, feeling more helpless than he has at any point in his life.

"I can't. I just can't," she says. "How am I supposed to leave the boys again?"

"Please, you—"

"I can't," she interrupts.

"I'll organize police protection."

"Never," she says, then lets out a surprised laugh.

"You wouldn't have to see them."

"Joona, listen to me, no cops, not on my property . . . except you."

He stands with his head bowed for several seconds, then opens his bag, takes out a pistol and hands it to her.

"It's loaded, eleven shots in the magazine. . . . Carry it with you at all times, keep it with you even when you're in bed. . . . See, here, all you have to do is release this catch, hold it with both hands, aim, and fire. Don't hesitate if you get the opportunity—shoot immediately, several times."

She shakes her head. "I'm not going to do that, Joona."

He puts the gun down on the stool next to her knife and takes a deep breath.

"The other thing I need to do is give you a warning. From now on, you have to look at anything that isn't absolutely familiar to you as a trap. Unexpected visitors, a new customer, someone who's changed their car or shown up at the wrong time . . . No matter what it is, you call this number."

Joona shows her a number on his cell phone, then sends her the contact.

"Keep that number, and make sure it's always the first option when you open your phone. . . . It won't be enough to save you immediately—Jurek's too quick for that—but this number belongs to a friend of mine, Nathan Pollock. He'll be able to see where you are, and that will increase the chances of their tracking and rescuing you."

"This all sounds crazy," she says simply, fixing her eyes on him.

"I'd stay with you if it wasn't for Lumi. I have to protect my daughter," he says.

"It's okay, I understand, Joona."

"I've got to go now," he whispers. "If you want to come with me, you'll have to come as you are, in boots and dirty pants. . . . I'll go back to the car and wait twenty seconds."

She doesn't answer, just looks at him, trying to hold back the tears and swallow the lump in her throat.

Joona walks out of the greenhouse. When he gets back into his car, he reverses to the circular driveway and stops.

He looks at his watch.

Snowflakes are falling through the glow from the big greenhouses.

The seconds tick past. He should have left by now.

He leans back against the cold seat and puts his right hand on the gear stick.

Everything is quiet and still.

He starts the engine again, and the headlights form a swirling tunnel down toward the edge of the forest. The fans whir as the car heats up.

Joona stares ahead of him, then glances at his watch again, changes gear, and goes around the driveway. He looks at the greenhouses in the rearview mirror, and slowly drives away from Valeria's nursery.

20

ERICA LILJESTRAND IS SITTING ON HER OWN AT THE COUN-
ter in the Pilgrim Bar, waiting for a friend from her biotechnology
class.

Sleet is running down the window facing the street.

She puts her phone down beside her glass of wine and looks at
the fingerprints on the screen before it goes dark.

She and Liv agreed to meet here at ten o'clock to discuss the
New Year's Eve party, but Liv is more than an hour late now, and
she's not answering her phone.

There are hardly any customers in the Pilgrim Bar this evening,
probably because the building's being renovated and the façade on
Regerings Street is covered up. The entrance is hidden by scaffolding and dirty white nylon netting.

The three guys at the table in the back have started glancing in
her direction, so she sticks with the bartender, chatting with him
and checking her phone.

Weird that a woman sitting alone in a bar has to think of herself
as fair game, she thinks. Erica knows she isn't exactly pretty, and
she's a long way from being a flirt. Even so, the simple fact that she's
there on her own is enough for them.

The bartender, who says his name is Nick, seems to assume that
he's irresistible. He's a suntanned, wrinkled man in early middle
age, with blue eyes and a fashionable haircut. His short-sleeved
shirt is tight across his bulging biceps, and only half covers the
tattoo on his neck that's faded with age.

So far Nick has told her about mountain climbing in Thailand, skiing in the French Alps, and the volatile stock market.

Erica glances surreptitiously at the older, pink-cheeked couple chatting over at one of the corner tables. They look happy with their bottle of wine and nachos with salsa and guacamole.

She calls Liv again, and lets it ring for a ridiculous amount of time. Dirty water is dripping from the scaffolding outside.

She puts her phone down and traces a scratch in the polished wood of the bar with her fingernail, then stops when she reaches the base of her glass and takes a sip.

The bell jangles as the door opens. Erica turns to look.

It isn't Liv, but a man the size of a bear. He brings in cold air from the street with him, then takes off his black raincoat and squeezes it into a plastic bag.

The man is wearing a dark-blue knitted sweater with leather patches on the elbows, cargo trousers, and military-style boots.

He says hello to the bartender and sits down a meter or so away from Erica, with one stool between them, and hangs the plastic bag from a hook under the bar. "It's a blustery night," he says in a deep, soft voice.

"Looks that way," the bartender replies.

The large man rubs his hands together. "What vodkas do you have?"

"Dworek, Stolichnaya, Smirnoff, Absolut, Koskenkorva, Nemiroff," Nick says.

"Black Smirnoff?"

"Yes."

"I'll have five doubles of Smirnoff, then."

Nick raises his eyebrows. "You want five glasses of vodka?"

"Room temperature, if that's okay." The man smiles.

Erica looks at the time on her phone and decides to wait another ten minutes.

The bartender places five shot glasses in front of the large man, then fetches a bottle from the shelf.

"And refill her glass, since we're celebrating," he says, nodding in Erica's direction.

Erica has no idea what he's talking about. Maybe it was just a joke that didn't quite work. She looks at him, but he doesn't look back. His face looks sad, and his thick neck has settled into folds. His hair is cropped, and he has beautiful pearl earrings in each earlobe.

"Do you want another glass of wine?" the bartender asks Erica.

"Why not?" she replies, stifling a yawn.

"Since we're celebrating," Nick says, then fills a fresh glass.

The large man has taken out a book of matches and is now chewing on one of them.

"I used to have a bar in Gothenburg," he says, then gets to his feet.

He stands still, as if he can no longer understand where he is. Slowly, he turns to look at the bartender, then Erica. His pupils are dilated, and the match falls from his lips. He keeps turning, looks at the older man at the corner table, then one of the young men, before licking his lips and sitting back down.

He clears his throat and empties the first glass of vodka, then puts it down on the bar.

Erica looks at the flat matchbook lying next to the line of glasses. The black cover is decorated with what looks like a small white skeleton.

"Are you spending Christmas in Stockholm?" Nick asks, putting a bowl of large green olives in front of Erica.

"I'll be going to my parents' in Växjö," she replies.

"Nice. Växjö's a good town."

"You?" she asks politely.

"Thailand, as usual."

"I don't think so," the large man says.

"Sorry?" Nick says in surprise.

"Not that I can see into the future, but—"

"Can't you?" the bartender interrupts. "That's a relief; you almost had me worried there for a moment."

The large man has lowered his gaze and is looking at his stubby fingertips. The young men get up noisily and leave.

"It's complicated," the large man says after a while.

"Isn't it though?" Nick says tartly.

The man doesn't answer, just picks at his matchbook. The bartender stands and looks at him for a while, waiting for him to look up; then he starts wiping the counter with a gray cloth.

"Nice earrings," Erica says, and hears the bartender let out a laugh.

"Thanks," the man says in a serious voice. "I wear them for my sister, my twin sister; she died when I was thirteen."

"That's terrible," she whispers.

"Yes," he says simply, and raises his shot glass toward her. "Cheers . . . cheers, whatever your name is . . ."

"Erica," she says.

"Cheers, Erica . . ."

"Cheers."

He drinks, carefully puts the empty glass down, and licks his lips.

"They call me the Beaver."

The bartender turns away to hide his smile.

"It's a shame your friend's late," the Beaver says after a pause.

"How did you know that?"

"I could say it's just deduction, a logical conclusion," he says. "I watch people. I saw the way you've been looking at your phone, the way you turned toward the door. . . . But I've also got a sixth sense."

"A sixth sense, like telepathy?" she asks, forcing herself not to smile.

Nick removes her first wineglass and wipes the counter.

"It's hard to explain," the Beaver goes on. "But, in layman's terms, I should probably call it precognition. . . . Along with clairvoyance, intrinsic knowledge."

"That sounds pretty advanced," Erica says. "So you're some sort of medium?"

She can't help feeling sorry for him. He seems completely unaware of how weird people think he is.

"My abilities aren't paranormal—there's a logical explanation."

"Okay," the bartender says skeptically.

They wait for him to go on, but instead he empties the third shot glass with very precise movements, then puts it down carefully beside the others.

"Almost every time I'm with other people, I know the order in which they're going to die," he says. "I don't know when it's going to happen—in ten minutes or fifty years—I can just see the order."

Erica nods, regretting that she encouraged him to talk. She only felt compelled to be a little friendlier because Nick was starting to act like a bully. She's wondering how soon she can leave without its looking like she's trying to get away from him when her cell phone buzzes.

21

ERICA FLIPS HER PHONE OVER, HOPING IT WILL GIVE HER AN excuse to leave the bar immediately. It's a text from Liv, apologizing for not showing up and saying she had to help a drunken friend get home.

Erica's thumbs feel numb when she replies that she understands and that they can meet up tomorrow instead.

"I have to go," she says, pushing her almost untouched glass of wine away.

"I didn't mean to scare you," the large man says, looking at her intently.

"No, it's . . . I believe everyone has abilities that they don't use," she replies vaguely.

"I know it sounded overdramatic, what I said, but I never seem to be able to find the right words to describe it."

"I understand," she says, looking at the screen.

"Sometimes I only have time to count a few people, but sometimes I can do everyone in a room. . . . It's like I see a big clock face with Roman numerals, and when the hand points to the number one, I find myself looking at the first person in the room who's going to die; I don't know how, but it's just what happens. Tick-tock, the hand moves to the number two, and I'm looking at another person. . . . Fairly often, I catch sight of my own face in a mirror before I lose contact."

"Can I settle up?" Erica says to the bartender.

"I scared you," the Beaver says, still trying to catch her eye.

"Can you leave her alone now?" Nick says.

"Erica, I just want to say that your number wasn't the first to come up in this room."

"Stop it," the bartender says, leaning across the bar.

"I'm stopping," the Beaver says calmly, and tucks the flat little matchbook into the chest pocket of his sweater. "Unless you'd like to know who number one was?"

"Excuse me," Erica says, and heads for the restroom.

The bartender watches her go, and sees her wobble and hold one hand out to the wall to steady herself.

The Beaver empties his fourth glass of vodka, then puts it down silently next to the last one.

"Okay, who's going to die first?" the bartender asks.

"You . . . which isn't really surprising," the Beaver replies.

"Why isn't it surprising?"

"Because I'm here to cut your throat," the Beaver replies calmly.

"Am I going to have to call the police?"

"You've already dosed her glass with Xyrem, haven't you?" the Beaver asks.

"What the hell do you want?" Nick hisses.

"Did you know that one of your girls died in the ambulance?" the Beaver says, turning the last glass on the bar.

"You're mentally ill," Nick tells him. "You may not even know it, but . . ."

He falls silent when Erica returns to her stool. Her cheeks are pale, and she sits quietly for a while, her eyes half closed.

"I'm fairly sure I'm going to succeed, because you're number one, and I'm number five," the Beaver says quietly.

The older couple call out their thanks, put their coats on, and leave the bar. Now there are just the three of them left.

"I should probably go," Erica says, slurring her words. "I'm not feeling too good. . . ."

"Would you like me to call a taxi?" Nick asks amiably.

"Thanks," she manages to say.

"He's only pretending to call," the Beaver says. "That's his way of getting you to stay here until the bar's empty."

"Drink up and leave," the bartender says.

"When my sister died, I—"

"Just shut up," the bartender says, getting his phone out.

"I want to hear," Erica says, and feels a fresh wave of exhaustion wash over her.

"I had a permanent stomachache when I was a child," the Beaver says. "It felt swollen and heavy ... and when I was thirteen it had gotten so big that I couldn't hide it anymore. They took me to see a doctor, who concluded that it was a tumor ... not an ordinary tumor, though, but my twin sister, a 'fetus in fetu.'"

He pulls up his knitted sweater and white vest to reveal a long, pale scar across the side of his fat, hairless stomach.

"Holy shit," Erica murmurs.

"Behind my peritoneum was a sort of mass of tissue, twenty-five centimeters long—that was where she was," he says. "I saw the pictures afterward, when she was dead: thin arms and big hands, small, sticklike legs, spine and a bit of face ... but no brain. My blood was the only thing keeping her alive."

Erica feels nausea rising in her throat. She stands up and tries to put her coat on, but one of the sleeves is inside out, and she stumbles, managing to grab the bar just in time.

"They also found parts of her in my brain," the Beaver goes on. "But they were too difficult to remove ... so they'll have to stay where they are. ... I can feel her most of the time. You can't exactly see it on an MRI, but I think her tiny brain is inside mine—that's why I have an extra sense."

Erica drops her handbag on the floor, and her glasses case and eyeliner roll out under the bar stool. She feels she's about to be sick, and wonders if she's eaten something that disagreed with her.

"God," she whispers. Her back is wet with sweat.

She sinks onto the floor to put her things back in her bag, but she's so tired she has to lie on her side and rest for a moment before she can get back up.

The floor feels cool against her cheek. She closes her eyes, then startles at a sudden noise. It's the bartender, shouting at the Beaver.

"Get out!" he roars.

Erica knows she has to get up, she has to go home. She forces her eyes open and sees the bartender backing away, with a baseball bat.

"Just fuck off!" he shouts.

The large man who said he was known as the Beaver sweeps several bottles off the bar, then moves quickly toward Nick.

Erica hears thuds and deep sighs.

The bartender crashes to the floor and rolls over, sending two chairs flying before he hits the wall.

The Beaver follows him with long strides. He grabs the baseball bat from Nick and hits his legs three times, yelling something in a broken voice before he smashes a table. He tosses the broken bat at Nick, then stomps on the remains of the table, kicking the pieces away.

Erica tries to sit up. She watches the Beaver drag Nick to his feet again before shoving him hard in the chest and screaming into his face.

"Okay, take it easy," Nick pants.

He can't put any weight on his right leg, and there's blood running down his face from a cut above one eyebrow. The Beaver grabs him by the neck with one hand and punches him in the face with the other. He pushes Nick down onto one of the tables, knocking glasses and a candleholder onto the floor, then shoves the table into the wall, flipping it over and sending Nick sprawling across the floor.

Erica has to lie down again, and watches as the Beaver stands astride the bartender, hitting him in the face.

Nick is trying to get away from the bear-like man. Blood sprays from his mouth as he coughs and begs him to stop. The Beaver grabs him by one hand and breaks his arm at the elbow.

Nick lets out a howl of pain and desperation as the Beaver yanks at the arm and tries to break it again.

Panting heavily, the Beaver takes hold of Nick's neck with both hands, then squeezes so tightly that his face turns white. The Beaver roars and crushes Nick's head against the floor. Then he suddenly lets go and steps away from Nick, who splutters and tries to catch his breath.

The Beaver staggers backward.

When he pulls something from his pocket, the little matchbook falls out and lands on the floor.

He flicks open a switchblade, then moves forward again, yelling at Nick. The Beaver's teeth flash in the glow of one of the wall lights.

"I'm sorry I was rude to you, I didn't mean it," Nick groans. "You don't have to kill me, I promise...."

Erica feels heavy steps across the floor against her cheek.

The Beaver reaches Nick, holds his raised hand aside, and stabs him with the knife. The blade penetrates deep into his chest.

Blood sprays up into the Beaver's face as he pulls the knife out. He lets out a roar of rage and stabs again.

Nick has almost lost consciousness, and is merely whimpering weakly now.

The Beaver spins him around, grabs his hair, and starts trying to scalp him. He cuts off a large chunk of skin and tosses it aside.

It's as if he's taken some sort of terrible drug.

The Beaver drops the knife, lets out a roar, then drags the lifeless body by one leg over toward the door.

Nick must surely be dead by now, but the Beaver goes on beating him and stomping on his stomach. He pulls a framed photograph of John Lennon off the wall, smashes it, sending pieces of glass flying in all directions, and tosses the remnants of the frame onto the bloody body.

He tips a table on top of Nick, then backs away, gasping, before turning around and looking at her.

"I'm not involved in this, please," she says weakly.

He walks toward her and picks the switchblade up from the floor. A string of blood is hanging from the blade.

"Please..."

Erica doesn't even have the energy to lift her head from the floor as he walks over to her and grabs her by the hair.

The pain really isn't that overwhelming as the blade cuts through tissue, sinews, and blood vessels. Far worse is the ice-cold wind in her face, combined with the feeling of being asphyxiated from within.

22

WHEN SAGA WAKES UP, SHE CAN HEAR RANDY IN THE kitchen. He often spends the night at her place, but otherwise sleeps in the old photography studio he rents. Randy comes in with a cup of coffee and a croissant with jam for her.

He's five years younger than Saga, and has a shaved head, calm eyes, and a skeptical smile. He's a detective, and is part of a team investigating online hate crimes.

"Whenever I go home to Örgryte, Mom brings me breakfast in bed," he says.

"You're spoiled." Saga smiles, and sips the coffee.

"I know your mom was—"

"I don't want to talk about her," she interrupts.

"Okay, sorry," he says.

"It doesn't help; that's why I have my rule. It's better to avoid the subject completely—I've told you that."

"I know, but . . ."

"This isn't about you."

"But I'm here," he says quietly.

"Thanks," she replies curtly.

When he's gone, she wonders if she might have sounded too defensive. There's no way Randy could know what she's been through. She texts him to say sorry and thank him for breakfast.

After work, Saga picks up her half-sister from school and takes her to see her hearing specialist. On the way home, she asks about the clown girls.

"Dad says they're not real," Pellerina says.

"That's right, they're not," Saga says.

"I still don't want them to find me."

Their dad isn't home when they get there. Saga hopes he'll be back soon. She wants to talk to him about the gift—to tell him she only reacted the way she did because it reminded her of her mom's illness.

Pellerina is standing at the kitchen counter, wearing a polka-dot apron and whisking cake batter while Saga greases the pan.

The doorbell rings, and Pellerina squeals that it's their dad.

Saga wipes her hands on a paper towel, then goes to answer the door.

It's Joona Linna.

His face is serious; his gray eyes are icy cold.

"Come in," she says.

He looks over his shoulder, then walks into the hall and closes the door behind him.

"Who else is in the house?"

"Just me and Pellerina," she replies. "What happened?"

He looks over at the wooden staircase, then the door to the kitchen.

"Joona, I realize that you really believe Jurek's still alive," she says.

"At first it was just a theoretical possibility . . . but now I've identified the pattern," he says, peering through the peephole in the front door.

"Wouldn't you like to come in and have coffee?" she asks.

"I don't have time," he replies, looking back at her again.

"I know recent events have stirred up old memories," she says. "But I really don't think Jurek's behind this. Look at the level of violence—it's aggressive in a way that Jurek never was. . . . And, yes, I know you're going to say it was his accomplice. I hear what you're saying, but I honestly can't see the pattern."

"Saga, I'm only here to tell you that you need to go into hiding—you need to find a safe place for yourself and your family. But I'm starting to realize that you won't be doing that."

"I'd never manage to get Dad and Pellerina to come with me. . . . I'm not even going to try—I don't want to frighten them."

"But . . ."

A door slams in the kitchen, and Joona's hand instinctively reaches for the pistol under his jacket before he hears Pellerina laughing.

"If Jurek's alive, it's my fault," Saga says in a low voice. "You know that. I was the one who let him out . . . so it's my responsibility to stop him."

"It isn't worth it," he says. "You're like a sister to me. I don't want you to try to stop Jurek. I want you to hide."

"Joona, you're doing the right thing from your point of view. You're convinced about all this, and you need to protect Lumi," she says. "But for me, the right thing is staying and trying to find the person who's really behind these murders. . . . And don't worry. I'm not ruling anything out, not even Jurek Walter."

"Then work with Nathan. I sent him everything I have."

"Okay, I'll talk to him."

"Saga!" Pellerina calls from the kitchen.

"I need to get back to her," she says.

"Don't think Jurek's like anyone else," Joona goes on. "He didn't treat you differently because you're beautiful. . . ."

"And there I was, thinking you'd never even noticed." She smiles.

"Jurek doesn't care about how you look, he's interested in your mind, your soul . . . your darkness, what he likes to call your catacombs."

"You do know I've spoken to him, don't you? More than you, actually," she reminds him.

"But back then you were merely a tool for him, a Trojan horse. . . ."

"Okay, fine," she says, raising her hands to get him to stop.

"Saga, listen to me. If you stay, you're going to see him again. I can't go without giving you three pieces of advice first."

"I'm listening."

She leans against the door frame and folds her arms over her chest.

"One: Don't try to talk to him. Don't try to arrest him. Don't worry about any ethical considerations. If there aren't any witnesses, you need to kill him immediately, and make sure he's dead this time."

"He's already dead."

"Two: Remember that he isn't on his own, and that—"

"If your theory's correct," she interrupts.

"—Jurek's used to having a brother who would obey him like a dog. These murders mean he's recruited an accomplice, and that means he can be in more than one place at the same time."

"Joona, that's enough now," Saga says.

"Three," Joona goes on. "You need to remember that you can't make deals with him, because they'll never work in your favor. He won't let go, and with each one you make, you'll end up deeper in his trap. . . . Jurek will take everything from you, but in the end it's you he wants to get at."

"I want you to leave now," she says, looking him in the eye.

"Just be careful."

23

AS JOONA PULLS OUT ONTO THE TRAFFIC CIRCLE, HE CAN'T help thinking he stayed too long at Saga's. He realized almost immediately that she wasn't going to heed his warnings, but maybe she'll remember some of what he said if she does encounter Jurek.

A dusty cement truck is parked in a cloud of exhaust fumes at the gas station, and a group of schoolchildren is approaching on the footbridge.

As Joona turns onto Nynäs Street, he spots the white van for a second time.

It was parked outside the church farther up the street as he hurried along the sidewalk after his meeting with Saga.

The branches of the trees were reflected in the windshield, but they weren't just moving in time with the wind—sometimes they shuddered and lurched.

There was someone inside the van.

That doesn't necessarily mean he's being watched, but, given the current circumstances, it's probably a fair assumption. He can't afford to dismiss anything as simple coincidence.

Joona changes lanes and pulls out onto the Johanneshov Bridge, keeping pace with the fast traffic as the dark water sparkles far below.

Two police cars rush past in the opposite direction, sirens blaring.

There's a shredded tire lying in the middle of the road.

In the rearview mirror, he sees the van pull out onto the bridge. It's several hundred meters behind him, but he's within sight of it.

Joona would never take it for granted, but he imagines he'd win in close combat if he met Jurek face-to-face. The reason he's running is that Jurek would never get into close combat with anyone he couldn't beat.

It's hard to defeat Jurek at his games because he exploits the fact that human beings love each other.

Joona passes a battered delivery van, then pulls in front of it and increases his speed.

The windows let out a little sigh and all sound is muffled as the car heads into the entrance to the Söder Road Tunnel.

He has precisely 1,520 meters to come up with a solution.

The dirty gray walls and green emergency exits flash past, and the glare of the strip lights pulses evenly through the car.

He speeds up and unfastens his seat belt as he passes the junction for Medborgar Plaza. The vehicles around him are making a monotonous roar.

Joona pulls into the right-hand lane and sees the signs for the exit to Nacka. He looks in the rearview mirror and veers even farther to the right, until he's driving on top of the dotted line separating the two lanes.

The turn is approaching fast, and the vehicles around him are sounding their horns and keeping their distance.

The dotted line becomes a solid line as it disappears beneath the front of the car. If he doesn't make a decision now, he'll drive straight into the wall dividing the two roads.

Joona glances quickly in the rearview mirror and brakes so hard that the tires skid across the pavement and into the hard shoulder. The ridged lines on the road make the entire chassis rumble before the car comes to a stop just centimeters from the low crash-barrier.

Heavy vehicles thunder past on both sides.

Joona slips out of the car and runs several meters at a crouch down the tunnel leading to Nacka.

Just as he tucks himself away in the darkness behind the row of columns, he hears a vehicle brake and stop behind his.

It stops on the hatch-marked area between the lanes.

A taxi heading for Nacka blows its horn irritably. Dust and garbage swirl through the air.

Joona draws his Colt Combat from the holster under his right arm, feeds a bullet into the chamber, then stops and listens.

All he can hear is the rumble of the traffic in the tunnel, and the sound of the fans in the ceiling. Lead-colored dust covers the floor and the garbage that's collected in the space behind the pillars.

There's a rustling sound from some old plastic bags behind him.

He's put his pursuer in an impossible position by stopping right where the tunnel divides, like a snake's tongue. Whichever road the person takes may turn out to be the wrong one. He's been forced either to give up or to surrender any attempt at stealth.

Now he's sitting there with the engine in park, unsure what to do.

It probably feels like a trap.

The pursuer doesn't know if Joona's hiding in the car, or if he's continued on foot and possibly even left the tunnel through the emergency exit up ahead.

Joona creeps forward slowly between the pillars. As long as he stays out of the lights, he's invisible.

Every time a vehicle passes, he pulls back slightly to stop himself from being caught in the headlights.

Black dust moves slowly in the backdraft from each car.

With his pistol pointed at the ground, Joona hurries forward the moment a motorbike passes him.

He has to know if the person who's stopped behind his car is Jurek.

Very slowly, he moves toward the van, noticing the filthy emergency telephone on the wall, the striped shadows across the rough concrete.

It's still impossible to see the other vehicle clearly.

He moves cautiously to one side to get a better angle and can now see part of the back of the van.

There's no doubt that it's the same one he saw parked on Saga's street.

Joona moves as far as he can and sees that the driver is still sitting at the wheel, but it's impossible to make out a face because of reflections in the glass.

A truck passes by, heading toward the city center. Its weight makes the ground shake, and its headlights illuminate the van long enough for Joona to see a large man with sloping shoulders. An air freshener dangles from the rearview mirror, obscuring most of his face. But Joona is certain that it isn't Jurek. Maybe he's just had his first glimpse of Jurek's new recruit.

JOONA LOWERS HIS PISTOL.

If it had been Jurek, he would have shot him the next time a large vehicle drove past, but because he's not sure that the man in the van is Jurek's accomplice, he tells himself he can't do that.

The van shakes slightly as the man inside moves.

Joona stands motionless, with his pistol aimed at the ground. He can hear rats rustling among the plastic bags behind him.

The van rocks again.

A large, noisy bus is approaching.

Joona moves back slightly.

The glare of the bus headlights fills the tunnel, and the light hits the cab of the van from the side.

The large man is no longer sitting behind the wheel.

He's gone.

The bus passes. The air fills with dust and rubbish.

The only sound is the heavy whirring coming from the large fans in the roof. Joona crouches down and tries to see under the van, but it's too dark. He can't tell if his pursuer is hiding there or not.

He waits for the next vehicle and aims his pistol toward the gloom between the front and rear wheels.

Joona can see the lights from another vehicle approaching in the distance, and as it advances, the beam bounces across the road until it reaches the van.

For a moment, the muddy chassis and tires are lit up.

There's no one there.

Joona lowers his pistol again and is just getting to his feet when the van starts to reverse; then it stops, turns left, and disappears into the tunnel leading to the city center.

Joona listens as the sound of the engine fades away.

He waits several minutes, then approaches his own car at a crouch with his pistol aimed in front of him, checks beneath the car, looks around, and then gets back in the driver's seat.

He reverses and drives to the Central Train Station, where he pulls up in front of the main entrance and stops in a no-parking zone.

He walks around the car, pulls out his cell phone, removes the SIM card, and destroys it.

He opens the trunk. There are two black shoulder bags in the space where the spare tire should be, one large, one small. He takes them both out, then gets back in the driver's seat. One of the bags contains a short knife designed for close combat, which he fastens to his lower left arm with tape. He puts his gun in the glove compartment, locks the car, and walks away.

The car will soon be removed by the Transport Police and stored in a compound outside the city until he collects it.

Joona walks in through the main entrance and glances up at the main departure board. He moves through the slow-moving crowd with his head lowered.

He walks straight to the plate-glass window of a bookstore in the station and stares intently at the reflections of the people moving behind him.

No one seems to be following him.

He walks over to the counter and buys a ticket to Copenhagen, paying for it in cash.

The train leaves in eleven minutes, and is already waiting at Platform 12.

He walks over to the platform, past the information board and ticket machines. A cold wind is blowing along the tracks. Crows are circling the dark, canopied roofs. There's a homeless person sleeping beside one of the trash cans, wrapped in a padded green quilt. Joona drops his cell phone into her cup, then climbs onto the train.

24

JOONA IS READING KEITH RICHARDS'S AUTOBIOGRAPHY. From time to time, he looks up to observe his fellow passengers. The woman in the seat next to him has her face turned toward the window and is talking on her phone in a monotone. On the other side of the aisle, an older man with dirt marks on the trousers of his pale-brown suit leafs through the free magazine from the pocket of the seat and then leans his head back and closes his eyes.

The train crosses the long viaduct and stops at Södertälje Syd Station. A large man sits down in a seat a few rows behind Joona.

A heavy smell of aftershave drifts through the car.

The conductor passes through, asking for new passengers, and clings to the luggage rack when the train jolts before he moves on to the next car.

The landscape is frosty and gray.

The conductor doesn't ask to see the man's ticket, so he must have boarded the train in Stockholm, but waited to get seated until they had passed Södertälje.

The thin thread of a migraine flares behind one of Joona's eyes. His vision loses its clarity, and he has to shut his eyes for a while before he can go on reading.

Keith Richards is describing a recipe for a dish involving sausages with great enthusiasm.

After a while, Joona stands up and glances down the car. He can't see the face of the tall passenger, who is looking out of the window and wearing a black wool hat.

Joona takes the smaller bag with him but leaves his jacket hanging on the hook by his seat and the larger bag up on the rack.

He walks to the buffet car and buys a cheese sandwich and a cup of coffee. When he turns back, he sees someone watching him from the noisy space between the cars. He can't tell who it is through the glass door, but as soon as he starts to move in that direction the figure disappears.

Joona returns to his train car and notes that the tall man is sitting in his seat as if he hasn't moved.

Joona sits back down in his seat and continues reading.

The train is approaching Norrköping. There are many hours to go before they reach Copenhagen.

The landscape flattens out.

The woman next to him is looking through a report from the Central Bank on her laptop.

Putting his book down on the seat, and leaving the coffee cup and half-eaten sandwich on the table, Joona takes the small bag and goes and stands outside the restroom, waiting for it to become free.

The train slows down and shudders as it changes tracks and approaches the platform. Just as the train comes to a halt at the station, Joona moves into the next car.

Passengers are lined up in the aisle, waiting with their bags and rolling suitcases to get off. The doors open with a wheeze, and Joona leaves the train under cover of the group. He stops behind a large vending machine on the platform, kneeling down so he won't be seen, pulls out the dagger, and conceals it against his body; then he waits.

The larger of his two bags is still on the rack above his seat, his jacket is hanging from the hook, and his coffee cup is on the tray.

The air is full of the smell of the train's brakes. There are cigarette butts and bits of tobacco on the ground.

The conductor blows his whistle, and the doors close with a hiss. Slowly, the train sets off from the platform as the electric cables hum.

Joona tucks the dagger away in his bag, then gets to his feet and runs toward the station. A bus is pulling away just as he turns the corner. There are two cars waiting at the taxi stand, and Joona opens the door of the first one, gets in, and explains quickly to the driver that he needs to get to Skavsta Airport in a hurry.

As the taxi pulls away from the station, Joona watches the train accelerate.

The taxi slows down to let an old woman with a walker cross the street. Some magpies are picking through the trash in front of a hot-dog stand.

The taxi is cruising along Norra Promenaden when the train stops in the distance, close to the imposing bulk of the police station.

Someone has pulled the emergency brake.

The taxi passes some large buildings, blocking Joona's view of the train. The driver tries to engage him in conversation by asking about taking a trip to someplace warm, but Joona keeps his replies short as he looks behind them.

Just before they head down into the tunnel under the rail yard, Joona catches sight of the train again. A man is running along the track toward the station. Joona knows he could get out and go after the man, could probably kill him. But then he would miss the plane to France—and Jurek might win the race to Lumi.

Thirty-six minutes later, the taxi stops outside the gray terminal building at Skavsta Airport. Tossing his bag over his shoulder, Joona goes in through the main entrance, passes beneath the plane hanging from the roof, and makes his way to the customer-service desk. He takes a numbered ticket and waits with his back to the wall, his hand clasping the dagger inside the bag.

People come and go. The pale sky glints in the glass every time the doors swing open.

A tired-looking man is trying to check a full set of golf clubs for a flight to the Canary Islands, and a very old woman needs help phoning her sister.

When it's Joona's turn, he walks up to the woman at the desk. She stares into his eyes as he asks for a ticket to Béziers, in the south of France.

"France? You wouldn't rather stay in Nyköping with me instead?" she says with a smile, then blushes.

"In another life," he replies.

"You know where I am."

After getting his boarding pass, he goes into the bathroom, carefully wipes all traces of his fingerprints from the knife, wraps it in toilet paper, and drops it into the trash.

Just as the last call for boarding is announced, he passes through security, making sure he's the last passenger on board. The door swings shut behind him, the plane starts to taxi, and the attendant steps into the aisle to begin the safety demonstration.

Joona turns to look through the window and feels the plane's engines start to roar, then the whir as the flaps extend. He's sent detailed instructions to Nathan Pollock. The first thing Nathan needs to do is make sure Valeria gets police protection, at the very highest level.

When Joona lands in France, he'll change his identity. He has a different passport in his bag, a new driver's license, euros, everything he needs.

If Jurek figures out that Joona has gone to France, he'll assume that Joona's going to meet Lumi in Marseille, but instead he will be driving his rental car in the opposite direction, to pick up a bag in Bouloc, north of Toulouse.

To the right of the Rue Jean Jaurès, just before you enter the town, is a small farm on the edge of a field.

Joona has buried an aluminum case there, next to the slurry pit.

It contains two pistols, ammunition, explosives, and detonators.

Once he's collected the case, he'll make his way to Geneva to meet up with Lumi.

25

SAGA'S KNEES ARE RESTING ON THE MATTE-BLACK GAS TANK, and she can feel the vibrations from the engine against her thighs. She's heading along the highway in sixth gear, parallel to the railroad tracks. She then leans gently to the left and takes the exit for Sollentuna, eases up on the throttle, downshifts, and turns so sharply that one of the silencers scrapes the asphalt.

She hasn't quite gotten used to how sensitive this motorcycle is. When her old Triumph reached the end of its life, her dad let her borrow his Indian Chief Dark Horse, since he only uses it on perfect summer days.

Her dad's sentimental about the brand, and the fact that it was a guy from Småland who cofounded Indian and built the first motorcycle. When Lars-Erik was young, he lived in San Francisco for a while and rode a tricked-out 1950 Indian. Now that he's middle-aged, he can afford to buy a new one, but he's become too used to creature comforts to use it.

She brakes on the steep hill leading to Nathan Pollock's driveway and pulls in behind his SUV.

They're due to have a meeting with their respective bosses at headquarters, but they wanted to look together through the material Joona has had couriered to Nathan before then.

The black villa is situated on a slope, and looks out across the dark, choppy waters of Eds Lake.

Saga hangs her helmet on the handlebars and walks around Nathan's car.

Dead plants are rustling on a flaking trellis behind a bench.

As Saga heads for the house, she sees a bag of groceries on the path, not far from the sunroom. Bread, a bag of frozen peas, and three packs of free-range bacon have spilled out onto the yellow grass.

She stops and listens. She can hear thudding sounds from inside the house. It sounds like a door being slammed five times; then the noise stops suddenly.

Saga sets off toward the sunroom but stops abruptly when she hears a woman's voice shouting inside the house.

Saga crouches down and pulls her Glock from its holster, chambers a round, and walks around the house with the barrel aimed at the ground.

She can see into the living room through the first window. A high-backed chair is lying on the floor.

Saga squeezes the trigger until it reaches the first notch, and walks past an apple tree to get a view through the second window. In the gap between the curtains, she can see Nathan's wife. She's standing in the door to the living room, wiping tears from her eyes.

Slowly, Saga moves sideways, and sees Nathan enter the room and empty a drawer of colorful underwear on the floor. His wife yells something at him, but he doesn't answer, just goes out again with the empty drawer.

They're obviously in the middle of a fight.

Saga puts her pistol back in the holster and walks to the front of the house. She's about to get back on the motorcycle and ride home when the front door opens and Veronica comes out with a pack of cigarettes in her hand. She sees Saga.

"Hello," Veronica says quickly, and lights a cigarette.

"Is this a bad time?"

"Not at all," Veronica says, without looking at Saga.

Nathan is standing on the porch behind her.

"She wants a divorce," he says.

"Should I come back later?"

"No, it's no big deal; she'll probably change her mind."

"I won't," Veronica says bitterly, and takes a deep drag on the cigarette.

"Maybe not, I'm sure you're right, why would you stay with me?" he says, holding the door open for Saga.

Veronica lowers her cigarette and looks at Saga with an exhausted expression.

"Sorry about the mess," she says. "I'll let Nathan explain the pile of underwear in . . ."

"Nicky, I just think—"

"Don't call me that," she interrupts sharply. "I hate it. I've always hated it. I only pretended to think it was cute in the beginning."

"Okay." He goes inside with Saga. He helps her out of the leather jacket she's wearing on top of her hoodie.

"You don't need a reason to get a divorce in Sweden, but . . ."

"I've got a thousand reasons!" Veronica calls from outside.

"But if one party objects, then the court will give the couple six months to think about it," he says.

Saga isn't sure how many times Nathan's been married, but she remembers his previous wife, a blond woman the same age as him. Before her, he was married to a forensics expert named Kristina.

They walk through the sunroom, with its cane furniture and potted ivy plants. The leaded windows rattle when the front door opens and shuts again.

"Veronica isn't keen on a six-month wait, and I can understand that. Things are very fraught right now," he says in a carefree voice.

"Are you upset about the divorce?"

"You know," he says, "I'm fairly used to getting divorced at this point."

"Well I'm not, and I'm upset," Veronica says from behind them.

"You weren't supposed to hear that," Nathan says over his shoulder.

"Of course I was," she says wearily.

"I just think you should think about it—that's why the law's been designed this way," he replies with irritating calmness.

"I've already thought about it. You know that perfectly well. This is just you throwing your weight around."

"She wants to sell the house and divide our assets before the divorce goes through," Nathan says to Saga.

"What difference would that make to you?" Veronica says, wiping the tears that have started to fall again. "It's going to happen, whether you like it or not."

"In which case, I'm sure you can wait another six months, Nicky."

"Am I going to have to hit you?" she asks.

"I've got a witness," he says, smiling, tossing his long silver-gray ponytail over his shoulder.

Veronica sighs, whispers something to herself, picks up an item of clothing, and puts it on one of the cane chairs. She grabs a mug of tea from the table.

"Don't ever marry him," she says to Saga, and leaves the sunroom.

Saga and Nathan walk through the living room, lined with bookcases and a brown-tiled fireplace.

"Her underwear," he says, gesturing toward the floor. "I thought she could make a start by selling that; then we could divide the profits."

"Don't be mean, Nathan."

"I'm not," he replies.

The deep lines on his face and wrinkles around his eyes make him look tired, but his eyes are as impenetrable as stone.

"Shall we take a look at what Joona sent?" she asks.

"It'll take a while."

He shows her into the kitchen, where there are ten boxes on the floor. He's started to unpack one of them, and the table is already covered with maps of the sites where the bodies were found, as well as railroad maps and photographs.

"Joona's written down a few notes," Nathan says, showing her a full page of writing in a notepad.

"Okay," she says, looking at a photograph of the graves in Lill-Jans Forest.

"The first thing he wants us to do is get protection for Valeria."

"That makes sense, looking at it from his point of view," Saga says.

"It isn't that straightforward, though," Nathan goes on. "He says it has to be done in secret, because she doesn't want protection."

He shows Saga a sketch Joona has made of Valeria's nursery, and the best locations to post ten police officers.

"That'd work." Saga nods.

"He says it's impossible to protect yourself against Jurek ... but that you can destroy a spiderweb with a stick."

"Jurek's dead," Saga mutters.

"The second thing he wants us to do is interview the church-warden who kept Jurek's finger in a glass jar."

"He's senile—it's impossible to get any sense out of him."

"Joona knows that, but he still thinks we could get something if we give the old man some time ... because Jurek's plan would never have worked without the churchwarden's involvement."

"I saw the body, the decayed torso, the bullet holes exactly where I shot him."

"I know," Nathan says, digging out the letter from the papers on the table. "This is what Joona says: 'The chapel on the island is the only entrance we've found into Jurek's world so far. . . . That's the crack he crawled out of, that's where you—'"

There's a loud thud from upstairs, followed by the sound of something shattering on the floor.

"I collect art glass," he says laconically.

"Shall we get going?"

26

IN THE NORTHEASTERN PART OF HUVUDSTA IS AN AREA known as Ingenting, "Nothing." The name can be traced back to an eighteenth-century estate. This is where the new headquarters of the Swedish Security Police is located.

Because information gathering is at the core of the Security Police's activities, the institution is characterized by paranoia. The fear of bugging is so widespread that they have more or less built a prison for themselves.

In fact, the same firm that built the prisons at Kumla and Hall constructed the secure seven-story building.

Saga and Nathan get out of the elevator and head past the windows along the open walkway. Saga still has the hood of her sweatshirt pulled up. Nathan's silver ponytail bounces against his back with each step.

Both of their bosses are already in the room when they arrive. It looks as if they've had a brief preliminary meeting.

Verner Zandén is sitting at the table in a suit and tie, his long legs crossed. One trouser leg has ridden up, revealing a striped black sock.

Carlos Eliasson is wearing a burgundy sweater and a white shirt. He's slouched in one of the armchairs, holding a clementine in his hand.

The large windows of Verner's office look out onto a building site, with some industrial units and the forest beyond. The world outside looks oddly soft around the edges through the reinforced glass.

"What's for lunch today?" Saga asks as she sits down at the oval table.

"That's a secret," Verner says, without smiling.

"One of the murders in question took place in the south of Sweden," Carlos begins as he peels the clementine. "And five took place outside our borders, two of them in—"

"Joona thinks Valeria de Castro needs police protection," Saga interrupts.

"So he told me in his voice mail . . . and she'll get it, just like anyone else in the country would, if there's a clear threat against her," Carlos replies calmly.

"Joona thinks there is."

"But the person responsible for the threat is dead," Carlos says, and pops three segments into his mouth.

"In theory, there's a small possibility that Jurek Walter is still alive," Saga says.

"Naturally, we don't believe that," Nathan interjects.

"So Joona is convinced that somehow Jurek is alive and behind the murders," Carlos goes on.

"And if he's right, the threat against Valeria is pretty damn real," Saga says, laying the sketched map of Valeria's nursery with possible police positions on the table in front of Verner.

"Obviously, what got to Joona was the fact that two of the victims had connections to him," Verner says, without looking at the map. "Of course, it's deeply upsetting that his wife's grave was vandalized, truly awful, but the man in Oslo had collected body parts from thirty-six different people."

Carlos stands up and throws the clementine peel in the trash.

"As for the second victim . . . it's undeniably difficult to explain why a German sex offender would try to call Joona shortly before he died," Carlos says.

"Why a Swedish police officer?"

"We have no idea. But the victim had been locked away in a psychiatric unit for years, and—according to the files I've received—at least three inmates there had been active in Sweden."

"And you can find Joona's phone number on the Internet if you know where to look," Verner says.

"We're not going to drop this, absolutely not," Carlos says, taking a seat at the table. "But we can't devote a lot of resources to it, either."

"Okay," Nathan says quietly.

"It would have been helpful to have Joona here for this meeting," Carlos says, picking up his cell phone for no apparent reason.

"He's probably left the country by now," Saga says.

"Because of this?" Carlos asks.

"I think he's doing the right thing," Saga says, looking him in the eye.

"You think—"

"Hold on," she says, cutting him off. "I'm sure I killed Jurek Walter, but I still think Joona's doing the right thing. He's not convinced Jurek is dead . . . so I'm glad he's gone to protect his daughter and left the investigation to us."

Carlos shakes his head doubtfully. "I wish I could make him see a psychologist when he gets back," he sighs.

"The killer is someone—or possibly more than one person—who's decided to clean things up around Europe," Verner says.

"But that's not Jurek's style. Why would he want to clean up society?" Carlos says.

"Joona believes that Jurek has recruited an accomplice," Saga says. "That he's spent several years testing candidates . . . and now he's killing the ones that didn't make the cut."

Verner gets a laptop from his desk. "Joona left Carlos a message saying that Jurek had whipped the man at the campsite the same way he used to whip his twin brother," he says, plugging in the laptop.

"Yes, I know." Saga nods.

"And when Joona found out about a murder in Belarus where the victim had similar wounds on his back, he took that as proof that Jurek is alive and is responsible for these murders," Carlos says.

"We've now received a recording from the Belarusian police. Some surveillance footage caught the killer on camera," Verner says, tapping the laptop. A large screen on one wall comes to life.

"You can see the murderer?" Nathan asks.

"The national park is closed at night. It's not quite ten o'clock, and the security guard is doing his rounds," Verner replies cryptically as he turns the lights off and clicks PLAY.

Three words in white Cyrillic lettering appear at the bottom of the screen, next to a timer.

The security camera is pointing at an ornate house built of dark wood, with elaborate carvings. The walls, veranda, railings, and pillars are covered with fairy lights, all of them switched off.

"A gingerbread house," Nathan murmurs.

"Their version of Santa Claus is Ded Moroz, and apparently this is where he lives," Verner says.

The snow-covered park is dark. The only illumination is coming from what look like electric lights with pointed glass domes that line the paths. A uniformed guard in a fur hat checks that the door to the house is locked, then walks back down the steps. His breath clouds around his mouth in the cold air. He walks along the plowed path lined by an ornate wooden fence.

"The Belarusian authorities haven't confirmed this," Verner says, "but we know that the victim was previously employed by the secret service to deal with critics of the government."

The guard stops and lights a cigarette before moving toward the left of the screen.

A large shape emerges from the darkness between the trees and follows him.

"Shit," Saga whispers.

The black-and-white recording is low-resolution, and the pursuer's movements seem to be subject to some sort of lag, like an elastic shimmer, as if part of his dark persona lingers.

"Watch this," Carlos says quietly.

The heavyset figure has pulled a pistol with a silencer from his bag. He is obviously moving silently across the snow, because the guard doesn't react.

"That's not Jurek," Saga says, staring at the recording.

The man catches up with the guard beside a plastic snowman and shoots him in the back of the head without any preamble. The end of the silenced barrel flares for an instant. Blood and bone burst from the guard's mouth, spraying across the snow.

The cigarette is still clasped between his fingers as his legs give out. The large man hits him in the head with the butt of the pistol.

The dead body falls into the snow, but the attacker doesn't stop. He takes a step to one side, puts the pistol away, then goes back and starts kicking wildly at the body.

"What's he doing? The man's dead," Nathan whispers.

The attacker grabs one of the guard's arms and drags him off behind the fence, leaving a dark trail of blood across the snow. His mouth is opening as if he's shrieking as he smashes the guard's head against a rock.

"Christ," Carlos says.

The man straightens up, evidently out of breath, then stomps on the guard's face and chest over and over again, before dragging the body out of the frame by one leg.

"The body was found sixty feet away, behind some trash cans," Verner says.

The large man returns, but it's still too dark for his face to be seen clearly. He wipes his mouth, then turns and walks back a short way, kicks and smashes one of the glass lanterns lining the path, yells something, and disappears.

The recording flickers and comes to an end.

"This disproves Joona's theory," Carlos concludes.

"It could be the accomplice," Saga says.

"The secret accomplice who kills other secret accomplices in Belarus," Verner mutters.

"I know how it sounds," Saga sighs.

"There's no logic to it," Carlos says, not unpleasantly. "If Jurek's alive and has an accomplice, then surely the accomplice would follow Jurek's plan, and he'd be burying people alive—not cleaning up society."

"We'd still like to conduct a preliminary investigation," Saga persists.

"Into the murder in Sweden, then," Carlos replies.

"This is a serial killer," she says.

"We can't go outside the country if no one's requested our help, especially since everyone seems happy to get rid of their worst criminals."

"Give us a month," Nathan asks.

"You can have a week, just the two of you. And that's being generous," Carlos says, glancing at Verner.

27

VALERIA HAS GATHERED HER CURLY HAIR INTO A THICK ponytail and changed into a clean pair of jeans and a white tank top. There's a cup of tea on the kitchen table, next to a paperback edition of *My Brilliant Friend* and her cheap reading glasses.

She's standing at the window, talking on the phone to her younger son, Linus, as she gazes out at the dark greenhouses.

Linus lives in Farsta, only twenty minutes away from her. She's promised to let him have an old dresser that's been in the attic for years.

"I'll pick it up next week," Linus is saying.

"Talk to Amanda about staying for dinner," she says.

"Will Joona be there?"

"He's away at the moment."

"How are things going with him?" Linus asks. "You've sounded happier recently."

"I have been," she says.

They end the call, and Valeria puts her phone down on the table and looks at her reading glasses. One of the screws fell out some time ago, so one hinge is held together with a paper clip.

She's used to being alone. Her years in prison have made loneliness a part of her, but when Joona comes back home she's planning to ask him if he'd like to try living together, to see how it goes. He can keep his apartment, but she'd love to spend more time with him, doing ordinary, everyday things.

She gets a glass out of one of the top cupboards and pours some wine from a box, then walks into the living room and switches on the record player. The speakers crackle; Barbra Streisand's 1980 album *Guilty* plays.

Valeria sits down on the arm of the sofa and thinks about how odd it is that she reconnected with Joona again after so many years.

She thinks of her car journeys to Kumla Prison, and the anxiety she felt when the steel gates clanged shut behind her. She felt the same panic every time she passed the guards. She would nod and smile at the immaculately made-up women there, with restless children milling around their legs. The waiting room contained a bathroom, several sofas, information for visitors, and a toy horse with worn rockers.

You weren't allowed to wear a bra with a catch on it, or tampons or pads. You had to put your shoes on a conveyor belt before you walked through the security gate and were searched.

But she still loved the dull visiting room. She loved Joona's attempts to make it nice with napkins, coffee, and cookies.

And now he is free.

He's spent the night with her, they've made love and worked in the garden together.

Valeria drinks some more wine and starts to sing along to "Woman in Love" before she realizes what she's doing and stops, embarrassed.

She goes out into the hall and stands in front of the mirror, where she blows a lock of hair away from her face, raises her chin, and concludes that she does in fact look happy.

The tattoos on her shoulders have become blurred over the years, and her arms are muscular from hard work, and scratched by brambles.

She walks into the kitchen, puts the wineglass down on the counter, and turns out the light that Joona always hits his head on.

The music in the living room is muffled by the walls.

She thinks of the fear she saw in Joona's eyes when he asked her to leave everything and go away with him. It frightened her. He really seemed to believe that Jurek was alive. She understands why he might think that: A trauma never really goes away. It just hides in the shadows, ready to leap out at a moment's notice.

It's good that he's gone to see Lumi. Valeria hopes it will help calm him down, spending a few days with her in Paris, seeing that she's doing well there.

The wind is whistling in the chimney.

Valeria is about to pick up her book and reading glasses when headlights shine through the kitchen window. They flicker between the trees like the images in a kinetoscope.

Her pulse speeds up as she sees the unfamiliar vehicle stop in the cul-de-sac. Its headlights are shining right into the first greenhouse, lighting up the plants and casting shadows.

Valeria goes out into the hall and pulls on her raincoat and boots, reaches for the flashlight on the shelf, and opens the door to the cold evening air.

The strange car is parked. A cloud of exhaust is billowing gently in the red glow of the taillights.

She thinks momentarily of the pistol in the drawer of her bedside table.

The gravel crunches under her boots.

The driver's door is open, the seat empty.

There's someone in the nearest greenhouse, a dark shape moving between the plants.

Valeria turns her flashlight on as she gets closer, but the beam fades almost instantly, so she shakes it and points the weak light toward the greenhouse.

It's Gustav Eriksson, from Hasselfors Garden Supplies. One of his colleagues is standing a little farther in among the benches.

Valeria waves to them, then walks closer and pulls the door open.

Gustav is a heavyset man in his sixties who always starts to rattle the coins in his pocket whenever he talks business. He has glasses and a salt-and-pepper mustache. He always wears baggy jeans and pink or yellow shirts.

Valeria's been buying compost and manure from Hasselfors for over ten years.

"Gustav?"

"Spring'll be with us before you know it," he says, rattling the coins in his pocket.

His heavily built colleague picks up a potted tomato plant, and some of the soil runs out through the hole at the bottom.

"I'm still working out how much I'll need," she says. "But it'll be a lot this year."

He lets out a low, embarrassed chuckle. "You'll have to excuse me for stopping by so late. I very nearly turned back, but when I saw that you already had a customer in here, I assumed it was okay to . . ."

There's a heavy thud, and Gustav stops mid-sentence. Then there's a second, wetter thud, and Gustav slumps onto the cupboard in front of her.

She doesn't understand.

His legs are jerking spasmodically, but his face is slack, even though his eyes are wide open.

Valeria sees the other man beside him, and is about to tell him to call an ambulance when she sees the hammer in his hand.

A dark pool of blood is spreading out beneath Gustav.

The man with the hammer is over six feet tall, with a thick neck and round shoulders. His nostrils are flaring and his face looks tense. His breathing is rapid, and his pearly earrings are swaying with his agitation.

It's like a dream.

She tries to move backward, away from him, but her legs feel surprisingly heavy. It's like she's wading through water.

The man tosses the hammer aside, as if he no longer understands what he's holding, and turns to her with a quizzical look.

"Don't go," he mumbles.

"I'll come back," she whispers, and turns slowly toward the door.

"Don't go!" the man bellows, and sets off toward her.

Valeria breaks into a run, and overturns the bench holding the blackberry bushes behind her. She hears him trip over it and roar like an animal. She rushes between the shelves, jumping over bags of compost.

She realizes that he's right behind her, and bumps into one of the shelves as she passes through the beam from the car's head-lights, knocking two terra-cotta pots to the floor.

She reaches the door, and has just managed to grab the handle when the man catches up with her.

She spins around and lashes out with the flashlight, hitting him hard in the cheek. He staggers sideways, and she kicks him between his legs. She sees him bend double and sink to his knees.

She turns back to the door again.

The old lock has caught, and she hits the rusty latch with her knuckles and tugs at the door.

She sees the man getting up.

Valeria turns the handle and hears herself whimper as he grabs one of her legs. With a single tug, he pulls her to the floor. She collapses onto her stomach and puts her hands out to brace her fall, then rolls onto her side and tries to kick him.

He yanks her backward, hard.

Her raincoat slides up, and she scrapes her stomach and chin.

Before she has time to get to her feet, he's on top of her, hitting her in the back. She gasps for air, and is finally catching her breath when he hits her again.

He backs away from her, growling, breaking the pieces of the fallen pots.

Coughing, she gets up on all fours and sees the man pull plants onto the floor as he makes his way back to Gustav. He starts kicking the lifeless body and roaring with rage.

She gets to her feet and reaches out to the glass to steady herself as he returns to her.

"Leave me the fuck alone!" she bawls, and tries to fend him off with one hand.

He catches hold of her arm and hits her hard across her left cheek. She stumbles, slams her head, and falls to the ground in a shower of broken glass.

He stomps on her chest, yelling that she's about to die, that he's going to slaughter her. Coughing and bellowing as he straddles her, he grabs her throat with both hands and starts to squeeze her neck.

She can't breathe, and struggles to get him off her, but he's too strong. She twists sideways and tries to reach his face.

He starts to hit her against the floor. The third time, the back of her head flares, and she loses consciousness.

She dreams that she's in an elevator, heading down to the ground fast, and wakes up because of an excruciating pain in one leg. The man is biting her thigh through her jeans; then he gets up with a growl and kicks at her feet.

Warm blood is oozing from the bite.

Only half conscious, she watches as he tears plants down from the benches and picks up a pruning knife from the floor.

The large man goes back to Gustav's body and slits his throat with a deep cut, then slices him open from his navel to his neck. He heaves Gustav up onto his shoulder and walks to the door. Little spasms run through his body, and blood pours down his back.

He passes Valeria and kicks the greenhouse door open. The hinges break, and the glass shatters as it hits the ground.

Valeria gets to her feet, and almost throws up from the pain. Blood is running down under her raincoat from the back of her head. She staggers forward, fumbling for support, and slips out through the door.

There's a muffled explosion from the driveway as the car starts to burn. Flames are tossed sideways by the wind. The large man smashes the windows with a shovel, then takes a step back as the flames shoot up, and fixes his gaze on Valeria.

She turns and starts to run into the forest, gasping with the pain from her thigh. Whimpering, she forces her way through the undergrowth, almost falling, but somehow managing to stay on her feet.

His heavy breathing is right behind her. She steps into a deep puddle and is trying to shield her face from low-hanging branches when he hits the back of her head with the shovel.

Knocked out, she falls headfirst through the dry branches onto the frosty lingonberry twigs. With another roar, he lashes out again but misses her head and loses his grip on the shovel.

When she comes to, she realizes that the man is dragging her through the forest by one leg. Valeria has lost her boots, and her raincoat is dragging behind her. She tries to grab a slender birch tree, but isn't strong enough.

28

ACCORDING TO HIS PASSPORT AND DEBIT CARD, JOONA IS now Paavo Niskanen, a Finnish landscape architect. Other than his body, there's nothing that can be linked to his true identity and life in Stockholm.

No paperwork, no electronics, not even his clothing.

ON THE A9 AUTOROUTE, IT'S ONLY FIVE HUNDRED KILOME-ters from Béziers, in the south of France, to Geneva, in Switzerland, but because he chooses to drive on smaller roads, the trip takes seven hours.

Joona keeps telling himself that everything's going to be all right. He knows that Nathan will have made sure Valeria has protection. It would have been better if she'd come with him, but she'll be safe until the police find Jurek.

He crosses the narrow extension of La Laire Rau River and the unmanned Swiss border, drives along the Chemin du Moulin-de-la-Grave, and approaches Geneva beneath a sky heavy with rain.

Joona parks on the Rue de Lausanne and slings his bag over his shoulder. He walks through the extravagant entrance of the rail-road station and into the café, and receives the envelope containing a key card from Lumi.

That means she's here. She escaped from Paris.

Before Joona walks into the marble-clad reception of the Hotel

Warwick Geneva, he puts his hood up. As he's heading to the second floor, he keeps his head lowered, so the security cameras in the elevator can't pick him up.

The carpet in the hall silences his steps. He stops outside Room 208 and knocks.

The peephole in the door goes dark.

He knows Lumi is standing to one side, covering the lens with something—a sofa cushion, maybe—in case the person outside is ready to shoot through the door the moment she looks through it.

The hallway is still empty, but he can hear faint music from somewhere.

The peephole gets lighter, then darker again.

Joona nods and Lumi opens the door. He goes inside quickly, locks the door behind him, and puts his bag down on the floor.

They hug. He kisses her on the head, breathing in the scent of her hair, and holds her tight.

"Dad," she whispers to his chest.

He smiles as he looks down at her. She has her light-brown hair pulled back into a neat ponytail, and she seems to have gotten slightly slimmer. Her cheekbones are more pronounced, her gray eyes darker.

"You look great," he says.

"Thanks," she says, lowering her gaze.

He walks farther into the double room, turns the light out, closes the curtains, and turns back to her again.

"Are you absolutely sure?" she asks seriously.

"Yes."

He can see that she's trying not to say anything. She just nods and sits down in one of the armchairs.

"Have you gotten rid of everything?" he asks as he grabs his bag from the hall.

"I did what we agreed," she replies slowly, her voice heavy.

"Did it go okay?"

She shrugs and looks down.

"I'm so sorry you're caught up in this," Joona says, pulling out a plastic bag. "Put these clothes on. . . . They're probably a little too big, but we can buy more on the way."

"Okay," she murmurs and gets to her feet.

"Change everything—underwear, hair clips. . . ."

"I know," she interrupts, then goes into the bathroom with the bag swinging from her hand.

Joona takes the pistols out of his bag. He slips one into the shoulder holster beneath his left arm, then tapes the other to his right shin.

Lumi emerges as he's adjusting his clothes. Her new sweater is baggy, and the pants hang loosely from her slender hips.

"Where's your gun?" he asks.

"Under the pillow on the bed."

"You've checked the hammer and spring?"

"You did that before I got it," she says, folding her arms over her chest.

"You don't know that."

"Yes, I do," she insists.

"Do it yourself—that's the only way to be sure."

Without saying anything, she goes over to the bed, pulls out her Glock 26, removes the magazine, takes the bullet out of the chamber, and disassembles the gun; when she has set the pieces on the bed, she starts by looking at the recoil spring.

"I'm starting to get used to disappearing," Joona says, trying to smile. "But I know all this may feel a little over the top."

Lumi doesn't respond. She just puts the gun back together, tests the mechanism a couple of times, and reinserts the magazine.

Joona goes into the bathroom and finds her discarded clothes in the bathtub. He puts them all in a trash bag, gathers up the rest of her things, grabs her shoes from the floor next to the door, and leaves the hotel again.

The air is chilly and the sky a steel gray. Dark streaks of clouds are hanging above the huge railroad station. The streets have been decorated for Christmas, with sparkling trees and garlands on the streetlights. The sidewalks are full of people, and there's still a lot of traffic. Joona walks with his head down. When he reaches the large pedestrian tunnel leading to the station, he discards Lumi's things in different trash cans.

On the way back, he goes into a Chinese restaurant and orders takeout. While he's waiting in the dimly lit bar area, he thinks about the time he spent with Lumi up in Nattavaara, and how they got to know each other again, talking about all the things they'd been through in all the years that had passed while they were apart.

Lumi looks like she's been crying when she lets him back into the room. He follows her to the couch and puts the food down on the table.

"Do you drink wine?" he asks.

"I live in France," she says quietly.

He takes out the cartons of food, then gets out glasses, napkins, and chopsticks.

"What's been happening at college? How's it all going?" he asks, taking a bottle of red out of the minibar.

"I'm happy there. . . . There's a lot going on at the moment."

"That's the way it should be, though, isn't it?"

"How about you? How have you been doing, Dad?" Lumi asks, opening the cartons.

While they eat, he talks about what's happened since he was released from prison, about his work as a neighborhood police officer, and about Valeria and her nursery.

"Are you going to move in with her?"

"I don't know. I'd like to, but she has a life of her own, so . . . we'll have to see."

She puts her chopsticks down and turns away.

"What is it, Lumi?"

"It's just that . . . you don't really know anything about me," she says.

"I haven't wanted to bother you. You've got a whole new life . . . which I'd love to be part of, but I understand that having a dad who's a police officer isn't something to brag about to your artist and author friends."

"Do you think I'm ashamed of you?"

"No, but . . . I just mean that I don't really fit in."

Her voice reminds him of Summa's. He feels like saying that but holds back. They finish eating in silence, then drink the last of the wine.

"We'll be leaving early," he says, starting to clear the table.

"Where to?"

"I can't say."

"No," she whispers, and turns her face away.

"Lumi," he says, "I know that you don't want to go into hiding, that it doesn't fit in with the way your life looks now."

"Have I complained?" she asks in a thick voice.

"You don't need to."

She sighs and runs the palm of her hand quickly over her eyes. "Have you seen Jurek Walter?"

"No, but his accomplice was following me, and—"

"What accomplice?" she interrupts.

"Jurek's been watching you," Joona goes on. "He's been mapping your life; he knows your routines, and he knows who you spend time with."

"But why would Jurek get an accomplice?"

"If he's going to get his revenge the way he wants, he needs an accomplice who's as loyal as his brother was," Joona explains. "He knew I'd drop everything and try to protect you the moment I realized he was still alive . . . and his strategy was to grab you before I could get to Paris, while his accomplice would seize Valeria in Stockholm. That had to happen simultaneously. He's a twin."

"So why was the accomplice following you, then?"

Joona puts the empty cartons in the trash, feels a sting of pain behind his eye, and grabs the writing desk with one hand to keep his balance.

"Because I realized Jurek wasn't dead just moments before he launched his plan," he replies, turning back toward her. "I called you, you did exactly what you had to do, and you escaped from Paris. . . . Sending the accomplice after me was an emergency solution, an attempt not to lose the only way he could find you. We were quick and managed to get a small head start, but that's all."

"There's no logic to any of this, Dad. . . . Besides the fact that there's no evidence that Jurek's alive, no one's seen him, not even you . . . I mean, why would the person who was following you have any connection to Jurek?"

"I know Jurek's alive."

"Okay, let's assume that—after all, that's why we're sitting here."

"I killed his twin brother, but not him," Joona goes on.

"And who am I in all this?" she asks.

"My daughter."

"I'm starting to feel like some sort of hostage," she says, then holds her hands up in a gesture of resignation. "Sorry, that was an exaggeration . . . but this is affecting my whole life. I have a right to know what we're doing."

"What do you want to know?" Joona says, sitting down on the sofa.

"Where are we going tomorrow, what's the plan?"

"The plan is to stay alive until the police catch Jurek. . . . I've given them lots of material, so they might be able to find him if they get a move on."

"How are we going to stay alive?" Lumi asks in a gentler voice.

"We're going to drive up through Germany and Belgium to Holland. There are some derelict buildings surrounded by fields in Limburg Province, not far from Weert."

"And that's where we're going to hide?"

"Yes."

"For how long?"

He doesn't answer. There is no answer.

"Will you feel calmer there?" Lumi asks, sitting down in the armchair again.

"Have I ever told you about my friend Rinus?"

"You mentioned him when we were practicing close combat in Nattavaara," she says, nodding.

After his time as a paratrooper, Joona was recruited for a top secret training course in the Netherlands, where he was trained by Lieutenant Rinus Advocaat.

"Rinus has always been a little paranoid and has created the closest thing you can get to a true safe house. It looks like a group of derelict buildings from the outside, but . . ."

"So what?" she sighs.

Joona is about to say something, but a second migraine hits him. A sharp pain behind his left eye, followed by a debilitating feeling, as if his ears are being filled with water.

"Dad? What's happening?"

He presses his hand to his left eye as the storm sweeps past and the pain eases.

"It's been a long day," he explains, then stands up and goes to brush his teeth.

When he comes back to the bedroom, Lumi is sitting on the edge of the bed with a watch in her hand.

"What's that?" he asks.

"A present," she replies.

"You'll have to leave it behind."

"It's safe," she replies firmly, pulling it over her wrist.

"I don't doubt that, but we have to make a complete break. That's the most important rule."

"Fine, but I'm not leaving my watch—you can check it, it's just a watch," she says, handing it to him.

He switches the bedside lamp on to see better. Then he turns the watch in the light, checks every link of the chain, and looks to see if any of the tiny screws on the back are scratched.

"No secret microphones or transmitters?" she asks, unable to hold back her sarcasm.

He hands the watch back to her without answering, and she puts it on her left wrist in silence. They pack their bags without speaking and get dressed as if they were about to leave. With their shoes on and pistols in their holsters, they lie down on either side of the bed.

29

SAGA BAUER AND NATHAN POLLOCK HAVE BEEN SITTING IN the National Operational Unit for fourteen hours now.

The three windows look out onto the covered inner courtyard, the enclosed rest area of the prison, and some roofs covered with ventilation units and satellite dishes.

The walls of the room are covered with maps, satellite images, photographs, and lists of names and telephone numbers for various contacts around Europe.

On the table are pads full of notes and highlighted ideas. A crumpled napkin in a mug has turned dark, and the only thing left on what was a plate of cinnamon rolls is some icing and a few pieces of old chewing gum.

"It isn't Jurek. It's a serial killer . . . and we've got one week to find him," Saga says, closing her stinging eyes for a few seconds.

"What's the next step? The quality of the pictures from Belarus is too poor—you can't even see his face."

"Six victims in six different countries, and the same MO. It's crazy," she says. "No witnesses, no pictures, no matches in the DNA database."

"I'll call Ystad again—there must be security cameras in an industrial park, for God's sake."

Exhaustion has made the lines in Nathan's thin face deeper than ever, and his sharp eyes are bloodshot.

"Go ahead," she sighs. "They'll only say that their forensic examination is ongoing, and that they don't need any help from Stockholm."

"We should go down there anyway."

"There's no point."

"If we had just one reasonably sharp picture, a single witness, a name, anything at all, then we'd be able to find him."

Saga looks at the map of the industrial park in Ystad again. A convicted double murderer was beaten to death in a workshop that he owned. His head was smashed to a pulp with a hammer, then severed from his body and hanged from a hoist. His dog was killed and impaled on a railing outside. Several windows in the building opposite were smashed, and a motorcycle on a neighboring property was vandalized.

Saga wonders if the perpetrator has abnormal levels of serotonin in his prefrontal cortex, and increased activity in his amygdala.

"He's extremely violent. . . . But there's another side to him as well," she says. "The victims are specific, so he must have done a lot of research, hacking or somehow gaining access to a whole range of databases. He's mapped the victims and probably established some form of contact with them well before the attacks."

Nathan's phone rings, and Saga has time to see a picture of his wife on the screen before he rejects the call and goes over to stand in front of the long list of countries, and names of police officers.

They've already crossed out four hundred names and eight countries.

Saga opens a PDF of a Europol report and thinks about all the sacrifices Joona has made over the years. He let go of his family, missed years of his daughter's life, and based his entire existence around trying to escape Jurek's vengeance.

It's clearly become an obsession. The fact that the grave robber in Oslo had Summa's skull in his freezer was simply too much for him. Joona's paranoia created a scenario in which these murders around Europe were committed by Jurek Walter.

But Jurek is dead, and this killer has nothing to do with him.

Nathan looks up from his computer and repeats that the common denominator between the victims is that they had all been found guilty of serious sexual or violent offenses.

"Without getting hung up on that . . . one plausible theory is that the perpetrator has some sort of warped moral motivation," Nathan says. "He thinks he's on a mission to clean up society, maybe even make the world a better, safer place."

"A superhero ... or the hand of God."

She and Nathan start searching the Internet for people advocating harsher punishment and the purification of society, but the number of results is too large to be of any use: hundreds of thousands of people declaring that the streets need to be cleaned up.

There are plenty of police officers among them. Colleagues complaining about the rules, about the courts, about politically correct colleagues, about excessive respect for the rights of criminals.

The phone rings, and Saga, seeing that it's a foreign number, picks up. Superintendent Salvatore Giani in Milan. He tells her apologetically that the investigation into the murder of Patrizia Tuttino outside the San Raffaele Hospital has gone cold. "We've examined the recordings from all the security cameras. We've talked to all the staff in the hospital. . . . There are no leads, no witnesses, nothing," he says.

"What about forensics?"

"I'm sorry, but we're no longer prioritizing this investigation," Salvatore explains.

"I see," Saga says. "Thanks for letting me know."

She puts her phone down, sighs, and meets Nathan's weary gaze.

"I'll have another go with Volgograd," he says, and is just reaching for his phone when Veronica calls again.

"Take it," Saga says.

"She just wants to tell me I'm an idiot for ignoring her calls."

"So stop ignoring them, then."

He takes a sip of cold coffee, tosses the plastic cup into the bin, and picks the phone up.

"Hello, darling."

Saga can hear from Veronica's voice that she's upset.

"I'm not ignoring you," Nathan says. "But I've got a job that . . . Okay, Nicky, we don't agree on that. . . . Fine . . . Other than that, was there anything in particular you wanted to talk about?"

He falls silent and puts his phone down.

"Well, at least we're friends again now," he says sardonically.

Saga stands up and goes over to one of the walls, where there are blurred pictures from security cameras, and photographs of the mutilated bodies.

"This isn't just going to blow over ... because this superhero isn't going to stop until he's caught," she says.

"Agreed," Nathan says.

"If the quality of the Belarusian footage hadn't been so poor, we might already have been able to issue a description," she says. "I mean ... he's going to make a mistake sooner or later, if he hasn't already."

Saga picks up her phone and weighs it in her hand. It's warm, and the dark screen reflects the lights in the ceiling. She looks at the notes on the pad in front of her and decides to call their contact at the National Police headquarters in Poland.

"I feel like a telemarketer," Nathan mutters as he calls the Russian narcotics unit, Gosnarkokontrol.

Nathan has already had twenty-three conversations with various Russian authorities—the FSB, SVR, and regional police chiefs in all the federal districts.

After several misunderstandings, he is put through to an elderly superintendent named Yakov Kramnik, and quickly explains why he's calling.

"Yes, we received your request via Interpol," the Russian superintendent replies. "I'm sorry I haven't gotten back to you yet, but we still have some of the old bureaucracy left in certain areas."

"Don't worry," Nathan says, rubbing his forehead.

"Thanks for understanding, that's good of you," he says. "It warms my heart. . . . Because we do actually have one suspected murder that matches several of your criteria. On Monday, an Igor Sokolov was found with his throat cut in a warehouse on the outskirts of Saint Petersburg. He'd previously served nineteen years in Kresty for narcotics offenses, but was also suspected of four murders. . . . It was an execution—one of his knees was broken, and the carotid artery severed. It looked almost like our special forces had done it ... but they'd never attempt to remove his spine."

"His spine?"

"Sokolov was subjected to extreme violence long after he was dead. I can send our report, if you like."

"Do you have any idea who the perpetrator might be?" Nathan asks, as Saga's phone starts to ring.

"Igor Sokolov fought for our country in Afghanistan, then developed a heroin addiction and got involved in serious crime . . . but he served his sentence and was rebuilding his life, and I respect that. . . . We have no leads on the perpetrator, but it looks like an old enemy from the underworld caught up with him."

In the window reflection, Nathan sees Saga stand up so abruptly that her office chair rolls backward and thuds into the wall.

"You've checked the security cameras in the area around the warehouse?" he asks.

"Nothing," the Russian superintendent replies.

Nathan ends the call with mutual expressions of thanks and hopes of continuing cooperation in the future.

He puts his phone down on the table, watches as it spins around, then turns to Saga.

She's standing with her phone pressed to her ear, and is leaning forward and scribbling something on the pad in front of her.

"We're on our way; we'll be there as soon as possible," she says.

30

TWO POLICE CARS ARE BLOCKING ONE SIDE OF REGERINGS Street, and the scaffolding and construction office with its barred windows are cordoned off with blue-and-white plastic tape, fluttering in the wind.

"I don't know. . . . It just sounded a lot like our perpetrator," Saga says.

"We spend hours making calls to every corner of Europe, but we don't even know what's going on in our own fucking backyard," Nathan says as he pulls over to the curb.

"Because they're convinced it's related to a protection racket," Saga says. "Apparently, this bar has been the target of extortion attempts before."

"Everyone guards their own little patch like a bunch of squabbling kids."

"Look, we're both tired, but we're here now, so let's try to be calm. I mean, this could be what we've been looking for," Saga says, opening the car door. "And, as far as I'm concerned, they're welcome to think Black Cobra are behind this, as long as they let us in."

An older man is waiting on the street under an umbrella— Senior Prosecutor Arne Rosander from the Central Stockholm bureau. He has thinning hair and a neat beard. He's wearing silvery glasses and an oilcloth raincoat over a checked blazer.

"I've heard about you, Saga Bauer, but I thought they were exaggerating," he says, holding the umbrella over her head.

"Have the victims been identified?" she asks.

"Erica Liljestrand ... twenty-eight years old, single ... studying biotech at the Royal Institute of Technology ... Niklas Dahlberg, also single, a bartender here at the Pilgrim Bar."

The dirty white nylon mesh covering the scaffolding is billowing like a sail in the wind.

"We haven't found any connection between the victims," the prosecutor goes on, shepherding them toward the crime scene. "All the evidence suggests that she was the last customer in the bar."

"Alone?" Nathan asks.

"She was supposed to be meeting a friend," Arne Rosander explains. "She probably just got caught up in it by accident."

They enter beneath the scaffolding. Rain is seeping through the makeshift plywood roof. Forensics has set up an airlock outside the entrance to the bar where people put on protective clothing and write their names on a list before entering the crime scene.

Well used to the procedure, Arne quickly slips into the protective outfit and waits patiently as Saga and Nathan sign the list.

"What do you think happened here, Arne?" Nathan asks, tucking his ponytail in before pulling the blue plastic hood over his head.

The prosecutor's warm eyes take on a rather despairing look.

"It's Black Cobra—you'll see the excessive brutality used—but it'll be hard to put a case together. We have to link the perpetrator to the organization, then show that he was given explicit orders to do this."

They step into the blinding glare of the floodlights. Around a dozen forensics officers are working inside the bar in silence.

"The bodies have been moved to the Forensic Medicine Department," Arne says quietly, "but otherwise I've kept the crime scene as intact as possible."

Saga inspects the locations where the bodies were found. The evidence suggests an extremely violent incident. Blood has been tracked across the floor. The bodies must have been dragged between the furniture, and in two places it looks as if they were at least partially dismembered.

There is a strong smell of alcohol and sour wine in the air from the smashed bottles behind the bar, and broken glass everywhere, strewn among the shattered furniture and splintered wood. If it wasn't for all the blood, you would have thought a tornado had blown through the room.

They stop next to the bent metal frame of a table that's lying beside a bloody wooden baseball bat.

Saga looks out across the room and tries to reconstruct the course of events. The bartender seems to have been the primary victim, or at least the focus of the perpetrator's aggression. The woman had her throat cut and was then dragged several feet through the room before her body was dumped.

"What do you think?" Nathan asks in a low voice.

Saga turns slowly and looks at the smashed-up bar. It seems to her that it all started with a fight, lots of punching and kicking, before it turned into an out-and-out assault with the baseball bat.

She looks at a large pool of blood by the opposite wall and notes that the blood sprayed out at considerable pressure, reaching the pink lampshades of the wall lights. That was where the most extreme violence occurred.

Forensics has probably already found the knife.

Several stabs to the heart and lungs.

Then the body was dragged toward the door. She follows the trail of blood and heavy footprints with her eyes.

The victims were still alive—one bloody hand tried to cling to a pillar.

"It's him," she says.

"Looks like it." Nathan nods.

"Is there any indication of sexual violence?" Saga asks.

"No," the prosecutor replies.

"You've checked all the security cameras in the area?" Nathan asks.

"Unfortunately, the only relevant ones are covered by scaffolding. But they probably wouldn't have given us much, considering it was dark and the weather was so bad."

"I see."

"But we've got three witnesses who saw a heavyset man on the street outside, shouting and being aggressive."

"I'd like to read their statements," Saga says.

"One of them was able to give a pretty good description," Arne says, searching for an audio file on his iPad.

They move closer to him. He presses PLAY, and they listen as an elderly woman starts to speak.

"At first I only heard shouting, a man screaming . . . which was very unpleasant . . . but then I saw him under the scaffolding. He was a big man, in his fifties, maybe six foot five, broad shoulders. . . . He was wearing a black raincoat—plastic, not nylon—and he jerked around as he walked. . . . When he reached the restaurant Nalen, I could see him clearly in the light. He had blood on his face. . . . He was shouting and kicking at parked cars. Then he picked up a stone and threw it at a group of kids on the other side of the street, and then he was gone."

"Can you describe his face?" the interviewer asked.

"I don't know. What struck me the most was the blood— I thought he'd hurt himself. . . . But he had a big head and a thick neck. . . . I don't know, it's very difficult. . . . I thought he looked like a Russian hooligan, but I'm not entirely sure what I mean by that."

THE DEPARTMENT OF FORENSIC MEDICINE AT THE KAROLIN-ska Institute is housed in an unassuming redbrick building on the northern outskirts of Stockholm. Advent stars and electric candelabras shine faintly from the windows behind the blinds. Trash from the overflowing cans has blown in among the bare rosebushes.

Saga and Nathan pull into the parking lot and get out.

A white Jaguar is parked crookedly on one side of the entrance, and as they push their way past it, Saga sees that there's a black briefcase lying on the roof of the car. She grabs the briefcase and follows Nathan into the building.

The floor of the empty hallway is worn from heavy use. The door frames and baseboards are badly scratched and dented.

The door to the professor's room is open. Nils Åhlén is sitting at his computer in his medical coat. His thin face is clean-shaven, his gray hair cropped short. He looks sad.

Someone has sprayed *Twisted Christmas* on his window in fake snow.

Saga knocks and steps into the room.

"I've got one just like that," Nils says when he sees the briefcase.

"Found it on the roof of your car," Saga says, putting the briefcase down on his desk.

"Well, it's not supposed to be there," he replies. He logs off his computer.

"We came straight from the Pilgrim Bar, where we spoke to Arne Rosander, who said you were looking at the bodies."

"Have you given up this idea about Jurek Walter?" Nils asks.

"It isn't him. We've got witnesses and some blurred security-camera footage," Nathan replies.

"When we find the real perpetrator, these murders will stop . . . and as soon as Joona hears that, he can come home," Saga says.

Nils nods, and his thin lips form themselves into a gloomy smile. He puts both hands on his desk and heaves himself to his feet.

"Then let's get going," he says, and leaves the room.

Saga and Nathan follow him to the autopsy room closest to his office. The automatic doors swing open. The white tiles on the walls glint in the glare of the fluorescent lights.

Saga walks over to the dead woman, who's lying with her eyes open, her lips shrunken. Her naked body is gray and pale, and the deep wound in her neck is gaping dark red. The plastic surface of the postmortem table, with its gullies and troughs, is covered in blood.

"Who confirmed the ID?" she asks.

"Erica Liljestrand's sister. She had trouble recognizing her— she kept saying there must be some misunderstanding, before I realized she was talking about the eyes."

"What about them?" Nathan says, leaning forward.

"Everyone gets brown eyes because of the hemolysin, regardless of what color they used to be . . . and that can confuse relatives."

"What can you tell us about her?" Saga asks impatiently.

Nils lifts up one of the dead woman's arms.

"Well, you can see here that the livor mortis is fairly faint. It's really only visible where the body was pressing directly against the floor."

"So she lost a lot of blood."

"I'm a long way from finished with my examination, but the cause of death is somewhere between loss of blood and inhalation of blood. Her neck was cut and her spine broken."

"The prosecutor's convinced it's a criminal gang making a show of strength."

"That could be right," Nils said, nudging his aviators farther up his nose.

"If it wasn't wrong," Saga says quickly.

"You sound like Joona," he says.

"No, but I know the prosecutor's wrong, because this is the same killer as the one down in Ystad. I've asked them to send you their postmortem report."

"It hasn't arrived."

"Well, it's the same perpetrator," she says. "And we need his DNA. The victims put up a fight. You must be able to find something."

"Yes, but that sort of analysis takes time," he says.

Saga's face is pale and tense; her eyes are blank from lack of sleep.

"We know that you're not finished yet," Nathan says. "But you think the man is the prime target."

Nils pulls his mask down under his chin and looks at them both. "Since the man and woman were basically killed at the same time, it's impossible to tell—from body temperature and decay—which of them died first, but of course that isn't what you're asking."

Saga lets out a loud groan.

"We want to know if the perpetrator really only wanted to kill one of them," Nathan says.

"The man, as you know, is in a far worse state, but that doesn't necessarily mean he was the primary target."

"What do you mean?" Nathan asks, noticing Saga turning to face the tiled wall.

"For instance, if the man was driven by jealousy and was planning to harm the woman, when he sees a man in her company he could be seized by a sudden, terrible fury against the man."

"In which case, she'd be the primary target even though he was subjected to a more violent attack," Nathan says.

"But if we're looking at a show of strength from a criminal organization . . . then it's far more likely that the man is the target and the woman merely a witness who needed to be silenced," Nils goes on.

"Yes," Saga says, still facing the wall.

"On the other hand, she had been drugged, which puts the spotlight back on her again. . . . I've just received the toxicology report, which shows that she had gamma hydroxybutyrate in her blood."

Saga turns and looks at Nils. "GHB? Was she even conscious when she was murdered?"

"She must have been incredibly tired, but I'm sure she was awake, because she was holding on to something tightly. Otherwise, she would have dropped it."

"What was she holding?"

Nils goes over to a cabinet and returns to Saga with a plastic bag containing a small matchbook, the kind where you open the lid and pull off a match to light it.

Saga holds the bag up to the light and angles it to avoid reflections. The little matchbook is a promotional product. The black front is decorated with a headless skeleton holding a skull in each hand.

As if he can't work out which one is his, Saga thinks. Like Hamlet confronted with a new problem.

There are three matches missing.

On the back is the word "Head" printed in white lettering. Perhaps this is the mistake they've been waiting for.

31

FOLLOWING THEIR MEETING WITH NILS ÅHLÉN, IT DOESN'T
take Saga and Nathan long to track down the unlicensed club,
Head, in its basement premises at 151 Ring Street, next to Lilla
Blecktorn Park. The underground death metal club is open on
Fridays and Saturdays, from midnight until six in the morning.

They have no way of knowing whether the matchbook belonged
to the perpetrator, but the victim's friends are pretty adamant that
she didn't go to metal clubs.

Nathan has gone home to talk to Veronica. He's going to handle the meeting with the prosecutor tomorrow morning, and has
offered Saga the morning off if she's willing to go to the club. The
plan is for her to go there tonight and talk to the bouncers, find out
if there are any membership lists or security cameras.

Saga took a three-hour nap to prepare for a late night. She has
showered and changed her clothes, and she's due to meet Randy
in an hour.

She picks up her phone and calls Pellerina. After a long pause,
her dad answers instead and says her sister's hands are covered in
chocolate cake mix.

"Is everything okay with her?"

"Same as usual," he replies.

"You sound a little low."

She hears him walk out of the kitchen. "Oh, it's just that I've been
trying Internet dating. There are apps for your phone," he tells her.

"What does Pellerina think about that?"

"I haven't mentioned it to her. It all feels a little embarrassing, actually."

"Everyone does it these days."

"I'm just wondering what you do when you meet up for real."

"I don't know," she replies, and goes over to drink a glass of water on her bedside table.

"Because I've been e-mailing a researcher at the Uppsala University Hospital, and I was thinking about asking her out for dinner."

"Do it," she replies.

"Would you be able to keep Pellerina company on Monday?" he asks with a smile in his voice.

"This coming Monday?"

"In the evening."

"I can't, I'm working late," she replies. She hears her sister in the background shouting that she's washed her hands now.

"It's not that I'm desperate or anything—I just thought it might be fun," her dad says.

"Can I talk to Pellerina?"

"But it's okay with you if I start dating?"

"Stop it—what do you think?" Saga says impatiently.

"Pellerina Bauer," her sister says, taking the phone.

"Hi, this is Saga."

"I've washed my hands now."

"Are you baking?"

"Sticky chocolate cake."

"Yummy."

"Yes," Pellerina says quietly.

"What's on your mind?"

"Dad's allowed to cry, too."

"Of course, but why do you say that? Has Dad been sad?"

"Yes."

"Do you know why?"

"He doesn't want to talk about it."

"I'm sure the cake will make him feel happier."

"Yes."

RANDY HAS BEEN RENTING HIS PLACE FROM AN OLD FRIEND who's put his advertising business on hold. He moved in after a recent breakup. A lot of the equipment is still there, or piled up in boxes lining the wall. The studio is in a dirty yellow brick industrial building in Västberga, filled with a mixture of studios, body shops, dentists and gynecologists, investment companies, and tire specialists.

Saga takes the big freight elevator up to the top floor and walks along the hallway to the old photography studio.

"Did you see the pizza guy?" Randy asks, giving her a hug.

"No."

Randy is a police officer, but he's also a passionate photographer. He takes pictures of Saga every time they're here together.

Twelve pictures, half frame.

The only furniture Randy brought with him is a double bed. It's sitting in the middle of the studio, surrounded by camera tripods, professional flashlights, reflectors, and backdrops.

The sky outside the big windows is dark.

They sit down on the bed and eat pizza and drink wine from coffee cups in the light of a floor lamp.

Randy reaches for a wine box that's perched on a black trunk full of lighting gear and fills their mugs.

"I can stay till twelve," she says, feeding him some pizza.

Randy was adopted from China, and is still in contact with his biological mother in Yuxi, in Yunnan Province. He grew up on the island of Lidingö and graduated from the Police Academy five years ago.

There are already several large photographs of Saga on the walls. They are so close up that the small hairs on her body are visible.

Beside the bed are several pencil sketches for his latest idea, which would have her lying inside a large heptagram of cherries, photographed from directly above.

Saga picks up one of the sheets and looks at the sketch. The lamp shines through the paper. Randy has drawn her face as an oval and the cherries as small dots forming a seven-pointed star.

"It's an old symbol of creation, the seven days," he says. "God created man and woman on the sixth day . . . and He made them both to rule over all the creatures on earth."

"Equal from the start," she says.

"We don't have to do this particular picture. . . . You can give the whole creation story the finger instead, as a little greeting to Ai Weiwei."

"No," she says, smiling.

"Or we could just eat all the cherries."

"Stop it. Let's do it now—it's a fun idea."

Randy lays the cherries out on the floor and then starts to rig up the camera, reflectors, and lights.

Saga gets up from the bed, takes off her jeans, and hangs them over a spare tripod. She unzips her old Adidas jacket and walks over to a full-length mirror leaning against the wall.

Without realizing that Randy has stopped working, she lets her jacket fall to the floor, then pulls off her worn old T-shirt. He can't help staring as she stands there in her underpants, applying cherry-red lipstick to her lips and nipples.

There's a bang, and she looks up. Randy has dropped one of the stands on the floor, and mumbles an apology as he picks it up.

"Are you cold?" he asks in a hoarse voice.

"Not yet."

"The lamps will warm things up soon."

She screws the lipstick back down, takes off her underpants, and follows his instructions to lie down in the middle of the star so that her nipples are in line with the cherries on the floor.

Last weekend, she took his picture as he sat naked with angel's wings on his back and a bottle of Calvados in one hand.

Randy has already mounted the camera on a pantograph that he moves along a rail in the ceiling to be able to photograph her from above. He climbs up a stepladder, looks at her, climbs back down, and moves the ladder.

"Ready for the first picture?"

"You want me to just lie here?"

"You're so incredibly beautiful, it's insane," he says, and squeezes the black rubber bulb at the end of the long shutter-release cable.

He climbs up and winds the film, climbs back down, moves the ladder out of the way, and adjusts one of the studio lights and a silver-colored screen.

"Great," he mutters. "This is going to be really great. . . ."

Saga raises one knee a little more.

"Good, that's great, stay like that."

"Are you coming with me to see Dad and Pellerina for the Lucia celebrations?"

"I told you, I'd love to," Randy replies, still taking pictures.

He's lost in the art now. He's already seeing the developed pictures. Her white skin and luminous beauty inside the pointed star of cherries. Her ribs stand out beneath her skin like rippled sand.

After the final picture, Saga gets up and eats some of the leftover cherries from a bowl. She has red marks on her back from lying on the hard surface.

"Are we almost done with the foreplay?" she asks.

"Maybe," he replies.

Saga angles the floor lamp away from her, lies down on the side of the bed, and waits while he disconnects the last of the cables. There are still a couple of hours before she has to go to the death metal club. Randy sits down on the bed and pulls his T-shirt off. She rolls onto her back and he kisses her neck and breasts.

She parts her legs slightly and closes her eyes, but she can still feel his eyes burning her skin. Randy kisses her stomach and the inside of her thighs, and she can feel his breathing as he starts to lick her, gently and rhythmically.

She disappears into the soft heat of his mouth.

The hot metal of the lamps clicks around them.

She puts one hand on his stubbled head and hears his breathing get quicker. The pulsating heat spreads through her whole body.

"Slower," she whispers.

He continues, light as a feather, and shifts sideways slightly, not noticing that he has knocked the floor lamp over with his foot.

She sees it fall, and feels him tremble between her legs as it hits the floor and goes out.

"God, that scared me." He smiles.

"I noticed." She laughs.

"Okay?"

She smiles and nods, helps him take his pants off, then pushes him down onto his back. She looks at his naked body, his muscles, his narrow hips.

Saga takes a condom out of the package on top of his iPad next to the bed, opens the wrapper, and meets his eye. She takes him gently in her mouth until he gets hard, then holds his erection with one hand and rolls the condom on.

She leans over him, opens her mouth, and feels the smell of the rubber and the taut, plasticky surface against her lips and tongue.

"Come here," he whispers.

She sits astride him and lets him slide all the way into her, squeezes him tight, and starts to move her hips.

She leans forward, resting her hands on his chest, and slides back repeatedly, sighing. He starts to breathe faster, holding her backside with both hands, then throws his head back and comes.

Saga didn't have time to reach an orgasm, wasn't even close—it all happened too fast—but she's learned that that's how he works. They'll start up again shortly, and she'll have longer the second and third times.

Randy pulls the condom off and ties it in a knot. They lie beside each other without speaking. His breathing is still fast. After a short while, he leans over her and starts to suck gently at one of her nipples.

Saga is stroking his damp neck when her phone rings from the pile of clothes on the floor. She gets to her feet, finds her jacket, and pulls out her phone.

"Bauer," she answers.

"I know it's late, but I just remembered what you said about getting in touch if we had the smallest detail that could help piece together a picture of the perpetrator," Senior Prosecutor Arne Rosander says.

"Absolutely," Saga says.

She takes a few more steps away from the bed. Her whole body is still tingling. Through the window, she sees that part of the building on the other side of the street is being redecorated. They've left the lights on, and there's a stepladder in the middle of the floor.

"It might be nothing," Arne Rosander goes on, "but I just spoke to our witness psychologist . . . and today she spoke to another woman who saw the perpetrator in the street outside the bar. This woman wasn't able to give any sort of description earlier—it's just what happens sometimes—but last night she had a dream about him."

"I'm listening."

Saga turns back to look at the studio again. Randy is lying naked on the bed, looking over at her with shining eyes.

"A large man with a thick neck, cropped hair, and a bloody face. . . . And listen to this, this is pretty interesting—he was wearing pearl earrings."

"Did she remember him wearing them in real life?"

"No, that was just in the dream, but the hair and blood match what the other witnesses said."

Saga thanks him for calling, then goes back to Randy. She settles down on his arm and feels his other hand make its way between her legs.

32

SAGA STOPS NEAR THE ENTRANCE TO THE CLUB. IT'S GOTTEN colder. Tiny, crisp snowflakes are drifting in the glow of the bare lightbulb above the unassuming door.

A tall bouncer in a protective vest with his blond hair pulled back in a ponytail is watching some young men in all black smoke behind some dumpsters. The bouncer's bare neck is blue-gray with tattoos.

Large nylon sacks of construction debris are piled along the edge of the street.

It's half past four in the morning, but music from the basement is still pounding.

Saga fell asleep after having sex with Randy a second time, and didn't wake up until a quarter to four. Before she left, she locked her pistol and police ID in his gun cabinet. She knows she'd never get permission from her boss to visit an underground club in her capacity as an officer. There was more than enough fuss after her trip to Chicago in pursuit of the Rabbit Hunter.

Saga approaches the entrance as an unlicensed cab pulls up in front of her. Three teens in long black coats get out and exchange a few words with the guy at the door, then go inside and vanish down the steps.

The bouncer steps aside so he's not blocking the light as Saga walks up to him.

"Are you sure you're not in the wrong place, princess?" he asks, his face breaking into a network of wrinkles as he smiles.

"Yes."

"Your decision," he says, and opens the door. The music instantly gets louder.

"Do you have security cameras?" she asks.

"No, why do you . . . ?"

"Nowhere inside?"

"We don't have a license for that."

Saga can't help smiling—an underground club is worried about licenses. She goes down a steep flight of concrete steps as the bouncer closes the door behind her.

She can hear some sort of roaring over the thud of the bass.

At the foot of the stairs is a security check. Ahead of Saga, the three teens are signing their names on a membership list. They then pay to enter and walk through a metal detector.

Framed pictures of famous visitors rattle as the music shakes the walls.

The security guard is a large woman with a double chin, a shaved head, round glasses, and black leather pants. A T-shirt that reads "Tribe 8" is stretched across her chest. Her thick, pale arms are covered with beautiful garland tattoos.

The boys laugh as she pats them down.

While she's signing herself in and paying, Saga looks at the list, which consists solely of first names and e-mail addresses. She walks through the metal detector.

THE THREE BOYS IN THE LONG COATS ARE YELLING TO ONE another over the music, and one of them pushes his way toward the restrooms.

Saga walks over and stands with her arms outstretched, and is quickly patted down by the guard.

"I signed the list, but . . ."

"What?" the guard says.

"I signed in," Saga says, louder. "But I don't know if I'm on the mailing list."

The guard shrugs and gestures to wave her on. More people are on their way down the stairs.

"Keep moving."

"Is there a mailing list that . . . ?"

The guard's face is shiny with sweat; her eyes are beady behind her round glasses.

"What the fuck are you talking about?" she asks.

Saga looks away and moves on into a coat room. She looks around. The door to the women's bathroom opens, and a young woman with dark lipstick emerges.

Saga catches a glimpse of the crowd in front of the bathroom mirrors before the door closes again. She steps over the legs of a man who's sitting on the floor with a phone pressed to his ear, and makes her way into the darkness of the main part of the club. She passes through two heavy doors with thick rubber fringes along the bottom, and has to stop for a moment in the sudden darkness.

The noise is extraordinary.

A band is playing onstage, and the rapid thud of the bass vibrates through her body. The crowd is pressing forward, jumping, and holding their hands in the air.

The room is packed. It's all but impossible to move.

A wave passing through the throng forces her sideways, and she's pushed up against the wall; then another wave sends her stumbling back into the sudden void.

The audience is pushing and shoving, dancing, singing along.

There are banks of speakers and other equipment mounted on the ceiling. Smoke streams through rotating beams of light.

There's no way she can have a conversation in here. Unless she finds someone in charge, there's nothing she can do except look for a heavyset man in his fifties. If he is here, it shouldn't be hard to spot him, because most of the clientele are young men with long hair and black clothes.

Saga apologizes and tries to make her way along the inner wall, as far away from the chaos onstage as possible.

The bass and double-pedal kick drum are keeping up a frenetic pace, and the guitar is playing rapid, repetitive power chords.

The singer is wearing black jeans and a T-shirt with "Entombed" emblazoned on it in ornate type.

A roar comes from the speakers, followed by guttural growling, a sort of deep, moaning throat song.

The audience moves backward, pressing Saga against the wall again. She struggles to hold them off, pushing the bodies away with both arms.

Just as the wave changes direction, she feels a hand between her legs. She turns around, but can't figure out who grabbed her. It's too dark, and everyone is already tumbling forward again.

A man with a beard and a shiny bald head is dancing and kicking the air. He loses his balance, falls to the floor, and rolls several meters.

Saga tries to make her way to the bar. She shoves her way forward along the wall.

The audience is jumping and pressing against the edge of the stage, yelling until their voices crack and waving their hands in the air.

The music is hammering against Saga's chest and neck.

A woman in a short black vinyl skirt spills beer as she tries to drink from a plastic cup. A man with greasy hair is standing behind her, squeezing her breasts. She makes a feeble attempt to resist, but then goes on drinking.

Saga pushes her way forward, shoving someone who's blocking her path out of the way, and ignores the bump in the shoulder she gets in return as she barges her way through the men.

She reaches the mixing booth, which has scratched plexiglass screens. Cables have been taped to the floor. The air is hot, laden with the smell of sweat, beer, and dry ice from the fog machine. The lights from the stage sweep across the crowd.

Over by the bar, Saga catches a glimpse of the silhouette of a man who's almost a foot taller than everyone around him.

She's almost certain his head is shaved.

Saga tries to make her way around the mixing booth but gets pushed back by the crowd. The music slows down and seems to hang in the air. The bass drum is silent, and the cymbals tinkle gently.

The singer pulls his T-shirt down over his stomach, stands right on the edge of the stage, raises his right arm, and then makes a slow chopping motion in front of him.

The audience parts on either side of the line, moving out of the way to free up a path down the middle.

There are some empty plastic cups and a denim jacket on the floor.

The two halves of the audience stand facing each other, panting, expectant.

Suddenly the music gets ridiculously fast again, and the men on both sides of the empty space rush toward each other, screaming as they collide and fall. One blond boy crashes to the floor, and several other men stumble over him. Another staggers away with his hand over his mouth and blood streaming between his fingers.

The music is thudding in her ears as strobe lights sweep the stage.

Saga pushes past the booth and gets elbowed in the cheek by a man trying to climb onto his friend's shoulders.

Sweat is running down her back when she finally reaches the throng around the bar. She scans the crowd for the heavyset man. People are leaning over the bar, passing large plastic cups of beer behind them. One young man with long, wavy hair looks Saga in the eye and says something inaudible with a crooked smile.

The singer divides the crowd again.

Saga makes her way toward a man with a tattooed head who's standing between the bar and the sea of people. She forces her way through to him and asks if he's seen an older man with a shaved head. She has to shout into his ear. He looks at her drunkenly, says something, then staggers away.

She realizes that he asked her if he looked like the sort of person who likes the police.

The music is rumbling slowly, gearing up for another crash.

Hazy lights sweep across the crowd, and Saga sees the tall man with the shaved head. He's standing in an alcove next to the door that leads to the staff area. The light flickers past, and then everything goes dark again.

The music explodes, and the screams from the stage drown out everything else as the two halves of the audience rush toward each other again.

They collide and fall.

One girl is dragged across the floor.

Two boys start kicking and fighting and have to be pulled apart.

Saga manages to push her way along the bar to the alcove. The tall man can't be any older than twenty. He's leaning against the wall, his thin, tattooed arms hanging by his sides.

She keeps going and checks the next alcove, looking at all the faces in the dim light.

The crowd is jumping and shoving. The guitars are playing rapid chord sequences. The singer is clutching the microphone with both hands and growling.

On a silver-painted podium to one side of the stage, a young woman is dancing in her underwear beside a vertical metal pole, circling it, hooking one leg around it, and spinning around as she slides down it.

Saga sees the man with the tattooed head pushing his way through the crowd toward the entrance. She sets off after him, but someone shoves her in the back, and she stumbles into a man who helps her regain her balance.

33

SAGA TRIES NOT TO LET THE MAN WITH THE TATTOOED head out of her sight.

The crowd pushes back, sweeping her up. Beer splashes in her face, and she almost falls. She collides with the mixing booth, hitting her head against the plexiglass.

She presses on along the back wall, tripping over a stray sneaker and fending off a man who's flailing around wildly, before she finally reaches the door and emerges into the coat room.

Cool air streams in from the entrance, and although the music is still thudding through the walls, it's much quieter there.

People are coming back down the stairs after going outside to smoke. They show their stamps to the guard.

There's a pile of the skeleton matchbooks in a cigarette machine.

The man with the tattooed head disappears into the men's bathroom with his phone pressed to his ear.

Saga follows him and is hit by an intense stench—a combination of urine and toilet cleaner. The entire floor is wet, and covered with damp paper towels, plastic cups, and bits of snuff.

There are several drunken young men lined up at the urinals. One of them is leaning against the wall with one hand as he aims his penis with the other. His urine swirls around the small portions of snuff in the urinal, hits the edge, and splashes onto the wall and floor.

The man with the tattooed head emerges from one of the stalls. The toilet seat is lying on the wet floor beside the toilet.

"I didn't hear your answer to my question," Saga says, moving to intercept him.

"What?" he mutters, looking her in the eye.

"I'm looking for a man in his fifties who—"

"She just wants a fuck," another man says.

"I don't know what you're talking about," the man with the tattooed head says.

"I think you do."

"Leave me the fuck alone," he says, and shoves her in the chest.

She follows him out into the coat room, applause and wolf whistles trailing behind her.

This is hopeless, she thinks, standing still. The matchbook didn't necessarily belong to the murderer, and even if it did, that doesn't mean he comes here regularly. But it's all they have to go on: a possible connection between the murderer and an underground club.

Hoping to catch a glimpse of him in the crowd is pointless. On the other hand, the club is about to close, which will make it easier to figure out who works here.

Someone must know something.

Saga returns to the main room. The audience is leaping around, fists raised in front of the stage, where the guitarist is shredding, both hands on the neck of his instrument.

The music slows and swells to a fanfare, the chord changes becoming heavier, more dramatic. The performance climaxes with a single howl.

It's five-thirty in the morning.

The band leaves, and roadies immediately begin to strike the stage.

The lights go up. The music is still ringing in people's ears.

Saga tries to see all the faces as people stream out. Security staff are now waking up men who have fallen asleep by the walls, helping the drunkest of them to walk.

The floor empties. The stage, its black paint peeling, is already deserted.

A few drunken teenagers are laughing and jeering as they make their way up the steps toward the street.

A red fire-extinguisher cabinet has been pulled from the wall and is standing on the floor.

Saga moves through the thinning stream of people and approaches the staff, who are still standing behind the bar. The woman who was dancing with the pole is now wearing a bathrobe, and the sound engineer with gray stubble is talking to the female security guard with round glasses.

The bartender is pouring them beer and Coke.

Saga sits down on one of the fixed bar stools, then turns to the man behind the bar.

"I'd like to be put on the mailing list," she says.

"We don't have one," he snaps, wiping the bar.

"How do you get information to your members, then? Through Facebook, or—?"

"No, not like that," he interrupts, looking at her.

"Why do you ask so many fucking questions?" the security guard asks.

"I'm trying to find someone who comes here," Saga says, loudly enough for everyone to hear.

"And who are you?" the bartender says, scratching his ear.

"A friend."

"Whose friend?" he asks, tapping the bar.

"We're closing now," the security guard says.

"I'm looking for a man in his fifties. He's been here," Saga continues. "He's heavyset, has a thick neck, shaved head."

"A hell of a lot of people come here," the bartender replies.

"You mean other than all the young guys in black clothes?" Saga asks.

"He's just trying to help," the security guard says sharply.

"All I'm saying is that the person I'm trying to find stands out," Saga explains.

"Fifty years old, shaved head, thick neck," the bartender says, pointing to a photograph behind him.

It's a picture of the singer Udo Dirkschneider when he was visiting the club. A plump man with cropped blond hair, a leather jacket, and a plastic cup of beer in one hand.

"The man I'm looking for is prone to fits of rage and breaks things," Saga says.

The bartender shrugs, and the security guard checks the time on her phone. A roadie who's been gathering cables from the stage comes over to the bar to get a glass of water. "What's going on?" he asks, looking at Saga.

"How often is there trouble here?" she asks.

"You mean the audience. . . . That's not trouble, that's just the mosh pit. I swear, it's one hell of a buzz," he says, emptying his glass and walking toward the door.

"We never have trouble here," the security guard says.

"He may wear pearl earrings," Saga says. From the corner of her eye, she sees the dancer turn away.

"You'll have to look for Daddy somewhere else," the bartender says, dragging a beer barrel out of the way.

The guard laughs and repeats the joke. Saga watches as the dancer heads for the staff room.

There was something about her face as she turned away.

As if she'd been caught.

Saga starts to follow her, and notices that the woman speeds up before she reaches the door.

"Wait a minute," Saga says sternly.

The dancer disappears into the staff room. Saga runs and catches the door before it closes.

"You can't go in there," the guard calls after her, turning to follow.

"I know," Saga says almost silently as she goes in.

The staff room is a windowless space with a row of metal lockers, a battered sofa, armchairs around a badly scratched table. There's a small kitchen in the corner and a bathroom in the back.

The dancer hurries into the bathroom and locks the door.

"Come out here—I need to talk to you," Saga says, banging on the door.

"You can't be in here," the guard says behind her.

"I know," Saga replies. "But I think she knows something about the man I'm looking for."

"Come with me and we can talk about it."

"In a minute," Saga says, and knocks on the door again.

"You're starting to cause trouble now," the guard says. "I need to do my job. The club's closed, and I can't let you be in here."

"I get it, but I need to speak to—"

"Are you slow on the uptake, or what?" the guard interrupts.

Saga brushes the hair from her face and glances at her. "This is important," she says. "I'd be really grateful if you could give me ten minutes."

She turns back toward the bathroom door, and when the guard puts one hand on her arm she pulls herself loose and looks her in the eye. "Don't touch me," Saga says coolly.

"I've tried to be nice—but what the hell am I supposed to do if you won't listen?"

"Open up!" Saga says, banging on the door.

The guard grabs her upper arm again. Saga turns and shoves her in the chest, making her take a step back to keep her balance.

The guard pulls a collapsible baton from her belt and opens it up to its full length.

"I can see how I'm going to have to deal with you and—"

"Just shut up," Saga interrupts. "It's late, and I'm starting to get really fucking tired, and if you don't stay out of the way . . ."

Saga sees the baton coming from the side and moves nimbly out of the way. She hasn't fought competitively for several years, but she still trains at the boxing club four days a week.

The guard moves after Saga. The baton swings down at her shoulder with full force.

Saga slides out of the way and throws an elbow into the guard's lower arm. The woman groans, and the baton spins through the air and hits one of the metal lockers.

The guard throws a left hook.

Instead of rolling past the punch, Saga just tilts her head back, beyond the guard's reach, to lure her into trying harder next time. A sort of Ali-shuffle.

The guard takes a step forward and swings again.

Saga jabs with her left hand to gauge the precise distance and moves simultaneously to one side, out of her opponent's central line.

"A little boxer," the guard says with a laugh, trying to catch her.

Saga lands a perfect right hook to her face. The woman's glasses go flying in a spray of sweat.

The guard looks confused; one leg is wobbling, and she staggers sideways from the blow.

Saga meets her unbalanced movements with a low left hook to her ribs.

The guard whimpers, sinks down onto one knee, and reaches out for a crate of toilet cleaner with one hand, gasping as blood seeps from her lip.

Saga is already on her again, with a right cross from above, aimed directly at the bridge of her nose.

The punch lands hard.

The guard's head flies back. Her body follows, and she tumbles backward helplessly, dragging a mop and bucket down with her.

Without giving the guard another look, Saga goes back to the bathroom door, bangs on it, and shouts at the dancer to open up.

"Fuck, fuck, fuck," the guard groans, trying to sit up as blood streams from her nose.

"Stay there," Saga says, then kicks at the bathroom door. There's a crash as the lock shatters and its metal components clatter to the floor.

"Don't hit me," the dancer pleads, sinking down beside the toilet.

"I just want to talk," Saga says.

34

IT'S STARTING TO GET LIGHT WHEN THE MCDONALD'S ON Göt Street opens for the day. Saga puts two cups down on the table. "Drink some coffee," she says, sitting down opposite the dancer from the club.

The dancer's name is Anna Sjölin. She's twenty-two years old and lives in Vårby. She's wearing jeans and a red padded jacket. Her gloves and knitted hat are on the table, and her long brown hair is gathered into a knot. Anna nods and puts both hands around the cup, as if she were trying to warm them up. Her thin face is pale as she hesitantly answers Saga's questions.

"How long have you worked at the club?"

"About a year," Anna says, tasting the coffee.

As she observes the young woman's expressionless face and slow movements, Saga massages the sore knuckles of her right hand.

"Pole dancing is a sport," Anna says without looking up.

"I know," Saga says.

"Not at the club, though. I just do simple things there, so I don't get too tired, because I have to dance all night."

"What do you do between shifts?"

Anna rubs her nose and looks at Saga. She has dark rings under her eyes from lack of sleep, and there are fine lines running across her forehead.

"Can you tell me why we're sitting here?" she asks, pushing the cup away.

"I work for the Security Police."

"The Security Police." Anna smiles. "Can I see some ID?"

"No," Saga says.

"How am I supposed to . . ."

"Tell me about the man with the pearl earrings," Saga says.

Anna lowers her gaze, and her eyelashes flutter. "What did he do?" she asks.

"I can't talk about that."

Anna looks out of the window just as the streetlights go out along the pavement. A homeless woman with an overflowing shopping cart stops outside the window and stares at them.

"You've seen a heavyset man with pearl earrings at the club," Saga says once more, encouraging Anna to go on.

"Yes."

"Is he there a lot?"

"I've seen him maybe five times."

"What does he do?"

"He just keeps to himself. He doesn't join in, doesn't dance. . . . He stays a few hours, drinking vodka shots and eating chili nuts."

She pulls the coffee toward her again, reaches for the sugar, then changes her mind.

"Have you ever talked to him?" Saga asks.

"Once, when some guys spilled beer all over him . . . He looks a bit—I don't know—like a big kid . . . with those earrings and . . . Oh, I don't know. . . ."

She falls silent again. There's a deep furrow between her eyebrows. Saga tries to think of a way to get Anna to tell her more, to give her something that will help them make progress.

"Did he get angry when they spilled beer on him?"

"No, he just tried to explain the pearls. They weren't listening . . . but I heard what he said. . . . They're a tribute to his sister, who died when she was thirteen. They were her earrings, and he said he didn't care if people laughed—he's happy to take whatever abuse he gets for them."

"What's his name?"

"He calls himself the Beaver," Anna says with a tired smile. "He doesn't exactly make things easy for himself."

She drinks some coffee and wipes her lips with her hand.

"Anything else?" Saga prompts.

Anna shrugs her shoulders.

"What?"

"We talked about a little bit of everything, I guess," she says, and seems to drift off in thought for a few seconds. "I'm not saying I believe it, but he told me he had a sixth sense. That he always knows who's going to die first when he enters a room."

"What do you mean?" Saga asks.

"He said it like it was obvious, and pointed at Jamal, a guy who . . . Well, he didn't know that I knew him. . . . Three days later, I heard that Jamal was dead: a blood vessel burst in his brain. He was born with it, apparently. No one knew about it, not even Jamal."

Anna puts the cup down, picks up her hat and gloves, and gets to her feet.

"We're almost done," Saga says.

Anna sits down again.

"Do you know what the Beaver's real name is?"

"No."

"Do you have his contact information, anything concrete?"

"No."

"Have you ever seen him with anyone else?"

"No."

"Did he hit on you?"

"He spoke about starting a club of his own, and asked if I'd be interested in changing jobs."

"What did you say?"

"That I'd think about it."

"Where does he live?"

Anna sighed and leaned back. "He seemed kind of rootless. He didn't have a fixed address, kept moving around all the time—at least, that's how I understood it."

"Did he mention any address at all? Did he say where he was living at the moment? Did he mention any friends, anything?"

"No." Anna stifles a yawn with her knuckles.

"Okay, let's go through the whole conversation again, bit by bit," Saga says. "He must have said something . . . something that would help me find him."

"Look, I need to get some sleep, I work at Filippa K during the week," she says, sighing. "He never said where he lived."

"How were you going to let him know about the job?"

"I don't know. It wasn't a concrete plan. He doesn't even have a club," she replies.

"So it was just talk?"

"I honestly don't know. He said he was an entrepreneur, a renaissance man. . . . He said lots of weird stuff. I didn't understand all of it. He talked about buying a deserted research center in Bulgaria, some state-run laboratory that was abandoned after communism, but I don't really remember."

"Is he from Bulgaria?"

"I don't think so, he doesn't have an accent. . . . Sorry, I'm too tired to think straight," she whispers.

"One of our psychologists will be getting in touch with you tomorrow. She'll help you remember," Saga says, getting to her feet.

35

IT'S EIGHT-FIFTEEN ON SUNDAY EVENING, AND SAGA AND
Nathan Pollock are reluctantly calling it a day.

There is a map of Europe on one wall, along with detailed maps
of the locations where the victims were found. On another wall are
a series of stills taken from the Belarusian security-camera footage. The recording was made in darkness and the picture quality is
poor, but the man who calls himself the Beaver is visible. They can
get a sense of his height and build. They can tell he has big, sloping
shoulders and glimpses of his thick neck, jawline, and the shape
of his head stand out against the background in certain pictures.

The glare of the desk lamp catches on the scratched lenses of
Nathan's reading glasses, and the reflection quivers on the ceiling
as he bumps the edge of the table when he stands up. He jerks his
head to get his gray ponytail to hang down his back.

The witnesses outside the Pilgrim Bar described an aggressive
man who resembles the suspect in the security-camera footage
from Belarus.

The Swedish police searched the home of the murdered bartender and found a bunch of snuff films—drugged women being
raped. He had twice been cleared of rape charges in court in
Stockholm.

The dancer Anna Sjölin has told them about her conversation
with the man who fits the description of the perpetrator. The Beaver wears pearl earrings, sees himself as an entrepreneur, and wants
to buy an old laboratory complex in Bulgaria.

For some reason, he seems to think he has special powers. It sounds like he has a fairly inflated view of himself, a sense of superiority, which would fit a murderer who sees himself as a superhero charged with cleansing society by taking out criminals the justice system has failed to punish hard enough.

When Saga spoke to Jeanette Fleming two hours ago, the psychologist was sitting at Anna's kitchen table out in Vårby. It was too early to discuss the conversation with the Beaver, but Jeanette said that they were making progress.

Nathan starts to pack his briefcase, explaining that he has to get home to Veronica to go over the divorce process. A few strands of gray hair have caught on his jacket.

"You should sign the papers," Saga says.

"I'm not in any hurry."

Saga has also decided to go home. She's thinking of going for a ten-kilometer run and then calling Randy. She really should talk to her dad as well, but she doesn't feel up to it. The last time they spoke, he tried to ask for advice on online dating, as if she'd ever tried that. The whole conversation left her feeling impatient. It was as though her dad thought that everything was already fine, that they had a normal relationship.

Saga goes over to the best picture they have of the Beaver's face. Grease from Blu Tack has stained the corners of the printout.

The camera caught him seconds before he kicked and smashed one of the outdoor lamps. Its glow lights up his face from underneath.

In spite of the poor resolution, it's possible to make out his round cheeks, his forehead, and the sparkle of what could be a pearl earring.

"Now we know that the Beaver is capable of sitting down and holding a conversation," she says. "He can even be badly provoked without getting angry . . . but we've also seen the sort of rage he's capable of."

"What else do we know?" Nathan asks quietly.

Saga meets his weary gaze. "He calls himself the Beaver, he's a heavyset man in his fifties, has cropped hair, and wears earrings—two pearls that belonged to his dead sister," Saga says.

"He claims to have a sixth sense, and is cleansing Europe," Nathan says.

"He speaks Swedish without an accent, probably has no fixed address, says he's going to start a club and buy an old research center in Bulgaria.... He says he's an entrepreneur, but that could just be talk.... I haven't been able to find any old laboratories that are for sale."

Silence fills the room again. The whole building is quiet; there aren't many people out at this time on a Sunday.

The windows of Nathan's office are streaked with dirt, and one has the imprint of a forehead. The telecommunications mast and the spire of the old police headquarters stand out against the dark sky. Fragments of small pale-brown leaves lie strewn on the windowsill around a potted plant.

"How long has Jeanette been talking to the dancer now?" Nathan asks, folding a napkin and tossing it in the trash.

"I don't want to interrupt them. Jeanette will call when she's finished."

They leave the room and walk down the hallway, depositing their mugs in the kitchen and switching the lights off behind them. On the way to the elevator, they pass Joona's empty office.

"We need to find some way to let Joona know that whoever is trying to clean up society isn't Jurek," Nathan says.

36

THE STREETS ARE ALMOST DESERTED WHEN SAGA FINALLY
heads home. A few snowflakes are swirling around the streetlights
and neon signs. At first the cold wind is painful, but after a while
her face starts to go numb and she feels an inner warmth. She's
already getting used to her dad's motorcycle and has come to
appreciate its low center of gravity in the urban traffic.

It occurs to Saga that Joona is bound to get in touch at some
point to ask about the investigation. Otherwise, he'd end up in hiding forever and would never know what they've discovered—that
they're dealing with a completely new serial killer.

She turns onto Tavast Street, where she parks and covers the
bike with its tarp. The thin silvery-gray material rustles in the evening wind.

Up in her apartment, Saga locks her pistol in the gun cabinet,
leafs through the mail, drinks some orange juice straight from the
carton, and changes into her running clothes.

Just as she's putting on her sneakers in the hall, her phone rings.
She hunts through her bag on the floor for it, and sees that it's
Pellerina calling.

"What are you doing?" her half-sister asks. Saga can barely hear
her.

"I'm going to get some exercise—you know, go out for a run."

"Okay," Pellerina says. Her breathing echoes down the line.

"Why aren't you asleep? It's pretty late," Saga asks tentatively.

"It's really dark," she whispers.

"Turn your heart light on."

"You can't forget to turn it off," her sister replies.

"I promise, you're allowed to turn it on," Saga says. "Can you go and see Dad and give him the phone?"

"No."

"Why don't you want to go and see Dad?" she asks.

"I can't."

"Is he downstairs in the kitchen?"

"He's not home."

"Are you alone?"

"Maybe."

"Tell me what happened. . . . Your painting class finished at eight o'clock, and then you went home with Miriam's mom as usual? Did Dad have your dinner ready, the way he normally does?"

"He wasn't home," her sister replies. "I think he's mad at me."

"Maybe Dad had to go to the hospital—you know, because he helps people who have problems with their hearts."

Saga can hear her sister's breathing.

"I heard giggling outside," Pellerina whispers, almost inaudibly. "I thought it was the clown girls."

"They're not real—you know that, don't you?"

Saga can't help thinking that the girls from school might have sent the chain e-mail.

"Did you turn the lights on?" she asks.

"No."

Suddenly Saga is worried that the girls might actually get inside the house and hurt Pellerina, hold her down and poke her eyes out, the way the e-mail said. She knows it's her imagination running wild, but still. Children are always testing their boundaries, and it's easy for that to get out of hand. It happens everywhere.

"Turn the lights on now."

"Okay."

"I'll be there as soon as I can—how does that sound?" Saga says.

They hang up, and Saga calls her dad as she pulls her white leathers over her running clothes. There's no answer, so she tries again as she hurries downstairs. She leaves a voice mail telling him to call her as soon as he can.

She looks up the number of the thoracic intensive-care unit at Karolinska, but is told that Lars-Erik Bauer isn't working tonight.

Saga removes the tarp, puts her helmet on, and starts the motorcycle.

While she's riding to Gamla Enskede, she thinks through the last conversation she had with her dad. She can't imagine how he could have misunderstood. He wanted to invite the researcher he'd met online out to dinner, and asked if she could babysit, but she said she would be busy tonight. Maybe she got the date wrong. Or she was distracted and said yes without realizing it.

There are snow-covered cars parked in front of all the houses, and the lawns are sparkling with frost.

Saga stops and opens the wrought-iron gate, and rides the heavy motorcycle into the drive.

She takes her helmet off and looks up at the house.

All the windows are dark.

The glow from a streetlight farther down the road reaches into the yard. The apple tree's bare branches cast a network of shadows over the brickwork.

Pellerina's pink bicycle, with tassels on its handlebars, is lying on the grass. Its tires are flat.

Saga walks toward the house. The faint light is behind her, and she sees her shadow get paler and longer.

She looks along the curved driveway down to the garage in the basement. There's a plastic soccer ball in front of the door.

She stops at the front door and listens. She can hear a faint thudding sound, like someone running on a treadmill.

She carefully pushes the door handle down and pulls.

The front door is unlocked.

The thudding sound stops the moment she opens the door.

She looks into the dark hall.

Complete silence.

The rug is slightly crooked.

Saga puts her helmet on the stool, takes off her boots, and walks in. The worn parquet floor is ice-cold under her feet. She turns the overhead light on, and a yellow glow spreads across the walls.

"Hello? Pellerina?" Saga calls.

The house is so cold that her breath clouds in front of her mouth. She passes the hallway and door leading to the basement and sees her dad's coat hanging over the back of a kitchen chair.

"Dad?"

Saga switches the light on and sees that the door to the back-yard is wide open.

She walks over to it and calls Pellerina's name again.

She hears some dull thumps from the boiler in the basement, then silence again.

Saga looks at the damp glass of the greenhouse, which is reflecting the light from the kitchen. She sees a black silhouette of herself standing in the doorway.

The bare bushes against the neighbor's fence are moving in the wind. The swing is creaking gently on its frame.

Saga gazes out into the garden, at the darkness between the trees, then closes the door.

The chain e-mail said that the clown girls come at night, grab you, then paint a laughing mouth on your face to make you look happy while they poke out your eyes.

She goes back to the hallway and stops at the door to the basement. Pellerina never goes down there. All that's there is the boiler, the washing machine, and a garage full of garden tools and furniture.

Pellerina is scared of the boiler, because on really cold nights you can hear its banging noise throughout the house.

Saga walks over to the staircase and sees that someone has walked up it in dirty shoes.

"Pellerina?" she calls upstairs.

Saga creeps up the stairs, and when her head reaches the landing she stops and looks along the thick floorboards. She sees the grain of the wood, the frayed edges of the rugs, the crack under the door to the bathroom.

She can hear a very faint voice, but can't tell where it's coming from. It sounds like monotone singing.

Saga turns back quickly and looks downstairs. She kneels down and checks that the door to the basement is closed.

She continues up the stairs to Pellerina's room, where she listens before carefully opening the door.

In the gloom, she can just make out the gray plastic case of the EKG machine, a pair of pink ballet shoes, and the closed closet door.

Saga sees that the bed has been slept in but is now empty. She hears a creaking sound from the attic. The loose cable of the satellite dish is swaying outside the window.

"Pellerina," Saga says quietly.

She switches on the lamp with the heart-shaped shade, and the pink glow spreads across the wall behind the chest of drawers, up to the ceiling.

Saga looks under the bed, and sees some candy wrappers, a dusty extension cord, and a plastic skeleton with red eyes.

She gets to her feet and goes over to the closet. She puts her hand on the bronze handle.

"Pellerina, it's just me," she says, and opens the door.

The hinges creak, and Saga catches a glimpse of the clothes hanging inside before a large shape sweeps toward her. She throws her head back, and her hand reaches automatically for her pistol. The huge teddy bear lands on the floor and sits there on its backside in front of her.

"I almost did a number on you," Saga says.

She closes the closet and hears the singing again. The voice is very weak, almost impossible to hear. She turns around slowly. She thinks it's coming from the guest bedroom.

Saga walks out of the room, past the dark staircase, then nudges open the door of the room where she usually sleeps. Someone's pulled the blankets onto the ground and is sitting under them on the other side of the bed.

"Not here, not here, not here," Pellerina is chanting in a high voice.

"Pellerina?"

"Not here, not here . . ."

When Saga pulls the covers back, her sister lets out a shriek of fear. Her hands are clamped over her ears, and she looks terrified.

"It's me," Saga says, taking her into her arms.

Her sister's heart is beating fast, and her small body is sweaty.

"It's just me, don't worry, it's just me."

Pellerina hugs her tightly and whispers her name over and over again.

"Saga, Saga, Saga, Saga . . ."

37

THEY SIT ON THE BED WITH THEIR ARMS WRAPPED TIGHTLY around each other until Pellerina calms down, then go downstairs to the kitchen. Her sister stays close to Saga the whole time and switches on every lamp they pass.

Saga opens the fridge and finds some leftovers: beef stew and boiled potatoes.

"You have to go to bed as soon as we finish eating," Saga says, taking out a carton of cream.

"Daddy was mad and didn't make any dinner," Pellerina whispers.

"Why do you keep saying he was mad?"

"I sent him a picture of my first painting."

"From painting class?"

"Yes, and he called and said it was a really lovely dog, and that he'd put it up in the kitchen. But when I told him it was a horse, he got angry and hung up."

"What? What did he say?" she asks.

Pellerina nudges her glasses farther up her nose.

"He just hung up," she says.

"There must have been something else going on. Sometimes the phone's battery just runs out. I promise, he wasn't upset," Saga says, smiling, as she starts to heat up the food.

"Why doesn't he want to come home, then?"

"That might be my fault. I think I forgot that Dad was going to meet a girl."

"Daddy has a date?" Pellerina smiles.

"Yes, I think so. You know I'm seeing Randy, don't you?"

"He's really cute."

"Yes, he is."

As the food warms up, Saga makes a sauce. She dissolves a stock cube in cream, then adds some pepper and a teaspoon of soy sauce.

"So what's Daddy's girlfriend's name?" Pellerina asks.

"I don't remember—Annabella, maybe?" Saga says, picking a name at random.

"Annabella." Her sister laughs.

"With big brown eyes, dark hair, and bright-red lipstick."

"And a sparkly gold dress!"

"Exactly."

Saga gets out two plates and two glasses, and some paper towels. She takes out the lingonberry jam and a jug of water.

"He probably put his phone on silent so he can kiss Annabella," Saga says.

Pellerina laughs out loud. The color's come back to her face now. They sit down, and Saga makes sure Pellerina takes her heart medication before they start to eat.

"Didn't Dad tell you about his date?" she asks after a while.

"No," Pellerina says, and takes a sip of water.

"But he told you I'd be coming tonight?"

"I don't know," Pellerina says, eating some of the stew. "I don't think so."

When they've finished eating, Saga helps Pellerina brush her teeth, then goes into her bedroom with her.

"I went and hid when I got scared," Pellerina says as she puts her pajamas on.

"I'll give you a little piece of advice," Saga says, brushing the hair from her sister's face. "If you really want to hide, you have to stay really quiet. You can't say 'not here, not here,' because then they'll know that you're there."

"Okay." Her sister nods, and lies back in bed.

"And don't hide under the blankets," Saga goes on. "Hide behind the curtains or behind an open door, and just stand there nice and still until I find you."

"Because you're the police."

"Do you want me to leave the light on?"

"Yes."

"Okay. But there's nothing to be scared of—you know that, don't you?" Saga says, sitting down next to her.

"Aren't you ever scared?" Pellerina asks.

"No, I'm not," Saga replies, taking her sister's glasses off and putting them on the bedside table.

"Good night, Saga."

"Good night, little sister," she says. Just then, her phone starts to ring in her pocket.

"Maybe Dad's had enough of kissing," Pellerina says, smiling.

Saga takes her phone out. It's Jeanette Fleming.

"It isn't him," Saga says. "It's my work. I need to pick up, but I'll come and see you again in a little while."

She takes the call as she walks downstairs, having left the door ajar.

"Sorry to call so late," Jeanette says.

"How did it go?" Saga asks.

"I probably need another couple of sessions."

"Can't we just tell her to take some time off at work?"

"You get better results if you fit their schedule, and I'm okay working nights."

"As long as you don't wear yourself out," Saga says.

"The baby likes it when I work, stays nice and quiet."

Jeanette's finally pregnant after wanting children for years. She's divorced now, and she'd been talking about going to Denmark to be artificially inseminated. Saga assumes that's what she did, but Jeanette's been oddly secretive about how it all happened.

"What did she say?"

"It might be better if you heard it for yourself. I'm sending the audio. Most of it is small talk, but there are a few minutes where she's remembering new things."

"Great, thanks."

Saga hangs up. She sits down at the kitchen table and looks out at the old apple trees in the light of the window. The recording begins in the middle of a sentence:

". . . and that, too. No, it isn't mine, it's . . ."

Anna knocks something over.

"Fuck."

Chair legs scrape the floor; then Saga hears footsteps and the sound of running water. Jeanette is a long way from the microphone—her voice is barely audible.

"Let's go back to what you said before, about his plan to buy a research center in Bulgaria?"

"He said all kinds of things," Anna replies, breathing heavily.

"But you remember him talking about the old laboratory in Bulgaria? Did you know what he wanted it for?"

"No idea; he seemed interested in the chemical industry. How the hell anyone could be interested in that. . . . He talked about a company in Norrtälje as well, one that makes—what's it called—the stuff that makes cars shiny?"

"Polish?" Jeanette suggests. Saga hears her sit back down at the table.

"No . . . wax."

"Car wax?"

"Yes, they make something that's in car wax. . . . He was talking about buying a majority of the company shares."

"Did he work there?"

"No, but he was hanging around there at the time."

"In Norrtälje?"

"He took the ferry from Sol Island," she replies.

"Where to?"

"I don't know."

"But he took the ferry to get home?"

"That's how I understood it, but he . . ."

Anna breaks off when the doorbell rings. She mutters that it's Marie, and leaves the kitchen.

Saga sits in silence for a while before she gets up and starts to clear the table. She rinses the plates and cutlery and starts the dishwasher, then goes back upstairs to check on her sister. Pellerina is sleeping soundly.

Saga walks around the house, turning out the lights and making sure the doors are locked and the windows are closed, before she goes to the guest bedroom. She picks up the comforter and sheets, makes the bed, and then tries to call her dad again.

It's strange that he hasn't been in touch, she thinks. Even if he is on a date, she would've expected him to at least check in.

His phone must be broken, or maybe he lost it.

If he'd had an accident, she'd have heard by now.

Saga switches the bedside lamp off and closes her eyes, but quickly opens them again. She thought she saw movement through her eyelids. When she looks up at the ceiling in the darkness, she sees the lamp swaying almost imperceptibly.

The vine creeping up the wall outside has grown around the window of the guest bedroom, and its dry branches scrape against the windowsill.

She thinks through that day's work: her conversations with Nathan, the short audio file from Jeanette, the Beaver's interest in the chemical industry, and a ferry outside Norrtälje.

The boiler starts to clank down in the basement. Its rattling is unnerving.

She should be asleep, but now that the thought's in her head she can't help it: she switches the light back on, grabs her phone, and looks up ferries from Sol Island.

Almost immediately, she finds a schedule. She sees that the ferry passes Högmarsö. It's just one of many islands that the ferry stops at. Even so, Saga's heart has started to beat faster.

Högmarsö was where Jurek Walter's body drifted ashore—where she met the churchwarden and was given the severed finger. That was where Joona thought she and Nathan should start their search. He thought that would give them an entry point into Jurek's world.

Saga realizes that her hands are shaking. She looks up Anna Sjölin's phone number and calls her.

"Fuck," the hoarse voice at the other end of the line says. "I was asleep. . . . What's going on? This is—"

"Did the Beaver say he lived on Högmarsö?" Saga interrupts.

"What?"

"Did he live on an island in the archipelago called Högmarsö?"

"I don't know," she says. "I don't think so."

"But he took the ferry from Sol Island?"

"That's what I thought he said. . . . Look, I need to get some sleep."

"Just one more thing," Saga says.

"What?"

"Are you listening?"

"Ye-e-e-s."

"Did the Beaver mention a churchwarden?"

"I don't know. . . . Wait, actually, yes, he said he was sleeping in a church."

38

JOONA AND LUMI ARE APPROACHING THE SMALL BORDER town of Waldfeucht along a narrow road.

The pastoral landscape is flat and wide, like a moss-green sea. White wind turbines stand out against the low winter sky.

A flock of crows takes off from a dark tree as they drive past.

They left their hotel yesterday morning and drove north, through Switzerland and into Germany. They stuck to minor roads close to Autobahn 5 up to Karlsruhe, driving for hours through small towns in the rain.

Joona keeps one hand on the wheel as he talks through strategy with Lumi. He goes over various escape routes and meeting places. He tells her how to get her bearings in the landscape when it's dark, using simple trigonometry of visible cell towers.

After the run-through they sit in silence, side by side, deep in thought. It's impossible to tell where the sun is behind the white sky.

Lumi's face is turned away.

"Dad," she says eventually, taking a deep breath, "I'm doing this because I promised I would . . . but I don't want to."

"I know."

"No, I don't think you do," she says, glancing at him sideways. "You've been waiting for this to happen. It's almost like you've been looking forward to it. . . . I mean, all the preparations, all the sacrifices you've been forced to make suddenly mean something."

They drive straight through a German border town. It takes

only a matter of minutes. Brown brick buildings and a beautiful church disappear behind them.

In the distance, a yellow tractor is rolling across a field. The sky reflects off a grain silo.

There's no border check between the countries. The narrow road simply continues. They pass a sign, welcoming them to the Netherlands.

"One thing I don't understand, Dad: the way you just left everything. I mean, you're the expert on Jurek. You know everything about him, but now that you think he's back, you just vanish and leave your colleagues to look for him."

"Even if I was there, I wouldn't be allowed to investigate," Joona explains. "But Nathan has my notes and background information, and he and Saga will be able to put together a team."

"While you're hiding," she says quietly.

"I'll do whatever it takes. I can't lose you," he says honestly.

"And Valeria?"

"I wish she'd come with me, but she'll have protection, and that's the important thing. Police officers, heavily armed. I can't make her do something she doesn't want to do, and I needed to move in order to keep you safe," he says.

"How can you live with that fear all the time?"

"You've pretty much only ever seen me when I'm frightened," Joona says, glancing at her quickly with a smile. "But the truth is that I'm very rarely scared."

They're driving through an avenue of bare trees, past the occasional dark-brick house. There are farms in the distance.

"Mom told me you were the bravest man in the world," Lumi says after a while.

"I wouldn't go that far, but I'm pretty good at what I do," Joona replies.

As they drive up through the southern Dutch province of Limburg, it starts to rain again. The windshield wipers scrape across the glass.

Rows of plastic-covered bales of hay lie on the dark fields like shiny white fruit.

"Have you and Saga ever hooked up?" Lumi asks.

"No, never." He smiles. "She's always been more like a sister."

Lumi looks at herself in the small mirror in the visor.

"I've only met her once, when she came to say she'd found Jurek's body. . . . I haven't been able to stop thinking about her. She's so ridiculously beautiful, perfect."

"You're perfect," Joona says.

Lumi looks out of the side window and sees a large crucifix by the side of the road, surrounded by iron railings.

"I don't get why she joined the police. She could have done anything, really."

"Just like me," he jokes.

"There's nothing wrong with wanting to be a police officer—you know that's not what I mean—but it doesn't suit everyone."

"As I understand it, Saga had a difficult childhood. Her mom suffered from mental illness. She never talks about it, but I think her mom committed suicide. . . . I've tried bringing it up with her, but she just says she doesn't want to talk about it. She's very particular about that. It's one of her rules. Thinking about her mom makes her unhappy."

"What was it like when your dad died?" Lumi asks.

"Dad," Joona says quietly.

"I mean, I know you were only eleven," she says. "Do you remember him? Really remember him, I mean?"

"I've been worried about forgetting. . . . When I was younger, I used to panic if I couldn't remember his face or his voice . . . but then I realized memory works in other ways. I still dream about him a lot, and then I can see him perfectly clearly."

The wiper blades are moving quickly, sweeping the rain away.

"Do you dream about your mom?" Joona asks after a while.

"A lot," Lumi replies. "I miss her so much, every day."

"I miss her, too," Joona says.

Lumi lowers her face and quickly brushes her tears away with the back of her hand.

Joona slows down at a junction just outside Weert. The red traffic light reflects off the wet road. A crow lands heavily at the top of a bare tree.

"I remember once when Mom and I . . . We'd been looking at this huge fire," Lumi said. "A warehouse was burning. Then, later . . . I think it was the same day . . . we sat and had ice cream on the steps of the cathedral. She told me about my wonderful dad, who was no longer around."

The light turns green, and they start moving again.

"Do you remember anything about life in Sweden?" Joona asks.

"Mom told me I used to have a little toy stove," Lumi says. "And that you used to play with me when you got home."

"You used to make me pretend to be your child, or a yappy dog, or I just had to lie on the floor while you fed me. . . . You were always very patient. I used to fall asleep after a while, and then you'd cover me up with plates and cutlery."

"What for?" She smiles.

"I don't know—maybe I was a table?"

They pass a truck close to a grubby-looking chapel. Water cascades over the windshield, and the slipstream makes the car shudder.

"It might just be something I dreamed about," Lumi says slowly, "but I think it's a real memory. Us saying good night to a gray cat."

"We did," he says. "I read you stories every night . . . and before you fell asleep we used to wave to the neighbor's cat."

39

IT STOPS RAINING AS THEY SLOW TO A HALT ON RIJKSWEG, which runs almost parallel to the E25. They're not far from the industrial zone on the outskirts of Maarheeze.

There are thirty or so sheep standing in a field, all facing the same way in the wind. On the other side of the highway is the gray surface of a large dam.

They turn off onto a narrow paved road. The badly dented signs indicate that it's a dead end, and that the area is private property. Tall grass brushes against the sides of the car.

Joona pulls up in front of a rusty gate, goes out into the cold air, and removes a spike that's been stuck into a chain in place of a padlock.

At the end of the road is a cluster of derelict buildings, with a wide view stretching out in all directions.

The place is perfect, carefully chosen. No one can approach without being seen from a distance, and it's only seven kilometers to the Belgian border.

They drive into the yard, and Joona parks behind the main building. The windows are covered with plywood, and the door is nailed shut.

A potholed gravel road loops around a meadow to the old workshop.

They take a shortcut across the meadow and step over an abandoned electric fence. The wires are missing, and several of the porcelain-insulated posts are lying in puddles.

"It isn't mined?" Lumi asks.

"No."

"Because that would give the hiding place away," she says to herself.

They follow a heavily rutted path through patches of ground elder and reach the gravel drive. The remains of a threshing machine are lying in the weeds beside the workshop.

Joona draws his pistol and holds it close to his body as they walk around the workshop. The windows upstairs are shuttered. Red-brown rust runs from the studs in the dirty white tin façade. The end of the building consists of two doors that are big enough to drive a dump truck through. One of the doors is hanging loose and moving back and forth in the wind.

The whole workshop looks like it's been abandoned for years.

Joona stops and looks back quickly. He takes in the meadow, the narrow path, and the car parked outside the main house.

He opens the door and looks inside the gloomy workshop. He sees that part of the concrete floor is covered with old oil-stains, a box of tin nails, and some rolls of industrial plastic.

The paint has been scraped off the pillar closest to the door, thanks to years of mechanical wear and tear.

"I think he has a surprise for us," Joona says, stepping inside.

Lumi follows him. She feels a nagging anxiety in the pit of her stomach. Dry autumn leaves have blown across the floor.

Instinctively, she sticks close to her dad.

The large workshop is almost completely empty.

The wind lifts the door behind them for a moment; then it swings shut with a creak, leaving them in almost total darkness.

The sound of their steps echoes off the walls.

"This doesn't seem good," she whispers.

The wind pulls the door open again, and white light from the sky reaches in. It moves across the floor and stops at an internal wall, before retreating again.

The room is spacious, but not quite large enough to fill the entire building.

Lumi tries to pull Joona toward the entrance. There's a strange sucking sound, and a moment later a hydraulic steel door crashes down behind them.

It hits the floor and locks into place. The way back is now blocked from floor to ceiling.

"Dad," Lumi says. Her voice is trembling.

"Don't worry," he replies.

The lights go on, and they see that the smooth walls are made of rough steel, welded at the corners. Four meters up are surveillance cameras and firing slots.

There's nothing to hide behind, nothing to climb up.

They see the reflection of their two gray shadows in the reinforced wall in front of them.

Lumi is breathing fast, and Joona puts a hand on her arm to stop her from reaching for her pistol.

A steel door opens in the wall, and a fairly short man in black sweatpants and a knitted black shirt comes limping into the room. His face is badly scarred. He has close-cropped white hair and is holding a pistol in his hand.

"I'm very unhappy with you," he says in deadpan English, gesturing toward Joona with the pistol.

"Sorry to hear—"

"Did you hear what I said?" the man interrupts, raising his voice.

"Yes, Lieutenant."

The man walks around Joona, inspecting him. He shoves him in the back, forcing him to take a step forward to keep his balance.

"How does it feel to lie on the floor in your own blood?"

"I'm not."

"But I could have shot you—couldn't I?"

"No one's going to come in here unless you repaint the pillar."

"The pillar?"

"The paint's been worn off the entire thing, all the way up, and if you look up to the roof you can see the whole mechanism," Joona says.

The man holds back a smile and turns to Lumi for the first time.

"My name is Rinus," he says, shaking her hand.

"Thanks for letting us come here," she says.

"I tried to knock some sense into your dad once upon a time," he explains.

"So he's said," Lumi says.

"What's he told you?"

"That it was like being on vacation," she replies with a smile.

"I knew I was too easy on him," he says, laughing.

RINUS TELLS THEM HOW HE BOUGHT THE PROPERTY THIRTY years ago. He was planning on running the farm himself, but that never happened. When he left the military, he was instead recruited by the AIVD, the Dutch national intelligence service. Although the AIVD reported directly to the Interior Ministry, Rinus worried that his work might require him to go into hiding for a long period of time.

"The intelligence service's own safe houses aren't safe enough, and you can't always trust your own team," he says, as if it were obvious. "I was leading an extremely sensitive secret investigation that appeared to implicate parts of our own organization, and I decided it was time to make sure I was prepared."

The property consists of four hectares of land. It's close to Belgium, Germany, Luxembourg, and France, helpful if he ever has to flee the country and seek asylum elsewhere. The main building serves as a front in case anyone gets curious. It's an abandoned, boarded-up house that he never uses. The real living quarters are hidden inside the old workshop.

Rinus shows them past the kitchen on the upper story into a passageway with doors that lead to four bedrooms, each containing two bunk beds. At the end of the hallway is a sealed emergency exit. Rinus has scrawled "Stairway to Heaven" on the door as a joke, because he's removed the escape ladder and taken it to the dump.

The only way *in* is through the workshop, but there's a hidden underground escape tunnel that runs two hundred meters to a patch of woodland in the field behind the building.

JOONA SETS THE TABLE FOR THREE. HE'S HEATING UP FRO-
zen lasagna in the microwave. He fills three glasses with water and
tells Lumi about training under Rinus. Once, he was dropped into
the sea five kilometers from the coast with his legs tied together
and his hands cuffed behind his back.

"A day at the beach," Rinus says, smiling, as he comes into the
kitchen. He's just moved their car to the hidden garage.

Rinus tells Lumi that he's lived in Amsterdam for years, though
his family comes from Sint Geertruid, in the southern part of the
Netherlands, not far from Maastricht.

"People down here tend to be Catholic. We're much more religious than those on the other side of the rivers," he explains as he
starts to serve the food.

"What does Patrik say about you disappearing like this?" Joona
asks.

"I like to think he'll miss me, but he's probably just relieved to
get rid of me for a while."

"I thought you make him breakfast in bed every morning." Joona
smiles.

"Well, if I'm already up," Rinus says with a shrug.

He looks at Lumi, who's blowing on a forkful of steaming-hot
lasagna.

"So—Police Academy after art school?"

"No way," she replies with a short laugh.

"Your dad's artistic, too," Rinus says, glancing at Joona.

"I'm not," he protests.

"You drew a—"

"Let's forget all about that, shall we?" Joona interrupts.

Rinus chuckles quietly to himself as he looks down at his plate.
The deep scars across his cheeks and one corner of his mouth are
as pale as chalk lines.

After the meal, Rinus leads them downstairs through a curtain
and into a dimly lit room with shutters over the windows.

One wall is lined with wooden boxes of weapons—pistols, semiautomatics, and sniper rifles.

Rinus goes through the tactical plan and order of command in case of attack, and shows them the monitor and alarm system.

Using the location of the shutters upstairs as the starting point, they divide their surroundings into different surveillance areas and set up the watch.

Joona watches the approach road and the barrier across the path through binoculars, while Rinus shows Lumi how the Russian detonators work, in case they have to mine the workshop.

"Electric detonators are better, but these mechanical ones are more reliable—even after they've been lying in a box for thirty years," he says, putting one down on the table in front of her.

The detonator looks a lot like a ballpoint pen, with a small fuse and a pin at one end.

"I assume that's where you attach the line," she says, pointing at the large ring.

"Yes, but first you stick the point about five centimeters into the explosive charge. Then you prime it with a line to the pin, as you said . . . then release the catch."

"And if someone walks into the line, the pin is pulled out."

"And the hammer hits the cap, which triggers the detonator," Rinus says. "The cap's no worse than the cap in a toy gun, but if the detonator explodes, you lose your hand, and if the explosives go off, you're dead."

40

RATHER THAN TAKE THE FERRY FROM SOL ISLAND LIKE THE Beaver did, Saga and Nathan opt to drive as far as they can across the bridges linking the islands and then catch the regular cable ferry from Svartnö.

Her dad still hadn't come home when Saga dropped Pellerina off at school. The school was closed for teacher training, but the after-school center was open all day, and Pellerina's special-needs assistant was working.

Saga's been trying not to worry, telling herself that her dad's phone might be dead, or that he went straight to work the morning after his date. But when she called Karolinska, he wasn't there. By now she's called all the hospitals in Stockholm, and spoken to the police.

She feels like the parent of a teenager.

All she can do is hope that he's fallen so head-over-heels in love that he's forgotten about everything else. That wouldn't be like him, but at this point she'd be relieved despite her anger.

Nathan brakes and turns off Highway 278, onto a gravel road that goes into a pine forest.

They're heading out to Högmarsö to talk to the churchwarden, and find out if the Beaver really did stay in the chapel for a while. If they're lucky, they'll soon know the Beaver's real name. Maybe the churchwarden is even forwarding his mail to a new address and can give them his contact information.

But Saga knows it isn't going to be easy. Erland Lind is suffering from dementia, and communicating with him has been hopeless for a couple of years.

They stop in front of the gate blocking the way to the dock. The road is empty. No one else is waiting to go across.

Saga looks at the dark island on the other side of the water. The cable ferry is approaching.

The location of Jurek Walter's remains is ominously connected to the search for the Beaver.

There's a scraping sound as the ferry pulls in. When the barrier rises, they drive onto the dock, and a man in a rain suit waves them on board. The ramp clanks against the quay as the car's weight presses it down.

The wet deck is painted black, and the railings and ferryman's cab are mustard-yellow.

Nathan and Saga stay in the car, which starts to shake as the ferry begins to move.

Beneath the surface of the water, two sturdy steel cables run parallel between the islands. The cables are raised and passed through the ferry's powerful winch before being dropped back down.

Saga looks back and watches as the swell makes the frozen yellow reeds on either side of the pier sway.

Saga has always been sure Jurek is dead. The reason she spent a year searching for his body was to convince Joona. It was her fault that Jurek escaped, so she felt it was her duty to prove to Joona that Jurek was dead.

She vividly remembers meeting the churchwarden on Högmarsö while he was gathering driftwood from the rocks. He told her he'd found a man's body five months earlier.

He'd put the body in the toolshed, and when the stench got really bad he burned it in the old crematorium. He cut off one of the fingers and kept it in his fridge in a jar of vodka, in case anyone came looking for the body.

Saga and Nils Åhlén studied the photograph he had taken of the swollen torso with three bullet holes in it.

Every detail fit.

And when the DNA and fingerprint turned out to be a 100 percent match, they were convinced. It was Jurek.

Saga wishes that Joona had waited a little longer before disappearing, that he'd seen the security-camera footage from Belarus.

She'll never forget the look on his face when he came to warn her. She almost didn't recognize him. In the wake of the theft of his wife's skull, he'd become paranoid.

He was suddenly convinced that Jurek had found a man the same age and build as he was, and shot him in the same places Saga had shot him. He'd then amputated his own hand or part of it, and left the amputated body part to soak in seawater for six months.

Joona's conclusion was that the churchwarden must have helped him, that Jurek either forced or persuaded Erland Lind to photograph the dead man's torso and then cremate it, cut off the finger from Jurek's rotted hand and save it, and then burn the rest.

Saga thinks back to Erland Lind's bloodshot eyes, from years of heavy drinking, his taciturnity, his shabby clothes. She tried to interview him on several occasions after that first meeting, but he'd already slid so far into dementia that it was pretty pointless.

The water is almost black this morning. There's no wind, and the surface is still. A thin mist is hanging between the islands in the distance.

The ferry slowly approaches Högmarsö.

Bare trees stand motionless beyond the empty dock.

The ferry slides up the rails beneath the water with a dull rumble, and the ramp scrapes across the concrete pier. The swell laps against the rocky shore.

Nathan gives Saga a look, starts the car, and rolls ashore. They drive up the hill, past summer houses that have been boarded up for the winter.

It only takes them a couple of minutes to reach the boatyard. The glare of a welding torch bounces between the buildings. There's a lot of clutter amid the covered boats.

Nathan turns left, past some small fields and a patch of woodland. The sugar-white chapel glints between the black tree trunks.

They drive up a hill and stop. A large anchor is propped up in the yellow grass. The cold air carries the smell of the sea. Distant gulls' cries can be heard from the harbor.

Saga walks up the gravel path and tries the door of the chapel. It's locked, but the key is hanging from a nail under the stair railing. She unlocks the door, and Nathan follows her inside. The wooden floor creaks beneath their feet. The pews have been painted green, and there are votives on the walls. They walk up to the simple altar, then turn back, stopping in front of a muddy blanket lying on the floor.

There are some cans of beans and meat stew by the wall, next to the hymnals.

Nathan and Saga go outside again, lock the chapel, and head to the churchwarden's cottage. The bell tower looms like a hunting platform between the trees.

The sun breaks through the mist as they knock on the door. They wait a few seconds, then go in.

The tiny house consists of a kitchen, a bed in an alcove, and a small bathroom. Uneaten food on the table has dried out. Next to the coffeemaker is a plastic bag full of moldy cinnamon buns. The narrow bed in the alcove has no sheets. He's been sleeping on the bare mattress with just a blanket to cover him. A watch with a scratched face is lying on a stool next to the bed.

The cottage has been abandoned.

Saga remembers the smell of cooking and damp from the first time she was here. Erland Lind had been drunk, but at least his mind was relatively clear back then.

The next time she came, he had been quiet and confused. His decline was very rapid. He must have ended up in a home. It looks like none of his relatives has sorted through his belongings yet.

"This is where he kept the finger," she says, opening the fridge.

The shelves are strewn with unlabeled bottles and packs of rotten food. She looks at the expiration dates of a carton of cream and a package of bacon.

"He hasn't been here for four months," she tells Nathan, shutting the fridge.

They leave the house and go to the garage. A dirty shovel with a rusty blade is lying on the floor, surrounded by dry soil. They can see part of Erland's illegal still behind the covered snowblower.

"This was where Jurek's body was. Liquid was leaking from it down into the drain," she says, pointing.

They walk outside again and look back toward the car and the chapel.

"Should we ask the neighbors if they know where he went?" Nathan asks in a low voice.

"I'll call the parish office," Saga says.

The remains of the crematorium's foundation are hidden in the tall weeds, but the brick chimney sticks up four meters from the ground.

"That was where he burned Jurek's body," Nathan says.

"Right."

They walk through the grass and stop in front of the sooty oven. Saga walks cautiously to the edge of the forest, examines the pitchfork sticking out of the compost heap, then moves toward the soil between the trees.

It's like the oxygen has been sucked out of the area. She sees a metal tube sticking out of the ground.

She grabs a tree for support.

She walks over, her heart pounding, and feels her heels sink into the loose soil. She kneels down, and smells the tube. She immediately backs away and spits on the ground.

Rotten meat.

The edge of the forest slides away as she turns around, searching for something to focus on. She takes a few steps, looking at the crematorium and the churchwarden's house.

"What is it?" Nathan asks anxiously.

She can't answer. She runs to the garage for the shovel, then runs back and starts digging the softly packed soil, shoveling it into the tall weeds.

Sweat trickles down her back. She makes a whimpering sound in her throat as she presses the blade into the earth with her foot and heaves the soil away.

Panting hard, she makes the hole bigger, then climbs down into it and keeps digging.

Seventy centimeters down, the shovel hits a coffin.

She sweeps the loose soil aside with her hand. The pipe leads through the lid, and the hole around the pipe has been sealed with silver duct tape.

"What is this?" Nathan asks.

She clears the top of the coffin, forces the shovel's blade beneath the lid, and breaks it open. She tosses the shovel aside, jerks the lid sideways, and pulls out the last of the nails.

Nathan takes the lid from her and puts it down beside the shallow grave.

They both stare down at the remains of the churchwarden.

Erland Lind's body is swollen and oozing. Some parts of it have almost dissolved, while others, including his hands and feet, seem to be intact. His face is emaciated, his eyes are black, his fingertips torn to shreds.

"Jurek," Saga whispers.

She clambers out of the grave and hurries back toward the chapel. She stumbles over part of the crematorium's foundation.

"Wait!" Nathan calls, rushing after her.

"He's got my dad!" she screams, and starts running for the car.

41

POLICE OFFICERS KARIN HAGMAN AND ANDREJ EKBERG ARE sitting in Patrol Car 30-901 on Palmfelts Alley, close to the Globe Arena.

It's a quiet morning. The rush-hour traffic heading into Stockholm has thinned out, the lines on Nynäs Street are gone, and, apart from one minor collision in which no one was hurt, things have been very calm.

Now they're driving slowly along the shaded road that runs beside the subway line, beneath deserted footbridges and dark, empty brick buildings. The area is still a mess after a concert the night before.

"Life's too long. I don't have the energy to have fun all the time," Karin sighs.

"You said you were going to tell Joakim how you've been feeling," Andrej says.

"It won't make any difference. . . . He doesn't seem to want anything anymore. He just doesn't care."

"You need to break up."

"I know," Karin whispers, drumming the steering wheel with her hand.

They pass someone dragging a trash bag behind him along the ditch, collecting discarded soda cans to get the deposit. He's dressed in a filthy military coat and a fur hat.

Karin has opened her mouth to say that Joakim will do anything to avoid having sex when they get a call from the command center. The operator's voice sounds unusually stressed. He says they have received a Priority 1 alarm from a colleague.

The pale glow from the Polman radio makes Karin's hand look as white as snow when she reaches for the gear shift.

The alert concerns a kidnapping at Enskede School, at the after-school club on Mittel Street.

The operator does his best to answer their questions calmly and efficiently, but clearly something about the situation has gotten to him.

As Karin understands it, they're dealing with the violent kidnapping of a twelve-year-old girl with Down syndrome. The suspected perpetrator may be armed, and is believed to be extremely dangerous.

The address appears on their screen. They're close. Karin switches on the flashing lights and turns the car around.

The operator tells them that they're coordinating their response with Södermalm Hospital and the National Operations Unit.

"You'll be first on the scene," the operator says.

Karin switches on the siren, puts her foot down, and sinks back into the seat as the car accelerates. There's a cyclist up ahead to their right, and a truck approaching from the opposite direction.

In the rearview mirror, they see the man collecting cans in the ditch watch them go.

She slows down at the large intersection to make sure that everyone has stopped to let them across before accelerating again.

Andrej asks the operator if he knows how many children are in the club, and is told that there are probably fewer than normal, because the school is closed for the day.

Karin thinks it sounds like a custody battle that's gotten out of hand, some aggrieved ex-husband.

They pass the yellow façade of the Catholic school, make a sharp right at the traffic circle, and speed up past the large sports field.

The silver fence in front of the soccer fields flickers past.

As Karin drives, Andrej keeps talking to the operator. They've received a number of calls from the public about a disturbance, and gunshots have been reported.

She's driving a little too fast when they reach the next traffic circle, and the tires lose their grip as she turns left.

They slide across the loose grit on the road and end up on the sidewalk, scraping a sign that points to Enskede Church.

"Take it easy," Andrej mutters.

Karin doesn't answer, just puts her foot down again as they drive along the edge of Margareta Park.

Several birds take off from a trash can.

They spot the tiled roof of the school above the surrounding buildings, and Karin turns the siren off. She makes a sharp right onto Mittel Street, slows down, and stops in front of the entrance.

They get out of the car and check their weapons and bulletproof vests. Karin tries to control her breathing.

The brown leaves at the base of the spiral fire escape are rustling in the wind.

Andrej confirms that they're on the scene. Karin watches him as he listens and nods before ending the call.

"The operator told us to be careful," he says, looking her in the eye.

"Careful? I've never heard that before," she says, not quite managing to summon up a smile.

"And that was from the officer who raised the alarm." She looks at the single-story building that houses the after-school club, which has been squeezed into a gap between the much taller school buildings on either side of it. Its brick walls have been painted yellow, and there's moss growing on the red-tiled roof.

Though there are lights on behind the curtains, no one is in sight. Everything is quiet.

"Let's go in and take a look," Andrej says.

They run across the sidewalk, then creep along the wall to the dark-red door, pistols drawn.

Andrej pulls it open, and Karin takes a couple of steps into the room.

A large plastic bin full of clothing sits in the middle of the floor. Boots and sneakers are lined up next to a drying rack.

Andrej moves past Karin, gesturing toward the next door, and she follows him into a large room with tables laid out with chess and backgammon.

The curtains in front of all of the windows are closed.

The only sounds are the rustle of their uniforms and the noise of their boots on the linoleum.

The door to one of the bathrooms at the far end of the room is closed.

They stop.

They can hear a clicking, bubbling sound.

Karin exchanges a glance with Andrej, and he immediately moves to one side. She walks closer to the bathroom door, still thinking about the operator's warning to be careful, and realizes that her hand is shaking as she reaches out to push the door handle.

42

KARIN YANKS THE DOOR OPEN, BACKS AWAY, AND AIMS HER pistol into the darkness, but the door swings shut again before she has time to see anything.

She reaches forward and opens the door again.

There's no one there.

The sink is running, and an even trickle of water is running down the drain, making a gentle tinkling sound.

"Where the hell is everyone?" Andrej whispers behind her.

They walk into the dining room. Three circular tables are spread out across the room. On one of the tables is a glass of chocolate milk and a plate with half a sandwich on it. Karin spots a shoe on the floor between the tables and chairs, close to the half-closed door to the kitchen.

Andrej goes over to the window, nudges the curtain aside, and looks out. There's no sign of the rapid-response team, but a white van is stopped at the end of the block.

"There's a van farther down the street," he says quietly.

Karin looks at the pistol in her hand, moves a chair out of the way, and walks over to him.

She stops and looks back toward the kitchen again.

She can see a bare foot among the tables.

"Andrej," she says in a tense voice.

She turns and hurries across the dining room, her pulse racing.

A large woman is lying on her stomach, completely motionless in the doorway to the kitchen. The sliding door is half closed, so that only the bottom half of her body is visible. Both of her shoes are missing.

Her heels are pink, the wrinkled soles of her feet almost white.

Karin looks at the embroidered pockets of the woman's jeans.

A horizontal-striped Marimekko T-shirt is stretched across her back.

Aiming her pistol toward the kitchen, Karin reaches out her other hand and slowly slides the door open.

She gasps when, instead of hair and the back of the woman's head, she finds herself looking at the woman's face.

It's been contorted. Her neck has been brutally broken.

"What the hell's happened here?" Andrej whispers.

"Check the next room," she says, unnecessarily loudly.

The woman's face is white. Her lips are closed, her eyes are wide open, and blood is running from her nose.

Karin keeps her pistol pointing into the kitchen as she crouches down to feel the woman's neck.

She feels cool. She must have been dead for several hours.

Thoughts are swirling through Karin's head. The alarm was raised too late; there's no point in setting up roadblocks, and they won't need the support of the rapid-response unit.

She stands up and is just about to head into the trashed kitchen when Andrej calls her. Karin turns around, steps past the dead woman, and accidentally walks into a chair, knocking it against the table with a bang.

Andrej is standing in the gloom of the dance-and-yoga room. The curtains are half drawn, and the pink glow of a mood lamp is shining off of a guitar hanging on the wall. A glitter ball is rotating up at the ceiling. Its tiny reflections are sliding across the walls.

Karin follows Andrej's gaze and looks at the far corner.

A man with a black beard and thick eyebrows is sitting on a yoga mat, leaning against an office chair. His forehead has been caved in at least five centimeters, and his face and chest are covered with dark blood.

Andrej mutters that they're too late and leaves the room.

Karin doesn't move. She can hear her pulse racing in her ears.

Even though she can see that the man is dead, she still goes over and feels his neck for a pulse.

She wipes her hand on her pants, then starts to walk back toward the entryway.

When she emerges into the cool air outside the building, Andrej is sitting on a bench.

They can hear sirens in the distance. A tattooed man is pulling a heavy hose from the van down the street.

"He killed the staff and took the girl," Andrej says without looking at her.

"Looks like it," she replies. "Did you report back?"

"I'm doing it now."

While Andrej talks to their immediate superior, Karin goes to the car for the roll of cordon tape. She ties one end to the spiral fire escape, runs it around the shed, trees, and building, then starts to write up notes about what happened.

The yellow glare of the streetlights illuminates the leaves on the road. At this time of year, the lights are on almost all day long.

The first ambulance turns into Mittel Street, drives up onto the sidewalk to get past their patrol car, and stops outside the cordon.

Karin goes over and explains the situation to the paramedics. They follow her into the after-school club and check the first body.

Together they move on into the dimly lit dance-and-yoga room.

Karin stops in the middle of the room and watches as the paramedics crouch down next to the dead man. The reflections from the disco ball are playing across his face and beard.

"We'll get the stretcher," one of the paramedics says in a heavy voice.

Karin goes over to the window and pulls one of the curtains back to let in the light from outside.

But as she opens the curtain, she feels adrenaline flood her system.

Her pulse is thudding in her ears.

A little girl is standing there, completely still. Her hands are clamped over her mouth, and behind her glasses her eyes are screwed shut.

"Oh, sweetheart," Karin manages to say.

The girl must have been hiding behind the curtain for several hours. When Karin touches her gently on the shoulder, she opens her eyes and wobbles.

"There's no need to be scared now; he's gone," Karin says.

The girl's lips are white, and she looks exhausted. Suddenly her legs give out and she sinks to the floor. Karin kneels down and holds the child, feeling her tense, trembling body.

"Can I carry you?"

She picks the girl up very carefully and walks out of the dance room. She makes sure the girl doesn't see the dead man, or the woman in the entrance to the kitchen.

"Who was here?" Karin asks as they move between the tables.

The girl doesn't answer. Karin can feel her warm, damp breath against her shoulder, and whispers to her again that she doesn't have to be afraid anymore.

43

LARS-ERIK BAUER WAKES UP. HE KNOWS THAT SOMETHING'S very wrong, but his sluggish brain can't process the information his senses are giving him.

It's cold. He's lying down, and the ground seems to be shaking beneath him.

The moment before he opens his eyes, he thinks about the strange phone call from Kristina.

She sounded different.

Something had happened.

He'd never heard her sound so lonely before. She must have apologized at least ten times for bothering him, and said that the battery in her car was dead. She'd given her son a ride to Barkarby Flying Club, just south of Järvafältet. On the way back, her car broke down in the middle of the forest. She couldn't get through to any of the towing services she called, and she ended up locking herself inside the car, too afraid to walk through the forest.

If he left immediately with his jumper cables, he'd have time to get to her, jump the car, and still get back in time to make Pellerina's dinner.

They were actually supposed to be meeting for the first time next week. He'd already booked a table at Wedholm's fish restaurant.

Something hits Lars-Erik in the back hard.

He opens his eyes, blinks, and sees the full moon glinting above him. Treetops are flashing past.

It's like a dream.

His jaw snaps shut when his head hits something hard.

He can't make sense of what's happening. He's being dragged on a tarp along a path in a pine forest. Time and again, his head and back hit rocks and roots.

He can't move his hands or legs, and he realizes that he's been drugged. His mouth is dry, and he has no idea how long he's been out.

His eyes close again; he can't keep them open.

He remembers hearing about the effects when an anesthetic gas like halothane is combined with opioids or muscle relaxants and injected into the spinal column.

Immediate anesthesia and lingering paralysis.

It must have been a trap.

Kristina tricked him, got him interested, lured him into the forest.

The last thing he remembers is parking his car on the dark forest road. The headlights were pointing at Kristina's car.

Then Pellerina sent him a picture of a painting she'd done at school, and he called her to tell her it was a lovely dog. In the side-view mirror, he saw that someone was walking toward the car from behind. Pellerina was explaining that it was a horse, not a dog, and that his name was Silver.

The person was approaching very quickly, turning red in the glare of the rear lights.

Lars-Erik opened the car door, but he doesn't remember what happened after that.

He remembers the tall grass lining the shoulder bending under the car door as it opened. A parking-lot ticket blew off the dashboard in the draft.

Then there was the faint sound of glass against glass.

He loses consciousness again and doesn't come to until the person dragging him through the forest stops and lets go of the tarp.

Lars-Erik's head sinks heavily to the ground.

He looks up at the moon and the black treetops surrounding the clearing. Everything is cold and silent.

He opens his mouth and tries to say something, but he has no voice. All he can do is lie on his back, breathing in the smell of the moss and the damp earth.

His toes are itching and tingling, but when he makes an attempt to move, his body won't obey him. All he manages to do is turn his head slightly to one side.

He hears footsteps on the soft ground.

He looks around at the trees.

A branch breaks, and then he sees a thin man walking along the path.

Lars-Erik tries to call for help, but he can't make a sound.

The figure passes a fallen tree, then becomes visible in the moonlight. His thin face is covered by a network of wrinkles.

The man walks past Lars-Erik without so much as glancing at him, then disappears from his field of vision for a moment before returning.

He's rolling a large plastic barrel.

Lars-Erik tries to tell him to get help. But the sound that emerges from his mouth is no louder than a whisper.

The man carefully lifts Lars-Erik's feet into the opening of the barrel, then pulls it up over his legs, all the way to his hips.

Lars-Erik still can't move. All he can do is toss his sluggish head from side to side, toward the mute, dark trees.

The old man says nothing and won't even look him in the eye. It's clear that he's just doing a job. He brusquely stuffs Lars-Erik's lower half into the barrel, handling Lars-Erik as though he were a slaughtered animal, a carcass.

With a hard jerk, he stands the barrel up, and Lars-Erik's legs give out beneath him. He slumps into the barrel, up to his armpits. His shirt slides up, and he cuts his stomach on the sharp edge of the plastic.

He still can't understand what's going on.

The old man tries to push him down into the barrel.

He's unexpectedly strong. Lars-Erik's arms are dangling over the sides, and half his upper body is still above the rim.

The man walks away and returns with a shovel.

Now Lars-Erik notices a deep hole in the ground next to the

barrel. On the grass beside it is a roll of plastic and a bucket containing a white liquid.

The thin man walks over to him again, raises the blade of the shovel, and brings it down hard on his shoulder.

Lars-Erik groans with pain as his left collarbone breaks. He's breathing heavily, and tears are running down his cheeks.

The man tosses the shovel onto the ground and leans over him.

The man squeezes his shoulder to get it past the edge. The pain is so intense that Lars-Erik's vision fades. His right arm is sticking straight up, but the man folds it down over his neck, then pushes his head down and puts a lid on the barrel.

Someone rocks the barrel a few times until it tips over, then rolls it into the large hole.

The impact makes Lars-Erik pass out. When he comes to, he can hear a clattering sound, like a heavy rain shower.

After a few seconds, he realizes that the barrel is standing upright in the bottom of the hole and the man has started to fill in the hole. The clattering sound becomes more and more distant, then stops altogether.

The moist air inside the barrel smells like plastic, and there isn't enough oxygen.

His body is still paralyzed. He twists his head in panic, and sees a small point of light on the side of the barrel.

As Lars-Erik stares at the light, he realizes that it's moonlight shining through a hole in the lid.

His contorted shoulder and broken collarbone are throbbing with pain. His fingers are ice-cold—his circulation isn't reaching them.

Lars-Erik realizes that he's been buried alive.

44

SAGA DRIVES PAST THE OPEN AMBULANCE ENTRANCE AT Södermalm Hospital, pulls up onto the sidewalk, and gets out of Nathan's car without closing the door. She runs by stretchers and unattended strollers into the children's emergency room, past a three-foot plastic frog.

One man is engaged in a heated conversation on his phone.

Jurek made his move early that morning, just thirty minutes after Saga dropped Pellerina off at the after-school center and left for Högmarsö.

He had plenty of time. If Saga hadn't told her how to hide and stay completely silent, Jurek would have snatched her that morning.

She would never have seen her sister again.

Ignoring the line, Saga walks straight up to the desk, shows her ID, and asks to see Pellerina Bauer.

Her sister is in the emergency room.

Saga runs along the hallway, pushing a cleaning cart out of her way. She slows down as she approaches the uniformed police officer standing outside the last door before Elevator B.

"Are you alone?" she asks, showing her police ID.

"Yes," the man replies.

"Idiots . . ." she sighs, then goes in.

The lighting in the cramped, windowless room is subdued. Pellerina is sitting up in bed with a yellow blanket around her shoulders. A glass of juice and a cheese sandwich on a paper plate lie on the bedside table beside her.

Saga hurries over and puts her arms around her. As she holds her sister, she allows relief to wash over her for the first time. She presses her face into Pellerina's tangled hair. "I came as quickly as I could," she says.

They hug for a long time; then Saga looks at Pellerina, forces herself to smile, and strokes her cheek. "How are you feeling?"

"Fine," the girl replies seriously.

"Really?" Saga whispers, fighting to hold back the tears.

"Can we go home to Dad now?"

Saga swallows hard. She has to force herself not to imagine what might have happened to her dad.

"Were you scared?"

Pellerina nods and lowers her gaze, takes off her glasses, and picks at the corner of one eye. Her pale eyelashes cast small shadows across her round cheeks.

"I can imagine," Saga says, brushing some hair from Pellerina's forehead.

"I hid behind the curtain, and I was as quiet as a mouse." She smiles, and puts her glasses back on again.

"That was really smart," Saga says. "Did you see him?"

"A little bit, before I closed my eyes . . . It was a man, but he was really quick."

Saga feels her heart speed up. She glances over at the door.

"We have to go now," she says. "Did the doctor look at you?"

"She's coming soon."

"How long have you been waiting?"

"I don't know."

Saga presses the alarm button and after a while, a nurse comes in, a middle-aged man with a round stomach and glasses.

"I want a doctor to look at her before we leave," Saga says.

"Dr. Sami will be here as soon as she can," the man replies. His patience is already strained.

"Pellerina is only twelve years old, and she's been waiting for I don't know how long."

"I know it's annoying, but we have to prioritize the most acute cases. I'm sure you can—"

"Listen to me," Saga interrupts sharply. "You're in no position to evaluate the urgency of this case."

She shows the man her ID. He studies it carefully, then hands it back.

"This child is a priority," Saga says.

"I can ask the triage doctor to come and make a new assessment—"

"There's no time for that," she interrupts. "Get any damn doctor who's qualified."

The man doesn't answer, just leaves the room, looking agitated.

"Why are you so angry?" Pellerina asks.

"I'm not angry, I promise. You know I sometimes sound angry when I get stressed."

"You swore."

"I know, I shouldn't have done that. That was very rude of me."

After a while, they hear voices outside the door, and then the doctor comes in, a short woman with light-brown eyes.

"I heard you wanted to talk to me," she says warily.

"I need you to examine her. We can't stay here. We're in a hurry, but first I want to make sure she's okay."

"I won't stop you as long as you can prove you're her guardian."

"Just do as I say!"

The police officer comes in with his hand on his holster.

"What's going on?"

"Guard the door!" Saga snaps. "You don't leave that door, and for God's sake fasten your vest!"

The police officer doesn't move.

"What kind of threat are we expecting?"

"I don't have time to explain . . . and it really doesn't matter. You wouldn't stand a chance anyway," she says, trying to force herself to calm down.

She looks the doctor in the eye and takes a couple of steps toward her, then tries to talk quietly so Pellerina won't hear.

"Listen, I work for the Security Police as a detective, and I need to interview this girl in a safe place—it's possible that she wit-nessed a double murder, and we have reason to believe that the murderer will come after her. . . . Trust me, you don't want us in this hospital any longer than necessary. We'll leave as soon as you're done. She's had an operation for a heart defect, Fallot's tetralogy. I know you've done an EKG, but I need to know if she's showing any signs of serious trauma."

"I understand," the doctor says.

While the doctor is talking to Pellerina, Saga leaves the room, checks the hallway, and looks over toward the entrance, scrutiniz-ing the people waiting beyond the glass in the reception area.

Her immediate evaluation was that the churchwarden had been dead for two weeks, but the dates on the food in the fridge suggest that he was buried in the grave more than four months ago.

The Beaver is Jurek's new accomplice. Joona was right all along.

The Beaver stayed in the chapel, keeping an eye on the grave, keeping the churchwarden alive.

Four months in a grave, she thinks.

And now Jurek has taken her dad.

She tries calling him again, but Lars-Erik's phone is still switched off.

Saga puts out an alert for her dad's car, then calls the Security Police and asks one of the technical experts to track his cell phone.

While she's talking, she sees a thin man walk through the door. She breaks off the call and cautiously draws her pistol. When she's sure it isn't Jurek, she slips it back into its holster.

She glances the other way along the hallway, then takes her phone out again and calls Carlos Eliasson's direct line at the National Operations Unit.

"Jurek Walter's back," she says bluntly.

"I heard what happened at your sister's school."

"She needs a safe house immediately," Saga says, looking over at the entrance again.

"That's not how it works. The personal-security unit needs to conduct an evaluation. Being worried isn't enough, you know that. The same rules apply to us as to everyone else."

"Then I'm taking a leave of absence; I need to find somewhere to hide."

"Saga, you're starting to sound like a certain superintendent with a Finnish—"

"Valeria," she interrupts, raising her voice. "Does she have protection? Tell me she has protection!"

"There's no tangible threat," Carlos says patiently.

"She has to have protection! This is your damn responsibility. . . . You know what? Just shut up, Jurek's back, that's what's happening."

"Saga, he's dead. You killed him, and you found his—"

"Just make sure Valeria gets protection," Saga interrupts, then hangs up.

She looks around the hallway again. Joona was right all along, and she and Nathan Pollock have wasted valuable time on a distraction. Joona took the threat seriously. He had his escape route prepared, and managed to save both himself and his daughter.

The police officer guarding the door looks at her with bemusement when she walks back into the treatment room.

The doctor is shaking Pellerina's hand; then she comes over to Saga.

"She's a lovely girl, really smart."

"She is, isn't she?" Saga says. There's a terrible weight on her chest.

"There are no problems with her heart," the doctor goes on. "But Pellerina has had a terrible scare although I don't think she saw any violence. She seems to have had her eyes shut the whole time. It's a little hard to tell, but she's not showing any signs of dissociation or disorientation, and she has no psychomotor problems."

"Thanks."

"I'd prefer that she see a psychologist, because she's going to need to talk about what happened to her."

"Of course."

"If she starts to get anxious or has trouble sleeping, you'll have to come back. Sometimes it—"

"Good," Saga says, cutting her off. She goes over to Pellerina.

She quickly wraps the yellow blanket around her sister and takes her past the doctor into the hallway, where she orders the police officer to walk with them to the car.

She puts Pellerina in the back seat, fastens her seat belt, then thanks the policeman.

Saga drives away from the hospital, thinking that they should head north, go someplace where she has no connections. She'll find an isolated summer cottage, break in, and hide out there with her sister. They can stay there while the police do their job. But first she needs to get a new phone, so she can't be traced. Saga pulls over to the curb in Skanstull and is googling shops that sell used cell phones when Carlos calls.

"Saga," he says in an unsteady voice, "I sent one of our cars to check on Valeria and ... I don't know how to say this, but she's gone, she's been taken. . . . We found a man's remains in a burned-out car. There's blood everywhere. The greenhouses are wrecked. . . ."

"Did you set up roadblocks?" she asks, almost whispering.

"It's too late; all this happened several days ago. . . . We should have handled it differently."

"Yes."

"I've arranged a safe house for your half-sister."

45

VALERIA TWISTS SIDEWAYS A LITTLE TO RELIEVE THE PRESsure on the sores on her heels and injured shoulders.

The low lid of the box stops her from moving too much. She has to sink down onto her back again.

It's totally dark, and she's long since lost all perception of time.

The pain in her thigh from where she was bitten was horribly intense at first, but has faded.

She wet herself twice, but that's almost dry now.

She doesn't think about hunger, but she's extremely thirsty. Her mouth is completely dehydrated now.

She sleeps occasionally, for an hour or so, maybe less—there's no way of knowing. Once, she heard a thudding sound, and a woman screaming in the distance.

The box is as cold as a fridge, maybe colder. She can keep her fingers warm, but her toes have gone numb.

Behind the sweet smell of the wooden box, she can detect the stale odor of soil.

She stopped calling for help fairly early on, when she realized that Jurek Walter had done this, just as Joona had predicted.

She's been buried alive.

This is Jurek's doing, and the gigantic man who came to her greenhouse is his new accomplice. He was horrifically strong and aggressive.

After he subdued her, he threw her into the trunk of a car and drove off along a bumpy road.

Valeria tried to open the trunk with her wounded hands, but lost her balance when the car lurched.

She tried again, but it was impossible.

Suddenly she remembered what Joona had said about situations like this. Sometimes he would tell her about the training he'd given his daughter up in Nattavaara.

The jack, she thought.

There's almost always a jack in the trunk of a car.

Valeria felt across the floor in the darkness, found the catches for the hatch, loosened them, then managed to move sideways and open the panel. She felt around the edge of the spare tire, fumbling across a wrench and a warning triangle before she found a nylon bag with the jack in it.

She positioned it as close to the trunk's lock as she could, turned the screw with her fingers until it reached the lid, and fixed the handle in place.

The car lurched, but though she slumped onto one shoulder, she held the jack in place and started to turn it. The trunk was so cramped that she scraped her knuckles with each turn.

The metal started to squeak as the lid was forced upward, but then the car came to an abrupt halt.

She continued turning the handle as fast as she could, but she had to give up when the engine was switched off and the driver's door opened.

She fumbled for a weapon, got hold of the wrench just as the trunk opened, and lashed out. But he was prepared. He grabbed the wrench, tossed it aside, yanked her hair back, and pressed an ice-cold rag to her mouth and nose.

When she came to, she was in this darkness. She's called for help, tapped out SOS, searched for anything she could use to open the box. She's pushed her hands and knees up and to the sides with all her strength; but the most she's heard is a faint creak in the wood.

She warms her fingers under her thighs and dozes off briefly, but the pain from the sores in her heels wakes her up, so she tries to move her feet.

Suddenly she hears a thudding sound above her, then heavy dragging. Her heart starts to beat faster when she hears voices. She can't make out the words, but she can tell it's a man and a woman arguing.

Valeria thinks she's been found, and is calling for help when there's a sudden bang: someone is stomping on the box.

"For fuck's sake, she needs water; otherwise, she'll die today, maybe tomorrow," the man says.

"It's dangerous, though," the woman says in an agitated voice. "It's too—"

"We can do it," the man interrupts.

"I'll hit her if she tries to get out," the woman says. "I'll split her head open!"

The sudden light when the box opens burns Valeria's eyes. She squints and sees a man and a woman standing above her.

Valeria is lying beneath the floor of a room with bullfighting posters on the walls.

A hole has been sawed through the tiles, insulation, and floorboards.

The man is pointing a hunting rifle at Valeria, and the woman is holding an ax. They look perfectly ordinary, like her own neighbors, or the sort of people you'd see in the supermarket. The man has a blond mustache and anxious eyes. The woman's hair is pulled up into a ponytail, and she's wearing pink-framed glasses.

"Please, help me," Valeria gasps, putting one hand on the edge of the box.

"Stay there!" the man commands.

The coffin is lying on the ground in the sealed crawl space beneath the house. Even though Valeria is weak, she tries to sit up. The man hits her in the face with the butt of the rifle. Her head jolts back, but she holds on to the edge of the box.

"Stay where you are, you bitch!" the man roars. "I'll shoot you— okay? I'll shoot!"

"Why are you doing this?" she says, sobbing.

"Lie down!"

Warm blood is trickling down her cheek. Valeria reaches up

with one hand and grabs the floor. The woman brings the ax down, but Valeria has already lost her grip when the blade cuts deep into the floorboard.

The man shoves her in the chest with the barrel of the rifle, and she falls back into the coffin, hitting her head on the bottom.

She had time to see the thick straps in the ground next to the coffin. They're the same type she uses in her nursery.

"Give her the water," the woman says in a tight voice.

Valeria is gasping for breath. She knows she needs to establish contact with them. She can't get hysterical. "Please, I don't understand. . . ."

"Shut up!"

A teenage girl with a block of wood in one hand approaches the coffin. She has a look of terror in her eyes. She tosses a plastic bottle of water into the coffin, then pushes the lid shut again with her foot.

46

PELLERINA WAS IMMEDIATELY PLACED IN THE MOST SECURE personal-protection program in the country.

Saga bought two used phones with pay-as-you-go accounts so that she and Pellerina can talk to each other.

After making sure she wasn't being followed, she drove around Stora Essingen, then headed to Kungsholmen and drove into the parking garage beneath City Hall Park, where she parked next to a black van with blacked-out windows.

The lenses of all the security cameras had already been covered.

Saga got out of the car and shook hands with the tall blond bodyguard.

"I'm Sabrina," she said.

"The threat level is extremely high," Saga said. "Don't trust anyone, and don't reveal the address to anyone, no matter who they are."

Saga got Pellerina out of the car, said a quick goodbye, and promised to come see her as soon as she possibly could. Then she opened the door of the van and strapped her sister in.

"I want *my* phone," Pellerina said when Saga gave her the used one.

"You'll get it when I come see you. It's broken, and I need to get it fixed," Saga lied.

Pellerina looked at her helplessly through her thick glasses and started to cry. "I was really careful with it."

"It's not your fault," Saga says, wiping the tears from her sister's cheeks.

Because Saga has been involved in personal-security operations before, she knows that the apartment assigned to Pellerina is at 17 P O Hallmans Street and has an advanced security system, with reinforced doors and bulletproof windows.

Saga gets back in Nathan's car and watches as the van backs out and disappears through the folding doors and up the ramp.

While she was driving from Högmarsö to Södermalm Hospital, she made three calls to the IT-and-telecoms department of the Security Police. They're trying to trace her dad's cell phone, but it can't be activated remotely, and it isn't giving off any kind of signal. The last time he used it was when he spoke to Pellerina in her painting class. At that point, his signal was picked up by a base station in Kista. She knows they're trying to get information from other towers so they can triangulate the signal and identify his exact location at the time of the call.

Even though Saga knows there's no point, she keeps trying to call her dad. The endless ringing reminds her of the night her mom died. She gets his voice mail and hangs up before she hears his greeting. She calls Nathan Pollock instead.

He's still out on Högmarsö with the forensics team. The sharp wind distorts his voice.

"How's Pellerina?" he asks.

"She's going to be okay. She's in a secure location now," Saga replies, swallowing the lump in her throat.

"Good."

"She was lucky."

"I know, it's incredible," Nathan says.

"But Jurek has my dad," she whispers.

"Let's just hope that isn't the case," Nathan says carefully.

"He's taken Dad and Valeria."

She draws a deep breath, clears her throat, and presses one hand against her eyes. Tears are burning behind her eyelids.

"Sorry," she says quietly. "This is all just so hard to accept."

"We're going to solve this," Nathan says. "We need to focus on—"

"I have to look for my dad," she interrupts. "It's all I can think about. He's probably still alive, and I have to find him."

"We will, I promise," Nathan says. "We've got plenty of people out here. We've already searched the churchwarden's home and the garage, but at this point there's nothing that can be linked to Jurek or the Beaver. Erland Lind didn't have a computer, but we found his phone under the bed."

"Maybe that will give us something," Saga says.

"The dogs have been through the forest, but there don't seem to be any more graves out here."

There's a lot of static on the line, and she hears shouting in the background.

Saga leans back against the headrest and runs her fingers over the rough leather of the steering wheel.

"I'll come back out, if I can help?" she asks. "We need to talk to Carlos about whether to issue a nationwide alert or—"

"Hang on a second," Nathan interrupts.

Saga sits with the phone to her ear. She hears him talking to someone. The wind keeps catching the microphone and making the voices vanish.

"Are you still there?" Nathan asks.

"Of course."

"You need to hear this. Forensics found something on the inside of the coffin lid," he says. "They've discovered two words. The churchwarden must have scratched the letters with his nails before he died—they're almost illegible."

"What does it say?" she asks.

"It says 'Save Cornelia.'"

"'Save Cornelia'?"

"We have no idea who—"

"Cornelia is the churchwarden's sister," Saga interrupts, starting the car. "She didn't have any contact with her brother. She lives fairly close to Norrtälje—that's not even twenty kilometers from the river where I shot Jurek."

47

SAGA DRIVES TO THE FERRY TERMINAL AT SVARTNÖ, TURNS the car around, and pulls over to the side of the road. She watches the dock and dark-gray water in the rearview mirror. When she sees the ferry approaching, she gets out of the car and walks down the slope.

Nathan is standing alone on deck, with both hands on the railing. The ramp lowers and scrapes the dock.

Nathan waves to the ferryman, then walks ashore. Saga hands him his car keys and gets in the passenger seat.

CORNELIA LIVES ON THE OUTSKIRTS OF PARIS, A SMALL RESIdential area just east of Norrtälje.

"There was nothing else on the coffin lid," Nathan says.

"Jurek probably threatened to kill Cornelia to make the churchwarden cooperate," Saga says, checking to make sure that her phone isn't on silent mode.

"So that was what he's thinking in the coffin," Nathan goes on. "He must have realized he was going to die—that was why he wrote the message. He hoped someone would find the grave and rescue his sister."

"Jurek must have terrified him to make sure he wouldn't tell the police the truth. Maybe he'd already been given a taste of the grave, or had seen his sister in one. His dementia developed pretty rapidly after I first met him."

They're driving past meadows edged with pine forest, and beneath the E18. Nathan's left hand is holding the bottom of the wheel. He's still wearing his slim wedding ring.

As they drive, they receive a few brief updates over the comms terminal in the car: Cornelia isn't answering her phone, and she hasn't been paying her bills. Before she retired, she worked as a nurse at Norrtälje Hospital. Cornelia is seventy-two years old and single. The screen shows a broad-shouldered woman with short white hair and reading glasses hanging on her chest.

"Who interviewed her?" Nathan asked.

"No one conducted a full interview," Saga replies. "I shot Jurek six months before the churchwarden found the body. There was no reason to think there was any connection between him and the sister."

"But she lives less than twenty kilometers from where he disappeared."

"I know, but we knew that Jurek was dying—how far could he have gotten? We spoke to everyone who lived within ten kilometers of the river. That alone meant seven hundred interviews."

She remembers that they discussed expanding the search area to twenty kilometers, but that would have included the highly developed area of Norrtälje and would have increased the number of interviews by a factor of twenty.

"I mean later, though, when the body was found and the churchwarden developed dementia," Nathan says, glancing quickly at her.

"I phoned and spoke to her," Saga says. "She hadn't been in touch with her brother for ten years and had nothing of interest to say."

They turn onto a narrow gravel road, with a strip of frosted yellow grass in the middle, that leads directly into the thick forest.

Saga stares at the dark trees slipping past.

Maybe Jurek is keeping Valeria and her dad on Cornelia's land.

Her mouth goes dry, and she reaches for the plastic water bottle.

It's not impossible. It wouldn't be unlike him to gather the graves in groups.

She's always wondered how he managed to remember all those unmarked graves.

"What are you thinking?" Nathan asks, giving her a sideways glance.

"Nothing—what do you mean?"

"You're shaking."

She looks at the bottle in her hand, drinks some more, then puts it down in the cup holder and squeezes her hands between her thighs.

"I'm worried about my dad," she says.

"Of course," Nathan replies.

Saga turns to look at the green fir trees and the scrappy heather and blueberry bushes.

It's unbearable that she's exposed her dad to this. It's all her fault. It's her responsibility, and she has to save him.

They're several kilometers from the other houses when the dark forest opens out into a clearing. Nathan slows down as a red house with white eaves and windows comes into view.

"The dog handler knew it was urgent, right?" she says.

"She left right away," Nathan says.

"I was just thinking that there should be dogs closer, maybe in Norrtälje?"

"Amanda's the best," he replies patiently.

They roll slowly toward the little house. A muddy Jeep Wrangler from the 1980s is parked in a carport with a canvas roof, beside a wall of stacked birch wood.

Saga draws her Glock from her shoulder holster and feeds a bullet into the chamber.

They stop on a weedy gravel drive leading up to the house. Saga gets out of the car. She holds her pistol close to her body, pointed at the ground, as she strides forward.

She hears Nathan shut the car door behind her.

She's fairly confident that Jurek isn't here. That wouldn't fit his pattern—it's too easy to trace.

She moves off to one side, looking for bare soil, signs of recent digging. Her eyes roam anxiously around the edge of the clearing, behind the carport, to the bare bushes beside the house.

She hurries around to the shaded back of the house without waiting for Nathan. The ground is drier there, covered **with** pinecones.

On the lawn between the house and the dark edge of the forest are two huge fir trees, with heavy, contorted branches. There's a stepladder lying in the grass behind the larger of the trees.

Saga walks past a water-filled wheelbarrow and looks inside a small greenhouse full of dead plants. She can't see any obvious sign of graves. There's no vegetable patch or bare corner of the garden.

"Saga? Talk to me," Nathan says as he comes around the corner.

"They could be buried in the forest," Saga says.

"I know how it feels, but we need to do this in the right order. We start by talking to Cornelia."

Nathan returns to the front of the house, leaving Saga to gaze out at the trees for a while.

Just as she's about to turn around and follow him, there's a crunching sound at the edge of the forest. Saga spins back around and raises her pistol, squeezing the trigger until she feels it catch, and focuses her gaze, scanning for movement.

All she can see are tree trunks.

She moves slowly sideways and hears the crunching sound again. She thinks it must be an animal—a hedgehog, maybe— and moves cautiously toward the edge of the forest.

She stops and stands completely still, scanning the trees **and** undergrowth.

Saga turns and starts to walk back to the front of the house.

Nathan rings the doorbell and takes a step back.

Saga stands next to him and notices a sign indicating that a duty nurse lives here. Cornelia's been running a private nursing clinic from her home, she thinks.

Nathan rings the bell again. The sound is clearly audible through the walls. He waits a moment, then tries the door.

It's not locked, and swings silently open on its three hinges.

"Put your pistol away," he says.

Saga wipes the sweat from her hand on her jeans, but keeps her pistol in her hand as she follows him into a waiting room with a television, two hard sofas, and a magazine rack.

They cross the pale-gray linoleum floor, check the visitors' bathroom, then walk through the door to the examination room.

There are two large paper fans blocking the views from the windows facing the carport. The sun just reaches above the treetops. The windowpanes are dirty, and there are dead flies on the sills.

Along one wall is an examination table covered with coarse protective paper, and on another a desk with a computer, phone, and printer.

Just beyond the desk is a door with a frosted-glass window at eye level.

The room behind the door is dark.

Saga sees her own hazy reflection in the clouded glass as she approaches and opens the door. She reaches in with one hand, feeling across the wall. The thought that someone could be standing in there watching her flits through her head. Her fingertips find the light switch. She flips it and raises her pistol.

She walks slowly inside and shivers as she looks around.

Cornelia's living room has been turned into an operating room. The curtains are closed and held shut with clothespins.

Motes of dust hang in the glare of the ceiling light.

Nathan stops next to Saga and looks at the well-used equipment.

The operating table may be only around ten years old, but the EKG machine isn't even digital, and prints out its readings on graph paper.

There's a round operating lamp next to an IV stand and a stainless-steel cart. On top of the cart are pieces of examination equipment: a capnograph and cylinders of oxygen, carbon dioxide, and air.

"This is too well stocked for a nurse's clinic," Nathan says beside her.

"I'm starting to realize where we are," Saga replies.

48

SAGA WALKS THROUGH THE OPERATING ROOM WITH HER pistol raised and pushes open the door to a small bedroom. The bed is neatly made with a crocheted bedspread. There's a pillbox on the bedside table, next to a Bible.

They go into the kitchen, which contains a pine table and four rib-backed chairs with red cushions tied to them. Above the sink is an old-fashioned storage unit, with glass scoops for flour, sugar, and oats tucked into wooden cubbyholes. A stained coffee cup and a plate with crumbs on it are sitting in the sink.

"He's taken her," she says.

"Amanda will be here with the dogs in an hour," Nathan says.

Saga lowers her pistol, pauses for a few seconds, then puts it back in her holster. She walks slowly over to the window and looks out at the huge pine tree and the stepladder lying in the grass.

The forest isn't particularly large, possibly no more than a thousand hectares, but it's started to get dark, and the search will take time.

They return to the living room and stop in front of the protective plastic that's been spread out on top of the fitted carpet beneath the operating table.

"Should we call Forensics?" Nathan asks.

"Yes," she sighs.

Saga looks at the closed curtains. Someone could already be standing outside, watching them, and they wouldn't even know it.

"So this was where Jurek ended up after you shot him," Nathan says.

Saga nods and goes over to a tall glass cabinet; she looks at the array of saws, scalpels, hooked suture needles, and hemostats. On the top shelf is an old-fashioned bound journal. The acrid smell of disinfectant hits her as she opens the cabinet and takes the book out.

On one page, in the column headed "Admission Date," Cornelia had written the date when Saga thought she had killed Jurek, and in the column for "Name and Place of Abode," she'd written "Andersson."

The most common last name in Sweden.

That's followed by a fifteen-page handwritten account of the first four months, followed by three pages of sporadic notes of treatment leading up to this summer.

Saga and Nathan stand side by side, reading about everything that happened in this room. They grow more and more astonished at the accuracy of Joona's guesses.

Cornelia had been standing in the nature reserve's parking lot by the water, smoking, when her dog picked up a scent. A body had been swept along on the current and stranded in the shallows just before the river made a wide curve.

She thought he was dead when she backed her Jeep down the gentle slope and out into the water. It wasn't until she lifted him onto the back of the Jeep that she realized he was conscious. In spite of the cold and his serious bullet wounds, he had somehow managed to persuade her not to take him to a hospital.

She must have realized from the gunshot wounds that he was probably wanted by the police, but still saw it as her duty to try to save his life. She told him that she was a nurse, and that she could patch him up just enough for him to be able to get to a doctor he trusted, but once they got to her house, he asked her to perform the operations herself.

The journal doesn't say how she got the equipment; maybe she had a set of keys to the storage room at her former hospital.

In the journal, she gives a scrupulous account of the patient's stats. He had three life-threatening injuries, and a number of less serious wounds. The shots fired by Saga are all accounted for. Two or three high-velocity projectiles had ruptured the front lobe of his left lung, and fractured his left shoulder blade.

Cornelia wrote that the patient had refused even basic painkillers. He lost consciousness several times during the operations that followed.

She describes the patient's condition as critical until she saved his lung and stopped the bleeding from his upper arm.

"She gave him her own blood . . . because she's Type O," Saga says.

"Unbelievable," Nathan whispers.

Later that night, she began to operate on his injured hand. Large parts of it had been destroyed by the shot, literally torn away. Traumatic injury to the artery, a complete rupture. There was no way of saving it.

"She amputated his hand," Saga whispers.

In minute detail, Cornelia describes how she removed the hand without specialized equipment, using a Gigli saw, then filed the exposed bones, isolated the blood vessels and nerves, inserted a double catheter for drainage, and, finally, shaped the stump using a flap of tissue and skin.

"Why didn't Jurek destroy the journal, burn the house down, do something to erase all this evidence?" Nathan wonders when they finish reading.

"Because he knows that none of this could lead back to him before he carried out his plan," Saga replies. "Jurek isn't afraid of prison or secure psychiatric care—that wasn't why he escaped."

She walks out of the house and looks off along the road through the forest.

A crow is cawing in the distance.

She looks in the Jeep, then circles the house. She stops in front of the window of the operating room and imagines how things unfolded.

Jurek must have started to look for a man the same age and build as himself fairly soon after the operation.

He probably drove around in Cornelia's Jeep long before he had fully recovered, searching among beggars and the homeless. When he found the right person, he shot him in the same places he had been shot, then let him die. Maybe he had the whole thing planned from the start, or maybe it occurred to him when his own hand had to be amputated.

Despite the large quantities of antibiotics, Jurek suffered a secondary infection after the amputation, which led to gangrene. Cornelia fought the infection as long as she could, but eventually decided to perform a second amputation, above the elbow. By this point, Jurek must already have left his own hand and the stranger's torso to rot in the sea.

In the spring, following the second amputation, Jurek took the decayed body parts to Cornelia's brother, the churchwarden. Jurek forced him to photograph the torso, cut the finger from the hand, put it in alcohol, and cremate the rest of the remains. The idea was probably that the churchwarden would contact the police to inform them of the body he'd discovered, but before he had time to do that, he met Saga on the shore.

The wind blows through the trees, knocking more pinecones to the ground.

Saga stands still in the garden.

The water in the wheelbarrow is as black as pitch.

The Earth has continued to turn, and the last of the evening sun lights up the large pine tree from a different angle—and now Saga sees the new shadow on the grass.

It reveals what's been hidden.

A body is hanging from a branch high in the tree.

That's why the stepladder is lying where it is.

Saga walks around the tree and looks up at the dead woman with the rope around her neck.

Cornelia hanged herself.

Her Wellingtons have fallen to the ground beneath her. She has ingrained blood on her fingertips and on her chest.

She must have done it around three weeks ago. She was probably already dead by the time the churchwarden scratched his message in the coffin lid.

He was the hostage, so that Jurek could force Cornelia to do what he wanted—not the other way around. He needed her, not the churchwarden.

The last entry in Cornelia's journal concerns trials of a YK prosthesis, with a functioning grip in the hand controlled by wires.

Perhaps that was when she realized that he was planning to kill more people, and that she had saved the life of a horrific serial killer.

49

SEVEN HOURS LATER, THE DOG HANDLER DROPS SAGA OFF on Timmermans Street, and she runs the last block to her building. She locks the door to her apartment behind her, checks it, then closes the curtains at every window.

She goes into the kitchen to call her colleagues who are involved in the search for her dad. No one has anything to report yet, but one of them tells her he will be getting results from eight base stations tomorrow.

Saga swallows the impulse to shout and swear at him. She explains very calmly that her dad has been buried alive, and that he might not survive the night.

"Please, try to put more pressure on them," she pleads. "I need the results tonight—it could save his life."

She hangs up and wipes the tears from her cheeks, then decides to take a quick shower. She cut herself badly in the undergrowth behind Cornelia's house, and she wants to clean the cuts on her legs and arms before they get infected.

IT WAS ALREADY DARK BY THE TIME THE DOG HANDLER arrived.

Saga was watching from the porch. The handler stopped behind the Jeep, got out, put a backpack down on the ground, and opened the back of the car for the dogs.

Amanda was a fairly tall woman in her thirties. She was wearing black hunting clothes, a black cap over her strawberry-blond hair, and heavy hiking boots with ankle supports and ski-boot fastenings.

Saga went up to her as she was giving the two police dogs some water after the drive. "You found us," she said, holding out her hand.

Amanda seemed shy. She averted her gaze a little too quickly, then introduced her dogs, a Belgian sheepdog and a black retriever. Billie specialized in finding dead bodies, picking up the smell of cadavers and dried blood. Her head was black, but her thick mane was almost reddish-blond. Ella, on the other hand, was trained to find people alive. She had even been flown down to help in Italy after the most recent earthquake.

Saga crouched down and talked to Ella, hugging her and patting her behind the ears. She told her she had to find her dad alive.

Ella listened and wagged her tail.

Saga, even though she wasn't dressed for it, decided to go into the forest with Amanda and the dogs. She had to be sure they didn't miss anything. She and Amanda used their flashlights to light their way, but it was the dogs who decided which way to go.

It took them almost six hours to search the dense forest. Saga tore her jeans and her hair kept catching on jagged branches.

Amanda had superimposed a grid on a satellite map of the forest, and she checked off the sections as they searched them.

They reached Björknäs without having found any trace of Valeria or Saga's father.

Saga was getting cold when they stopped. She patted the dogs, who were starting to get tired. Ella had white froth at the corners of her mouth and was wagging her tail, and Billie seemed nervous—was whimpering and twitching her pointed ears.

Saga turns the shower off and dries herself. She puts Band-Aids on the deepest cuts, puts on a pair of loose sweatpants and an old T-shirt, and puts her shoulder holster and pistol back on.

She gets her bulletproof vest and stuffs it into a canvas bag, along with a knife and several boxes of ammunition.

On the floor in front of the door, she lays out her motorcycle helmet, overalls, and boots.

She needs to be ready to leap into action if they get any sort of tip-off, if anyone sees the Beaver or Jurek or finds her dad.

She opens her gun cabinet and takes out a small Sig Sauer P290. She feeds a bullet into the chamber, releases the safety catch, and tapes the gun under the kitchen table.

She puts the roll of tape down, then stops and forces herself to take a breath.

She's starting to act like Joona. If anyone could see her now, they'd think she was paranoid.

She needs to pull herself together and think clearly.

Pellerina is safe.

She repeats this to herself several times.

Pellerina is safe. And she's not going to give up until she finds her dad.

It's a terrible situation, but she can cope.

One day, all this will be nothing but a memory, she tells herself. A painful memory, but it will fade a little more every year.

She takes a wine box out of the pantry, pours herself a glass of red, and takes a sip.

Saga sits down at the kitchen table with her wine, and takes out the pay-as-you-go phone to call Pellerina, even though they've already spoken twice today. She hasn't told her sister that it would be too dangerous to visit her, and that's why she hasn't come by. She doesn't want to scare Pellerina, but she knows that a single visit could give away the safe house's location.

She misses her sister badly, wishes she could cuddle and joke with her, but she can't let herself give in.

"Sabrina's really nice," Pellerina says.

"Do you think you'll be able to sleep okay if she's with you?"

"Why can't you be with me?"

"I have to work."

"At night?"

"Is that okay?"

"I'm twelve now."

"I know, you're a big girl."

"We can say good night if you have to work," her sister says.

"I can talk a little longer."

"It's okay."

"Good night, Pellerina. I love you," she says.

"Saga?"

"Yes?"

"I was thinking," she says quietly, then falls silent.

"What are you thinking?"

"Do I have to stay here so the clown girls don't get me?"

50

SAGA MAKES SURE HER FRONT DOOR IS LOCKED, THEN PUTS her holster and pistol under the other pillow on her bed.

She took her time to calm Pellerina, and steered the conversation toward her favorite movie, *Frozen*, before they finally said good night.

Now she turns the light out, and rolls over onto her side. She feels fatigue sweep through her body and closes her eyes. But she quickly starts thinking about her dad again, and her heartbeat starts to pulse in her ears.

This is his second night in a grave.

The temperature will fall below freezing. The ground will harden. The grass will sparkle with frost.

She has to find him.

And then she has to find and kill Jurek. He's hiding out there somewhere. She needs to lure him into the light and finish what she started.

Saga has just entered a deep sleep when she dreams that a rough hand is stroking her cheek.

It's her mom, only she's older now. When Saga realizes that she's still alive, she feels an intense wave of gratitude. She tries to explain how happy she is.

Her mom stares at her, shaking her head. Then she walks backward through the window and gets tangled up in the blinds.

Saga jolts awake and opens her eyes. It's dark in the bedroom. She's only been asleep for an hour.

She blinks and tries to figure out what woke her up. It can't be her phone—it's charging and the screen is dark.

She's telling herself that she just needs to get back to sleep when she sees the thin figure sitting in the chair next to the window.

She starts to wonder if it's her dad, but then fear overcomes her. She knows who it is.

Her heart is pounding. She carefully slips her hand under the other pillow, but her pistol is no longer there.

"Little siren, always lethal," the man in the chair says.

It's a voice she's heard many times in her nightmares, a voice she'll never be able to forget.

The chair creaks as he leans over to one side to turn the lamp on.

"Still just as beautiful," he says.

Jurek Walter's pale eyes and wrinkled face are turned toward her. He's sitting up straight, with her pistol and holster in his lap. He has a deep scar running across one cheek, and part of his ear is missing. He's wearing a checked shirt, and the shiny plastic of his prosthetic left hand looks like a doll's compared with his rough right hand.

Saga sits up carefully. Her heart is beating so fast that her breathing is ragged. She knows she has to calm down. She has to play along until she can get to the pistol in the kitchen.

"I thought I killed you," he says. "But I was in a hurry. I was sloppy."

"I thought I killed you," she replies, and swallows hard.

"You almost did."

"Yes, I read Cornelia's journal," Saga says, breathing through her nose. "But I don't understand why you put yourself through all this. You could have gone to the hospital, gotten proper care, avoided the pain."

"Pain doesn't frighten me; it's part of life," he says calmly.

"But when will you be finished, when will this really be over?" she asks, a shiver running down her spine as his pale eyes focus on her again.

"Over?" he repeats. "I live to restore order . . . and I'm inexhaustible. I was robbed, and that created a hole that needs to be filled."

"I understand," she replies, almost silently.

"I had to survive.... Joona took my brother from me. You know that I'm going to take everything away from him."

At that thought, he almost smiles for a few seconds.

She thinks about how he believed he'd killed her. He pummeled her, so hard that she passed out, but she's sure he never thought he'd killed her.

For some reason, he let her live.

And, for some reason, he wants her to believe that that was a mistake.

She has to remind herself that Jurek lies all the time. And it doesn't matter whether you believe the lies or uncover the truth—you're still in his trap.

She has to concentrate on finding some way of getting to the kitchen with enough of a head start to reach the Sig Sauer.

"You still run your finger along your left eyebrow when you're thinking," he says.

"Good memory," Saga says, lowering her hand.

"Do you know, I noticed that you were looking at me through your eyelids when I came into the bedroom.... If you'd woken up then, you'd have had your Glock in your hand...."

Jurek breaks off, stands up, and walks calmly over to the gun cabinet, where he locks the pistol away.

"It's fascinating, isn't it, the little evolutionary details of our eyelids?" he continues, turning to face her. "We can see changes in the light with our eyes closed—movement, silhouettes—and the brain registers sensory perceptions in our sleep."

Saga turns her face away to hide her agitation. She tells herself not to lose control. She needs to stay calm, but she can't understand how he knows her secrets.

When she was little, she often had a lot of trouble falling asleep: she would lie awake, listening to things, and trying to see them through her eyelids. Whenever she thought she saw something, she had to open her eyes and check her bedroom.

She's never told anyone about this compulsive behavior. None of her boyfriends know, and she's never written about it in any of her diaries.

Almost all children have compulsive thoughts, but what makes the memory of this one so painful is that she later realized it was a survival instinct. When her mom had her manic episodes, she used to imagine all sorts of things, seeing enemies everywhere and getting aggressive. Saga needed to wake up if her mom crept into her room at night, so she could calm her down.

Saga knows Jurek is trying to provoke her. She needs to focus, keep the conversation going. She can't let him trick her.

He wants her to believe that he can see right through her.

But of course he can't.

She needs to think.

Maybe she told him the thing about eyelids when she was in the secure unit, when she was drugged. She was heavily medicated. It must have affected her judgment and caused lapses in her memory.

That's the only logical explanation. It's enough, she thinks, and meets his gaze again. His pale eyes are observing her as if he's trying to determine just what effect his words have had on her.

"Your sister was hiding behind the curtain," he said. "I realized that afterward. . . . Very good, you've trained her well."

"What are you doing here?" she asks.

"Do you really want to know?"

51

SAGA DECIDES SHE'S HAD ENOUGH. SHE PUSHES THE COVERS back, lowers her feet to the floor, and stands up. She doesn't have to play by his rules.

"Sit still," he says.

She's going to the kitchen to snatch the pistol from under the table, and she's going to shoot him in both thighs.

Once he's lying on the floor, she'll shoot him in his good arm.

Which will render him harmless.

She'll put him in the bathtub and let him bleed until he tells her what she wants to know. He'll talk, and as soon as she finds out where her dad is, she'll kill him.

"I just want some water," she mutters, turning toward the door.

Joona had said not to wait but to kill Jurek instantly, as soon as she got the chance. He knew that she would be less likely to find her dad alive if she listened to Jurek, even if she had the advantage.

Jurek gets up from the chair. She can feel his eyes following her, lingering on her face, neck, the Band-Aids on her arms.

"Stay here," he says.

She turns toward him, and looks him in the eye.

"I'm not going to try to escape," she says, smiling, then casually strolls into the hall.

She hears him follow her. She doesn't know how much of a head start she has. The light from the floor lamp shows her shadow sliding across the wall, closely followed by his.

She nudges the bedroom door open and walks toward the kitchen.

She realizes that Jurek is right behind her. He's not going to let her go into the kitchen alone.

She glances at the closed front door, and the clothes and helmet on the floor.

Maybe she could run away from him and grab the gun. She knows she would have no chance in close combat.

She hesitates, because the kitchen door is closed, and the moment is gone. When she passes the dresser with her keys and some scented candles on top of it, she can hear his breathing behind her.

She opens the door to the kitchen, calmly turns the light on, and walks over to the sink without looking at the table.

Jurek watches her as she waits for the water to get cold. She fills a glass, then turns to face him and drinks.

His checked flannel shirt is hanging down over his narrow prosthetic hand, whereas the right sleeve is pushed up to the elbow. His time as a soldier and his work as a mechanic made him tough, she thinks, looking at his coarse right hand, the muscles, and the thick veins beneath the wrinkled skin of his forearm.

When she casts a quick glance at the table, she sees that one of the chairs is in the way. She'll have to shove it aside to reach the gun.

Saga drinks some more, then gestures toward the table with the glass in her hand.

"Should we sit down instead?"

"No."

The pistol weighs so little that it took only one strip of tape to fasten it. That will save her vital seconds. Even if she tears the tape off with the pistol, it won't get in the way when she shoots.

Jurek goes over to the counter and takes a glass from the cabinet. She moves a little farther away, a few steps closer to the table.

The moment she hears the sink run, she walks quickly and silently toward the hidden weapon. She puts the glass down, shoves the chair aside with one hand, and reaches under the table with the other. Just as she's about to grasp the gun, she's shoved from behind and thrown forward violently.

She tumbles over two chairs, and her shoulder blade hits the wall. She sinks to one knee, tries to get to her feet, and fumbles across the table for support.

The glass container full of cornflakes falls to the floor and shatters.

He yanks her hard by the hair, and brings his prosthetic down on her ear so forcefully that she collapses, sending one chair flying as she tries to stay on her feet.

Her whole head is ringing from the blow.

He lashes out again, and Saga wrenches her head out of the way and hits him in the face with a right hook.

But his hand grabs her neck and starts to squeeze her throat. He pulls her toward him and hits her across the cheek and neck with the hard prosthesis, making her vision flare.

He jerks her sideways by the neck and hits her again. She tries to protect herself with her hand but can feel her legs starting to buckle.

He strikes her head again, and she falls, hitting her temple on the wooden floor. She blinks but she can't see anything.

She realizes that he's dragging her back to the bedroom by her hair.

Jurek pulls off his belt, wraps it around her neck, and ties it to the back of the chair by the window.

She can't breathe.

She can make out Jurek standing in front of her, just watching. The prosthesis has come loose in the struggle and is hanging from its straps and the shirt.

Saga tries to insert her fingers under the belt to stretch it. She's struggling to get air into her lungs, and kicking out with her legs. She tries to knock the chair over, but all she can do is bang it against the wall.

Her field of vision contracts. She sees a flickering image of Pellerina against a white sky before Jurek loosens the belt around her neck.

She coughs and gasps for breath, leaning forward over her knees as she spits bloody saliva onto the floor.

"Sit up," he says calmly.

She straightens up and coughs again. Her face and neck are throbbing with pain. Jurek is standing by her bookcase, pulling the duct tape from the little pistol with his mouth.

Her vision is still shaky.

With three short steps, he's in front of her, squeezing her cheeks together and pushing the short barrel into her mouth.

Then he pulls the trigger.

The gun clicks, but it isn't loaded. He's removed the bullet.

She gasps. She can feel sweat trickling between her breasts.

"I don't know where Joona is," she manages to say.

"I know," Jurek says. "You don't even know which continent he's on right now. I know him. He doesn't tell anyone anything. It's the only way. . . . If I thought there was the slightest possibility that you knew something about Joona, I wouldn't hesitate to cut your face off, piece by piece."

"So why did you take my dad?"

"I don't mean any harm," he says. "I'm almost done with you. You helped me get out of the secure unit; that was your only function."

She wipes the blood from her mouth with the back of her hand. Her whole body is shaking from shock.

"So what are you doing here?" she asks.

"My brother has no grave," he says. "I just want to know where he is."

"They might have scattered his ashes in the Garden of Remembrance somewhere?" Saga suggests in a hoarse voice.

"I tried to find out."

"I have absolutely no idea."

"I want to know where he is," Jurek says. "There must be documentation. . . . I don't believe in God, but I'd like to bury my brother for my parents' sake. . . . Igor had a difficult life. Those years in the children's home in Kuzminki broke him. . . . And the Serbsky Institute made him who he was. . . ."

"I'm sorry," Saga whispers.

"You have access to files through both the Security Police and the National Operations Unit," he says slowly. "I'll give you your father in exchange for my brother."

"I want my father alive."

The wrinkles in Jurek's face deepen into what might be a smile.

"I want my brother alive. But I'll settle for documentation showing where he's buried."

Saga nods. She realizes that Jurek reacted so quickly in the kitchen because he wasn't looking at the sink at all—it was just a ruse to find out where the gun was hidden.

"You're going to do this for me," Jurek says. "Even if it means surrendering classified material, even if it costs you your job and your reputation."

"Yes," she whispers.

"Tomorrow—we'll meet around the same time, somewhere else."

"Where?"

"I'll send you a text."

52

AS SOON AS JUREK IS GONE, SAGA LOCKS THE DOOR, LIMPS to the gun cabinet, checks that her Glock is loaded, and puts her holster on. She checks the door and windows again, then goes into the bathroom to inspect her injuries.

After she washes her face and rinses her mouth, she tosses the bloody towel into the bathtub and sits on her bed with all the lights on. She searches the Security Police database.

By the time she gives up, three hours later, it's morning. She can't find any information about where Jurek's brother's body is.

Saga gets out of bed and pulls on a pair of jeans and a soft sweater. Her whole body is sore. She attempts to conceal the bruises on her face and neck with makeup, then leaves the apartment.

THE LARGE INVESTIGATION ROOM AT THE NATIONAL OPERA-tions Unit is deserted. Saga walks past the map of Europe that covers the wall and stops in front of the blurred pictures of the Beaver from the Belarusian security-camera footage.

Every detail they've noted so far takes on a completely new meaning now that they know Jurek is behind everything.

They had thought the Beaver was a murderer who was trying to cleanse society, who saw himself as some sort of superhero. But he was actually a slave, a domesticated predator.

Saga can hear voices in the hallway. It's Nathan, chatting with a colleague over by the coffee machine as he waits for his espresso.

Their investigation has suddenly become the largest in the country. They have almost unlimited resources, but Saga knows they won't save her dad.

She has to find Jurek's twin brother's remains. She can't tell anybody about the deal with Jurek.

Nathan comes in and drops his heavy bag on the floor, then looks at her.

"What happened to you?" he asks, putting his cup down on the desk.

"I went through the forest with Amanda and the dogs—wrong clothes entirely."

"You look like you've been in a boxing match."

"Feels like it, too," she says, and turns her face away.

Nathan drinks some coffee, then sits down. "I picked up two reports from the lab."

"Have you read them?" Saga says in a hoarse voice.

"I leafed through them. They seem fairly confident that they've identified Cornelia's cause of death."

"She hanged herself?"

He pulls out a thick folder from his bag, opens it, and takes out the two preliminary pathology reports. He puts his reading glasses on and flips through one of them, tracing the lines with his index finger. "Let's see," he murmurs. "Yes, here it is. . . . 'The cause of death was total blockage of arterial flow to the brain.'"

"Can I look?"

Saga sits on the edge of the desk and starts to go through the material. She stops when she reads that Cornelia's brother had been lying alive in his grave behind the churchwarden's cottage on Högmarsö for at least three months. He died of dehydration one week after Cornelia committed suicide.

"They helped Jurek, and now they're both dead," she says.

She thinks about the deals Cornelia and Erland must have made with Jurek. Their attempts to be helpful in order to save themselves and each other could have been the cause of their deaths.

They had no idea how dangerous he was.

Joona said that every deal you make with Jurek only leads you deeper into the mire. Saga knows she shouldn't trust Jurek, but she can't think of another way to save her dad.

She imagines an old-fashioned fishing net in shallow water. The wooden rings form a tunnel from which you can't escape. Each section is designed so the fish can swim into it easily, but it's impossible to get out of.

Saga's cell phone buzzes with a text saying that the police have issued a national alert, and that they've brought in Interpol.

"A national alert," she says in a subdued voice.

"Yes, I heard."

"They still haven't identified the Beaver?"

"No."

Saga goes over to the map of Lill-Jans Forest and the Albano industrial park. Once upon a time, Jurek kept a large number of victims buried alive there.

She looks at the railroad tracks and the distribution of burial sites. She stares at the markers on the map, trying to understand how Jurek could keep track of all the graves. They're spread out across something like three million square meters.

And this was just one of his cemeteries.

He must have had maps somewhere, or lists of coordinates. But in all their years of searching, they've never found anything like that. They haven't even found his actual home. The apartment where he was registered was just a façade.

And there was no trace of Jurek in the old workers' barracks where his brother hid out. Forensics experts and teams of dogs searched the whole quarry, the surrounding buildings, and the bomb shelters, but it was as if Jurek had never even been there.

"Nathan, what actually happened to Jurek's twin brother?" she asks. "To his body, I mean. Where is it now?"

"No idea," he replies, laying out photographs on the table.

"If the body still exists, I'd like to take a look at it," Saga says once she's confident she can keep her voice steady. "At the injuries—you know, the old scars on his back."

Nathan shrugs his shoulders. "There's a comprehensive report from Karolinska and at least a thousand pictures in the archive."

"I know. I'd just like to see it with my own eyes.... Do you know who was in charge of the postmortem?"

"I don't remember, but probably Nils."

"Probably."

Nathan rolls his chair over to the computer and logs in, sits in silence for a while, types something, then clicks.

"Nils Åhlén," he confirms.

"Can I see?" she asks, going over to stand behind him.

He gestures toward the computer and moves out of the way. She pulls up a chair and starts looking for information about whether the body was retained for some reason, but finds nothing. Just tables documenting his injuries and the weight and condition of every organ.

She tells herself she's going to have to call Nils the next time she's alone. Maybe she should just go into the bathroom and call him now?

Out of the corner of her eye, she sees Nathan pinning the pictures from Jurek Walter's file on the wall.

His official police photographs show him from the front and in profile.

He's older now, has more scars, and is missing his left arm. But the calmness in his wrinkled face and pale eyes is unchanged.

"The meeting's about to start," Nathan says.

Her phone rings as she's switching the computer off.

"Bauer," she says.

"We found your dad's car," a female officer tells her, panting as though she'd run to give her the news.

BARKARBY FLYING CLUB, THE ROAD, AND THE AREA AROUND Lars-Erik's car have been cordoned off. The police haven't found any visible signs of struggle, but they discovered Saga's dad's smashed cell phone in the frozen mud ten meters from the vehicle.

The crime-scene investigators have been through the entire area.

The search party sets off from the gravel road beyond the fluttering cordon tape.

The winter grass is stiff with frost. Red and yellow brick buildings rise up above the treetops like somber witnesses.

Saga hasn't been able to reach The Needle. He's flying back from a conference in Melbourne and won't be home until eight o'clock this evening. The thought that Nils might know something about Jurek's brother is the only thing that's stopping her from panicking right now.

Police officers with dogs and volunteers from Missing Persons form long chains. They've all been told to look out for pipes sticking out of the ground, or soil that seems to have been disturbed recently.

Ninety people in yellow vests start to move across the grass, through areas of woodland. They poke at dense patches of undergrowth with sticks and search alongside roads and paths.

When they take a break after searching the sandy slopes of the nearby motocross course, Saga steps away to call Randy. When he doesn't answer, a heavy loneliness fills her chest.

"They've found Dad's car. I'm going to stay out here as long as the search is going on. . . . Please, call me when you get this," she says, then goes back to her place in the chain.

IT'S EIGHT O'CLOCK IN THE EVENING, AND SAGA IS WAITING in the Falafel Bar. She slips off her high stool and takes the bag of food from the counter.

The search was called off at six-thirty, and they still hadn't found any trace of her dad.

Saga feels she has no choice but to play Jurek's game.

She goes back to her apartment, where she locks the door, checks all the windows and closets, looks under the bed, closes the curtains, and switches all the lights off. Then she calls The Needle.

"I literally just switched my phone back on," Nils says in his nasal voice. "The plane's still taxiing."

"I need to ask you something."

"We'll be done with the postmortems tomorrow or—"

"Listen," Saga interrupts. "I'm calling because you did the postmortem on Jurek's twin brother."

"Igor."

"What happened to his remains?"

"I don't remember," Nils mutters. "But I assume we followed the usual procedure."

"Can you find out?"

He sighs. "Someone stole the body from the cold-storage room," he says in a subdued voice.

"Stole?"

"Right after we'd finished the postmortem."

"Why would someone want to steal his body?" she whispers.

"I don't know."

Saga takes a few steps forward, then turns and leans against the window. The glass feels cool against her sweaty back.

"Could it be a coincidence?" she asks. "Medical students messing around? Someone who just wanted a dead body?"

"Why not?" he replies.

"Nils, just tell me what you know. This is really fucking important."

"I don't know anything," he says slowly. "And that's the truth. . . . I only mentioned the theft to one person, the only person I thought needed to know about it. I thought he'd be upset, but he took it very calmly."

She stares into space. She knows that he's talking about Joona, and that Joona's the one who took the body. But she doesn't know why.

"Do you have any idea where the body might be now?"

"I haven't made any attempt to find it, because there was no practical need to," Nils replies bluntly.

They hang up, and Saga stands in silence for a while.

The body is gone.

She had been sure that Nils would be able to help her, that there was a reasonable explanation for where the body ended up.

But now her dad has been buried alive, and she has nothing to offer in exchange for his release.

She takes the plastic carton of falafel out of the bag and sits down at the kitchen table.

She looks at her phone. She hasn't called Pellerina today, because she doesn't feel up to lying to her again. She needs to rescue their dad first.

53

DARKNESS WILL SOON FALL ON THE FIELDS AND MEADOWS. The landscape already looks diluted and watery.

As usual, the wind is blowing from the southwest, swaying the bare branches of the weeping willow gently.

Joona and Lumi are on their last shift before night while Rinus rests.

They're in the surveillance room, the largest in the building. Their empty coffee mugs are on a box of ammunition.

The regimented timetable and monotonous tasks mean that days in the safe house tend to blur together.

"Zone Two," Lumi says, closing the shutter over the opening. She puts her binoculars down on the plain wooden table, with its fixed felt covering, rubs her eyes, and looks at the time.

Zone 2 covers the fields toward Eindhoven and a distant greenhouse.

All the zones overlap, taking into account the idiosyncrasies of the landscape. It's impossible to keep an eye on their entire surroundings at all times, but as long as they stick to the plan, the risk of anyone's approaching the workshop without being spotted is minimal.

"Zone Three," Joona says, looking at his daughter.

She's sitting on her chair, staring at the floor.

"Ninety minutes to go before we wake Rinus," Joona says.

"I'm not tired," she mumbles.

"You should still try to get some sleep."

Lumi doesn't answer, just stands up and walks past the table where Joona's phone is charging. She stops in front of the large monitor. It's divided into sections, showing the workshop and the inside of the garage from various angles.

The smooth, reinforced walls blur together in the gloom.

Rinus has repainted the pillar that had been worn smooth by the hydraulic shutter.

The old, crooked door is swaying in the wind.

Lumi walks past the row of hatches covering the firing holes aiming onto the garage and sits back down on her chair without looking at her dad.

"How long are you planning to keep us in hiding?" she asks after a pause.

Joona looks out through one of the openings with his binoculars, lingering on a dense patch of bushes in front of a water-filled dike.

"This is starting to feel like Nattavaara," Lumi goes on. "I mean, if Saga hadn't found us we'd still be there—wouldn't we?"

Joona lowers the binoculars and turns toward her. "What am I supposed to say to that?" he asks.

"I'd never have gone to Paris."

Joona raises the binoculars and scans the next zone, a furrowed field and the clump of trees where the underground passageway emerges.

"What if the higher-ups in the police don't listen to Nathan?" Lumi continues, talking to his back. "What if they don't believe you? I mean, then Valeria wouldn't have any protection. . . . Would she be okay if that's the case?"

"No," Joona says.

"And you don't care—I can't get my head around that."

"I couldn't stay. I had to leave in order to . . ."

"To save me—I know," she says.

"You're on Zone Four."

"Dad," Lumi says as she gets to her feet, "I'm doing all this because I promised I would, because it matters to you, but this isn't going to work forever. . . . I'm already falling behind with my classes. I have a social life. This is so fucking ridiculous, on every level."

"I can take your zones," he says.

"Why would you do that?"

"If you want to draw, read, eat . . ."

"Is that what you think I'm talking about?" she snaps. "That I want to sit and draw instead of doing my duty?"

"It doesn't bother me," he says.

"Well, it bothers me!" Lumi says, snatching her binoculars from the table.

She walks past Joona, stops at the window next to the filing cabinet, and opens the shutter.

The drainpipe sticks up like a huge straw beside the partially collapsed outbuilding behind the workshop. An old tractor tire is lying on the edge of the field. In the distance, she can see headlights on a minor road flickering between the tree trunks.

Everything is peaceful.

Lumi closes the shutter and puts the binoculars down. She can't bring herself to say the name of the zone she's just checked. She just walks across the room, pulls the curtain aside, and walks out.

Joona moves on to Zone 5. He looks through the binoculars, lingering on the neighboring farm in the distance, where an old bus is parked in the yard.

In his notes to Nathan, he asked him to leak information to the evening tabloids as soon as Jurek was dead and The Needle had categorically confirmed the death. At least once a day, Joona thoroughly checks the papers' online editions, but there's been nothing so far, which means that Jurek is still alive.

And Joona knows what Jurek is capable of.

He keeps hearing him whisper that he's going to take his wife and daughter. That he's going to grind Joona into the dirt.

But Joona also understands his daughter's frustration. She's been living her own life for the past two years, a life she could only have dreamed about before.

And to her, Jurek isn't a real threat.

He wasn't dead, as they had believed when they left their hiding place in Nattavaara, and yet nothing had happened to her. She's been living the kind of life any young, independent woman might.

Joona checks the farmyard and bus in the distance again before closing the shutter and putting the binoculars down.

He goes through the curtain down to the ground floor to the kitchen for a cup of coffee.

Lumi is standing by the counter with her phone clutched to her ear. Her cheeks are red as she meets his gaze defiantly. He marches over to her, snatches the phone, and ends the call.

"I need to speak to my boyfriend—and you can't just—"

Joona throws the phone on the floor and stomps on it, smashing it to pieces.

"You're crazy!" she yells. "What's wrong with you? You act so fucking cool all the time, but you're really just scared. You're just like some old guy hiding in a bunker with guns and canned food, so you can survive a fucking war that isn't even real."

"I'm sorry I dragged you into this, but I had no choice," Joona says calmly and somberly as he pours the last of the coffee from the pot.

Lumi hides her face in her hands and shakes her head.

"You think everything I do is dangerous," she mutters.

"I'm just worried about you."

She takes a deep, shaky breath. "I didn't mean to yell, but it makes me so angry. This isn't working. In fact, it's totally fucking claustrophobic," she says quietly, sitting down at the kitchen table.

"We don't have a choice," Joona replies, drinking some of the bitter coffee.

"I haven't told you about Laurent," she continues in a calmer voice. "He's my boyfriend. He's important to me."

"Is he an artist, too?"

"He does video art."

"Like Bill Viola."

"Well done, Dad," she says in a subdued voice. "Like Viola, only more modern."

Joona walks over to the sink and rinses his mug. "You can't do that again," he says.

"I can't bear the thought of him panicking—I mean, what's he going to think when I've just vanished?"

Lumi's hair is falling out of her ponytail, and the tip of her nose is red.

"If you call Laurent, Jurek will kill him. And before he dies, Laurent will reveal the number you called him from."

"You're crazy," she says, swallowing hard.

Joona doesn't respond. He goes back to the surveillance room, picks up the binoculars, opens the shutter for Zone 1, and starts all over again.

54

IT'S ALMOST DARK ENOUGH TO SWAP THE BINOCULARS FOR the night-vision goggles.

Joona is checking the boarded-up main house and abandoned garden furniture.

He hears Lumi enter the room and glances over at her. She's stopped just inside the curtain with her hand on a stack of chairs.

He goes back to watching. He checks the barrier and the narrow path that leads to the main road.

"Are you okay? Are you sure you're really okay, Dad?" Lumi asks, wiping tears from her cheeks. "You haven't been out of prison for that long, and you were in there for years. . . . All you said was that you had to help an old friend, but I'm guessing it was really about Jurek."

"No," he replies, moving on to Zone 2.

He checks the immediate vicinity through the binoculars. He looks at the dark bushes along the dike before he raises the binoculars toward the distant greenhouse.

"Whenever you lose your judgment, it's always about him," Lumi goes on. "I know what happened to Samuel Mendel and how badly that affected you. I know you felt you had to sacrifice us to—"

"Quiet," Joona interrupts sharply.

A light is flickering at the top of the binoculars' lenses. It looks like a blue rainbow, and is only visible for an instant. He looks through the window beside the binoculars and just catches sight of a cell phone going dark in a large hand.

"Wake Rinus; we've got visitors," he says in a low voice. He's identified two figures in the darkness.

Lumi hurries out of the room, drawing her pistol.

Joona can make out the curve of the taller man's head against the slightly lighter background. The figure moves toward the workshop before disappearing behind something.

He hears Lumi come back with Rinus.

"I can't see them anymore, but they're close," Joona says.

"How many?" Rinus asks.

"Two."

Lumi takes a semiautomatic rifle from a wooden crate, inserts a full cartridge, and puts the gun on the table. Then she takes out another one, inserts a cartridge, and lays it next to the first.

"I don't think it's Jurek," Joona says, looking Rinus in the eye.

Lumi moves over to the monitor as she checks the emergency bag containing her passport, cash, water, emergency flares, and a pistol.

Joona raises the binoculars again and quickly scans the whole zone before moving on to the next.

The weak glow of the monitor is lighting up Lumi's anxious face. She's concentrating on the external cameras that show what's happening just outside the workshop and garage. The low light makes the images gray and grainy.

Suddenly two figures emerge from the darkness.

Their pale outlines move along the side of the workshop and step over something lying on the ground.

"I can see them," she says.

Rinus stands next to her, fastening his protective vest.

The heat-sensitive cameras make it look as if the two figures are moving through a snowstorm. They seem to be emitting a kind of pale dust.

They stop in front of the large garage doors.

Lumi sees them on the cameras inside the building as the loose door sways in the wind.

Joona is double-checking the other zones so they're not taken by surprise by any more intruders.

Rinus picks up one of the semiautomatics from the table.

They can't see what the two men are doing outside the garage.

On the monitor, Lumi sees one of them hold the door open for the other.

"They're coming in," she says under her breath.

The two intruders turn around, and the monitor flares white when one of them raises a camera and takes a picture.

Joona releases the reinforced shutter. It slams shut instantly behind the intruders, the clang echoing off the walls.

The two men cry out and stumble backward against the solid wall, scrabbling around it in panic.

Rinus switches the floodlights on, and Lumi and Joona see that they've caught two teenagers. One is hammering against the door with his hands, and his hat has fallen off. He has a full red beard and torn jeans. The other is gasping for breath. He's shorter, with dark hair, and is wearing a denim jacket with a fleece lining.

They turn around in the enclosed space, trying to understand what's going on.

Rinus opens one of the firing holes, and the young men's agitated voices suddenly sound louder.

He calls out something in Dutch, and the two men stop at once and put their hands in the air.

"Don't frighten them," Joona says.

The two follow a series of short commands from Rinus. They turn to face one wall, kneel down, put their hands behind their backs, and then lean forward to rest their chests and a cheek against the wall.

That's one of the best ways to control enemies—when they're in that position, it takes them much longer to launch any sort of counterattack.

Joona knows that the two young men have nothing to do with Jurek, but they could still be dangerous. He keeps them covered with one of the semiautomatics while Rinus goes downstairs to meet them.

Rinus walks in, then lowers and puts away his pistol before patting them down.

"What are you doing here?"

"We're looking for a good place to hold a party," the young bearded man says in a subdued voice.

"Stand up."

They both cautiously get to their feet, and their breathing speeds up when they see Rinus's scarred face.

"A party?" he asks.

"Factory Dive—one night, one stage, three acts," says the younger one, in the denim jacket.

"Sorry," the bearded man blurts out. "We thought this place was abandoned. We live in Eindhoven; we've driven past it tons of times."

"It says 'Private Property' on the signs."

"They always say 'Private Property' and 'No Trespassing,'" the shorter one says.

55

SAGA PUTS HER PHONE AND PISTOL DOWN ON HER KITCHEN table. It's late evening. The wind is rattling the window, and a strip of dark glass is visible between the curtains.

She's felt paralyzed since her conversation with The Needle. She has nothing to negotiate with now. She needs to change her strategy.

She doesn't understand why Joona took the body. Joona has always been aggressive when it comes to Jurek. He's been prepared to do things no other police officer would do.

Jurek has a very orderly mind, and he only makes mistakes when he loses control. Joona probably took the body to prompt another of those moments. He'll have buried it somewhere, unless maybe he froze it. He could never have predicted that she would need it. If only he would get in touch, Saga thinks, trying to eat some of her cold food.

Her cell phone starts to buzz on the table. She starts, then smiles with relief when she sees that it's Randy.

She nudges the tub of cold food aside and picks up the phone. "Randy?"

"I just got your message. I've been in the darkroom—how are you doing?"

"Okay, I guess, given the circumstances," she murmurs.

"Do you want me to come over?"

"No, I . . ."

"I'd be happy to."

"I have to work," she says.

"It's after eleven o'clock," Randy says quietly.

"I know."

"Can you please let me know what's going on?"

AFTER TALKING TO RANDY, SAGA DRAGS THE ARMCHAIR from the living room into the hallway. She turns the volume of her ringtone up as far as it will go and puts her phone on the dresser. Then she makes a quadruple espresso, puts her shoes and coat on, and sits down in the armchair, staring at the front door, pistol in hand.

Randy told Saga to call him whenever she wanted, if she just wanted to talk, or—if she felt like having company—he could come and sleep on the sofa.

But Saga is starting to realize that she needs to deal with this on her own.

Otherwise, she won't get her dad back.

They finished searching the woodland around Cornelia's house with dogs, and they've been across Järva Field with officers and volunteers.

It's almost unbearable.

He could be lying in a coffin like the churchwarden, struggling to get enough air through a narrow tube.

The strong coffee is cold by the time Saga drinks it. She puts the cup down, glances quickly over her shoulder, then settles back into position in front of the door.

She knows she should be exhausted after everything she's been through in the past twenty-four hours, but her brain can't relax.

If Jurek gets in touch tonight, she's going to say she's expecting information about his brother's remains tomorrow.

She can't tell him that Joona took the body.

She's not going to negotiate with Jurek. She knows better than that. But she needs to convince him that he'll never find out where his brother is if her dad dies. It's her only leverage.

At two o'clock in the morning, she's almost asleep when her phone suddenly buzzes.

Her hands start to shake. The bright light of the screen makes her pupils contract. The letters slide sideways as she reads: "Hasselgården, entrance C1, ward 4, 2:30."

She gets a sheet of paper from the printer, writes down the address and time, and leaves the sheet on the kitchen table.

If she doesn't come home or get in touch, someone will find the note.

She grabs her pistol and two cartons of ammunition. As she runs down the stairs, she looks up Hasselgården and discovers that it's a home for people with dementia.

Saga pulls the tarp off, starts her motorcycle, and rides into the cold winter night.

She shifts into fifth gear on the straight part of Bergslags Street, and her head jerks backward as the bike accelerates.

The streetlights flash past.

The name "Hasselgården" suggests hazel trees, and makes her think of a red wooden building with creaking floorboards and traditional fireplaces. But as Saga approaches the home, she discovers it's a dirty high-rise complex with salmon-pink plaster and brown window frames.

Fifteen meters from the entrance labeled C1, she stops, turns her bike around, puts her pistol in her saddle bag, and leaves her helmet on the handlebars. She doesn't take the weapon with her, because she knows she won't have a chance to kill Jurek tonight. She must follow his rules until he tells her where her father is.

The door of the main entrance is unlocked.

She glances at the building map and fire-escape plan, then takes the elevator up to the fourth floor.

Saga knows she misjudged Jurek. He was stronger and faster than she remembered.

She's only still alive because he wants something. Maybe it really is about his brother's remains, but she has to be prepared for the possibility that he wants something more.

She'll listen to him, talk to him—she needs him to believe that he's messing with her head, finding his way into the darkness inside her. But she can't give in.

She has to find her dad, and then she has to take Jurek out.

She knows she can't afford any more mistakes. The next time she reaches for a gun, she needs to be sure that she's going to kill him.

Though he's extremely dangerous, she can exploit the fact that he's interested in her.

Not in that way. This isn't a fairy tale about beauty and the beast. He sees something special in her.

That was what Joona meant when he said that Jurek is interested in what's going on inside her, in her inner catacombs.

She needs to exploit that.

Saga repeats to herself that she can't let herself be sucked in, can't let herself be provoked, but she's going to have to let him inside, just a little, to make him feel comfortable enough to reveal something. It's dangerous, but she has no choice.

She succeeded last time, and she's planning to succeed again.

She's going to stick to the truth.

Exchange darkness for darkness.

56

THE ELEVATOR DOORS SLIDE OPEN, AND SAGA STEPS OUT
onto the fourth floor. Three meters in front of her is a glass door
with a sign that says "Ward 4." She can see her own reflection in
the door, but can only just make out the hallway behind it.

A woman's screams cut through the walls.

The elevator doors close behind Saga. The light shrinks to a
narrow strip, then vanishes altogether.

Suddenly she can see the darkened ward through the door.

An old man is standing and looking at her with his nose pressed
against the glass. When she meets his gaze, he turns and hurries
away, dragging a tube along the floor behind him.

She opens the door cautiously and makes sure that it shuts behind her.

The weak light reflects off the gray linoleum floor. A black hand-
rail runs along one wall. The row of sprinklers in the ceiling casts
shadows that look like spiked flowers.

One of the doors on the left is open.

Saga moves forward slowly, trying to see if there's anyone hiding
behind the door. She's getting closer, but just before she gets there
it slams shut with a bang.

A man is talking. It sounds like he's rearranging the furniture.

The next door is also open.

She approaches it warily, each step revealing more of the small
waiting area.

A thin woman is asleep in a wheelchair in the middle of the

room. She has a blue-black mark on the back of one hand from an IV.

Someone's giggling farther along the corridor.

She moves on slowly, glancing at the emergency exit and noting that the door opens outward.

She's spent countless hours in the gym and on shooting ranges, but she knows that Jurek is much stronger than she is. Jurek's fitness comes solely from combat situations, where he had to kill to survive.

She steps over a crutch lying on the floor and continues down the hallway.

There are splashes of red-brown liquid on the scratched skirting board and textured wallpaper. The elevator whirs into motion behind her.

She reaches the unlit staff room. She can hear a beeping sound, some sort of alarm.

"Hello?" Saga says tentatively, and walks through the doorway.

Faint light is coming from one side, illuminating a dining table with a Christmas tablecloth and a bowl of oranges.

She feels a chill rush of adrenaline when she catches sight of the bloody footprints across the L-shaped kitchen.

The fridge is open and beeping. That's where the alarm is coming from.

A pool of blood leads off to the side.

Saga looks at her own reflection in the dark window, and the empty doorway out into the hallway.

She walks around the corner and sees a middle-aged woman lying on the floor behind an overturned chair. The glow from the fridge doesn't reach the woman's face, but Saga can see her dark-blue scrubs and T-shirt. Her laminated name badge glints on her chest.

Saga moves closer and sees that one of the woman's pant legs has ridden up. Her shin has been snapped in two. The jagged bone is sticking through the bloodstained nylon of her socks. The linoleum floor beneath her is covered in blood. Saga repeats to herself that there is nothing she can do: the woman is already dead. If Saga were to rush out to get the National Response Unit here, Jurek would be gone and her father dead.

Saga turns and feels her legs shaking as she walks back out into the hallway. She opens the cabinet on the wall and takes out the heavy fire extinguisher, to have some sort of weapon.

Behind one door comes what sounds like a child crying, but it must be one of the patients, a senile woman with a high voice.

Saga reaches the dayroom, which has an electric Advent candelabra in the window. A large man is sitting on the sofa with his face turned toward the switched-off television.

"You can stop right there and put your hands up," he says in a low voice.

She puts the fire extinguisher down on the floor as he stands up and turns toward her. There's no doubt in her mind that he's the Beaver.

He's big—bigger than she'd expected. He's wearing a crumpled black raincoat, and the pearl earrings are swaying from his earlobes. He's holding a handsaw.

"Saga Bauer?" he says.

He blows his cheeks out, drops the saw on the floor, and walks toward her. The look in his narrow eyes is sad and serious.

"I'm going to check you for weapons, and I want you to stand completely still," he says.

"I assumed I should come unarmed," Saga says.

He stands behind her and starts to run his big hands over her neck, under her arms, down her chest, stomach, and back.

"This is an intimate situation, and I'm not particularly comfortable with it, either," he explains as he starts to feel between her legs and buttocks.

"That's enough," she says.

He doesn't answer, but runs his hands down her thighs and shins, then stands up and checks her hair, before finally asking her to open her mouth and checking inside by the light on his phone.

"Jurek told me not to bother with the other bodily orifices," he says.

"I'm not armed," she repeats.

He starts to walk, and she follows him. Saga can see that he has a fat wallet in his back pocket.

The Beaver shows Saga into a dark room that smells of pipe tobacco and hand sanitizer.

"Jurek will be here shortly," he says, switching the light on.

"Is he your boss?" Saga asks.

"He's more like a strict older brother. I do whatever he tells me to."

Saga walks past the small kitchen area and discovers that there's an old man lying in a bed crying. He has gray hair, thin arms, and a faded nightshirt. A large bandage is hanging loosely from his cheek.

"Where is everyone?" he says, sobbing. "I've been waiting and waiting, but where are Louise and the boys, I'm so alone. . . ."

"Stop whining, Einar," the Beaver says.

"Yes, yes, yes," the old man says, pressing his lips together.

The Beaver takes off his black raincoat, crumples it up, and pushes it behind the radiator.

She thinks about the man in Belarus, and the trail of destruction in the bar on Regerings Street. It's clear that the Beaver has had one of his rages here with the patients. He has wreaked havoc and killed people, but he seems to be calm again.

"I know I don't look it, but I'm more intelligent than most. A hundred seventy on the Wechsler scale."

"Everyone's different," Saga says warily.

The Beaver squints at her, then smiles, revealing crooked front teeth.

"But I'm unique," he says.

"How so?"

"You wouldn't understand."

"Try me."

"I have an allele, a variant gene that means I can incorporate specific mutations. It's like IVF, only natural. . . . I was born with a sort of sixth sense."

"What do you mean?"

"The simple version is that I'm on the precognition spectrum.

Most people don't believe me when I tell them, not that it matters. I have an ability. I know who's going to be the first one to die almost every time I enter a room."

"You know who's going to die first?"

"Yes," he replies seriously.

57

THE BEAVER PURSES HIS LIPS AND CLOSES HIS EYES, AS IF he's trying to see into the future. A few seconds later, he opens his eyes again and nods sadly.

"Einar," he replies, then leans his head back in a silent laugh.

When the old man hears his name, his upper body starts to rock, and he begins to whimper again.

"Can you guess why I wear my pearls?" he asks.

"As a tribute to an important person in your life," she replies.

"Who?"

"Will you tell me where my dad is if I guess right?"

The door opens, and Jurek walks in, wearing the same flannel shirt, work pants, and heavy shoes.

He goes over to the kitchen area and pours a glass of water without so much as looking at them. His prosthetic hits the counter with a dull clang when he turns the faucet off.

"Isn't staying in this place unnecessarily risky?" Saga asks. "Why don't you live in your own home?"

Jurek drinks the water, then rinses the glass.

"I don't have a home," he says.

"I think you have a house," Saga goes on. "But it's probably not completely isolated. You seem to think taking the Beaver there would be a risk."

"A house?" Jurek repeats in a low voice, turning his pale eyes to her.

"Your early childhood was spent in Leninsk," she says. "Near the cosmodrome. Your name was Roman, and you lived in a house with your brother, Igor, and your father."

"Yes, well done," Jurek says dryly. "I had guessed that Joona found the gravel pit by tracking my father's movements."

He looks down at the floor and tries to adjust the straps on the prosthesis.

"But here in Sweden . . . why didn't your brother live with you?" Saga continues.

"He wanted to live at the quarry. He needed to be near Father's things, an environment he recognized—I suppose some places have a sort of magnetic attraction."

The Beaver goes over behind Jurek and tries to adjust the straps under his shirt. The prosthesis seems to have twisted slightly, and he's trying to loosen it.

"Just take it off," Jurek says curtly.

With a calm smile, the Beaver starts to undo the straps across Jurek's back.

"A prosthesis never obeys the way you want it to," the Beaver explains to Saga. "It's almost as if the power relationship is reversed. You start to adapt to its limitations."

He rolls Jurek's flannel shirt up, gently releases the arm's fixture, and pulls it out from the sleeve.

Saga catches a glimpse of the end of the stump before the shirt falls back into place. It's very high up the arm, not far below the shoulder. Cornelia stretched the skin and made sure the stitches and sutures were on the inside of the arm.

The Beaver puts the prosthesis in the sink and ties a knot in the loose sleeve of Jurek's shirt.

"You know there are more modern prostheses?" Saga says.

"I don't really miss the arm anyway," Jurek replies. "It's just a cosmetic issue, an attempt not to attract attention."

Saga looks at the bloodstained plastic hand sticking out of the sink, and the sand trickling from the cup of the arm.

"Why did you put Cornelia's brother in a grave?" she asks.

"Cornelia was threatening to commit suicide, so I took her to the island and made her watch while I buried him."

"But it didn't work," Saga says.

Jurek makes a resigned gesture with his hand, then grabs the knot in the other sleeve.

"I'd have liked to keep her," he says. "But when she realized I'd tracked her daughter down in Fort Lauderdale, she hanged herself. . . . She thought that would save her daughter, but it didn't."

"But you're not really interested in killing people," she says hoarsely.

Those pale eyes focus on her once more, and she holds his gaze without blinking.

"That's a good observation," Jurek says.

The Beaver takes out a frying pan and puts it on the hot plate, then gets eggs, cheese, and bacon from Einar's fridge.

"I don't even think you wanted to kill me before, like you mentioned the last time we met," Saga says, taking a shot in the dark.

"Maybe not," he replies. "Maybe that's the thing about sirens? You don't want them to die—and that's what makes them so dangerous. You know they're going to ruin your life, but, still, the thought that they might disappear is unbearable."

The Beaver turns on the fan above the stove, then starts to melt some butter in the pan.

"Let's go to the dayroom," Jurek says.

They leave the Beaver cooking and go out into the hallway. Jurek calmly pushes a wheelchair out of the way.

"I remember what you said about the first time you killed someone," Saga says as they walk.

"Is that so?"

"You said it was strange . . . like eating something you didn't think was edible."

"Yes."

"So how is it now?"

"Like physical labor."

"Did it ever feel good?" Saga asks tentatively.

"Oh, yes."

"That's hard to imagine," Saga says.

"'Good' might not be the right word, but the first person I killed after Father's suicide . . . it felt calming, like when you've solved a complicated riddle. . . . I hung him up on a spike and told him why it was happening."

"So that was when you explained to him the way you saw things—about how you were going to restore order, or however you put it," Saga says.

Jurek doesn't answer.

They reach the dayroom.

An old woman is standing on the other side of the sofa, poking her cane at the floor in front of her, muttering something, then poking again.

Jurek gestures to a table where there's a small laptop. They walk around the dark aquarium and sit down opposite each other. Jurek's empty shirtsleeve ends up on the table, and he brushes it off with his right hand.

Saga looks over at the old woman behind the sofa and swallows hard. From this angle, she can see that the woman is poking at a severed head with her cane. She doesn't seem to understand what's on the floor in front of her, but is still anxious, as if she can't quite put her finger on what's wrong, and somehow imagines she can set it right by poking at it.

The slowly rolling head belongs to a man in his thirties with a neat black beard. His glasses have fallen off and are lying in the pool of blood.

58

SAGA CAN HEAR THE SOUND OF HER OWN BREATHING. THE dead are beyond help. She will get the police and rescue teams there as soon as she can. She looks at the dark aquarium and tells herself that she can handle this meeting, that she just needs to keep calm.

"Has it ever felt good for you?" Jurek asks.

"Just once—when I shot you," she replies, looking him straight in the eye.

"I like that," Jurek says.

"Because you tricked me into thinking I'd killed my own mother," she says, but then regrets it immediately.

She doesn't want to talk about her mother.

She never wants to talk about her mother; it doesn't do any good.

The old woman catches hold of the glasses with her cane and backs away.

"I just assumed you deliberately let her die," Jurek says, leaning back in his chair. "It would have been perfectly natural, but I was wrong."

"Yes, you were."

"I know you were only eight years old," he continues. "And, in purely legal terms, you had no responsibility for her. But, obviously, you could have saved her."

"You don't know what you're talking about," Saga says, feeling the weight of each breath.

"You're right. I don't know anything about you. I'm not claiming to. I assume you went to school, like all Swedish children."

"Yes."

"Well, are you saying that no one noticed anything? That no one noticed that you sometimes hadn't slept for days, that you came to school with bruises on your face and—"

"Mom never hit me," she interrupts, then purses her lips.

"She was pretty heavy-handed, though? You said you never wanted to take your jacket off because you were ashamed of all the bruises."

Saga tries to smile in an attempt to hide her agitation. Jurek takes nourishment from other people's darkness.

He thinks he can shock her, knock her off balance with his cruelty, but she's already thought about all of this. That's why she keeps that door firmly closed.

"Mom never hit me," she says in a calmer voice.

"I didn't say she did. You survived. It was okay, but you had the ability to save her," he goes on, wiping his hand on the front of his checked shirt.

"I know what you're doing," Saga says.

"All you had to do to save her was to tell someone about your situation," Jurek says slowly. "But for some reason you thought that would be disloyal. And that was what killed her."

"You don't know anything," Saga says.

Her lips are dry, and when she moistens them she can feel her mouth trembling.

He can't possibly know anything. But she remembers the morning she had been awake for three days, and her mom felt better and made pancakes for breakfast. Before Saga went to school, her mom made her promise not to say anything about what had happened that night.

It was a long time ago, and Saga no longer remembers exactly what happened. She just remembers that her mom said Saga would end up in a children's home if she said anything.

She slowly gets up from the chair and turns away.

Maybe it was just a throwaway remark. But if that was the case, why did she say she'd lose custody if Saga said anything?

"I'm not saying you wanted to kill her," Jurek says to her back. "But you didn't save her, and I think that's perfectly understandable, given what she'd done to you."

Saga realizes she's let Jurek inside her head.

She looks up at the simple floral pattern of the wallpaper and tries to compose herself.

It doesn't matter, she tells herself. This is part of the plan—she can handle it.

She knows that the way he mixes the truth with lies gives him the ability to gain access to the catacombs. There's still no danger. She can put a stop to it here. He won't get any deeper now.

Still, she realizes that he's right. Someone at school must have known that things weren't okay at home. She remembers having bruises on her neck and upper arms, and she knows she used to be incredibly tired. They tried to talk to her, of course, took her to see the school nurse and the counselor.

She turns back toward Jurek, clears her throat quietly, then looks him in the eye.

"My mom was bipolar. I loved her, even though it was hard sometimes," she explains calmly.

Jurek runs his hand over the top of the computer. "It isn't inherited," he says.

"No."

"But there are genetic vulnerabilities that increase the risk of a child's having the same condition by ten."

"Genetic vulnerabilities?" she says with a skeptical smile.

"Abnormalities in the configuration of the genes that control how we perceive time. They're supposed to work on a frequency of twenty-four hours, of course, but if they don't, then the risk of bipolar disorder increases."

"I sleep well."

"But I know you have periods of hypomania . . . when you get incredibly focused, think fast, and are easily irritated."

"Are you trying to tell me I'm crazy . . . ?"

Jurek's eyes remain firmly focused on her. "You have a darkness inside you that's almost a match for mine."

"What does your darkness look like?"

"It's dark," he says with the trace of a smile.

"But are you healthy, or are you mentally ill?"

"That depends who you ask."

Jurek stands up and walks over to one of the doors. He listens, glances out into the hallway, then returns to Saga. The empty sleeve swings as he walks.

"Is your brother's illness inherited?" Saga says when he's sitting down again.

"Igor was just downtrodden."

"Why didn't you take care of him?"

"I did. . . ."

"I was in the gravel pit with the forensics team. I looked inside those barracks, went down into the old shelter. I saw everything."

"Nothing escapes Forensics." Jurek sighs and leans back.

"Your brother lived in utter misery," Saga says. "Did you ever go there to make sure he had a hot meal, to sleep under the same roof?"

"Yes."

"You treated him like a dog."

"He was the best dog I ever had."

"And now you want to bury him like a human being?"

He smiles joylessly at her.

"I've requested all the files," she goes on. "But the request needs to be authorized. It'll take a few days."

"I'm not the one in a hurry, am I?"

"You only get the information if I get my dad back," she says, feeling her chin start to tremble. "I know what it sounds like, but the best thing would be for you to let him go immediately."

"You think so?"

"I promise, you'll get all the information relating to your brother's body. But if my dad dies, you won't get anything."

"So don't let him die, then," Jurek says simply.

He opens the laptop and turns the computer toward her.

A video feed is already running.

Saga can see that the other computer is trained on a cramped space with rough concrete walls, lit by a bare bulb hanging from the ceiling.

"What's that supposed to be?" Saga asks, even though she knows the answer.

Black shadows are moving across the concrete wall—as if they were reacting to her voice; then, a moment later, a figure appears off to one side of the screen.

It's her dad.

He's started to grow a white beard. His glasses are gone, and he's squinting in the harsh glare of the bulb. His brown corduroy jacket is dirty and sandy. Something scares him, and he flinches as if he's expecting to be hit.

"Dad," Saga cries. "It's me, Saga."

When he hears her voice, he starts to cry. She can see his mouth moving, but there's no sound. One arm is hanging limply, and there's some dried blood on his face and white shirt.

"Please, don't get upset," she says to the screen.

Her dad approaches the computer. She sees the light of the screen illuminate his face. Trembling, he reaches out with his dirty hand. He tries to say something again, but she still can't hear.

"Dad, listen," she cries. "I'm going to find you, I promise. . . ."

Jurek closes the laptop, then sits and studies her with patient curiosity, as if she were part of an experiment he was running. His pale eyes linger on her face.

"Now the darkness will close around him again," he says calmly.

59

SAGA PULLS THE KEY OUT OF HER APARTMENT DOOR AND hangs it around her neck. She covers the keyhole with duct tape, then tapes over the mail slot and turns around. She repeats to herself that she needs a plan. As soon as she knows what to do, she will talk to her boss, and the ward will be full of police and ambulance staff.

She has a deep crease between her eyebrows, and lack of sleep has left her skin looking almost transparent. The T-shirt under her jacket is wet with sweat around the neck.

She's already searched her apartment. That was the first thing she did when she got home.

She goes into the kitchen and opens one of the drawers. The sheet of paper with the Hasselgården address on it flutters as she walks past.

She takes out two sturdy kitchen knives, goes into the bedroom, and tapes one to the back of the open door.

She and Jurek have met twice now. Maybe she could have killed him on the first occasion if she'd hidden her pistol better, if she'd noticed him entering the apartment.

It's possible that she actually noticed his presence in her sleep that first time, through her eyelids, but dismissed the warning. She's been sleeping with Randy too much; she's no longer as alert as she used to be.

Saga tapes the other knife to the side of the toilet, steps back to check that it can't be seen, then turns out the bathroom light.

Her phone is lying on the dresser in the hall. She hasn't gotten any more messages.

Saga's eyes are burning from lack of sleep. She goes into the living room to get the floor lamp. The wooden floor is covered with her dirty footprints. She puts the lamp in the hall, switches it on, and points it directly at the door, so it will dazzle any intruders.

Thoughts are swirling through her head. Images are tumbling toward her in a torrent.

Her dad's frightened face.

His left eye was wounded, drooping slightly.

He was moving like someone who was dying.

Saga swallows hard and forces herself not to cry. Crying is completely pointless. If she can't sleep, then she needs to make use of her time, concentrate, think.

She sits down in the armchair with her pistol in her hand, the bag of ammunition by her feet.

Saga looks at her phone again, but the screen is still dark. She puts the pistol on the arm of the chair and wipes her sweaty hand on her pants.

She really should try to get some sleep, maybe dig out her morphine pills. That would calm her down.

Jurek isn't likely to contact her again tonight. He thinks she isn't going to be getting any more information about his brother until tomorrow.

She picks up her pistol again and stares at the front door.

There are air bubbles trapped beneath the silvery tape.

She slowly closes her eyes, leans her head back, and sees the light from the floor lamp through her eyelids.

She detects a slight change, and immediately opens her eyes again.

It was nothing.

Saga knows that the Beaver is the one who killed all those patients, probably during a rampage. Jurek doesn't mind killing, but it doesn't excite him.

Jurek probably wanted to frighten her, to remind her how dangerous he is—that he's serious about holding her dad hostage until she comes up with information about his brother's body.

She realizes her hands are shaking when she checks again to make sure that her phone is charged and the volume turned up.

It's five-thirty.

Joona wouldn't be happy with the way she's handling this. He would tell her to kill Jurek the first chance she gets, even if it meant her dad's life.

That's impossible for her. It's not a choice she can make.

Joona would have said that the cost rises every second Jurek's still alive. It doesn't stop until you've lost everything.

Maybe she's wrong, but it feels as if she and Jurek were sitting at a chessboard again. She was trying to lure him out through an opening in her defense.

That was the plan, anyway.

But what was she getting in return?

It must be something. You can't move a piece without leaving a gap.

She feels she missed an important detail, something she brushed past, something that could be pieced together with what she already knows.

Her fatigue is suddenly gone.

Jurek managed to get her to talk about her mother even though she had drawn a sharp line there.

It was strange how easily that happened.

She had felt that she had control over the situation, that she had merely been denying false claims about her mom, and yet she revealed something new—that her mom had been bipolar.

It probably doesn't matter, but it's always a risk to reveal personal information to him.

Sometimes she feels like a butterfly he's trying to catch. But sometimes it's as if he already has her in a glass jar.

Jurek is smart. Every conversation with him is a precarious balancing act.

He fed her a series of false suppositions before claiming that her mom had hurt her.

He was just guessing—but now he knows.

She rubs her face hard with one hand. She has to think.

All her memories of the conversation are growing weaker by the minute.

Jurek sounded cold when he said his twin brother was a dog. That was part of his strategy. He wanted to see how she reacted to his harshness—she's sure of that. But when he talked about different homes, that was probably genuine. He said that some places have a sort of magnetic attraction that draws you back time after time.

"Damn," she mutters, getting out of the armchair.

There was something she'd meant to remember.

But the sight of the dead bodies seemed to erase her ability to think strategically.

Saga glances at the door, then goes into the kitchen, puts her pistol on the counter, and opens the fridge.

She had just let Jurek talk about her mom's bipolar disorder when she asked about his brother.

What did she get in return?

He was almost obligated to give her something.

Saga pulls a cherry tomato from the vine, pops it into her mouth.

She tried to provoke him by saying he hadn't taken care of his sick brother, said she had seen the misery Igor lived in when they searched the old workers' barracks at the gravel pit.

That was when it happened.

Jurek's voice took on an unexpectedly derisive tone when she spoke about the police's forensics team going through every corner of the gravel pit.

Nothing escapes Forensics, he said, seeming to imply that they had actually missed something important.

Saga pulls the Saran Wrap off a plate of leftovers and starts eating with her fingers as she tries to think through the entire conversation again.

Jurek claimed that Joona managed to find his brother after their escape from the cosmodrome in Leninsk because of their father's work at the gravel pit.

She chews cold pasta, swallows, then pops some lemon-garlic chicken into her mouth.

The Beaver was standing behind Jurek, helping him undo the

straps. He spoke about prosthetics, and the fact that you start to adapt to their limitations.

A pointless contempt for weakness, Saga thinks. In her mind's eye, she sees the Beaver putting the prosthetic in the sink. Some sand had trickled out of it.

She saw it, but didn't understand at the time.

Jurek is living out at the gravel pit—that's the only plausible answer.

He's been there the whole time, she realizes.

She puts the empty plate in the sink with trembling fingers and pulls the carton of leftover falafel out of the fridge. She chews quickly, then bites the end off a piece of green pepper.

The gravel pit is the epicenter—the place that exerts a magnetic force on Jurek, she thinks. That's where everything began and ended. That was where their father and Jurek's twin brother died.

When he said nothing escapes Forensics, he meant the exact opposite.

There must be another bunker, one that they didn't find. Maybe it's even farther underground, beneath the ones Forensics has already searched.

Saga can't help grinning to herself.

It could all fit.

She goes through the conversation again as she eats dried-up hummus and carrot sticks. She drinks juice straight from the carton and wipes her sticky fingers on her jeans. She goes over to the table, turns the sheet of paper over, and starts to write down the key points, and what she's discovered, starting with the sand trickling out of the prosthetic.

Jurek hasn't revealed anything obvious. But if she looks at the whole picture, it's possible that he let something slip.

He claimed he'd visited his brother, but there was no trace of him, either in the buildings or down in the bunker.

The perfect hiding place. Jurek knew that the police wouldn't find the hidden room at the pit, because they'd already tried looking with all the resources at their disposal and had concluded nothing else was there.

The concrete wall that had been visible behind her dad could be a part of a Cold War bomb shelter.

And once the connection with her dad had been broken, as Jurek said, "Now the darkness will close around him again."

He didn't say anything about a grave, nothing about digging.

Saga is almost certain her dad is in the gravel pit in Rotebro. She hurries out into the hall and grabs her phone from the dresser.

60

AFTER ENDING A CALL TO HER BOSS, VERNER, SAGA SITS down in the armchair with her phone in her hand, feeling a rush. He had listened carefully to what she had said, only patronized her once, and agreed with her analysis on almost every point.

When she explained the plan she had worked out, he was silent for a few seconds, then gave her the go-ahead to put together a small team. She would have access to officers from the National Response Unit, as well as an experienced sniper.

"I'm shaken up and pretty tired . . . but maybe we can finally put an end to this. Hopefully we can save my dad, and maybe Valeria, too," Saga had said.

She stands up and goes into the kitchen. The sky is getting lighter through the closed curtains.

By the time the police arrived at the care home, Jurek and the Beaver had long since gone, leaving the two bodies behind.

The operation this evening isn't a guaranteed success. She has to keep in mind that she could be completely wrong. Still, right now she feels a huge sense of relief at having a plan at all.

She's going to prepare a trap that can evaporate like mist in a matter of seconds if circumstances change. But with a little bit of luck, she'll be a few seconds ahead of Jurek. They'll be the last seconds of his life.

The plan entails her being in position at the gravel pit with the sniper and rapid-response team when Jurek contacts her with the location and time of their next meeting.

She'll tell him she'll see him there, and if he shows himself, he can be taken out.

Saga opens her laptop again and examines the satellite and drone pictures of the pit. It's a fairly large area, with extreme drops in elevation.

She looks at the long gray block of the workers' barracks, which form a narrow strip between the forest and the pit where sand was extracted.

Beneath them are the bunkers.

She calls her boss again and says she needs another two snipers.

Verner replies that she'll have the whole team at her disposal when the time comes.

Saga puts her laptop and a gold-embroidered sofa pillow in a blue Ikea bag, grabs her *Game of Thrones* mug from the kitchen, and unplugs the floor lamp.

IT'S ALREADY NIGHT BY THE TIME SAGA AND NATHAN POLLOCK approach the meeting point on the narrow road west of Rotebro.

Nathan's phone buzzes with a text message from Veronica. She's sent him a red heart.

"I signed all the papers," he says.

"Good."

"I have no idea why I was being such a pain."

The team is already there. Their black vehicles glint like splashes of ink in the distance.

Nathan turns onto a bumpy road and drives past the wall of the church and some signs warning of military maneuvers.

It's just after midnight. If Jurek follows the same pattern as he has the previous nights, they still have plenty of time before he calls to take up their positions.

Scattered streetlights illuminate the deserted parking lot.

Nathan stays in the car while Saga goes to see the team. She shakes hands with each of the six men from the National Response Unit, their commanding officer, and the forensics officers from the

Security Police. Then she goes over to the three snipers, who are standing a little apart from the others.

Two of them are from the Special Operations Group in Karlsborg, plainclothesmen in their thirties. Linus, tall and blond, holds Saga's gaze for slightly too long when they say hello; Raul has deep scars across his cheeks and hides his mouth with his left hand when he smiles.

Behind them stands Jennifer Larsen, from the Stockholm Police. She's dressed in black, has her brown hair in a thick braid, and has sports tape fastened around her right hand.

"Do you feel like joining us?" Saga says.

"Anywhere you say." Linus smiles.

"Good," Saga says, without smiling back.

"Just tell me who we're going to shoot," Raul says.

"I'm going to need some time to set up my equipment and sort out the ballistics," Jennifer says.

"How long?"

"Twenty minutes should do it."

"You'll have more than half an hour after my briefing."

"Perfect."

The three snipers follow Saga back to the rest of the group. The entire area around the medieval church is quiet.

The reflection of the half-moon looms on the thin ice covering the lake.

So far, Jurek has suggested a new meeting place each time, to avoid potential traps. If Saga is right, and Jurek is hiding out in the gravel pit, her plan might just succeed.

When Jurek contacts her, she's going to claim that she knows where his brother's remains are, but say she needs proof that her dad is still alive before she'll agree to an exchange.

Perfectly reasonable.

What Jurek doesn't know is that they've already got snipers outside his hiding place. The moment he shows himself, one of the snipers will have time to take him out.

The only thing that will happen if she's wrong about his hiding place is that the operation will be called off.

The most dangerous scenario is if the snipers miss or merely injure Jurek and he gets away.

If that happens, the rapid-response team will storm the building.

But if Jurek gets away and her dad isn't there, she'll probably never find out where he is.

And all trust between her and Jurek will be gone.

The same thing is true if Jurek realizes they're there—if perhaps he has some sort of alarm system or hidden-camera surveillance.

But this is her only chance.

Saga gathers her team in a circle, hands out maps of the gravel pit, and carefully goes through the positioning of each sniper. Jurek won't be able to leave the old workers' barracks without finding himself in a line of fire. She shows the rapid-response team which way to go in and where to gather, as well as entry routes for ambulances, and a place for a helicopter to land.

While they talk about the operational tactics, she thinks about how Joona said to ignore the rules and throw caution to the wind when it comes to Jurek. Killing him is the only thing that matters. It's worth any potential consequence.

"So you don't want us to shoot the other one, the tall guy?" Linus asks.

"Not until the prime target has been neutralized."

"Neutralized?"

"You should consider this a hostage situation," Saga explains. She can hear the tension in her voice. "You're not to hesitate, you're not to miss, and you'll only get one chance."

"Okay," Linus says, holding his hands up.

"Listen, everyone . . . let me remove any trace of doubt. Your shot needs to be fatal—that's what I mean by neutralize."

The circle around her falls completely silent. A cold wind is blowing from the churchyard, lifting the frozen leaves from the ground.

"When it comes down to it, this isn't a complex operation," Saga continues in a slightly milder voice. "The various stages are clear. We break it off if anything goes wrong. You've all been briefed. I'll be with Sniper Number One—that's you, Jennifer—and we maintain strict radio silence until the order to proceed is given."

61

THE SNIPERS RETURN TO THEIR CARS AND GET OUT THEIR
rifles, helmets, and camouflage nets. They change into warm, waterproof clothing in the dim light from the two vehicles' trunks.

Saga sees Raul do a little roll of his hips with his hands behind
his neck once he's pulled his pants on.

She goes over to the group from the National Response Unit
to confirm their tactics.

The men are specially trained for hostage situations in which
storming the location is the only option.

"It's possible that the hostage is in bad shape, and a pressure
wave could do serious harm," she says.

"We'll start with welding arcs on the hinges and bolts," the
group leader says.

Saga is about to discuss the use of explosives as a last resort, but
stops when she hears the snipers arguing.

"What the hell are you doing?" Jennifer asks angrily.

Linus looks at his friend with a grin and shakes his head.

"What did you just do?" she asks.

"Nothing," he replies.

Saga sees him calmly zip up his camouflage pants. He has broad
shoulders and is at least a head taller than Jennifer.

"I'm thirty-six years old, and I have two children," Jennifer
says. "I've worked as a police officer for eight years. No one just
pinches another person's nipple. That's a tactic used to humiliate
and exclude women."

"All that matters to us is how good a shot you are," Linus says coldly.

"Listen," Saga says, stopping in front of them. "That was fucking uncalled-for and fucking unprofessional. . . . No, shut up. Jennifer's right. Every woman's had to deal with that shit. No one likes it, so lay the fuck off in the future."

Linus's cheeks are flushed. "So call my boss and get me fired. I'm one of the best, but now that you ladies are ganging up . . ."

"We'll deal with this later," Saga says.

The men check their equipment with sullen looks on their faces. Saga goes over to Jennifer's car and sees that she's mounted a night sight on her rifle and has wrapped four magazines in camouflage tape.

"I need three snipers," Saga says. "There's no time to find a replacement for him."

"Don't worry," Jennifer says, pulling a stray strand of hair from her mouth.

She secures a knife to her belt, above her left hip, then puts her protective vest on and fastens the straps at the side.

"You're going to be lying just over four hundred meters from the target area," Saga says.

"I'll make the necessary adjustments," Jennifer says.

"You handled those idiots well," Saga says in a quieter voice.

"I used to just let it go," Jennifer replies wearily. "I even felt ashamed of it. But now I have way too much going on in my life to put up with that shit. My mom has Alzheimer's, and the rest of my family is already fighting over the inheritance."

"I'm sorry to hear that," Saga says.

"But the worst thing right now is probably that my husband's determined to run the Stockholm Marathon."

"They all have their little projects," Saga replies. "I mean, my guy's got it into his head that he's a photographer."

"Not naked pictures?" Jennifer asks with a wry smile.

"Yes, but *very* artistic." She smiles.

"My husband went through that phase, too. . . . The marathon is much worse. I hope you manage to avoid that one."

Just as Saga is about to reply, her phone buzzes in her hand. She reads the short text message from Jurek: "Lidingö golf club 2am."

She walks slightly away from Jennifer to compose herself. She thinks through her reply, then taps with trembling fingers: "I know where your brother's body is now. Before any exchange I need to see that my dad's okay."

She reads her message twice, takes a deep breath, then clicks send. There's no way back now, she thinks. She's just lied to Jurek, and it's going to be very hard to maintain that lie if anything goes wrong.

While she's waiting for him to reply, she looks out across the fields.

The forest is dark behind the church. The amber-colored lighting on the façade makes the little building shimmer like molten glass.

There's a chance she might be able to fix everything.

Her phone buzzes again. Saga looks at the screen and shivers when she reads: "Make sure you have a laptop handy."

She walks across the parking lot, her heart pounding. She raises her voice so everyone can hear her. "Listen, we heard from the hostage taker. The situation is now live. You know what to do."

62

SAGA IS IN THE LEAD VAN, WHICH IS PARKED ON A FOREST trail on the top of the Stockholm Ridge, approximately one kilometer from the edge of the large gravel pit where she thinks Jurek is hiding out.

She's been sitting there for forty minutes now.

Just to be on the safe side, the forensics officers and team leader have left her alone. They've cleared the inner panel inside the van and have set up a white backdrop. Saga is leaning against it, sitting on her cushion with her laptop on her knees and the *Game of Thrones* mug beside her. The only light comes from the screen and the floor lamp she's brought from her apartment.

If she doesn't move the laptop, it will look like she's sitting at home, in her apartment, when she and Jurek see each other on camera.

She thinks through what she's going to say if Jurek asks her to take the laptop into a particular room. She hopes it will be enough to tell him that the battery's charging, and that they might lose their connection if she moves.

The cars passing by on the highway are almost inaudible, but when an ambulance passes, Saga can hear its siren from the van.

The snipers should be in position now, and the rapid-response team will have split into three pairs in the forest up above.

Saga thinks through the upcoming conversation again. She's going to suggest an immediate exchange, but she can't appear to be in too much of a hurry. Jurek relishes their conversations, the feeling that he's dissecting her soul.

She controls her breathing by feeling the gentle movements of her stomach, and exhaling slowly.

When the incoming Skype call chimes, Saga feels oddly calm, almost as if she's taken sedatives.

She moves her cold fingers over the pad, and clicks to accept the call.

Jurek's face appears on her screen. He's disconcertingly close. She can see the network of wrinkles and scars on his forehead, chin, and one cheek.

Jurek's eyes inspect her calmly.

He's wearing an unbuttoned black hooded raincoat on top of the same checked shirt. One sleeve of the raincoat is hanging empty. She can just make out the shape of the stump beneath the fabric.

"You should have found your dad's car by now," he says.

"I knew it wouldn't lead us anywhere, but I joined the search because it was expected of me," she replies honestly.

Saga hears tired coughing coming from somewhere behind Jurek. He doesn't react to the sound, his pale stare doesn't deviate from her face for a moment.

"I've been thinking about what happened when you found my brother," he says.

"You'd been given a high dose of Cisordinol and happened to mention Leninsk," Saga says.

"No, that . . . You couldn't have understood what I said."

It's impossible to tell if he's feigning surprise, or if he genuinely didn't know that.

"That was how we found you."

He breathes in and leans closer to the screen. Saga forces herself not to look away.

"You know that Joona executed my brother?"

"How do you mean?" she asks quietly.

"According to the postmortem report, he shot Igor in the heart from such close range that the powder from the barrel penetrated his skin."

Saga has read the postmortem report, and knows that Jurek is right, in purely technical terms. There were no witnesses when Igor died, and Joona refused to answer any questions at the obligatory debriefing required when firearms are discharged.

"I know Joona intended to arrest your brother," she says in a steady voice. "Something must have happened, or he wouldn't have fired."

"Why not? People flatter themselves by claiming they adhere to moral codes. But everyone is basically jealous, cowardly, full of hate ... bound by their environment and ready to defend their territory with aggression and destroy other people ... because, in the end, when you're still alive and sitting down to dinner with your family, other people's suffering means nothing."

"I want to see that my dad's okay," Saga whispers.

"I want to see that my brother's okay," he says, turning his computer.

Bare concrete walls flicker past the camera in the top edge of the laptop before it stops on Saga's dad.

He's lying curled up on his side on the concrete floor, next to a blue plastic drum. His bare feet are sandy, and his corduroy jacket is even filthier than the night before.

"Lars-Erik, sit up," Jurek says.

Saga sees her dad curl up, but he makes no effort to sit.

"Sit up now," Jurek says, kicking him gently in the shoulder.

"Sorry, sorry," her dad whimpers, and sits up against the wall, trembling.

He squints into the light, and almost topples over, but puts his hand on the floor to support himself. He has traces of blood under his nostrils, on his cracked lips, and in his white stubble.

Her dad is looking in surprise at Jurek, who turns his back on him and returns to the computer.

"Are you giving him water?" Saga asks.

Jurek sits down in front of the screen again. His pale eyes study her face.

"Why do you care so much about your dad all of a sudden?" he wonders. "A few years ago, you didn't even know if he was alive or dead."

"I've always cared about my dad," she says, swallowing hard.

"And I need to be sure that you're going to let him go if I give you want you want."

"The Beaver will drive Lars-Erik to a gas station, where he'll be given a phone to call you."

"Okay," Saga whispers.

Jurek leans closer to the screen and studies her intently.

"How did you find out where my brother's remains are?" he asks after a pause.

"I can't tell you that," she says. She notices that the laptop has started to tremble on her lap.

The silence between them grows. Jurek very slowly tilts his head to one side without taking his eyes off her.

"How do I know you're not trying to trick me?" he asks calmly.

"Because you wouldn't be asking that question if you thought I was."

Jurek's lips form a thin smile. Saga decides that if she's wrong, if Jurek and her dad aren't here in the gravel pit, then she'll go through with the exchange anyway. She'll lie about knowing where his brother's body is, say it's being stored in a secret cold-storage room at the Karolinska Institute.

Jurek stands up and takes the laptop with him as he leaves the room where her dad's lying. Saga catches a glimpse of a small room with concrete walls before he closes and locks a thick steel door and walks down a dark tunnel.

"We'll soon be finished with each other," he says into the computer. "But I need to see you one last time to find out why someone took Igor's body."

"I promise you'll get your answers," she says. "Should I go to the Lidingö Golf Club now?"

"You'll get a new address," he replies, and ends the call.

63

SAGA QUICKLY PULLS ON HER CAMOUFLAGE GEAR AND BUL-
letproof vest, fastens the holster around her hips, and pulls on her backpack. She takes out a compass, then starts to run through the forest.

Her flashlight illuminates a path across the black ground. She veers around a tree and jumps over some huge roots.

In four hundred meters, she'll have to switch the light off, and then it will be pitch-black.

She counts her steps and turns around, keeping her head down to push through a dense thicket backward. Then she turns around and runs again.

She slows down when she's a hundred meters or so from Jennifer's position. She checks the compass, switches the light off, and ducks under a low pine branch.

She moves forward cautiously, holding one hand out.

To her left, she can see a floodlight in the gravel pit, but it's too far away to be of any use to them.

Her phone buzzes, and she stops, breathing cold air into her lungs. Then she takes it out and reads: "Järfälla ice rink, 3am."

She keeps moving. She can be at the ice rink in fifteen minutes. If she's wrong, or if for some reason they miss Jurek, she'll go there as if nothing has happened.

When the ground starts to slope downward, she slows her pace even more, moving carefully so she doesn't make any noise.

Even though Saga knows where Jennifer is, she still has trouble spotting her. She's cut some branches to give herself some cover, is wearing camouflage gear and a net over her helmet, and is lying on her stomach with her legs wide apart. The barrel of her rifle is sticking through a clump of heather.

Saga approaches at a crouch. Jennifer acknowledges Saga's presence, but doesn't take her eye off the night sight for a second.

It is impossible to see the barracks in the darkened gravel pit four hundred meters away with the naked eye.

Saga can't even see the outline.

Everything is black.

Saga knows there's a fence in front of the pit's ledge, almost fifty meters below the original ground level.

There's a floodlight on a post maybe two kilometers away, but it's little more than a white dot against the black sky.

They're maintaining radio silence until the final order.

Saga lies down on her stomach a short distance from Jennifer. She smells the pine needles and damp earth. She brushes a branch away from her face and takes her night-vision binoculars out.

With them, Saga looks into the darkness and sees a radiant, emerald-green world. Most of the light seems to be coming from the floodlight on the post in the distance. But in its glow, the barracks and broken asphalt are now visible.

This was where they started to extract sand industrially many years ago, and this was where Jurek's father ended up when he fled to Sweden.

The old barracks have been abandoned for years. Some are still almost intact, but others are in ruins, barely more than their foundations are left. Almost all the windows are broken, most of the roofs have collapsed, and piles of bricks lying around have been overgrown.

A crow caws in the distance.

Saga scans the target area, following the line of the buildings and scrutinizing the weeds and piles of scrap and rubble. In the luminous green, everything looks oddly plastic. The shadows make the ground look like the surface of a pool.

In the forest on the other side, she can just make out the other snipers. The lighter circle close to the ground must be the lens of the night sight, which would fit with Linus's position.

Jurek hasn't had time to get out yet, but it won't be long now.

There are no cars parked nearby. Maybe he left one in the industrial park by the highway, or possibly in Rotebro. Either way, he'll have to leave soon if he's going to get to the ice rink in time.

Saga checks to make sure that her pistol is still in its holster, and glances quickly at Jennifer. She can just make out her cheek and one eyebrow in the faint glow of the night sight.

Saga scans the barracks once again through the night-vision binoculars. She checks it piece by piece—the doors, collapsed walls, piles of bricks. The green world is peculiarly lifeless.

She stops.

It looks like there's a candle burning in one of the windows.

She's at the point of breaking her silence when she realizes what she's actually looking at. The floodlight is being reflected in a splinter of glass left in an otherwise shattered window.

She needs to pull herself together. There's no room for mistakes.

She checks the last building in the row—the one that's been almost razed to the ground—before starting again.

It's so quiet that she can hear Jennifer swallow.

Saga doesn't know how the snipers' night sights will react to Jurek's black raincoat. What if he's swallowed by the shadows because of the sharp contrast?

That would make it much harder to get a clean hit.

He's thin and very quick.

They won't have much time.

There's a noise in the forest, a branch breaking.

Saga looks back into the darkness, suddenly worried that Jurek could get out of the quarry through a hidden tunnel.

Maybe she's made a huge mistake. What if she's ruined her chances by being greedy, wanting too much?

Her dad is in bad shape.

Valeria is probably in an even worse condition—if she's still alive.

They've got ambulances waiting nearby.

There are two helicopters in the air. Though they're out of earshot, they're only a minute and a half from the gravel pit.

The moss crunches quietly beneath her as she moves one elbow.

Saga looks at the barracks again, going from door to door, then pans to one side to look at the entrance from Älvsunda Road. Someone's dumped some trash down the slope. The overgrown gravel drive leads to a wire-mesh fence that's supposed to stop people from entering the quarry. A sign with the name of the security company is lying in the grass. The rusting remains of a car are a little farther away. Weeds are growing through the chassis.

Saga looks at the barracks again. Everything is frozen in shades of pistachio and seaweed.

The sifting machines and huge crushers with their conveyer belts are down in the pit, and farther away is the entrance from Norrviken Road, which is where the office and weigh station are.

Jurek must be here, she thinks. He locked a huge steel door behind him when he left her dad. It looked like an old bunker, with a sandy concrete floor.

But there are more than sixty-five thousand bunkers in Sweden. He could be anywhere.

What if she read too much into her observations? But no. She's been through the list hundreds of times, and both Verner and Nathan agreed that the operation was justified.

For some reason, Saga finds herself thinking back to last summer, when she and Pellerina found a dead swallow in the garden in Enskede. Pellerina filled the shallow grave with flowers and wild strawberries before gently laying the bird in it.

A torn sheet of plastic is swaying in one of the doorways.

The wind seems to be getting stronger, whistling through the forest behind them.

Suddenly bright light makes the entire landscape seem blindingly bright. It's as if it was caught in the glare from a soundless explosion.

64

SAGA LOWERS THE BINOCULARS AND SEES THAT A CAR HAS turned in from the main road and is now rolling toward the fence. The headlights sweep across the old paint cans, empty bottles, pieces of old tires, and a white oven with its door hanging open.

The woman in the passenger seat unbuckles her seat belt.

The young man says something.

At first Saga doesn't understand what they're doing. It looks like the woman is trying to climb over the driver's legs. Greasy blond hair hangs over her face. Then she holds on to the steering wheel with one hand and turns around, pulling her dress up over her white backside, and sits astride the man.

This can't be happening, Saga thinks.

They could ruin the entire operation.

Saga checks the barracks again. She sees a darting light out of the corner of her eye, and when she turns quickly back to the car she realizes that the guy is filming them having sex on his phone.

The door of the third barrack has swung open, possibly from the wind.

Jennifer is breathing slowly.

The operation will have to be called off soon.

Light fills the landscape again, turning it radiant white. The car backs out. They're already finished; the windshield is misted up.

Not exactly a feature-length film, Saga thinks to herself as she looks at the window of the building where Jurek's father hanged himself.

Time is running out. They should have seen Jurek by now.

Saga hears Jennifer's breathing speed up, and quickly scans the target area again, but everything looks quiet.

There's a slab of concrete lying on the asphalt. It's cracked in the middle, and Saga can see the rusty reinforcement rods in the gap.

The wind has picked up so much that Jennifer has to adjust the range on her rifle.

Saga looks at the time. She can stay for another four minutes before she has to set off for the ice rink.

The likelihood that Jurek is here has shrunk dramatically.

A large bird moves through the treetops above them.

She tries to see into the dense green darkness behind the barracks, but the outline of the buildings shimmers in the night sight.

It's time for her to leave if she's going to make it to the meeting in time; she knows that, but she keeps scanning the area again, just as rigorously as before.

Piece by piece, she checks Jurek's father's old home. The ragged curtain is swaying in the wind. She's about to move on to the next building when something catches her attention at the end of the row. She pans across to a building that's collapsed completely.

Dark-green light spreads out across the foundations, the remains of one wall, collapsed tiles, and a fallen roof beam.

Saga holds her breath.

The image flickers, and just as it's stabilizing again, she sees movement, just above the ground.

"The far building," Saga says, and hears Jennifer move the barrel of the rifle through the heather.

A thin figure is emerging from underground, step by step.

There must be some stairs there.

"I see him," Jennifer says quietly.

The man straightens up and becomes a thin silhouette against the pale-green glow from the distant floodlight.

Only when he takes a few steps forward is Saga sure it's him. The moss-green shimmer surrounds his outline, but she recognizes the black raincoat and the empty sleeve fluttering in the wind.

"Fire," Saga says over the radio, staring at the flickering image.

He's heading toward the edge of the forest, and will soon be hidden behind the next building.

They've got less than three seconds.

The hood is pulled up, but the raincoat is open. The checked shirt is visible when the wind grabs the loose sleeve.

"Fire," she repeats, just as Jennifer fires her rifle.

Saga sees the shot hit fairly high up on his torso; she's almost certain that the jacketed bullet has passed right through his body.

Jurek takes a small step to one side, then carries on.

The shot echoes off the buildings.

Saga can't breathe; she almost drops her binoculars. She looks over toward the barracks again with her bare eyes, but everything is dark—there's nothing in sight.

She raises the binoculars again, hands shaking. Linus fires from the other direction.

Blood flies out behind Jurek.

He stops.

She can see him clearly.

Jennifer fires again, and hits him right in the middle of his chest. He falls sideways, like a slaughtered animal, and lies absolutely still.

"Target One down, Target One down," Saga reports to the team leader, and gets to her feet.

She drops the binoculars on the ground and rushes through the edge of the forest and down the slope, triggering little avalanches of stones as she goes.

She doesn't care about the risks, about the Beaver. She'll leave that to the rapid-response team.

As she runs, she draws her pistol.

She can't see him now, but keeps telling herself that he must be dead, he must be dead.

Crouching, she runs along the side of the building, pulls her flashlight from her belt, and switches it on. She climbs over an old pallet, then sees the body in the wavering beam.

It's still there.

Crouching to get under a fallen beam, she stumbles, reaches out to the wall for support, and steps over a sodden mattress.

The rapid-response team comes running up behind her. Saga can hear the rustle of their equipment, the thud of their boots, but she doesn't take her eyes off the body for a moment.

He's lying by the remains of the foundations, twisted on one side. Blood has spattered the heap of bricks.

She suddenly imagines that he lifts his head, that his neck strains and the back of his head lifts off the ground, just for a moment.

Her heart is beating fast. The butt of the pistol is slippery in her sweaty hand.

Joona's words about Jurek's being a child soldier flash through her mind. He doesn't care about pain, and will do whatever it takes to survive.

A sheet of plastic billows out, blocking her view.

She stops, holds the flashlight alongside her pistol, and tries to find a line of fire. She sees the reflection off the plastic, catches sight of him on the ground, and fires three shots.

She sees the body jerk with the impact, and feels the recoil against her right shoulder.

She moves forward, holding the plastic back with one hand, and tries to blink away the flare of the shots.

The blasts have rendered her half deaf, and the shots are fizzing like bubble bath in her ears.

A pane of glass cracks beneath her right boot.

She reaches the body and keeps the pistol trained on it as she kicks the lifeless corpse onto its back, only to find herself looking at her dad's face.

She doesn't understand.

It isn't Jurek. It's her dad lying there. They've shot her dad.

He's dead. She's killed him.

The ground lurches and she falls to one knee.

Everything collapses around her.

Saga reaches out her hand, and her fingertips touch his bearded cheek just as everything turns black.

65

SAGA IS SITTING MOTIONLESSLY ON A CHAIR IN THE EMER-gency room of the Karolinska Institute. She still has the blanket from the ambulance around her shoulders.

Nathan Pollock is standing beside her, trying to get her to drink some water.

Her bulletproof vest and backpack were left in the gravel pit, but she's still wearing her camouflage clothing. Her pistol and holster are hidden by the blanket.

She's pale and in a cold sweat. Her forehead is dirty, and her cheeks are streaked with tears. Her lips are pale, her pupils enlarged from shock.

She doesn't answer any of the doctor's questions, and doesn't even seem to notice when he disentangles her arm from the blanket to take her pulse.

Her hand is limp, and there are traces of brown blood under her fingernails.

The doctor straightens up, takes out his phone, and calls one of the duty psychiatrists.

Saga hears what he says about dissociation and amnesia, but she doesn't bother to protest—there's no point.

She just needs to think for a minute.

The doctor leaves them alone, shutting the door behind him.

Nathan crouches down in front of her and tries to smile at Saga's frozen features.

"You heard what he said. You're a victim, and it's perfectly natural to experience guilt about surviving. . . ."

"What?" she mutters.

"It isn't your fault. You're a victim, there was nothing you could have done."

Looking at the scratches and marks on the floor, Saga vaguely remembers yelling that it was her fault when they forced her into the ambulance. She was crying and repeating that Jurek was right, that she hadn't cared whether her dad was dead or alive.

"It was a trap," Nathan says gently, trying to catch her unseeing gaze.

Jurek hadn't made a mistake when he led her to think about the gravel pit. The whole thing had been planned in minute detail. He made sure she saw the sand trickling out of the prosthetic arm.

He probably made up his mind when she tried to reach the pistol in her kitchen. That was when he was sure that she wanted to kill him.

And the game irrevocably changed direction.

Jurek understood precisely how she thought.

He knew what the trap should look like, and how he should lure her into fulfilling his plan.

A checked shirt and a raincoat.

Her dad's collarbone and shoulder were broken, and his arm was strapped tightly to his back, so that the sleeve would hang loose.

Jurek led her dad up the stairs and let him go, while he himself left via a passageway to the pump house at the edge of the forest—he had dug the tunnel beneath the rubble and ruined buildings.

With the help of tracking dogs, the police were able to reconstruct Jurek's passage through the forest and along the edge of the gravel pit to the neighborhood of Smedby.

Saga was slumped on her knees beside her dead father. Time stretched out into a huge, gaping hole. She was no longer aware of the rapid-response team, searching and securing the barracks.

They made their way down the stairs, checked the hallways, and forced open the steel door inside the shelter.

No one was there.

No Jurek, no Beaver, no Valeria.

There were no more bunkers; Forensics hadn't missed anything.

The rapid-response team even drilled into the reinforced cement floor of the bunker, but there was nothing but sand beneath it.

In order to deceive Saga, Jurek had been keeping her dad in the same bunker where his brother had kept the previous victims.

Jurek's real hiding place remains unknown.

The glare of the fluorescent light in the ceiling is falling across Saga's face almost directly from above. There are dry pine needles in her hair. Beads of sweat merge and trickle down her cheek.

A nurse comes in and introduces herself. She asks Nathan to leave them alone, then tells Saga that she's going to give her a sedative to help her sleep.

Nathan gets to his feet and gently squeezes her shoulder before he leaves.

While the nurse prepares the injection, Saga starts to think about eyelids again, and the fact that they're transparent, that you never quite stop being aware.

"I have to . . ."

She stops and slowly stands up, holding the nurse off with one hand as she makes her way out of the room.

She leaves the emergency room with the blanket around her shoulders. She walks out into the cold morning air and leaves the hospital complex.

Saga knows what she has to do, what she should have done a long time ago.

She needs to get Pellerina, leave the country, and go into hiding somewhere.

Karlberg Palace shimmers bright white in the morning mist when she crosses the bridge over the railway line. The hospital blanket falls off in front of the broad flight of steps leading to the palace, but she doesn't notice.

Her gray camouflage clothing is dark with blood on the arms

and chest. She sat with her dad in her arms, pressing his head to her chest, until the paramedics arrived.

She crosses the narrow Ekelund Bridge to reach Stadshagen, then walks along Kungsholms Strand until she gets to P O Hallmans Street.

She rings the doorbell but gets no answer. Just as she's about to ring again, she changes her mind.

She no longer knows what she's doing there.

Pellerina is safer inside the apartment. She isn't in danger.

Really, Saga just wants to hug her, hear her voice, feel her love.

Holding back tears, she takes out her pistol, checks the magazine, and makes sure it's working.

Then she starts to walk toward police headquarters.

She has just one task, and it can't wait. She needs to tap into her steel core, track Jurek down, and kill him.

66

JOONA PUTS THE NIGHT SIGHT DOWN ON THE TABLE AND gazes out across the landscape. There are no lights on at the neighboring farm in the distance, but the sky is starting to brighten slightly on the horizon. The haze in the air catches the light of the town.

It looks like all of Weert is in flames.

On the other side of the dimly lit room, Rinus switches surveillance zones, pulls a chair over to the window, and opens the hatch.

Lumi is standing in front of the monitor.

She hasn't spoken to Joona properly for two days, and isn't looking at him. She responds to direct questions, and her answers are curt.

Joona scans the grass in front of the old bus, then looks across the front wheels, headlights, and windshield and along the flat roof.

The starry sky looks as if it's covered in gauze.

Joona thinks back to their life in Nattavaara, the last time they were in hiding from Jurek. He trained his daughter so she'd be as prepared as possible if the worst happened.

They grew closer.

He remembers the crystal-clear black sky, and how he taught her to navigate by the stars.

In the Northern Hemisphere, you can always get your bearings from the North Star. It's always directly to the north, and doesn't move in relation to the rotation of the Earth like other stars.

"Can you still find the North Star?" he asks.

She doesn't answer.

"Lumi?"

"Yes."

"It's at the end of the Little Dipper; you just have to—"

"I don't care," she says, cutting him off.

He raises the rifle's night sight again and checks his zone, piece by piece. They can't let themselves get complacent.

Yesterday he read in one of the papers about a major police operation outside Stockholm, but there was no indication of what it had been about.

He's lost track of the number of times he's looked for Nathan's message in one of the evening papers: an unconfirmed rumor that a hitherto unknown serial killer has been killed during the course of a police operation.

But no one's printed anything like that, so Joona has to assume that Jurek Walter is still alive.

He has to protect Lumi, but if the Swedish police don't manage to stop Jurek soon, they'll cut back on Valeria's protection.

The current situation isn't sustainable for much longer.

Joona thinks about all the information on Jurek he's looked through over the years. He even had Jurek's father's letters from Leninsk to his family in Novosibirsk translated.

Vadim Levanov was a rocket engineer, extremely interested in space exploration. Joona recalls one letter about George O. Abell, the American who discovered the Medusa Nebula, which forms part of the constellation of Gemini. Back then, it was thought to be the remnants of a supernova, but it was actually a planetary nebula—gas that's been expelled from a red giant at the end of its life.

Joona thinks about the fascination expressed in Vadim Levanov's letter as he explained that the constellation of Gemini would soon change, since a nebula of this type has such a short life—just a million years.

Joona moves to Zone 3, opens the hatch, and looks out at the telephone pole and a stand of trees.

"Dad, you probably did the right thing last time," Lumi says, taking a deep breath. "Jurek had an accomplice—that's why Samuel Mendel's family went missing even though Jurek was being held in isolation. We know that now. And I understand that . . . that you probably saved my life, and Mom's, by cutting all ties with us."

Joona lets her speak as he watches the clump of woodland where the hatch from the hidden tunnel is concealed. A plastic bag has blown in and caught on some brambles.

"But it was still a high price to pay," Lumi goes on. "Mom got used to it, to grieving . . . but her life was put on pause. . . . I was just a child, I adapted, forgot about you."

Joona checks the edge of the patch of trees. The front scoop of a large excavator is lying on the ground. He always spends a long time looking at it, because it would be a good position for a sniper.

"Are you listening?" she asks.

"Yes," he replies, lowering the night sight.

He closes the hatch, turns, and meets her blank gaze in the gloomy room. When her brown hair is hanging over her forehead, she's the spitting image of Summa.

"Sometimes I got teased for not having a dad," she says. "It sounds so old-fashioned, but single moms really weren't that common back then . . . and we didn't have one picture of you. How was I supposed to explain that?"

"It had to be done," Joona replies.

"According to you," she points out.

"Yes."

"Can't you try to understand how this feels for me? You call me and tell me to drop everything and . . . Oh, forget it, there's no point harping on it," she says. "But all this because you've decided that Jurek isn't dead. Maybe you're right this time, too—we don't know—but the situation is very different now. I'm an adult, and I make my own decisions."

"That's right," he says in a low voice.

She leaves the monitor and walks over to him. She stands there with her arms wrapped around herself, and takes a deep breath. "I mean, life isn't just about surviving, it's about living," she says. "I know I've said lots of things—I've been angry. I know you're worried about me, that you're doing this for my sake, and I'm not ungrateful, I'm really not. But I'm not as convinced as you are that Jurek has come back from the dead."

"He has," Joona says.

"Okay, but even apart from that . . . at some point, you have to make a decision—am I going to let fear define me?"

"What if you die? What if he takes you?"

"Then that's just the way it is," she says, meeting his gaze.

"I can't accept that."

She sighs and goes back to the monitor.

Rinus is sitting perfectly still, looking out at his zone through his binoculars. He doesn't understand Swedish, but he would know enough to stay out of this anyway.

Joona opens the hatch for Zone 2 and looks out across the fields toward Eindhoven. The greenhouse is so far away it's like a pinprick of light. He picks up the night sight and stares at it. A luminous golden mirage. Even though he's got the focus adjusted as far as it will go, he can't see if the dark outlines behind the glass are just plants or if there's someone standing there.

He knows he can't force Lumi to stay here. He can try to persuade her, but when it comes down to it, it's her choice.

She'll end up going back to Paris soon, no matter what he says. And before that, someone has to stop Jurek.

Once, when he was a child, Joona was on the island of Oxkangar, in the Finnish archipelago, and the water in the inlet was perfectly smooth. He was walking along the shore, as usual, looking for bottles with messages in them. A duck was floating maybe twenty meters out, a mallard, a brown female with five small ducklings in a nervous little row.

He doesn't know why he's always remembered that.

One of the ducklings fell behind and was attacked by a seagull. The mother returned to the lone chick and chased the larger bird away, but then another gull attacked the rest of the ducklings. Joona yelled and tried to scare the gulls away. The mother flapped back to the four ducklings, but then the first gull attacked the lone duckling and snatched it up in its beak.

The mother rushed back, and the gull dropped the duckling. Its neck was bleeding, and it was squeaking in its high voice. Joona grabbed some stones and tried to throw them at the gulls, but he couldn't reach.

The mother was getting desperate. The second gull was attacking the four ducklings again, pecking at them and trying to catch one. The mother had to give up. She left the lone duckling to save the other four. The first gull turned sharply in the air, dived at the injured duckling, pecked at it, caught it by one tiny wing, and flew away with it.

That's precisely the tactic that Jurek uses.

Joona moves on with his surveillance, opening the hatch of Zone 1 and looking out at the old house and narrow road. Before he has time to raise the night sight, he spots lights, bouncing up and down.

"A vehicle," he says.

Rinus starts systematically checking the other zones while, without a word, Lumi feeds five cartridges into the sniper rifle and passes it to Joona.

He quickly mounts the sight on it, rests it on the window, and watches the car as it comes closer along the narrow road. The headlights bounce in time with the potholes in the asphalt. He can see at least two people through the windshield.

"Two people," he says. They stop in front of the barrier.

The beam of the headlights illuminates most of the road leading to the main house. One door opens, and a woman gets out of the car. She looks around, climbs over the ditch, and takes a few steps into the meadow. She unbuttons her jeans, pushes them and her underwear down around her ankles, then crouches down with her legs apart.

"Just stopped to pee," Joona says, lowering his rifle and removing the sight again, without taking his eyes off the two people.

The second person is still in the car. The glow from the dashboard lights up the end of a nose and a pair of eyebrows.

The woman gets up and zips her jeans, then goes back to the car, leaving a piece of toilet paper on the ground.

Lumi mutters something and goes off toward the kitchen as Joona watches the car reverse out of sight.

When the lights have disappeared, he takes the cartridges out of the rifle and puts the gun back.

Joona walks across the room and goes into the kitchen. Lumi is standing in front of the whirring microwave. It lets out a ping. She opens the door, takes out a plastic mug full of steaming hot noodles, and puts it on the table.

"You're right," Joona says. "I'm scared of Jurek. I'm scared of losing you, and that's exactly what he's exploiting. . . . I've been so certain that the only way to protect you was to disappear, hide—you know all this."

"Dad, I'm just saying that this won't work long-term," she says, sitting down at the table.

"I know, and I understand that, of course I do, but if you agree to stay here for a little longer, I'll go back to Sweden and meet Jurek."

"Why are you saying that?" she asks, trying to swallow her tears.

"This has turned out wrong, I have to admit that. I thought Saga and Nathan would be able to track Jurek down fairly quickly. I mean, he's in one of his active phases, and they've got all the material, plenty of resources, but I have no idea why things haven't gone the way I hoped."

"What are you going to do?"

"I don't know, but I realize I can't run away from this. It's up to me to stop Jurek."

"No."

He looks at her for a while, her lowered gaze, the sad set of her mouth, the hand holding the steaming mug of noodles, the chopsticks on the table.

"It'll be okay," he says almost silently, then goes back through the curtain to the surveillance room.

Rinus has moved his chair to Zone 3. He lowers his binoculars and listens as Joona explains his new plan.

"I trained you, so you'll do a good job," Rinus says in his terse way.

"If I'm still welcome after all this, I'd love to come and visit you and Patrik in the spring."

"As long as you can put up with him calling you Tom of Finland," Rinus says, and, for the first time in several days, the trace of a smile crosses his scarred face.

IT'S DAWN BY THE TIME LUMI WALKS TO THE CAR WITH Joona. The barrier has been opened, and the narrow paved road lies like a thread of silver through the damp meadow.

He looks over toward the main road. Thin veils of mist are hanging over the fields.

Joona's plan is to drive back to the south of France, then catch the first available flight to Stockholm, as quickly as he can, without giving away their hiding place.

They both know that it's high time he got going. Lumi's cheeks are pale and the tip of her nose is red.

"Dad, I'm sorry I've been so awful," she says.

"You haven't been." He smiles.

"Yes, I have."

"You were right. It's good that you didn't back down," he says.

"I didn't mean you should leave immediately, though. We could stay here a little longer—that wouldn't be a problem, would it?" she says, swallowing hard.

He wipes the tears from her cheeks. "Don't be upset. It's going to be okay."

"No, it isn't."

"Lumi."

"Let's stay, please, Dad. We . . ."

Her voice breaks and the words turn into hacking sobs. Joona hugs her, and she holds him tightly.

"I can't bear it," she says.

"Lumi," he whispers to her head, "I love you more than anything, I'm so proud of who you are, and there's nothing I want more than to be part of your life, but I have to do this."

He holds her until she runs out of tears and starts to breathe more calmly.

"I love you, Dad," she says between sniffs.

When they finally let go of each other, reality kicks in again—the narrow road, the waiting car.

Lumi blows her nose. She smiles and does her best to pull herself together. Their breath forms clouds in the cold air.

"Remember, if something happens, none of this is your fault, not in any way whatsoever," Joona says. "It isn't your responsibility. This is my choice, and I'm doing it because I believe it's the right thing to do."

She nods, as he walks around the car and opens the door.

"Come back to me," she says.

He looks her in the eye, then gets in the car.

The engine starts, and the taillights color the road beneath her feet red.

Lumi stands with her hand over her mouth and watches him leave.

The car disappears from sight.

When she can no longer see him, she closes the barrier, pegging it with the rusty bolt, then walks back to the workshop.

67

SABRINA SJÖWALL KNOWS THAT HER JOB IS TO PROTECT PEL-lerina Bauer at all costs. She knows the girl is in serious danger, but it's not up to her to ask questions about the circumstances.

Unquestionably, the most important aspect of witness protection is keeping the address of the safe house a secret. The girl's location isn't mentioned in any lists or reports. Only those directly involved with the operation know where she is.

The apartment is on the ninth floor, and consists of five rooms and a kitchen. It's unnecessarily large for just one child, but sometimes whole families are protected here.

The front door looks exactly like the others in the hallway, but it should, in theory, be able to withstand an attack from a rocket launcher.

The whole setup is designed to feel like ordinary life. The furnishings are simple but pleasant—brown leather sofas, throws, wooden floors, and soft rugs.

It all seems normal, although the world does take on an oddly soft shimmer, thanks to the thermoplastic windows.

Sabrina is dressed in civilian clothing, but she has her Sig Sauer P226 Legion by her hip, and her portable radio unit slung over the left shoulder of her jacket.

She's five foot ten, and has blue eyes and dark-brown hair, which she wears in a braid down her back. She runs every morning, even with her bad knees, goes to the gym, and trains at action shooting.

She's always struggled with her weight, but she's lost four kilos since she stopped eating sweets, back in the summer.

For the past six years, Sabrina has worked in the Personal Protection Unit in Stockholm. She's had more than twenty previous assignments, but this is the first time she's been in this particular apartment.

Being a bodyguard for someone in the witness-protection program is extremely demanding. The social aspects are as important as the technical side of things. You are responsible for your charge's mental health.

Sabrina calls Pellerina, telling her that dinner is ready.

She's piled their plates with fish fingers, rice, peas, and crème fraîche flavored with saffron and tomato.

Pellerina comes running in, wearing her fluffy slippers, and intentionally steps on the threshold of the kitchen door to make it squeak. It could be the tiny brass nails, or maybe the wood is splitting, but for some reason that spot makes a high-pitched squeak whenever you step on it.

Sabrina has never spent any time with someone with Down syndrome before, and she's actually always been unsure of how to act. But Pellerina is wonderful.

It's very obvious that the girl is trying to hide how worried she is about her dad and older sister, but every so often she will tell Sabrina that her dad's a cardiologist, and that sometimes he has to work nights. She used to go to a day care that was open at night, but now Saga stays with her instead. Pellerina spends a lot of time thinking about her missing dad. She worries that he's fallen off his bicycle and broken his leg, and wonders if that's why he hasn't come to get her.

Pellerina eats four fish fingers, but doesn't touch the peas, just arranges them in a circle around the edge of her plate.

"My dad's a hen. I used to have to feed him peas and sweet corn," she says.

Once Sabrina's finished clearing up in the kitchen, it's time for *Swedish Idol* in the living room. Pellerina takes her glasses off and pulls the footstool over to Sabrina. She's the judge, and has to sit on the stool while Pellerina mimes and dances to Ariana Grande songs.

An hour later, it's time for Pellerina to go to bed, after brushing her teeth and getting washed up. Sabrina pulls the curtains in the bedroom. They sway gently, and the rings tinkle on the pole.

"You can still be scared of the dark even though you're twelve," Pellerina says quietly.

"Of course," Sabrina replies, sitting down on Pellerina's bed. "I'm thirty-two, and sometimes I get scared of the dark."

"Me, too," Pellerina whispers, fiddling with Sabrina's silver cross.

Pellerina tells her about the chain e-mail that frightened her: that if you don't send it to more people the clown girls will come and hurt you at night. Sabrina reassures her, and eventually manages to make her laugh. They say good night and agree to keep the door open slightly and leave the bathroom light on.

Sabrina walks across the soft carpet in the living room. She checks that the front door is locked, even though she knows it is.

She doesn't know why she feels so uneasy, but she's got an anxious feeling in the pit of her stomach.

She gets a glass and the large bottle of Coke Zero from the kitchen, and settles down on the living-room sofa to watch a dating show on television.

It's ridiculous, but her face gets hot and she has to take her jacket off.

She fans herself with her hand, then leans back again.

The pale light of the television plays across her slightly sullen-looking features. The shadows of her head and shoulders rise and fall on the wall behind her.

She goes to the kitchen again and makes herself a sandwich at the pine table. She checks Facebook and Instagram, then brushes her teeth.

She's always been struck by her own loneliness when she's on an assignment like this, but it feels worse now, maybe because of the nagging feeling in her stomach.

She's a shy person. Her sister's been trying to get her to try Internet dating. But Sabrina feels she has some sort of need to be alone.

She can't explain it. She often finds socializing exhausting.

Like the time her neighbor invited her out to dinner.

She hopes she evaded the situation without seeming too weird. But that conversation with her neighbor has been bothering her for weeks, to the point where she can hardly bring herself to go out into the stairwell now.

Maybe her shyness is related to her job; maybe she just needs to be alone when she's not working, sleep in her own bed without having to worry about anyone else.

Her mom also takes up a lot of her time, even now that she's moved into an assisted-living facility, where she has her own apartment but has access to a cafeteria, and a shared space for activities.

Her mom has always been a little New Age; it makes her happy, breathes fresh life into her. But since she moved into the facility, she's hooked up with a group of spiritualists.

Sabrina isn't sure what to think about that. Her mom told her she's been in contact with her dead father, Sabrina's grandfather, and that he's very angry. He keeps shouting at everyone, and calling Sabrina's mom a whore.

Sabrina inherited the large silver cross she wears from her grandfather. She isn't really even a Christian, but she always wears it—it's like some sort of protective talisman.

Sabrina has tried to ask her mom who the spiritualists' medium is, but all she's been told is that it's one of the residents.

Mediums usually offer support and comfort. This sounds more like manipulation, some sort of personal attack.

Sabrina feels sorry for her mom, for being tricked into believing that her father is angry with her.

It's very sad.

Three weeks ago, her grandfather apparently told her mother to hang herself.

After that, Sabrina had enough. She said she was going to report the medium and the managers of the home, and that she wasn't going to visit her mother again unless she stopped seeing the spiritualists.

She went back last Sunday anyway.

Her mom had a new wig, with tight light-brown curls down to her shoulders. It didn't look anything like the hair she used to have.

Her mom offered her "afternoon tea," and got out a three-tiered cake stand.

They looked in the old photograph album from when Sabrina was little, then worked their way back in time, to her parents' wedding, then her mom's graduation.

When they came to a black-and-white photograph of her grandfather, her mom didn't want to look any further.

She just clung to the album without saying anything.

Sabrina had never seen that photograph before.

Her grandfather was standing under a ladder that was leaning against a building, with an angry frown on his face. He was wearing a strange, tight-shouldered jacket with the silver cross outside it, and was holding his hat in one hand.

Sabrina tried to get her mom to turn the page, but she didn't want to, just sat there, staring at the picture.

Before Sabrina goes to bed, she does another circuit of the flat, checks on Pellerina, makes sure all the windows are shut and locked, then turns on the monitor so she can see the door to the street and the landing just outside the reinforced door.

There's a stroller parked on the other side of the elevator.

Last night, the doorbell rang, someone down in the street, but there was no one there. Probably someone pressing the wrong button.

Sabrina turns the monitor off, goes into her bedroom, and plugs her phone in. She lies down on the bed fully clothed, with her pistol still in its holster, and switches the light out.

The screen on her phone glows for a while before going dark. Sabrina stares up at the ceiling, closes her eyes, and thinks about the fact that someone's coming to relieve her tomorrow.

68

SABRINA OPENS HER EYES IN THE DARKNESS.

Someone's banging on the apartment door.

She gets up from the bed, wobbles, and reaches out to the wall with one hand.

"What the hell? What time is it, anyway?"

She adjusts the cross around her neck as she walks past Pellerina's room. She crosses the darkened living room, bumping into the footstool with a dull thud.

Her jacket is still lying on the sofa.

There's another knock on the door.

Sabrina scratches her stomach and puts her hand on her holstered pistol as she walks out into the hall.

She turns on the light so she can see the buttons, then switches the monitor on the wall beside the intercom on.

The black-and-white image flickers, then becomes sharper.

It's her mom.

Her mom is standing in the stairwell, banging on the door. She's wearing that weird curly wig and staring into the camera. Her face is visible in the light of the intercom's buttons, but the stairwell behind her is completely dark.

How on earth has her mom found her way here?

And how did she manage to get through the entrance, up the elevator, and find this particular apartment door?

Sabrina swallows hard and presses the button for the microphone.

"Mom, what are you doing here?"

Her mom looks around. She doesn't understand where her daughter's voice is coming from. She bangs on the door again.

"How did you get here?"

Her mom holds up a scrap of paper with the address on it, then puts it back in her purse.

Sabrina tries to understand how this has happened.

"Mom, you need to go home," Sabrina says.

"I hurt myself, I . . ."

When her mom takes a step back, she's almost swallowed up by the darkness in the stairwell. Her face becomes a gray shadow.

She leans into the light again, feels beneath the wig, and shows Sabrina her bloody fingers.

"Oh God, what happened?" Sabrina says, unlocking the door.

Just as she begins opening the door, she looks at her mom in the monitor and sees a thin man stepping quickly out from the darkness. She has started to pull it shut again when someone grabs the handle on the other side. "No one dies," her mom cries. "He promised me that. . . ."

Sabrina braces one hand against the door frame and pulls with all her strength, but the other person is too strong. The gap is slowly getting wider.

She isn't going to be able to hold them back—the handle is already starting to slip out of her sweaty hand.

Sabrina tries to pull the door shut once last time.

Impossible.

She lets go and rushes back into the apartment, stumbling over Pellerina's fluffy slippers and hitting her shoulder against the wall, knocking a framed poster to the floor.

Sabrina runs straight through the dark living room into Pellerina's bedroom. She lifts Pellerina's warm body out of bed, hushes her, then hurries along the hallway, past her own room, and into the bathroom.

She closes the door silently, locks it, and turns the light out.

"Pellerina, you need to be completely silent. Can you do that?"

She can feel the girl shaking.

"Yes," she whispers.

"You need to lie in the bathtub and not look up—we can pretend it's a special bed for you to sleep in," Sabrina says.

She lays some large towels in the bathtub, then lifts the girl over the edge so she can lie down.

"Is it the girls?" Pellerina asks in the darkness.

"Don't worry, I'm going to take care of it. You just try to stay really quiet." Sabrina moves away from the door. She unfastens her holster and draws her pistol, feeds a bullet into the chamber, and releases the safety catch.

"Are you okay, Pellerina? Are you lying down?"

"Yes," the girl whispers.

Sabrina's portable radio is in the jacket she left lying on the sofa last night. She's supposed to keep it with her at all times, so she can always contact the command center.

This wasn't supposed to happen.

She's been careless.

Her phone is lying on the bedside table, in full view. If the man has been in there, he's probably taken it.

She can't believe that she let herself be tricked into opening the door.

She thought her mom was confused—maybe she'd fallen. In any case, she needed help. But someone must have given away the location of the safe house, seen her go in, then traced her mother and fetched her from her assisted housing.

There's a dull clang from the bath when Pellerina moves.

"You have to lie still," Sabrina whispers.

Sabrina thinks about the door handle slipping from her grasp.

Her eyes are slowly getting used to the darkness. Some very faint light from the lamp in the entryway is reaching the bathroom.

The faint glow comes through the strip under the bathroom door. There's just enough light for Sabrina to see that there's someone standing right outside.

69

SABRINA STANDS ABSOLUTELY STILL IN THE DARK BATH-room, staring at the light under the door.

She's breathing as quietly as she can. Sweat is running down her back.

She hears a metallic sound somewhere in the apartment.

The man must be in Pellerina's room. She can hear the rings moving along the rod as he opens the curtains.

Sabrina puts her ear to the bathroom door.

He's searching Pellerina's room. The magnetic lock on the closet clicks as he opens the door, and the empty plastic hangers clatter against each other.

Then footsteps again. It's impossible to tell in which direction they're headed.

Sabrina aims the pistol at the door and moves back. She stares at the unbroken strip of light beneath the door.

Her heart is beating fast.

The man is systematically searching through the apartment. It's only a matter of minutes before he finds them. She needs to get the radio from her jacket, get back to the bathroom, and sound the alarm. If he's not armed with a gun, she can probably hold him off long enough for backup to arrive.

She can tell he's walking through the living room again. The sound of his footsteps vanish as he crosses the rug, then reappears.

He's heading toward the other bedrooms, and possibly the kitchen.

"Wait here," she whispers to Pellerina.

Sabrina hesitates for a moment, then pushes the handle down and carefully inches the door open. She keeps the barrel of the pistol aimed at the crack in the door, her finger resting on the trigger.

Sabrina steps out, sweeps the passageway with the pistol, making sure it's secure.

The heavy silver cross sways between her breasts.

She closes the bathroom door and looks along the dimly lit passageway toward the two bedroom doors and the opening to the living room.

It's quiet.

Sabrina passes the first door and sees that her cell phone is gone. She keeps going, constantly looking between the living room and the other bedroom door.

She stares at the doorway to Pellerina's room and shivers as she passes it.

Slowly, she approaches the living room.

Every door represents a point of danger.

She sticks close to one wall and keeps the pistol aimed in front of her. Now she can see the soft living-room rug and one end of the sofa. Her jacket should be on the other.

Sabrina looks back. The handle of the bathroom door has moved slightly.

She keeps going. She needs to get into the living room.

Everything is silent.

Sabrina bends her arms, holds the pistol in front of her face, and tries to control her breathing.

The threshold of the kitchen door creaks. The man must have stood on it.

She reacts instantly, quickly takes the last few steps along the hallway, and hurries into the dark living room.

She checks around the walls, then sinks to one knee and sweeps the pistol from right to left around the room.

The glow from the light in the entryway reaches across the floor, all the way to the half-closed kitchen door.

Bloody footprints lead in both directions across the parquet floor.

Sabrina stands up, walks around the large sofa, and sees that the radio is still hanging over the left shoulder of her jacket.

Just as she's about to reach out for it, she hears a kitchen chair slam into the table.

He's been here all along.

The kitchen door opens, and Sabrina sinks down behind the sofa.

His footsteps come closer.

She glances at the pistol in her right hand. The barrel is resting on the soft rug.

She's breathing too quickly.

He's in the living room now. His steps are slower on the wooden floor, and fall completely silent when he crosses the rug.

He's only three meters away.

Sabrina tries to shuffle sideways, so he won't see her if he moves toward the bathroom.

Her pulse is thudding in her ears, making it hard to hear what he's doing.

It sounds like he's walked into the footstool.

Now he's approaching the sofa, heading straight for her.

She realizes she's about to be discovered. If he takes just another few steps, he'll see her lying on the floor.

So it has to happen now.

She leaps to her feet, holding the pistol with both hands.

But there's no one there. She sweeps the room with the gun.

He's gone.

With trembling hands, she frees the radio from her jacket and starts to walk back to Pellerina.

It takes just a couple of seconds, but it's still too late: she realizes he was crouching down at the other end of the sofa.

He's right behind her now.

She spins around with the pistol, but her hand is blocked abruptly, and the blade of a knife is thrust up into her armpit.

The pistol falls onto the rug, bounces, then slides across the wooden floor.

The pain in her armpit is so intense that Sabrina can't resist when the man drags her sideways and kicks her legs out from under her.

She falls heavily, and lands across the coffee table. The edge hits her like a blow from a baseball bat. The fruit bowl shatters.

She tumbles onto the floor. Even though she tries to cushion her fall with her hand, she still hits the back of her head on the floor.

The oranges from the fruit bowl are rolling across the rug.

She lets out a gasp and tries to get up.

Warm blood is pulsing from her armpit.

For a minute, she thinks she can hear the waves rolling on the sea, but then she realizes it's just her own breathing.

The man stamps hard on her shoulder and looks at her. His wrinkled face is perfectly calm.

He bends over and moves the heavy silver cross aside so it won't damage the blade, holds her still, then brings the blade down hard between her breasts, through her breastbone, and straight into her heart.

A large wave rolls in and breaks with a hissing sound.

The man stands up.

Sabrina can only see a hazy figure, a thin outline.

He got the knife from the kitchen, didn't even bother to make sure he was armed when he arrived.

She thinks about the photograph of her grandfather standing under the ladder; then the wave washes over her, and everything turns black and cold.

70

ON THE PLANE'S DESCENT INTO STOCKHOLM, JOONA SEES that the country is covered with snow, but the bigger lakes still haven't frozen; their black water contrasts with the white landscape. Fields and patches of forest drift past in leaden colors.

After going through customs, Joona heads to the storage lockers, taps in the code to one of them, and takes out the bag containing his identity papers and the keys to the apartment on Rörstrands Street. He switches back to his true identity and takes a taxi to the long-term parking lot in Lunda Industrial Park.

He pays the fee, gets into the car, and unlocks the glove compartment.

His pistol is still there.

Dusk has already started to fall by the time Joona arrives at the Department of Forensic Medicine. A suspended streetlight is swaying in the wind, its light swinging back and forth across the almost empty parking lot.

Joona gets out of the car and buttons his jacket over his shoulder holster as he strides through the main entrance.

The Needle has just pulled off a pair of disposable gloves when Joona walks into the main pathology lab.

"Are you coming?" Joona asks.

"Are you up to speed, Joona?" Nils replies, dropping the gloves into the bin.

"All I know is that Jurek is still alive. You can tell me the rest in the car."

"Sit down," Nils says in a hoarse voice, pointing to a metal chair.

"I want to get going right now," Joona says impatiently, but stops when he sees the look on the professor's face.

Nils looks at him sadly, then takes a deep breath and starts to tell him about everything that's happened.

Joona listens as Nils tells him that no one believed Jurek Walter was behind the murders because of the recording from Belarus, which showed the man known as the Beaver killing a security guard.

When Nils takes his glasses off and tells him that Valeria was never given protection, Joona slumps heavily onto the chair and covers his face with both hands.

Nils tries to explain that Joona's theory was dismissed because all the evidence seemed to disprove it: the footage, the method, and all the witness statements, which seemed to point to the Beaver as the sole perpetrator.

It wasn't until the churchwarden was found buried that Jurek's name cropped up again. Now they know that it was the churchwarden's sister who took care of Jurek's injuries and amputated his arm.

Joona's face is impassive, and his pale-gray eyes look glassy as he lowers his hands and meets Nils's weary gaze.

"I have to go," he says quietly, but doesn't move.

Nils tells him about what happened in the greenhouse, then at the school. Joona nods slowly as he hears about the circumstances surrounding Saga's father's death.

When Nils tells him that Pellerina is missing and her bodyguard has been murdered, Joona gets to his feet, leaves the room, and hurries for the exit.

Nils catches up with him in the parking lot and gets into the passenger seat as Joona starts the engine.

The winter evening is dismal. The world seems alien to Joona. It feels like the whole world has been abandoned.

During the short drive to police headquarters, Nils tells Joona what little Saga has said about her encounters with Jurek. "She doesn't want to talk, doesn't want to write any reports," Nils explains heavily. "She's blaming herself for everything that's happened."

Wet snow starts to fall as they drive along Klarastrands Road. Their headlights stretch out into oily smears.

Now Jurek has returned from the dead and has taken the people closest to her, as he always does. But he's deviated from his normal pattern, Joona thinks as he listens to Nils.

He tricked her into killing her own father.

That's indescribably cruel.

But Jurek isn't a sadist.

At first Joona wonders if Jurek is behaving differently because he's fascinated by Saga.

Maybe it hurt more than usual when she tried to trick him? Was that why he was taking such brutal revenge?

"No," Joona whispers.

This goes much further than that. Jurek set this entire drama in motion to unbalance her.

No one can defend themselves against Jurek.

They cross Sankt Eriks Bridge and approach Kronoberg Park, and the old Jewish cemetery where Samuel Mendel and his family are buried.

Snow is blowing toward them along the road. Even though they slow down, it feels like they're still moving quickly.

Joona parks outside police headquarters, and he and Nils walk in through the large glass-covered entrance.

They take the elevator up and walk past Joona's old office, knock on the door of the conference room, and walk in.

Saga barely reacts when she sees him. She just looks up briefly, then resumes writing different names on a whiteboard.

"Saga, I'm so sorry, I've just heard—"

"I don't want to talk about it," she says, cutting him off.

Nathan gets up from his computer and shakes hands with Nils and Joona. His face looks ravaged, and he seems to be on the brink of tears. He tries to say something, but stops and covers his mouth with his hand.

Joona turns back toward Saga and sees that she's written the names of everyone who has been found buried, in the order in which they were reported missing.

"Where do you think that's going to lead?" he asks.

"I don't know," she whispers.

"There are plenty of us working on this now," Nathan says. "The chiefs are with us, along with the National Homicide Commission, Forensics, plenty of detectives. Things are heating up. . . ."

"While we're rummaging through the trash," Saga says without looking at them.

"I hear what you're saying," Joona says. "But the four people who know more about Jurek Walter than anyone else are together now in this room."

Saga puts her pen down and looks at him with bloodshot eyes. Her lips are cracked, and her throat and one cheek are covered with yellow bruises.

"It's too late," she says hollowly. "You came back too late."

"Not if we can save your sister and Valeria," he replies.

71

NATHAN HAS ORDERED SOME SALADS, AND THEY EAT WHILE they work. Nils is talking on the phone to a colleague in Odense as he spears pieces of lettuce with a plastic fork.

Joona has dragged the desk lamp over, and it's shining down on the boxes he's going through: water-damaged notes, fuzzy pictures, printouts from the population registry, smudged letters written in pencil in Cyrillic script.

Freezing rain falls against the small windows and runs down the dirty sills.

Saga doesn't touch the food, but she sips at some mineral water as she sends a formal request for reports to the Saint Petersburg police.

Joona clears the table, puts Saga's salad in the fridge, then continues looking through the details of the new investigation. He makes his way along the wall of photographs from the new crime scenes and stops in front of the pictures from the nature reserve in Belarus.

"Jurek leaves nothing to chance, even though it sometimes looks that way," Joona says. "But he's still human, and he makes mistakes.... Some of those mistakes are traps, but others are doors.... I know he's here in the details."

Nathan is still adding new information to the database. After a while, he wonders aloud if it's time to reach out to the media, and plead with Jurek not to harm Pellerina.

No one bothers to argue with him, even though they all know it would be pointless.

Saga goes over to one of the windows and looks out.

"We don't have time to be sad," Joona says.

"Okay," she sighs.

"I understand that this is terrible, but we need you," he says.

"What more can I possibly do?"

"You've spoken to him three times; maybe . . ."

"It won't lead anywhere," she exclaims. "We won't find a damn thing. I thought I had a chance, but I didn't—he was way ahead of me."

"It can sometimes feel like that."

"He makes you believe his lies, he makes you lose your footing," she says, rubbing one eyebrow hard. "I thought I was smarter than this, but I made every mistake I could have."

"He makes mistakes, too," Joona says. "It's possible to read him. . . ."

"No, it isn't."

Nathan gets up from his chair, loosens his tie, and undoes the top button of his shirt. "Joona wants us to try to figure out how Jurek thinks," he says. "So—okay. Every criminal has their own rules, their own system. . . . Jurek had lots of people buried in the same place—Lill-Jans Forest. I mean, why there, of all places? How was he able to remember where all the coffins and barrels were?"

Saga sweeps a heap of reports off of one of the tables.

"This is stupid," she says in a trembling voice. "We aren't the ones making the rules here; why are we even pretending that we are? We're just going to end up doing whatever he says."

"So what's he saying?" Joona asks.

"Just stop!" she interrupts. "All I need to know is where you took Igor's body. That's what he wants. . . . I don't give a damn about anything else, I just want to get Pellerina back. She's terrified of the dark, she's . . ."

"Saga," Joona says. "This isn't about Igor's body. That's a lie, it's just something he said to manipulate you."

"No, it's important to him," she sobs.

"It isn't important. He isn't sentimental or religious. Why would he care about someone's remains?"

Joona knows that Jurek exaggerated his interest in his brother's body because he already knew that Joona had taken it. That was the only reason he said he was prepared to swap Saga's father for his brother.

The idea was that, if Saga started to look for the body, she would realize that Joona had taken it. She'd have to contact him to get her dad back, and thereby reveal where he was hiding.

It was a smart and cruel ploy—a brutal plan—and it would probably have succeeded if Saga had had any idea where he was.

She was just a means to an end, again.

Joona looks at Saga's anguished face and thinks: I'm the one Jurek's obsessed with, and he needed an accomplice to share that obsession. That's why my number was in the German pedophile's phone, that's why the grave robber took Summa's skull. But Jurek chose the Beaver—and there are no limits to what his accomplice is prepared to do.

"But I spoke to Jurek," Saga goes on in a tense voice. "He wants Igor to have a proper burial. I need to be able to tell him where the body is if he calls again."

"He won't call."

"Great, so he's lying about everything," she says quietly.

"Not all of it—that's why you have to tell us about your conversations."

"There's no point. I have a good memory, but Jurek is in a completely different league. He remembers everything I've ever said to him, from the moment we first met. It's crazy—every gesture, every intonation. . . ."

"The first time you met him, he mentioned Leninsk, and that was enough—we stopped him," Joona points out.

"That was just luck."

"No, *you* did that, *you* got him to talk. He wanted to get inside your head, and he happened to give you something he hadn't planned to."

"That's what I thought at the time," she says quietly. "But he tricked me. This whole thing has been one trap after another."

"Did you write down your conversations?"

"I didn't want to," she whispers.

"But you can remember them?"

"Stop it," she mutters, biting her lip.

"I know you can remember everything if you try."

"That's enough," she says.

"Tell us where he lives," Joona says in a sharp voice.

"Who?"

"Jurek."

"If I knew that, I'd—"

"But what do you think?" he interrupts. "You talked to him, you should have some idea. . . ."

"I don't know!" Saga yells.

"Maybe you do," Joona persists.

"Stop it!"

"Just tell us what you—"

"I don't want to! I don't want to. . . ." She is sobbing.

"Saga, I'm going to ask you some questions, and you need to try to answer them."

"I can't deal with any more of this shit right now."

"Of course you can."

"Be gentle with her," Nathan says.

"Shut up," Joona says, and stands in front of Saga. "You talked to Jurek, and I want to know where he's hiding."

"The rest of us will leave," Nils says.

"You're staying," Joona snaps.

Saga is staring at him wide-eyed. Her breathing is labored, as if she's just finished a long run and is exhausted. "I can't bear to think about him, don't you get it?" she says. "He humiliated me. I can't stand myself. . . ."

"Try to think about him anyway," Joona insists.

Saga takes a deep breath and looks down at the floor.

"Okay, fine," she says. "I got the impression he was living in a house, because he reacted when I said that, but it could have been another trap."

"What did you say exactly?"

She raises her head and looks at him with tired blue eyes.

"I said I thought he had a house, and that it probably wasn't all that isolated, because he would have thought it was too risky to let the Beaver live there."

"What did he say to that?"

"He just turned what I'd said back on me and got me to believe he was hiding in the gravel pit. It seemed logical. He tends to live in places that have a special meaning for him."

"Yes, he does," Joona says.

Joona goes over to look at the maps, then bends down and picks up a folder containing ownership registries, rental contracts, and tax payments from one of the boxes.

"Maybe that's because he fled Leninsk, and then was thrown out of Sweden, and had to make his way back here?" Nathan says quietly.

"Jurek never lived in that apartment in Södertälje," Joona says as he leafs through the folder. "There were no personal belongings there, no trace of him. . . . He probably only ever went there to pick up the mail."

"And he didn't live in the gravel pit, either—that was just a lie," Nathan continues. "We've been in with bulldozers. The barracks have been demolished, the whole area dug out. There are no more bunkers."

"But he did live there as a child; we know that much," Joona says thoughtfully.

"Yes," Saga whispers.

"And while he was recovering, he lived with the churchwarden's sister," Nathan reminds them. "Under the name of Andersson— the most common surname in Sweden—just to mess with us," Nathan sighs.

"He's not messing with us," Joona says.

72

THE HOURS PASS, AND THE WORK OF PULLING THE MATERIAL together continues in silence.

Joona blows on his coffee and looks at the map with the locations where the rejected accomplices were found or murdered.

The lights flicker.

He turns to the map of North Djurgården and looks at the pins that mark each individual grave in Lill-Jans Forest and the industrial park.

"How was Jurek able to find the graves in the dark?" Joona asks.

Nathan searches for his reading glasses among the papers on the table, but, as usual, they're perched on his forehead.

"We've tried to figure out coordinates using his system. We've run it through the best programs we have, looking at geometry, trigonometry, prime numbers, all that sort of thing."

"He isn't a mathematician," Joona says, studying the pattern of the graves.

"There is no fucking system," Saga sighs.

"Hold on," Joona says quickly, still staring at the map.

"Look, there's no sense in being stubborn," Saga says. "It's time to retreat. We need to ask the public for help."

Joona moves along the wall. He looks at the pictures from the gravel pit, Cornelia's house, and the apartment in Södertälje.

"Sometimes I understand his way of thinking," he says in a low voice. He feels he's on his way to interpreting the currents, nudging toward the answers.

He goes back to the map of Lill-Jans Forest, and follows the old railroad tracks with his finger, looking again at the locations of the graves.

"Are they randomly placed?" Nils asks.

"It's the twins," Joona says, and starts to pull the pins out.

"What? What do you mean?"

"Gemini, the constellation," Joona says, pulling out more pins. "That's how he remembers where the graves are. Each grave corresponds to a star in the constellation."

Joona pulls out the last pin, takes the map down off the wall, and holds it up to the light, so that it shines through the small holes in the paper.

"Do you remember Jurek's father's letter about the Medusa Nebula?" Joona asks.

"Yes," Nathan says.

"That's part of the same constellation."

Joona puts the map down on the table and draws lines between the tiny holes; the image resembles a cave painting of two people holding hands.

"Gemini—the Twins," Nathan says slowly.

Saga stands behind Nathan as he looks up a photograph of the constellation on his phone and enlarges it. He puts the map over his phone and enlarges the image a bit more. The holes in the map match the stars almost exactly.

"This is crazy." Nathan smiles, looking at the others.

"We took his bishop," Saga mutters.

She sinks onto a chair and runs her hand gently across the table.

"Saga . . . we're still deep in the catacombs together," Joona says. "And it's your move again. Your move."

"Now we know it's possible to understand him," Nathan says hoarsely. "He was following a pattern. . . ."

"An order," Saga says quietly.

"What?" Nathan asks.

She swallows and closes her eyes to help her find the right words. "Morals have no meaning for him, we know that," she says, looking Joona in the eye. "But he does subscribe to a certain sort of order."

"What are you thinking?" Joona asks.

She rubs her forehead hard. "I don't know," she sighs.

"Back up, go back," he says quickly. "What were you thinking when you used the word 'order'? You didn't use that word by accident. What sort of order did you mean?"

She shakes her head, wraps her arms around herself, looks down at the floor, and sits in silence for a while, before she finally speaks.

"When we were in the psychiatric unit, Jurek and I used to talk about what it was like the first time he killed someone," she begins, and looks up.

"He said it was like eating something he didn't think was edible," Joona says.

"Yes, but now, when I talked to him about it again, in the care home, he compared killing to physical labor. . . . He doesn't kill for fun, but I asked him if it had ever felt good."

She falls silent again.

"And it hadn't," Joona says.

Saga meets his gaze. "No, but the first time, the very first person he killed in Sweden after his father's suicide . . . he said it made him calmer, as if he'd solved a riddle. . . . A riddle about how to restore order, I thought . . . because that was when he realized he wasn't just going to kill those who wronged him, he was going to take everything away from them instead."

"Do we know who his first victim in Sweden was?" Nathan asks.

"No," Nils replies. "We still haven't found enough bodies."

"Could . . . could the first victim's name have been Andersson?" Saga asks, wiping her mouth with her hand.

"You're thinking that's why Jurek chose that name?" Joona asks. "That he took his alias from his first victim."

"Just as he had once assumed the name Jurek Walter."

"Good thinking, Saga," Joona says. "Very good."

She nods. There's a feverish look in her eyes now. Nathan starts to search for the name in Jurek's files.

"No Andersson," Nathan whispers in front of the computer.

"Then it's a victim we don't know about," Joona says.

"Come on, we need to think," Saga says, pausing to draw a ragged breath. "When Jurek returns to Sweden after all those years and finds his dad dead, when he realizes that his father had been so lonely he was driven to suicide . . . who's the first person he thinks of, who does he want to destroy?"

"The people who made the decision to separate Jurek and his brother from their father, the officials in the old Immigration Office," the Needle suggests.

"It can't be them. They committed suicide several years later, they're on the list," Joona says.

"So who does he kill first?" Nils asks.

"Maybe the foreman at the pit? That's what I would have done. Check him out—the man who took Jurek and his brother," Saga says, wiping her mouth with the back of her hand again. "I mean, he was the one who started it all. He could have just told their dad to keep his kids under control; that's what a lot of people would have done, and that would have been the end of it."

"Can we figure out his name?" Nathan asks, clicking around on the computer.

"It must be possible," Saga says.

Nils starts searching old reports on his own laptop.

"I know I have the notes somewhere," Joona says, pulling a bunch of notebooks out of a box.

"Jan Andersson," Nils says, looking up from his computer.

"That was the foreman's name?" Saga asks breathlessly.

"Yes, but it's wrong," Nils says. "He wasn't the first victim. . . ."

"What?"

"Because he's alive," Nils says, reading on. "Jan Andersson and his family are still alive; that's why the investigation never picked him up."

"Would Jurek have ignored the man who reported his family to the police?" Nathan wonders skeptically.

"Well, Jan Andersson is retired now. His daughter lives in Trelleborg," Nils continues. "His wife's dead, but his brother's still alive. He has a large family in Lerum."

"I think Jan Andersson has been dead for many years," Joona says slowly.

"What do you mean?" Nils asks.

"Jurek hasn't just taken his name, he's taken his whole identity," Joona says. "That's why it looks like he's still alive."

"You mean Jurek is drawing his pension, paying his bills. . . ."

"Yes."

"In that case, he's probably living in Andersson's house in Stigtorp," Nils says, turning his laptop toward them.

73

VALERIA IS FREEZING ALL THE TIME NOW, AND SHE CAN'T feel her feet. The darkness and silence beneath the floorboards mean that she's also lost all track of time. The pressure sores on her back keep waking her up.

To make her water last as long as possible, she waits until her thirst is almost unbearable before drinking any. Her rationing extends the chances of her being found, but it's also made her weaker.

She tells herself that by now someone must have realized what happened in the greenhouse. They must have seen the blood and the body. Her sons are bound to have contacted the police, and everyone will be looking for her.

Valeria lies still and listens for any sign of life, but soon she dozes off. She's dreaming about a rowboat full of water when she suddenly wakes up to the sound of a girl's voice, very close to her.

"Daddy? Daddy?"

Valeria drinks a little bit of water to get her voice back.

"Daddy? Saga?"

"Hello?" Valeria says, and clears her throat cautiously. "Can you hear me?"

The girl falls silent abruptly.

"My name is Valeria. I'm locked up, too . . . right next to you."

"I'm freezing," the girl says.

"Me, too, I'm really cold, but we're going to get out of here. . . . What's your name?"

"Pellerina Bauer."

"You were calling for Saga—do you know Saga Bauer?"

"Saga's my sister," the girl says. "She's going to rescue me, because she's a police officer."

"Who took you, Pellerina—do you know?"

"No."

"Did you see him?"

"He's old, but quick. . . . Sabrina was taking care of me. I was hiding in the bathtub, and I kept as quiet as a mouse, but he still found me."

"What happened?"

"I don't know. I woke up and it was completely dark. . . . I'm twelve years old, but I'm still a little scared of the dark."

"I was scared of the dark when I was twelve, but you don't have to be scared now, because I'm here, and you can talk to me as much as you want."

Valeria has figured out that the man and woman who gave her the water are dangerous. Jurek must have lied to them, frightened them. They think they're safe as long as they do what he tells them, as long as they hold her captive and keep her in a coffin. But Pellerina is only a child. It's hard to imagine what Jurek might have said to them to make them treat her like this.

TIME PASSES IN THE DARKNESS BENEATH THE HOUSE. THE long hours merge together. Valeria is feverish, and her head aches. Pellerina is chilled to her core, and very thirsty.

All they can do is try to hold on until they're rescued.

At first, Valeria talked about her greenhouses to help calm Pellerina down. She described the different plants, the fruit trees and raspberry bushes. Now she's making up a long story about a girl named Daisy and her puppy.

The puppy has fallen into a hole, and Daisy is looking everywhere for him. Pellerina keeps talking to the dog, trying to comfort him and tell him that the little girl is going to find him soon.

Valeria has determined that Pellerina was in some sort of safe house when Jurek came for her. That means that her disappearance hasn't gone unnoticed. The police know what happened, and presumably are conducting an intensive search for the girl. But time's starting to run out. Valeria can feel her general condition deteriorating rapidly now, and she knows that a child won't last long without water.

She describes how Daisy keeps looking in different places, and finding different clues: the dog's favorite toy, a bone, his collar.

Valeria falls asleep in the middle of the story, but wakes up when someone walks across the floor of the room above them.

There's a scraping sound as the floorboards are lifted.

"Be ready—I'm about to open it," the woman says sharply.

"I'm ready," the man says.

"Shoot if she tries to get out."

Valeria's mind is racing. She hears them loosen the cords around the other coffin. They're afraid of Pellerina, too. What has Jurek told them?

"Okay, open up," the man says.

They nudge the lid open.

"Hold her down," the woman yells.

"I'm trying, I'm trying!" the daughter replies.

"Let me out!" Pellerina is sobbing.

"Hit her!" the mother cries. "Hit her in the face!"

There's a loud slap, and Pellerina starts to whimper in pain.

"Lie still!" the man roars.

"Hello?" Valeria calls out. "What are you doing?"

"Give her the bottle of water."

More thuds, and Pellerina starts crying even louder.

"Calm down, Anna-Lena," the man says.

"For Christ's sake, she was the one who burned him, she was the one who . . ."

"I don't want to be here," Pellerina cries.

"Just drink," the woman snarls.

"I don't want to! I don't want to!" Pellerina cries. "I want to go home to—"

Pellerina gasps as someone slaps her again; then she starts to cough.

"She's bleeding," the daughter whispers.

"Can you hear me?" Valeria calls. "Why are you hurting a child?"

"And you can shut up!" the woman yells.

"Can you tell me why you're keeping a little girl down here?" Valeria asks. "Her name is Pellerina, and—"

"Don't listen to her," the woman interrupts.

Valeria quickly tries to weigh the possible consequences before she speaks, but there's no time to really think things through, and she decides to risk it anyway.

"Pellerina doesn't have anything to do with this. Her dad overdosed, and she's just staying with me until he gets out of rehab."

"We know everything," the man says.

"Good, because I'm not going to make any excuses," Valeria says. "I'm a junkie . . . and I was desperate when it happened."

"What's she saying?" the daughter asks.

"I'm so sorry for what I did, I swear. . . ."

"Shut up!" the woman shouts.

They close the lid of Pellerina's coffin again, and Valeria hears them tighten the cords.

"The man you met—his name is Jurek—he just wants his money. I don't know what he's going to do with me, but that's my own fault. I borrowed a lot of money for smack, and I just took off. . . . I get that you want to punish me, but if you let Pellerina die, you're no fucking better than I am."

"He said we shouldn't listen to them," the teenage girl whispers.

"When the withdrawal kicks in you start to panic. It's like something takes over, you'll do anything for half a gram. . . . I burned him to get money, and his phone. . . . Pellerina doesn't know anything about this."

"He said she burned those letters into Axel's face," the teenage girl says.

"No, it was me, she can't even write. . . . I branded him with those letters so he'd get money from the ATM."

"Shoot her, shoot her through the lid," the woman says, sobbing.

"Calm down," the man says. "We can't; you know what we have to do."

"Give me the rifle," the woman says. "I'm going to shoot her."

"That's enough!" the man roars.

The woman continues crying, and walks away.

"It's cold down here, and we're freezing," Valeria says. "I don't think Jurek wants me to die, because if I die I won't be able to pay back the money I owe him."

"What the hell are we supposed to do?" the man asks.

She hears them start to put the floorboards back over the hole.

"Pellerina's only a child. Her parents are addicts," Valeria says in a stronger voice. "I don't know why you're doing this to her. . . . If you won't let her out, then at least give her some warm clothes and some food."

She starts to cry as the footsteps fade away across the floor and everything goes quiet again.

"Drink some water. I know they were mean to you, but you need to drink," she says into the darkness.

Pellerina doesn't answer.

"Did they hit you with the stick? Pellerina? Were they mean to you? Can you hear me? You know I was lying to them when I said I burned that boy? They seem to think you did it, but we know that wasn't true. It isn't good to tell lies, you're not supposed to, but I did it so they'd let you out. Sometimes you have to say silly things. But I promise you, I've never hurt anyone like that. . . . And neither have you, right?"

"No," the girl whispers.

"But they think we have, that's why they're not letting us go."

74

AFTER A QUICK BRIEFING, THE NATIONAL RESPONSE UNIT team sets out from their base in Solna.

Two black vans and a white command vehicle are now driving quickly past Rinkeby and Tensta, following a black Volvo.

Nils has gone home, but Nathan is in the white minibus with the team's commanding officers.

Joona is driving the first car in the convoy, with Saga sitting next to him. Her eyes are closed. They've both been given direct orders to stay in the background and not take an active part in the operation.

"Saga, how are you doing? Really?" Joona says.

"Fine," she snaps.

"You know I can handle this alone?"

"I have to find my sister," she replies in a subdued voice.

Both Saga and Joona are having trouble believing that they're going to find Jurek in the house, but they still sense that they have some sort of advantage now. Beating Jurek no longer feels absolutely impossible.

Joona has uncovered a vital part of Jurek's system. It looked chaotic or fiendishly complex, but Jurek was actually following a simple pattern: the stars in a constellation that Jurek and his twin brother felt an affinity toward.

It's perfect on every level.

The stars that make up the Twins' heads are called Castor and

Pollux. According to Greek mythology, Castor and Pollux were twin brothers who were raised by the gods.

Only one thing separated them.

Pollux was immortal, but Castor was mortal.

When Castor was killed in battle, Pollux went to Zeus and asked to be allowed to share in death with his brother, so that his brother might in turn be allowed to share his own immortality. The twins take turns, each spending every other day in Hades.

The convoy crosses the bridge at Stäket, passes a soccer field, and takes the exit for Kungsängen.

Saga is holding a map on her lap that has two houses circled in red.

Even though she lost the game of chess against Jurek, she still managed to identify the truths his lies were based on.

Saga understood that Jurek's first murder meant something to his psyche. He got the feeling that there was a way for him to restore justice. She connected that first murder with the anonymous name of Andersson. Joona realized Jurek had adopted his first victim's entire identity.

Nathan managed to track down Jan Andersson's daughter, Karin, who works for Bjurfors Real Estate in Trelleborg. When he contacted her, she said she hadn't spoken to her father in twenty years. He had always been an alcoholic and a loner, but he still sends her a Christmas card every year. That's the only sign that he's alive. She tried to call him at first, but he never answered, and never called her back. Though she sent letters and invited him to christenings and summer parties, he never answered. Eventually, she gave up.

Three of the vehicles turn off in the small village of Brunna, while the fourth continues on to the military base at Granhammar Castle.

The retired foreman Jan Andersson owns two small houses in Stigtorp, just outside Kungsängen. They're set slightly apart from the other houses, but they're not completely isolated.

Many years ago, Jurek murdered him and stole his identity. He draws his pension and pays his bills. This is the identity he uses whenever he has to show any ID or travel abroad.

The frozen ground slopes down toward the water. In the steepest sections, bare rocks stick out from the ground, but otherwise the pine forest is dark and dense.

They stop on a forest trail just north of Stigtorp. Saga stays in the car while Joona goes to talk to the rapid-response team who are going to storm the house.

Twenty meters into the forest is a cliff from which you can see the entire little community, eleven houses in four groups.

A white van is parked on the gravel in front of the three buildings that belong to Hultström's Tractors.

The two houses owned by Jan Andersson are tucked against the edge of the forest.

The rapid-response unit can be down in Stigtorp in less than five minutes.

The officers from the other van have already split up. One group is waiting in a boat out in Garns Bay, and the other is approaching the two houses on foot through the forest.

When Joona reaches the team, the officers are sitting on the ground in their heavy bulletproof vests, chatting among themselves. Their breath forms clouds in the icy air. They're all clutching semiautomatic rifles in their laps. One of them is lying on his back with his eyes closed, as if he were trying to sleep. Another officer is eating some dried fruit. He offers some to the man sitting next to him.

The men need to be able to bounce back and forth between moments of high adrenaline and relaxation.

The group leader, called Thor because of his big beard, has a gentle manner. Joona listens as he gives out orders in a surprisingly soft voice.

"Was I the only one watching the match when the alarm went off?" one of them says.

"It's always the same," another one says with a smile. "The minute you light the grill or take a beer out of the fridge."

"This counts as a party for me," one red-haired officer says.

"Definitely, as long as the bastard's actually in the cottage," the first one says.

"Don't assume this is going to be an easy job," Joona says.

"We've spent years training for this kind of thing, for going in and incapacitating someone who's taken hostages," the man with red hair replies, looking over at Thor.

"I hope that's what's going to happen, but I don't think it will be," Joona says bluntly.

"Come over here," Thor says to him.

They walk behind the black van. The wind carries sounds from the highway.

"What are you doing?" Thor asks gently.

"Jurek Walter is dangerous," Joona replies.

"So we've been told."

"Good," Joona says.

"Anything else?" Thor asks.

"I respect your team; based on everything I've seen, you're good. . . . But Jurek is far more dangerous than you imagine."

"I'll raise that with the team."

"I'd be happy to come with you."

"Thanks, but we'll be okay," Thor says, and pats Joona on the shoulder with a smile. "I mean, we're talking about one, maximum two perpetrators, right?"

Joona looks at one of the officers, who's kneeling down and playing with a police dog.

"Jurek is an elderly man now," Joona says slowly. "But he has more combat experience than you can imagine. . . . He's been a soldier for years, starting when he was a child. He's killed hundreds. . . . It's all he knows."

"Okay," Thor whispers.

"If he is in that house, then most of you are going to die," Joona says, looking him in the eye.

"I certainly hope not," Thor says, without looking away. "But we've already said goodbye to our families."

"I know."

All the officers in the rapid-response unit have recorded videos for their families in case they're killed in service. They're stored back at headquarters.

Thor opens the back door of the van and takes out a box of flash grenades, then responds to a call on the radio from the operational commander.

The other team is in position.

The officers silently get to their feet and put on their balaclavas and helmets. Their semiautomatics swing soundlessly on their leather straps.

75

THOR AND HIS TEAM FOLLOW THE STEEP PATH DOWN
toward the water. The path is covered with pine needles and cones.
Thor can't stop thinking about the tall detective with the Finnish
accent.

Most people tend to be impressed when they meet the rapid-
response team, but Joona had only seen their weaknesses. He
seemed genuinely concerned for their safety.

That annoyed Thor.

And he doesn't usually let himself get annoyed.

In a childish attempt to seem brave, he told Joona that they'd
already said goodbye to their families. But he knows that neither
he nor anyone else on his team is prepared to die. They all avoid
thinking about death, and tell themselves that they take these risks
to help make the world a safer place.

Thor thinks about their brief farewell messages. They were
given templates to help them, so they could prepare in advance
of the recording. The whole situation felt very unnatural, and he
probably sounded strange and detached when he said goodbye to
his mother and his wife, Liza.

He knows he looked into the camera when he addressed Liza.
He spoke slowly, the way you were supposed to. He told her several
times that he loved her, and apologized for letting her down.

It was only when he started talking to his daughter that the tears
came. A chasm opened up, quite unexpectedly. All he felt he could

do was try to explain a little bit about himself, so that she'd have something left of him when she grew up.

The team reaches a junction and turns right where the terrain flattens out. Three hundred meters farther on, the forest opens onto the broad clearing with the scattered group of buildings. Areas of gravel and yellowed grass slope down toward the choppy water.

Thor rests his finger on the grip of his semiautomatic.

He gestures for his team to spread out along the side, staying close to a rusty diesel tank perched on some concrete blocks. The tall, corrugated-metal garage hinders their view as they walk past. Thor swings his rifle quickly around the corner and finds himself looking at a yellow dump truck.

The team moves on. The gravel crunches beneath their heavy boots, and their equipment rattles as they move.

The two houses that Jurek has taken over lie at the far end of the clearing. The front one blocks the second one from sight almost completely. So far, Thor can only make out its tiled roof and satellite dish.

The windows in the first are dark, and reflect the cloudy sky.

Thor's group makes no attempt to conceal their approach.

It doesn't matter if they're spotted, because all possible escape routes are covered. The terrain is rough on almost all sides, with bare rocks and steep drops. The forest along the shore is the only real escape route, and that's where the other team is posted.

Thor's orders are to storm the house, rescue the hostages, and incapacitate the perpetrator.

He has his rifle raised as he marches toward the first building. He keeps his gaze fixed on the house. The plaster has crumbled from the end of the building, revealing the brickwork underneath. There's a grubby lace curtain hanging in the single window.

The dog starts to pant and raises its nose.

"What's wrong?" Thor whispers, moving cautiously sideways across the yard so he can see the other house.

He looks back at the lace curtain.

Did he just spot movement behind it?

His heart starts to beat faster.

He stops and points his rifle at the window.

He's just about to move on when he sees a shadow behind the curtain, a quick flicker in the little room.

He gestures to the team to make them aware that they have a potential hostile ahead.

Thor moves forward slowly; out of the corner of his eye, he sees one officer move off to the left, and another sink down on one knee.

Thor's crosshairs are trained on the window with the peeling wooden frame.

A shadow appears behind the curtain, then a head.

He's about to pull the trigger when he realizes what it is. There's a deer inside the room.

Through the lace curtain, he can see the animal's ears twitch nervously. Its breath billows around its black nose.

He stretches his arm out sideways with his hand clenched, and the team spreads out, divides, and passes the house on both sides.

Suddenly there's a clatter of hooves as the deer turns and rushes out into the forest.

Thor walks around the house and discovers that one wall is completely gone. There are piles of leaves in the corners, and weeds and saplings growing from the open floor.

He trains his rifle on the next house, a red cottage with a sunroom. It's half hidden by trees, as if it's being swallowed by the forest.

The house is neglected, but seems to be intact.

All the windows are covered by dark-blue blinds.

Beside the house is a bare patch of cement that's protected from the wind. Rainwater has frozen into ice in a grill next to the front door, near a plastic chair that's blown over.

They all know what's expected of them. Once the door is forced open, Thor will go in with two of his men.

He presses up against the wall beside the door.

Two of his men are aiming their semiautomatics at the house. Thor pulls on a protective mask and affixes the flashlight to his rifle.

When the team leader gives the final order to storm the building, the windows are shattered by tear-gas grenades. They detonate almost simultaneously, making a deep sucking sound. Shards of glass fall to the ground. The pale smoke filters out past the blinds.

Thor is already sweating.

One of the officers saws the front door open with an angle grinder.

Flash grenades explode in a storm of noise and blinding light.

The door is lifted out, and Thor enters the house.

The light on his rifle picks out a smoke-filled tunnel through the hall and into the kitchen.

Two officers follow him, securing the lines of fire to the sides of the house.

He can already feel the tear gas burning the bare skin not covered by his mask.

After securing the kitchen and the bathroom, Thor approaches the bedroom. The floorboards creak under his weight. He gestures to one of the officers, who steps up and stands beside the door.

He focuses the light from his rifle on the door handle and brass lock.

Thor is breathing faster now, feeling that he can't quite get enough oxygen.

He counts down from three, puts his finger on the trigger, then walks up and kicks the door open. A gray cloud billows out toward him, and for several seconds he can't see a thing.

76

JOONA AND SAGA COME DOWN TO JAN ANDERSSON'S HOUSE
after the operation is over. The National Response Unit is still
searching the rest of the area with the dog.

Everyone knew that the likelihood of taking Jurek by surprise
and incapacitating him was small, but they also knew they had to
conduct the operation immediately, in case they had a chance to
rescue Pellerina and Valeria.

Joona looks inside the first house as he passes. There are sacks of
grass seed and compost on the floor, grill tools hanging on a hook
on the wall, and a rusty bird feeder swaying from the lamp hook.

Thor is standing in the doorway of the larger house with his
protective mask in one hand. His neck is red and his eyes are
streaming.

"We're all still alive," he says in a hoarse voice when he catches
sight of Joona.

"I'm pleased."

"You'll have to put surveillance on this place and call us if he
comes back."

"He won't come back," Joona replies.

"You haven't been inside yet. Are you sure this was his place?
We didn't find anything—no weapons, nothing."

Joona knocks over the charcoal grill. The ice breaks, and black
water runs out. Among the clumps of wet ashes on the grass is a
vacuum-sealed pistol.

Thor's pale-blue eyes stare at the gun.

"How did you know that?"

"Jurek isn't a grilling kind of guy," Joona says, drawing his Colt Combat and releasing the safety catch.

The grill is a good hiding place for a reserve weapon, which is easy to grab if you have to leave quickly. Jurek had moved the grill from the dilapidated house, but he left the cooking utensils behind.

The wind comes straight off the water here, and no one would have a grill right in front of the door: the paved area was more sheltered.

Saga pulls her pistol from her shoulder holster and follows Joona into the house.

The floor in the gloomy hallway creaks. A single military jacket is hanging on a hook, and there's a pair of muddy boots on a rack.

They enter the kitchen. The blinds have been torn down, and a tear-gas canister is lying amid the broken glass on the linoleum floor.

On top of the dirty stove there's a frying pan with a thick layer of grease in it, the color of wax. A coffee cup, a fork, and a clean plate have been left on the table out on the deck.

There are dead flies and wasps along the bottoms of all the windows.

Joona opens the fridge and finds butter and eggs. Saga finds a bag of bread in the pantry and holds it up to the window to check the date.

"Baked yesterday," she says quickly.

Joona goes back out into the entryway. He gently nudges the bathroom door open with the barrel of his pistol. There are several bright-yellow disposable razors on the sink. Next to the faucet is a toothbrush perched in a streaked glass.

Saga goes into the bedroom.

There's a row of photographs on top of a dark wooden chest of drawers.

Jan Andersson's family—his daughter and his wife.

Joona comes in behind her and holsters his pistol as he spots the tear-gas canister in the middle of the unmade bed.

"He's been living here all these years, but he hasn't changed a thing, not one detail," Saga says, opening the closet. "He kept the fridge stocked and hung his clothes in the closet next to Jan Andersson's."

They search the room, even though, deep down, they know they're not going to find anything useful.

There's a Bible in the top drawer of the nightstand, as well as a pair of reading glasses and a bottle of Tums. Joona feels under the drawer and leafs through the Bible.

They spend two hours looking for maps, addresses, anything at all that could lead them to Valeria and Pellerina.

The sense that they're finally closing in on Jurek slowly fades away.

When Joona and Saga walk outside again, the rapid-response team is gone, and everything they found inside the smaller house is neatly lined up on the paved area. Nathan has moved the plastic chair and is sitting in the midst of the sacks and buckets, sheltered from the cold wind.

"They checked all the other buildings, spoke to any neighbors who were home," he says. "Jurek seems to have kept to himself. In all these years, they've only seen him, at a distance, a few times."

Saga walks slowly along the row of lawn mowers, paint cans, and boxes full of old electronics.

"If there's anything that could help us, it should be here," Saga says. "This is his place."

"That's why there are no graves nearby . . . just like there weren't any in the gravel pit," Joona says.

"Home and burial sites are kept separate," Nathan says, nodding.

"Yes," Saga sighs.

"We've got experts examining Jan Andersson's bank account to see if there's a link between purchases and locations," Nathan says.

"We won't find anything. That would be too easy," Joona says, looking toward the dark forest behind them.

"Come on, Pellerina and Valeria have to be somewhere—there must be something that can lead us to them," Saga says.

"We know he used the constellation Gemini to keep track of the coffins in Lill-Jans Forest," Nathan says, thinking out loud. "He's systematic—these locations fit a pattern. We just need to figure out what it is."

"We know him, we're getting closer," Joona says. "He assumed the foreman's identity, called himself Andersson. . . ."

"Because that's when everything changed for him," Saga says.

"But where the hell are the rest of the graves?" Nathan asks.

Saga pulls out her map and unfolds it. The large sheet of paper rustles in the cold wind.

Joona looks at the red circles around the Andersson property, then follows the road leading toward Jakobsberg and the gravel pit in Rotebro.

"He's done it again," he says in a low voice.

"What?" Saga asks.

"The Twins, just on a different scale. This time the constellation is much, much bigger," Joona replies, pointing at the red circles on the map. "This is us, at the place where Jurek lived for years; it corresponds with Pollux, the head of one of the Twins. . . ."

"Slow down," Nathan says.

"Look," Joona says, pointing to the workers' barracks at the gravel pit. "This is Castor, the head of the other twin. And of course this was where Jurek's brother lived. It's the same thing again—he keeps using the same constellation, the same mental picture."

"Like a kind of memory palace," Nathan says.

Joona adds the other stars that make up the constellation, then draws lines between them so the image becomes clearer: twin boys with their heads almost touching, holding hands.

"This star, the gravel pit, that's Igor's head," Joona repeats. "And, at this scale, his left hand is in Lill-Jans Forest in Stockholm."

"Because he was watching over the graves there," Saga whispers.

"These are the coordinates we're looking for," Joona says, pointing at the map. "We have seventeen precise points, and we've already searched three of them. I promise you, Pellerina and Valeria are somewhere among the ones that are left."

77

EMILIA IS WEARING A BLACK KIMONO AND HAS HER RED hair loosely pulled back after showering. She's holding a dog-eared textbook, *Mathematics 3*, that she found on the kitchen table.

Her stepson, Dorian, who's in his last year of high school, is doing his homework in his room with a friend.

The "Do Not Disturb" sign he stole from a hotel has fallen off the handle.

Emilia opens the door and enters the room. There's a pair of boxing gloves on the wall, and she has to step over some clothes on the floor before she turns the corner and the room opens up.

She can hear the sound of waves and heavy sighing.

Dorian and his friend are sitting on the floor with their backs to her. They didn't notice her coming in.

She stops when she realizes they're watching porn on a laptop: the screen shows a blond woman having sex with two men at the same time.

Emilia can't help spying on the boys for a moment. She can just make out their serious faces from her angle behind them and off to one side. Their eyes are open wide, and their pants are tight across their crotches.

The woman in the video is being taken from behind by one man, while the other is using her mouth.

Emilia stares at the young men as they concentrate on the screen, then slowly steps backward, but she accidentally kicks a skateboard with her foot.

Dorian quickly shuts the laptop.

She walks toward them, pretending not to have noticed anything, and tells them they left the textbook in the kitchen. They're clearly both embarrassed, and lean forward to hide their crotches. They thank her for the book and say they're going to keep studying.

"Dorian, what are you two up to?"

"Nothing," he replies quickly.

"I know you're hiding something."

"I'm not."

"Move your hands," she says, in a slightly sterner voice.

Dorian blushes but does what she asks. His jeans are so tight that the zipper in his crotch is clearly visible. Emilia crouches down with an expression of feigned concern on her face.

"What's this?" she asks, and swallows hard.

She runs her hand gently across her stepson's crotch and tries to hide the fact that she's breathing faster as she squeezes his stiffness. His blond friend is staring at them, unable to understand what's going on.

"Can I see?" she asks, running two fingers across the taut denim.

Dorian looks away, undoes the button of his jeans, and has just started to pull the zipper down when the picture freezes.

The director stops the rough cut of the introduction to the scene and closes his computer. He's putting together a first cut because the producer is going to be calling in today to see how things are coming along.

Emilia comes back into the studio from the dressing room in a thick bathrobe. Her heavy mascara has left a line of black dots just below one eyebrow.

She watches as the director puts his reading glasses down next to the computer and says something to Ralf, the cameraman.

They're behind schedule, but Ralf doesn't seem bothered. Emilia has met him many times before. He's over sixty and has been married to the same woman for more than twenty years. His face is tan and slightly puffy. He's wearing a Smiths T-shirt stretched tight across his stomach, washed-out jeans with a brown leather belt, kneepads, and a pair of black Crocs.

Emilia hasn't worked with this director before. He looks stressed. Apparently he's mostly worked on commercials until now.

Swedeep Pictures is a recently established production company that's still looking for its own studio. They're just in an old industrial building with a polished concrete floor. It may have been used as a warehouse by a wholesaler before. Outside, beside the front door, is a weathered metal sign with a picture of a doctor smoking.

It isn't an ideal location for recording, but the rented cameras are decent quality and the scenery looks real enough. It probably came from a genuine television set, borrowed or stolen from some lot somewhere.

They record thirty and sixty seconds of the sex scenes at a time, then have a ten-minute break.

It would be impossible otherwise.

Emilia has spat out her nicotine gum and drunk some water.

They're done with the long oral scenes.

According to the script, first she sucks her stepson off, then moves on to his friend while her stepson licks her.

Now they're going to do vaginal penetration, followed by anal and more oral, then double penetration, and finally cumshots to the face.

Very original, she had muttered to herself during the read-through.

The director and Ralf spent the morning setting up, and when she arrived at eleven, they went through that day's scenes with her. They don't exactly have high standards for her acting, but she still gets directed:

Look at the door, look at him, stretch your wrists.

Smile when you say his dad's at work.

It's always the stepmother who's the dangerous one, just like in the fairy tales.

They usually film using three cameras, except when they're doing the extreme close-ups. Then Ralf uses just one camera with the Steadicam.

The new guy calls himself Dorian. He's only twenty, with short dark hair, green eyes, and tattooed arms.

She checked his medical certificate. It was issued on Monday by the same doctor she goes to.

Dorian was brought in after the original guy was fired on the first day. The producer got angry and dragged him out by the hair, because he was snooping through the things in the closets next to the dressing room.

The producer attended the first day of shooting. He said that they'd been given permission to use the premises by a friend and that they needed to respect that.

Presumably, the friend still has things in the closet next to the women's dressing room. There's no lock on the door, but no one's allowed to go in there—that was one of the conditions.

The friend probably didn't know what his space was being used for.

The producer walked up to all of them in turn, looked them in the eye, and said that the closet was absolutely off limits.

Emilia prefers professional partners, ones who just do their job. The biggest problem with beginners is that they sometimes think it's about sex and make a real effort to get her excited. She's worked with guys who thought she could actually have an orgasm while they were recording.

The chances of that happening aren't particularly high.

Back when she first started, she actually came close a couple of times, when she was performing with her ex. He was the one who got her into the business. Before she met him, she had no self-confidence at all.

But now, although she feels what's going on, and her nerves get stimulated during vaginal intercourse, there's no excitement at all. She doesn't get wet.

It's just about the money.

And at least she gets paid well, unlike the guys. She's never understood why they do it. Being in porn isn't exactly the sort of thing you can brag about.

She does her best to avoid seeing the videos. It makes her feel weird, seeing herself on-screen. She remembers the first time she watched when they were editing and saw a huge, shiny penis slipping inside her.

The same thing, every time.

Emilia has been thinking a lot about an article she read recently on two female directors who make feminist porn. She got curious and considered contacting them, but couldn't pluck up the courage. She was too worried that they would look down on her.

Emilia hangs up the bathrobe and lies down on the bed again. The soccer poster on the wall has fallen off, but it doesn't really matter, since they're about to do the close-ups.

She grabs the plastic tube and squirts more lubricant into her vagina. The makeup artist comes over and wipes away any excess, then applies more powder.

Dorian is standing beside the bed, masturbating to get his erection back. His face shows no emotion as he stands there with his back hunched.

She shivers until the heat from the lamps warms her up.

While she waits for Dorian to be ready, she looks around at the set—the lights, the reflective screens, the soft boxes. She looks at the row of small windows up by the ceiling, and sees a piece of Christmas tinsel hanging from a vent in the wall.

The director and Ralf are waiting in silence. There's nothing to say; they all know what they have to do.

Dorian breaks into a sweat as he masturbates, and the makeup artist goes over and pats his cheeks and chest with more powder.

No fluffers anymore, Emilia thinks. She feels a little sorry for the men, who have to eat tons of Viagra and jerk off to perform.

It's easy enough to fake ejaculation, but they have to get an erection by themselves.

Emilia is careful not to take any responsibility for the guys who have trouble. She tries to stay out of it and does her best to hide her irritation and impatience when they take too long.

But Dorian is sweet and eager to impress.

Earlier that day, he had some trouble. His hands were cold, and he kept shaking and muttering to himself.

"Come on," she says gently to him now.

"It's not going to work," he replies, giving her a pleading look.

"Idiot," the director mutters.

Ralf sighs and adjusts one knee pad.

"Come on, it's okay," she says. "Let's pretend it's just you and me. . . ."

Dorian walks around the bed and lies on top of her; she helps him in and keeps a grip on his semi-erect penis.

"You know, you really have a great cock," she whispers.

"This isn't working," Ralf says, starting to remove the camera from the Steadicam.

Dorian lies down heavily on top of her, his stubble against her cheek, and slowly starts to move his hips.

"It's just you and me here," Emilia whispers.

She can feel his heartbeat start to speed up, and she puts her arms around him, even though that's against her rules. She usually just tries to relax as much as she can, to stop herself from getting tired, and to avoid injuries.

"Don't stop now."

Emilia groans in his ear and feels him growing and getting hard.

"God, this is great," she lies, and catches Ralf's eye.

"Okay, camera rolling," the director says.

"Lie on your side," Ralf says, kneeling down with the camera in front of the bed.

"Keep going, keep going, I'm going to cum soon," she whispers.

"On your side," the director repeats.

Dorian lets out a groan, and she feels him ejaculate, three hard pulses, and his back feels sweaty under her hand. His body relaxes, and he gets heavier, then rolls onto his side and whispers an apology.

"Jesus, this can't be happening." The director sighs wearily.

Emilia lies back. She can't help laughing, but stops immediately when she sees that the heavyset producer has come into the studio.

He's standing just inside the door in a black raincoat. His broad shoulders are dusted with a thin layer of snow. His pearl earring swings.

She goes completely cold when she remembers what she did yesterday. Without looking at the producer, she gets off the bed and puts her bathrobe on. Dorian's semen is trickling down the inside of one of her thighs.

Emilia doesn't know why the order not to look in the forbidden closet had the opposite effect on her. Maybe it's just that she doesn't like being treated like a child.

When Ralf needed a long break to copy the recordings from the memory card, she went into the hallway, past her dressing room, and stopped in front of the metal door. There was just a hole where the lock should be. She was only planning to bend over and look through it, but found herself reaching for the handle and opening the door instead.

She couldn't help it, despite what had happened to her first leading man.

The closet was dark, but she could barely make out something to her left.

There was a dusty smell of freshly sawed wood in the air.

She turned on her phone's flashlight, and its glow trembled across the bare concrete walls.

In the far corner was a dark-blue tarp covering what looked like furniture or boxes.

Emilia could still hear the director talking to the two guys in their dressing room. She hesitated for a moment, then crept farther into the closet.

She grabbed one corner of the tarp, but it was too heavy for her to lift with just one hand.

She put her phone down on the floor. Its cold light shone straight up at the ceiling.

Using both hands, she managed to fold back one corner.

She quickly picked up her phone and aimed the light at it.

It was a coffin made of unpainted plywood, resting on two sawhorses.

On the floor beneath it was a circular saw and some boxes full of nails, brackets, straps, and blocks of veneer.

She crouched down and shone the light farther under the tarp. Next to a row of large blue plastic barrels was another half-finished coffin. This one was clearly made for a child.

78

THE TEMPERATURE OUTSIDE HAS FALLEN TO SIXTEEN degrees Fahrenheit, but the heat inside makes Joona's face flush as he hurries along the hallway. His pistol is knocking against his ribs under his jacket. A flyer about this year's Christmas collection comes loose from the wall and drifts to the floor as he passes.

Carlos is standing beside his aquarium and has just finished feeding his fat goldfish when Joona opens the door.

"No, you have to share," Carlos says, tapping the glass.

Joona called him from the car to tell him that they've cracked Jurek's code, and that there's a chance they can rescue Pellerina and Valeria.

He requested that Carlos immediately put together an operation involving the collective efforts of the Stockholm Police, the National Response Unit, and Special Operations to check out the coordinates of the fourteen remaining stars.

Carlos said that, because this would mean the largest police operation in Swedish history, he would have to organize it via the National Police Authority and get the green light from the Ministry of Justice.

"Have you spoken to them yet?" Joona asks.

Carlos looks away from the fish, sits back down in his chair, and sighs.

"I explained that you'd identified fourteen locations for Jurek Walter. I didn't mention the constellation—I don't think it would have helped."

"Probably not."

"I tried," Carlos says awkwardly. "I stressed how urgent this was, but the justice minister was very clear. He isn't going to authorize any more operations. . . . Hold on, Joona, I know what you think. . . . But try to see it from his point of view. This is about kidnapping, not terrorism."

"But we—"

"There's no obvious threat; the general public aren't in danger," Carlos interrupts.

"Call and say we'll accept a smaller operation focused on eight locations."

Carlos shakes his head. "There aren't going to be any operations at all, not until we have definite proof of where Jurek or his victims are."

Joona gazes out through the window behind Carlos, at the dark treetops in the park, the frosted grass hillocks.

"This isn't good," Joona says in a low voice.

"We've already used the Rapid Response Unit twice this week," Carlos reminds him. "With nothing to show for it."

"I know."

"You have to understand."

"No," Joona replies, looking him in the eye.

Carlos lowers his gaze, runs one hand across the top of his desk, then looks up again.

"I can reinstate you," he says.

"Good," Joona replies, then leaves his boss's office.

He takes the elevator to the tenth floor, and walks to the investigation room.

With the help of their technical experts, Nathan and Saga have put together a precise map with the constellation, using the house in Stigtorp and the workers' barracks in the gravel pit as their starting points. There were only two hundred meters between the twins' heads in Lill-Jans Forest, but this time there are eight thousand meters between the heads, and eighty-six thousand meters from head to foot.

"This version of the constellation is four times the length of Manhattan," Nathan points out.

They pinned the map on the wall next to the photographs of the gravel pit, the stills from the Belarusian security cameras that show the Beaver, and the photos of the various crime scenes.

Jurek's brother, Igor, represents Castor, whose hand corresponds with Lill-Jans Forest. That's where Igor presided over a graveyard modeled on a smaller version of the Gemini constellation. The stomach is located on Ekerö, and the feet are down in Tumba and Södertälje.

Saga takes her jacket from the hook on the wall and pulls out the hat she'd stuffed into one sleeve.

"Print out the exact addresses and coordinates," Joona says.

"We're going to have a meeting with all the teams as soon as we can," Nathan says, standing up from his place at the large table. "I'm going to need at least three command vehicles."

"Actually, we're going to have to handle this on our own," Joona says.

Saga sighs.

"So it's over before we've even started," Nathan says, sinking down in his seat again.

"Nothing's over," Joona says. "The only difference is that we're going to have to search the locations one at a time, just us."

"Fourteen sites," Nathan says.

Saga puts her jacket and hat on the table, grabs the list from the printer, and hands it to Joona.

"You both agree that Pollux in the constellation of Gemini represents Jurek, because the star for Pollux's head is located at his house."

"And the other twin . . ."

"Castor," Joona fills in.

"His head matches Igor's home in the gravel pit," she concludes.

"The interesting thing is that Castor's hand, in the large version of the constellation, is located where we found the graves that Igor was responsible for," Joona says.

"Yes."

"That makes me think that there's a symbolic logic, that these stars are more than just coordinates for Jurek."

"I agree," Saga says.

"And because we need to make a quick decision . . . I think we have to follow that logic, and assume that, now that Igor's dead, Jurek has abandoned the stars that make up Castor."

"Which leaves us with eight locations," Nathan says.

"Take another look at Pollux," Joona says. "Where are Valeria and Pellerina?"

"I'd start with the hands," Saga says.

"One hand is on a building in an industrial park in Järfalla; the other is on a summer house just south of Bro," Nathan says, showing them the map.

"Joona?" Saga says.

"We go to the industrial park," he says. "That marks the spot where the twins are holding hands, as if the dead brother is handing responsibility to watch over the graves to Jurek."

The three of them run out of the room, putting their jackets on as they hurry down the hall.

SAGA AND JOONA ARE IN ONE CAR; NATHAN IS IN ANOTHER. They're following the GPS instructions as they head along Järfalla Road, beside the railroad tracks, into a run-down industrial park.

Trash has blown into the weeds along the tall fence.

They pass low buildings made of concrete and metal sheeting, and paved areas with shipping containers, stacks of pallets, and a row of abandoned trailers.

They slow down and turn right by an auto-repair sign, then pull up in the empty parking lot in front of JC's Car Service. The three of them get out of their cars.

It's very cold. A snowstorm is approaching from Russia, and the Swedish weather service has issued a Level 2 warning.

They pull on their bulletproof vests and check their weapons.

Nathan opens the trunk of his car and takes out a Benelli M4 Super 90, a semiautomatic shotgun used by rapid-response units around the world.

Joona grabs the bag holding the bolt cutters, crowbar, lock-pick gun, and angle grinder.

Saga checks her Glock, then slips it back in her holster.

Nathan wraps his shotgun in a waterproof jacket.

They head out.

The industrial building at 14 Åker Street is owned by an export company registered in Poland; its ownership is unclear.

It's located precisely where the two twins' hands meet when the constellation is superimposed on the map.

There's no one in sight.

The run-down building is tucked behind a tall fence with three rows of barbed wire above it. Immediately below the zinc roof, a band of narrow windows runs the entire length of the building. At one end are a loading bay and a large retractable metal shipping dock. The entrance to number 14 is blocked by a heavy gate that bears the logo of a security company.

Joona puts the canvas bag down, takes out the bolt cutters, and cuts through the lock. When it has clattered to the ground, he kicks the pieces into the ditch, opens the gate, and walks in.

A commuter train passes behind the building, making the bushes by the fence shake.

There's a dented metal ad for Camel cigarettes, featuring a doctor smoking. The rust from the screws has run down over his face.

They stop and listen, but there's no sound from inside the building.

Saga uses the lock-pick gun on the door.

Nathan unwraps his shotgun.

Joona puts the canvas bag full of tools on the ground, draws his pistol, looks his colleagues in the eye, then opens the door and goes in.

He checks the small lobby.

There's nothing there except for an empty coatrack and a fuse box. The main circuit breaker is switched off.

Saga and Nathan stay close behind Joona as he goes over to the next door. Joona can hear Nathan's breathing.

Holding his pistol at eye level, he gets ready to cover the right-hand side of the room, while Saga takes the left, and Nathan the area in front of the door.

Joona carefully presses the handle down, then shoves the door open and points his pistol into the large space.

They count down from three.

The windows up by the roof let in sounds from outside. There are worn patches across the bare cement floor.

Saga follows Joona in, and they systematically check the dark corners.

Nathan walks toward the middle of the room and sweeps the space with the barrel of the shotgun.

It's empty.

Their footsteps echo off the bare walls.

Joona turns around.

On one end of the room is a huge door made up of horizontal metal strips that can be raised up into the roof.

The floor has been scrubbed clean.

There's a piece of tinsel hanging from an air vent, jerking around in the draft.

Without a word, they cross the floor toward a dark hallway, and search two more empty rooms and a bathroom, using the same system as before.

Judging by the marks on the linoleum floor, there were once shower stalls next to the drains in the floor.

The last room is an empty storeroom, littered with sawdust.

They return to the large room. Joona walks to the middle of the floor and turns around, looking at the narrow windows, the blank walls.

"I'll check around the back," Saga says, and heads off.

"Has this place ever had anything to do with Jurek?" Nathan wonders.

"Yes," Joona says in a low voice.

"I mean, the whole idea with the constellation could be wrong," Nathan says.

Joona doesn't answer, just walks over to the retractable door leading to the loading bay. The floor is scratched, the metal threshold buckled.

He follows the black rubber seal with his eyes, then turns back to look at the room again.

Dust particles are floating in the weak sunlight.

The floor is perfectly clean. It hasn't just been swept, it's been scrubbed. Recently, too.

Joona walks over to the drain in the floor. When he kneels down to sniff, he detects a strong smell of bleach.

He removes the grille, pulls out the filter, and sees that it, too, has been cleaned.

Nathan mutters something about going outside, and walks out.

Joona gets to his feet and glances over at the loading bay again, then walks slowly after Nathan.

He stops at the open door to the lobby. This part of the building is darker.

Joona looks at the hinges. He closes the door, then opens it again.

There's a long strand of hair stuck to one of the screws holding the metal threshold in place.

Joona stands right by the wall and inspects the edge of the door.

There are three small ovals, not far from the floor.

At first he thinks they're just knots in the wood that are visible through the paint, but something about the angles of the ovals prompts him to bend over and photograph them, with his phone.

The corner lights up, then goes dark again.

He hears a loud scraping sound outside. Like a bulldozer dragging a scoop across the ground.

Joona enlarges the image on his phone and sees that the ovals are actually bloody fingerprints. Someone has been dragged through this door and tried to hold on here.

He can't see any blood in the lobby, but it looks as if a fitted carpet has recently been removed: fragments of glue are still visible on the cement.

Joona goes out into the cold air and sees a flock of crows circling a white industrial building some distance away. They're focused on a dumpster that's being lifted onto a truck. That's where the noise is coming from.

Saga comes around the corner of the empty building. She shakes her head, and she seems to be holding back tears.

Several of the crows land and start pecking at the ground where the dumpster was.

The truck rolls out through the gates of the HVAC company and turns slowly onto Åker Street.

Joona runs out into the road and stops in the middle of it. He gestures at the driver to stop.

The heavy vehicle comes to a stop with a hiss. The driver rolls his window down and looks out. "What the hell's your problem?" he shouts.

"I'm a detective with the National Operations Unit, and—"

"Did I break any laws?"

"Take the key out of the ignition and throw it on the ground."

"I pay your wages, and—"

"If you don't follow my instructions, I'll shoot your tires out," Joona says, pulling his pistol from its holster.

The keys rattle as they hit the pavement.

"Thanks," Joona says, climbing onto the truck.

He heaves the heavy metal bar aside to open the dumpster, pulls the hatch open, and is met by a terrible stench.

Beneath a pile of old drainpipes, insulation and packaging, damp cardboard, and a broken toilet seat are six black trash bags.

The bottom of the dumpster is covered with blood.

A naked arm is sticking out from a tear in one of the bags. It's been broken at the elbow, and is dark with internal bleeding.

The hand is small, but not small enough to be a child's.

The six trash bags are large enough to contain a body each.

Six people killed at the place where the twins hold hands.

The building was scrubbed clean, and the bodies dropped in a dumpster.

Joona pulls out his cell phone and calls The Needle. While the call goes through, he looks down into the dumpster again, staring at the broken elbow and the odd angle of the lower arm. He thinks about the bloody fingerprints on the door frame. When he looks at the pale hand resting on the black plastic again, he sees that two of the fingers are moving.

79

VALERIA WAKES UP IN THE DARKNESS WITH A SPLITTING headache. They've put some thick socks on her feet, and laid a blanket over her. Still, she's so cold that she's shaking.

"Pellerina? Are you cold?"

Valeria fumbles for the water bottle, unscrews the cap, and drinks the last drops.

"Pellerina?" she says, louder this time. "Are you there?"

When the girl doesn't answer, Valeria's smile is so wide that her dry lips crack. They've brought Pellerina into the house. That must be what has happened. Valeria has been given a blanket, so, clearly, at least they listened to some part of her plea. She was taking a risk when she pretended to be a drug addict—it could have gone terribly wrong.

She still doesn't know what they think she did, but if she had told them the truth and denied everything, they'd never have listened to her.

Valeria did her best to make her story sound plausible by using her experience as an addict. She's sure they had already noticed the ugly scars on her arms. She has never tried to hide them, because she thinks she deserves the contempt they sometimes prompt in other people.

Her own sense of shame is so much worse.

The family had probably already been having trouble believing that Pellerina was involved. When Valeria confessed that they were both being punished for her own drug debts, things seemed clearer to them.

The last time they removed the floorboards and opened the coffin, she had sat up, even though they were yelling at her to stay down, calling her a junkie whore and saying they were going to shoot her in the head.

"Do it, then," she had replied. "Then you'll be responsible for my debts to Jurek."

"Just shut up!" the woman had said.

"I need you to know that I'm sorry for everything I—"

"You want us to forgive you?" the man interrupted. "Is that it? You're scum, you're not even human."

"Stop talking to her," the woman whispered.

"I didn't want to do bad things," Valeria said. "It was just that I couldn't borrow any more, and the withdrawal kicked in, and I was just so desperate. . . . I never worried about AIDS or overdosing, or even about getting beaten up or raped . . . but withdrawal terrified me. It's like being in hell."

"I hope you're there now," the man says.

"It's really cold, I can't feel my legs anymore. . . . I don't think I can survive another night. . . ."

"That's not our problem," the woman said, weighing the ax in her hands.

"Did Jurek tell you to kill us?"

"We're just guarding you," the man replied.

"We're not supposed to talk to her," the teenage girl blurted out.

"I don't want to frighten Pellerina," Valeria had said, "but she's small. She'll freeze to death soon—you understand that, don't you?"

"Lie back down," the man said, taking a step toward her and raising the rifle.

He was so close she could see the blond hair on his arms.

"I mean, you could take us into the house. I'm so weak I probably can't even stand up at this point. Just tie me up. You're armed, after all. . . ."

They threw a bag of food scraps into the coffin, forced the lid down again, and tightened the straps.

Valeria's fingers were too weak to untie the knot, so she had to rip the bag open with her teeth.

She ate some of the boiled potatoes and sausage and almost threw up, but concentrated on keeping the food down.

Her stomach warmed up, and her thoughts drifted off. She realized that the food was drugged, and they were either sedating or killing her.

She had a short dream about a pink hummingbird and a beautiful Chinese tapestry moving in the wind, before she jerked awake and opened her eyes in the darkness.

The seal around the lid of the coffin started to glow white and blue. She thought she could hear the straps falling onto the dry earth beneath the house and the clatter of a winch.

In her drugged state, she thought that they were opening Pellerina's coffin. She thought she could hear her crying as they lifted her up into the house.

Valeria has no idea how long she's been unconscious.

It feels like at least a day.

Her head aches and her mouth is dry.

She realizes that they drugged her so that they could put more clothes on her. They must have believed her story.

Pellerina isn't down here with her anymore. Maybe they even let her go. Now Valeria has to try to save herself. She'll try to turn her story against Jurek, and get them to understand that he was using her.

80

SAGA WASHES HER FACE IN THE SINK IN THE BATHROOM OF the intensive-care unit on the fourth floor of the Karolinska Hospital.

Once again, she tells herself that she needs to pull it together. But the tears well up again, and she has to sit down on the toilet and try to breathe slowly.

"I can do this," she whispers.

She had been around at the back of the industrial building when she heard Joona shout that he'd found something in a dumpster.

It was as if she'd fallen through the ice on a lake and was sinking through the freezing water. The sudden fear was like an immense, all-encompassing wave of fatigue. She wanted to give in, lie down on the ground, and stop time.

But she clung to the low fence at the railroad embankment.

And when she heard Joona say that one of them was still alive, she began to walk, as if through deep sand.

She didn't notice her bag falling to the ground. It must have just slid off her shoulder.

All she could think was that she should have let Jurek kill her.

It was all her fault.

Black crows were perched on the ground.

Saga walked around the corner and stepped out onto the road. She saw the garbage truck, and could just make out the driver through the windshield.

Joona was shouting something; Nathan turned and walked toward her, holding his hands up to keep her calm and stop her from getting any closer.

"My sister," she mumbled, trying to get past him.

"Please, just wait, you have to . . ."

"Who's still alive?"

"I don't know, but the ambulance is on its way, and . . ."

"Pellerina!" she cried.

Now she thinks back to how Nathan stopped her from going there. She ended up sitting in Joona's car, a few hundred meters away, shivering.

Three police cars and six ambulances arrived.

Their blue lights flew across the buildings, casting quick shadows along the pavement.

She watched through the car's windshield as the paramedics did their work.

At first, the activity around the truck was frenetic.

But everyone except the naked woman was dead. Saga could tell from the way they were handling the bodies.

There were three people standing in the dumpster, cutting the trash bags open and lifting body after body out.

Saga tried to see if any of the bodies looked like a child's, but she was too far away, and her view was obscured. One ambulance backed away, and uniformed officers cordoned off the area.

She didn't manage to catch a glimpse of the bodies until they were lined up on the ground. Then she saw a narrow leg hit the rusty edge of the dumpster, and a black trash bag stuck to a heavyset man's back.

The first ambulance left the area, taking the woman away. She heard the sirens start to blare as it pulled out onto Järfalla Road.

Saga couldn't tell if Valeria or Pellerina were among the dead.

She opened the car door and got out. She didn't want to go, but she had to.

It felt like she was wading through water, thick, blue, sluggish. She wasn't sure she'd be able to make it.

Joona was standing to one side and didn't see her coming. She tried to read his face.

He looked sad, focused.

Saga walked up to the cordon. One of the uniformed officers recognized her and let her through.

She heard herself thank him, and walked on, stopping a few steps away from the bodies, which were bloody and horribly pale.

Neither Pellerina nor Valeria was among the dead.

She checked several times.

The body at the far end was a young man in his twenties, with green eyes and dark hair. His throat had been cut, and his face and one side of his head had been badly beaten.

Saga staggered and reached out to the fence for support, then walked off through the weeds, back to the road, where she stood for a while with her hands resting on the hood of one of the police cars. She could see her face hazily reflected in the white paint. She knew she should go back and help, but when she turned around, the paramedics were lifting the naked man onto a stretcher.

She sank into a crouch with her back against the front wheel of the police car, covered her face, and wept with gratitude that Pellerina wasn't among the dead.

Joona came over and sat on the ground next to her. He brought a blanket from the ambulance to wrap around her.

"I thought she was one of the bodies," she said, wiping her tears away.

"It's okay to feel relieved."

"I know, it's just that . . . this isn't like me. But I just can't bear the thought of anyone hurting her," she said, trying to swallow the lump in her throat. "Pellerina is the most wonderful . . ."

"We're going to find her."

"What's the plan?" Saga asked, trying to pull herself together.

"If they can save the woman's life, I need to talk to her," Joona said. "And after that I'm going to the summer house where Pollux's other hand is located."

"I'll come with you," she said, but she didn't move when he stood up.

"You don't have to."

Saga rinses her face in the sink again, then dries it off with paper towels. As she walks down the hall, she thinks about all the other people affected—parents, children, wives, boyfriends, and siblings of the dead people in the dumpster—who would be getting terrible news that day. This time, she has been given a reprieve. She can still hope for a happy ending.

THE UNCONSCIOUS WOMAN HAS BEEN IDENTIFIED AS EMILIA Torn. She was driven to the intensive-care unit at Karolinska Hospital, where the decision was taken to sedate her. Both her arms and one leg are broken, and she has severe trauma to the back of her skull. She's been bitten in the neck and cut across the stomach, and has lost a lot of blood.

Joona comes running over just as the doctor is about to go into the operating room.

"Wait," he says. "I need to know if there's any chance of talking to the patient. I'm a police officer, and—"

"Then you know how this works," the doctor interrupts.

"There are more lives at stake."

"She's already been sedated and is about to be anesthetized, so—"

"I was the one who found her. I only need a couple of minutes," Joona interrupts, pulling on protective clothing.

"I can't let you impede our work," the doctor says. "But you can try before we intubate."

They go into the operating room, where the staff are busy preparing. An anesthesiologist disinfects the woman's groin, then inserts a catheter into a vein.

The woman's face is pale and yellowish, and she's sweating from the morphine. Some of her red hair is stuck to her cheek with congealed blood. Her broken arms are mottled with internal bleeding.

"Emilia? Can you hear me?"

"What?" she replies, almost inaudibly.

"Was there a child in the building, a little girl?" he asks.

"No," she whispers.

"Think, was there a little girl with Down syndrome?"

"I don't understand. . . . He killed Ralf. . . . He stomped on his face, then cut the guys' throats, then attacked me and . . ."

"Who did? Who did this?"

"The producer, he just went crazy, he . . ."

"Do you know his name?"

"Auscultate heart and lungs," the doctor says, looking at the carbon-dioxide monitor.

"Do you know how I can reach the producer?"

"Who the fuck are you, anyway?" she murmurs.

"My name is Joona Linna, I'm a detective with—"

"It's all about you," she says in an uneven voice.

"What do you mean?"

"He kept shouting, saying you'd be ground into the dirt, that you'd—"

Her body starts to shake, and she coughs up blood all over her chin and chest. Joona steps back to get out of the doctors' way. He leaves the room and hurries along the hall to the waiting room.

Saga and Nathan are sitting side by side on the sofa, staring at their phones. Saga's face is tense; her eyes are bloodshot.

"It doesn't look like Pellerina was there," Joona says.

Saga nods to herself, then puts her phone away and meets his gaze. Nathan moves the pile of brochures from the small table and lays out the map with the constellation of Gemini drawn on it.

"Seven locations left," he says. "Presumably, we start with the other hand, the summer house?"

"Maybe we've been thinking about this wrong," Joona says.

"How do you mean?"

"I'm convinced we're going to find something there, but this is personal for Jurek—he said he wants to grind me into the dirt."

"The feet?" Nathan says, looking up at Joona.

They bend over the map again and scrutinize it. The star marking Pollux's left foot is in the middle of a road in Södertälje. But his right foot is located on a detached house just north of Nykvarn.

81

WHILE THEY WERE AT THE HOSPITAL, THE STORM SWEPT across Stockholm, bringing huge amounts of snow. The temperature dropped even more.

Joona is driving quickly through the heavy snow along the E20, heading toward Nykvarn. The snow has already settled between the lanes and along the shoulder.

Saga checks her pistol, then inserts the magazine.

Joona swerves into the incoming lane and passes a truck.

A cloud of dirty snow flies up onto the hood and windshield.

According to the property registry, the house that Pollux is standing on is owned by a middle-aged couple with two children.

Tommy and Anna-Lena Nordin run their own recruiting business. Their daughter, Miriam, is fifteen, and goes to the high school in Tälje. Their son, Axel, is eight, and attends Björkesta School in Nykvarn.

Joona accelerates a little more, and they can hear the engine ramp up.

Just before the Almnäs junction, he sees a flashing blue light in the rearview mirror. He slows down and pulls over to the side of the road.

In the back seat, Nathan smiles, cradling his semiautomatic rifle on his lap.

The police car stops behind them, the front doors open, and two uniformed officers get out. The female officer strolls toward them, while the man unfastens his holster.

All they know is that they've stopped a dirty BMW that was doing 180 kilometers an hour, and that the car is registered to an ex-con. They're about to discover that the three people sitting inside are heavily armed.

Considering the circumstances, it really didn't take Ingrid and Jim of the Södertälje Police long to re-evaluate the situation.

At first, Joona was reluctant to accept their help, because they had no idea how dangerous the operation could turn out to be.

"They're experienced officers," Nathan said. "And we've been promised backup as soon as we have proof of Jurek's location. . . . We need their help to get inside the house."

So now Saga is sitting in the back seat of the police car, going through the details of the operation with the two officers. They're following Joona's BMW.

Snow flies up behind the two cars.

Ingrid and Jim have a thermos of coffee and a bag of saffron Lucia buns on the console between them.

Saga continues sketching out possible scenarios. "The most dangerous possibility is that Jurek and the Beaver have taken over the house and are waiting for us inside, heavily armed," she says.

The police car skids and almost slides out as it turns right at Turinge Church and follows Joona's BMW along a narrow road.

"As long as we don't have to do the triathlon," Jim says in a thick rural accent.

"Nothing's worse than the triathlon," Ingrid replies, in the same drawl.

They laugh, then apologize and explain that they sometimes pretend to be Sture and Sten, two old men from Skaraborg.

"They can't stand physical exercise," Ingrid says with a smile.

"We invented them when we started training for a triathlon together," Jim explains. "We've been doing it for four years now, coaching each other. . . ."

"And now Sture and Sten are terrified because we signed up to do a triathlon in the French Alps."

"Nothing's worse than the triathlon," he says.

"Sorry, we're a little ridiculous." Ingrid laughs.

"Well, we're not *that* ridiculous," Jim says, in his exaggerated accent.

They have to drive around the entire golf course. Beyond the clubhouse there are no further tire tracks in the snow. Bright-orange poles mark the edges of the road, to stop people from driving into the ditches and fields.

JOONA AND NATHAN PULL OVER. THE SNOW CRUNCHES beneath the tires before the car comes to a stop.

As soon as the police car with Saga passes, they get out, step over the ditch, and head up into the forest to make their way around to the back of the house without being seen.

It's almost twenty degrees Fahrenheit. The cold is stinging their faces and making their eyes water. The snow is nowhere near as deep among the trees, where it's littered with fallen pine needles and cones.

As they walk, Joona scans the ground for air pipes, disturbed soil, or bare ground.

A few snowflakes drift down through the trees.

After fifteen minutes, they see the back of the house between the trees. They move cautiously before stopping at the edge of the forest.

The thick snow has blanketed the landscape. The silence is deafening.

The house is modern and fairly large—two stories, with a black-paneled roof and a gray façade.

Nothing about it suggests violence and death.

The snow on the lawn at the back of the house is untouched. It gently undulates over the garden furniture.

Joona takes out his binoculars and starts to check the windows, one after another. The curtains upstairs are all drawn.

He takes his time, but he can't see any sign of movement, or any shadows.

Everything is quiet, but there's something unsettling that he can't quite put his finger on.

When he looks down, he sees that snowdrifts have built up against the porch doors. Through the frosty glass, he can make out a conservatory with a sofa, two armchairs, and a polished cement fireplace. There are blankets folded neatly over the arms of the chairs, and the glass table is clean and bare.

Joona lowers the binoculars and looks at Nathan. His face looks somber, and his nose is red with cold.

"Nothing?" Nathan says, shivering.

"No," Joona says, but then he realizes what was unsettling him.

It wasn't anything he saw. Rather, something was missing from the picture. An ordinary middle-class family with two children, and there wasn't a single Christmas decoration in sight on December 12. No Advent candles, no stars in the windows, no string of lights, no outdoor decorations.

THE POLICE CAR HAS DRIVEN RIGHT UP TO THE HOUSE AND parked in the snow-covered driveway.

Saga and the two officers are sitting in the car, looking at the house.

The snow is falling more heavily now.

Through the kitchen window, they can see a girl wearing headphones, doing her homework.

The snow on the drive is untouched. No vehicles have come or gone since it started falling.

One of the double garage doors is open. Saga can make out a golf cart, a few sun-bleached cushions for outdoor furniture, a huge grill, a lawn mower, and a shovel with a rusty handle.

The radio crackles, and Joona's voice breaks the silence.

He and Nathan are in position at the back of the house. They can't see anyone, and there's nothing remarkable except the absence of any Christmas decorations. They're staying hidden in the forest, but are ready to go in through the back door if necessary.

Saga gets out of the car with the two uniformed officers. Ingrid starts to cough as she breathes the cold air into her lungs.

"Okay?" Jim asks quietly.

She nods, and the three of them walk toward the house. Through the window, they see a man removing cutlery from a dishwasher. He's wearing a pastel-blue shirt with the sleeves rolled up.

They stop in front of the door, stamp the snow from their shoes, then ring the doorbell.

Saga moves to the side and puts her hand in her jacket to grab her pistol.

Their breath looks like smoke around their mouths.

Saga's face is stinging from the cold.

They hear footsteps coming from inside as someone approaches the door.

Saga reminds herself that Jurek or the Beaver could be inside the house, and that Pellerina and Valeria could be buried in the garden or in the forest behind the house.

The lock clicks, and the door is opened by the man from the kitchen. He's tan, and has a blond mustache and tired rings under his eyes.

He's standing on the white marble floor in stocking feet. Behind him is a broad staircase leading up to the second story and down to the basement.

"Tommy Nordin?" Saga asks.

"Yes," he replies, looking at her quizzically.

"We got a report about a disturbance."

"A disturbance?"

"We need to come in and talk to you and your wife."

"But there hasn't been any disturbance," the man says slowly.

"We still need to talk to you. We received a report," Saga says.

The girl who had been sitting at the kitchen table comes out into the entryway. She seems drowsy, and is moving strangely. She's taken her headphones off. Her straight blond hair hangs down on her cheeks, and she's penciled in her eyebrows and applied makeup to cover the acne on her chin. Her lips are thin, and she's dressed in jeans, white socks, and a Hollister polo with a dirty collar.

"Ask Mimmi," the man says, nodding toward the girl. "Ask

her. . . . Anna-Lena and I split up. I haven't seen her in two months. She moved to Solna with our son."

"So it's just the two of you living here?"

"Yes," the father replies.

"Then you won't mind if we come in and take a look around," Jim says.

"Don't you need a warrant from a prosecutor to do that?"

"No," Saga replies curtly.

"We can question and even arrest someone without a permit," Ingrid explains.

"That sounds like a threat," the man says, but he steps aside to let them in.

82

SAGA UNBUTTONS HER JACKET IN THE ENTRYWAY SO SHE can quickly reach the pistol in her shoulder holster.

She blows on her cold fingers as she looks over at the staircase. There are no lights on upstairs or down in the basement.

Ingrid is leaning against the wall with one hand as she wipes her shoes on the doormat.

There's a sudden clatter: Jim has accidentally knocked a broom over. Dust and hairs are caught in its bristles.

They follow him into a large, open-plan kitchen and dining room. The two areas are separated by a full-length white screen.

"We have a home-entertainment system that can be quite loud," the father says, running his tongue over his front teeth.

The girl says nothing, just slowly walks back to the island and sits down on the bar stool in front of her textbooks again.

Joona's right. Even though the parents have separated, it's strange that they haven't put up any Christmas decorations in the kitchen or dining room.

It feels like time is standing still in here.

There are white orchids in the window.

"Would you like coffee?" the man asks.

"No, thanks," Saga replies.

The thin screen between the kitchen and dining room is semi-transparent, and sways gently in even the slightest draft.

The man continues emptying the dishwasher, lining up the clean glasses on the counter.

"Could you leave that for the time being?" Saga says.

He turns around and looks at her. There's a deep crease between his eyebrows.

"Have you had any visitors recently?" she asks.

"What do you mean by visitors?"

"What do you think?"

He scratches the top of one arm, then goes back to emptying the dishwasher.

Saga watches him. She changes position slightly and sees that he's broken out in a sweat.

"No visitors?"

She moves the screen aside with her hand and walks into the dining room, past a large table with a stone top, then turns toward the man again.

"If it wasn't a fight with your wife, what was it?" Saga says, addressing her words to the screen.

"Like I said, we were probably watching a movie," the father says.

Viewed through the screen, the kitchen looks like it's covered in thick fog. Saga sees the girl glance unhappily at her father.

"Every day?" Saga asks.

"It varies."

"Which days this week?"

Ingrid straightens up and puffs her chest out beneath her uniform. Jim is watching the man with one hand on his holster.

Saga goes over to one of the windows overlooking the snow-covered garden. Flakes are still falling, only to be swallowed up by the existing whiteness. The branches of the fir trees are weighed down. She leans closer to the pane and feels the cold through the glass. A trail of dark footprints leads from the entrance, around the garage, and over to a playhouse.

Her heart starts to beat faster.

What have they been doing in the playhouse?

The number of footprints indicate that they've been there several times.

She goes back into the kitchen, and feels her hand trembling as she puts it down on the marble counter.

Very cautiously, she slips her other hand inside her jacket and grabs her pistol. From this position she can cover both father and daughter, as well as the entrances to the living room, hall, and entryway.

"When did you stop using the playhouse?" Saga asks the girl.

"Don't know," she replies quietly, staring at her books.

"After the first summer?" Saga suggests.

"Yes." The girl nods, without looking at Saga.

"So what do you keep in there?" Saga asks the girl.

"Nothing," she says quietly.

"Look outside," Saga says. "There are deep footprints in the snow."

The girl doesn't look, just keeps her eyes trained on her books.

"The neighbors have two little girls; they sometimes use it," she whispers.

"In the winter?" Saga says, letting go of the pistol.

"Yes," the girl says, still not looking at Saga.

"Hasn't this gone on long enough?" the man says, rubbing the back of his neck hard.

"We'll be out of here soon," Jim says amiably.

"You can start by showing my colleague your bedroom," Saga says.

"Look, I'm really not happy with this. . . . It's an invasion of privacy. I haven't done anything."

The girl lowers her head slightly and covers her ears, but seems to realize what she's doing and puts her hands back down on the counter.

"We'll just take a look around, and then we'll leave you in peace," Jim says.

Saga thinks she can hear knocking through the walls. She holds her breath and listens, but it's quiet again. Maybe it was just snow falling from the roof.

The father dries his hands on a checkered dish-towel, then tosses it on the counter and walks toward the entry.

His dark-blue socks are so worn that Saga can see his white heels through them.

Jim glances at Ingrid, then follows the man out of the kitchen. The two men's footsteps echo in the kitchen as they go upstairs.

The girl hasn't turned the page of her book once. She's still staring at the opening page, about Sweden's years as a great power.

"Your name's Miriam?" Saga says.

"Yes," she says, and swallows hard. "Everyone calls me Mimmi."

"And you're in high school?"

"First year."

Ingrid has walked over to the frosted door leading to the living room.

"What subjects?" Saga asks.

"Soc-social sciences."

"Did you hear those thuds?"

The girl shakes her head, and Saga notices that she has grubby Band-Aids on her thumbs.

"What year do they say Sweden first became a great power?" Saga asks.

"What?"

"Which century?"

"I don't remember," the girl mumbles and closes the book.

"Do you remember if you had any visitors in the past week?" Saga goes on.

"I don't think so," she says in a monotone.

"Mimmi," Saga says, taking a step closer to her, "I'm a police officer, and I can tell that something has happened here."

The girl's been biting her pen; the end is chewed and squished. She keeps staring at the table.

"What happened here?" Saga persists.

"Nothing," Mimmi whispers to herself.

"Why don't you have any Christmas decorations up?" Ingrid asks amiably.

"What?"

"Why don't you have any Advent stars, or gingerbread cookies?"

The girl shakes her head as if the question was annoying and irrelevant.

Saga wonders if it's possible that they're just an ordinary family that hasn't yet been drawn into Jurek's world—a family blissfully unaware that their house is located in Jurek's constellation.

But it's obvious that they're hiding something. They both have a panicked look in their eyes.

"Can you show me your room?" she says.

"It's in there," the girl says, pointing at the door leading to the hallway.

"Show me."

The girl gets to her feet without a word.

"Who plays golf?" Ingrid asks.

"The whole family, but I do some extra work coaching kids."

Saga and Ingrid follow the girl through the door to the hall. It's fairly long and ends at a bathroom. A thin line of LED lights runs along the bottom of the left-hand wall.

Two doors lead to the children's rooms. According to the signs, the first is Axel's, the second Mimmi's.

The floor outside the boy's room is ice-cold. A sign that reads "No Entry" has been taped to the door.

Saga gestures to Ingrid to stay in the hall while she goes into Mimmi's room with the girl.

They pass a small closet under the stairs. The girl automatically closes the door as she passes it.

On the wall above the unmade bed is a poster of a very thin David Bowie holding a thick book with a black star on it. He looks almost like a priest.

There's a bottle of sleeping pills on the bedside table.

In the corner, on the back of a chair, hangs a Halloween mask—some sort of zombie, a bloody skull jutting out from a man's torn mouth.

"So you're past the princess stage," Saga says.

"Yes," the girl replies.

It sounds as though someone's banging on a door a long way away.

"Did you hear that?" Saga asks, looking at her.

"No," the girl says slowly.

Saga looks through the window. Large snowflakes are falling in the light.

"And just you and your dad live here?"

The girl doesn't answer, only prods the mask absentmindedly.

The ceiling creaks. Saga assumes that Jim and the girl's father are on their way back downstairs.

"Sit down on the bed," she says.

The mattress creaks as the girl does so. The bottoms of her white socks are filthy.

"Mimmi . . . you know you're going to have to tell me what happened," Saga says seriously.

"I wish I were dead," the girl whispers.

83

INGRID IS STANDING IN THE HALLWAY, LISTENING, AS SAGA talks calmly to the girl in her bedroom. It seems to Ingrid that this family has been badly damaged by the divorce. All their happiness is gone.

She looks hesitantly at the door to Axel's room. She isn't sure if the detective meant for her to go in there, or just wait.

Dust is drifting along the floor, lit up by the white glow of the LEDs.

She presses the handle down and goes into the boy's room.

It's dark and cold.

She can hear a faint scraping, rasping sound.

Large model airplanes are hanging from the ceiling on nylon threads.

Ingrid can hear Saga talking to the daughter through the wall.

It smells like rotting flowers.

She steps farther in.

The window is wide open, letting the ice-cold wind in. The catch is rattling with every gust, and the curtains are billowing.

Several sheets of paper have blown off the desk.

Something's wrong.

The airplanes swing in a fresh gust, and the door to the hall slams shut. The closet door creaks.

As she walks farther into the room, Ingrid looks at a poster of Wonder Woman.

A boy is lying on the bed, staring up at her with reddish-brown eyes.

He's almost entirely covered with flowers.

His face is covered with black burn marks, and his greenish torso is swollen with gas.

He must have been dead a week, maybe longer.

"Bauer, you need to see this," Ingrid calls out loudly.

The curtain billows again, then sinks back.

From the corner of her eye Ingrid sees the closet door open. A chill runs down her spine. She turns around and just has time to see the stern expression on a woman's face before the ax hits her in the head. The back of Ingrid's head hits the wall bearing the superhero poster. The thick blade has penetrated her brain, and everything goes dark and silent. She doesn't even notice her legs buckle beneath her. She ends up lying on her back, with her neck against the wall at an unnaturally sharp angle, blood gushing onto the floor.

AFTER ADMITTING SHE WANTS TO DIE, THE GIRL CLAMS UP entirely. She stops answering questions, just sits there with her head bowed, tight-lipped. When Saga hears her colleague call her, she tells Mimmi to stay where she is and wait until she comes back.

"Promise not to move," Saga says.

She hears a loud thud against the wall, and the corkboard above Mimmi's desk shakes.

Mimmi stares at Saga with a look of horror, then clamps both hands over her ears.

Saga goes out into the hallway, but Ingrid isn't there. She looks toward the kitchen, then notices that the door to the boy's bedroom is slightly open.

"Ingrid," she says quietly.

Saga moves closer. She can feel the cold wind from the dark room. She hesitates, then steps into it. The curtains are fluttering in front of an open window; snow is swirling in, and there are petals drifting across the floor.

Behind the heavy scent of hyacinths is the stench of death.

A pale reflection slips across one wall.

Saga takes another step into the room and notices the ax swinging toward her from one side.

All her years of boxing have taught her to judge the direction of the blow correctly. She instinctively lowers her head and takes a step back off to one side. The blade of the ax misses her face and slices into the drywall, before coming to rest on an internal beam.

Saga stumbles out into the hallway before the woman has time to pull the ax loose. She reaches out for the wall to keep her balance and backs away as she draws her Glock from its holster.

Aiming the pistol at the door, she retreats a little farther and glances quickly over her shoulder.

There's no one behind her.

The bathroom door is closed, but the light is on inside.

"Ingrid?" she asks in a loud voice.

There's no answer, and Saga turns back quickly toward the boy's room.

The woman has managed to sneak out into the hallway. She's standing still, looking at Saga with the ax over one shoulder. Her face is taut, focused. Tiny specks of blood are spattered across her glasses, her neck, and both arms.

Saga backs away slowly, raises her pistol, and puts her finger on the trigger.

"Police!" she declares, squeezing the trigger past the first notch. "Stand still and put the ax on the floor!"

Instead of obeying her, the woman charges. She's approaching with long strides, breathing hard through her nose.

Saga supports her pistol with her left hand, quickly lowers the barrel, and shoots her in the thigh. The bullet passes straight through the muscle, and blood sprays out behind her. The woman lets out a groan, but keeps moving.

Her pant leg turns dark with blood.

Saga backs into the bathroom door.

The woman's lips tighten as she comes forward. She raises the ax, bringing down the ceiling lamp. It crashes to the floor and goes out.

Saga shoots the woman twice in the chest. The recoil slams her right shoulder blade into the door.

The cloud of powder dissipates.

The woman reaches out for the wall with one hand, drops the ax, and slumps down heavily onto the floor. Her blood-spattered glasses drop into her lap, and her head falls forward, then jerks sideways several times.

THE MOMENT THE FIRST SHOT GOES OFF, JOONA KICKS IN the narrow glass door to the conservatory. The door flies open, and the glass shatters, casting shards everywhere.

Joona runs in with his pistol drawn. Nathan rips the plastic bag from his semiautomatic and runs after him.

Joona points the pistol at the sofa, then aims at the door to the kitchen.

Nathan is covering their backs as they hurry past the fireplace. Joona stops in front of the door and catches Nathan's eye.

"We go in together," he says quietly. "You take the left side, ninety-five degrees."

He counts down with his fingers, then opens the kitchen door. They run in and secure the scene.

Empty.

Joona signals for Nathan to guard the door to the hallway as he walks around an island with some schoolbooks and a cell phone on it.

He points his pistol toward the screen leading to the dining room. Their movements have made the fabric sway.

The garden outside is dark now, and it's hard to see anything through the screen. Joona can just make out the table, chairs, and sideboard.

He hears two more pistol shots from the hall.

"What the hell's going on?" Nathan whispers, looking around.

Joona slips behind the screen and trains his pistol on the door to the hallway. He looks over at Nathan, and sees him turn his back to the hall door just as it starts to open behind him.

"The hall!" Joona calls out.

Nathan barely has time to start turning around before the father comes into the kitchen and fires his shotgun at him.

A hail of bullets rips the back of Nathan's skull off.

Blood and brains spray over the island and across the screen.

Joona rushes forward as Nathan falls to the floor.

His pistol is aimed at the father's chest, the line of fire through the thin fabric perfect, but Joona doesn't shoot.

Nathan's dead body falls heavily to the ground and ends up on its side.

Without letting go of the shotgun, the father wipes away the blood on his face with his shoulder.

He doesn't see Joona until he's emerged from behind the screen.

Before the father has time to aim the gun at him, Joona shoves it aside with one hand and hits him across the face with the pistol.

The shotgun goes off and blows a hole in the ceiling.

The man staggers sideways and tries to grab the gun.

The blast rings in their ears as fragments of plaster and dust rain down on both of them.

Joona slams his right elbow into the man's cheek. It's a solid blow.

The man's head smacks against the wall, and he sinks to one knee. He doesn't even realize that Joona has seized the shotgun.

Blood is running into his mustache from both nostrils, and his eyes look dazed. He reaches out for the wall and tries to stand up. Joona takes a step forward and kicks him hard in the chest, and he jerks backward and slides back across the floor.

"Stay there," Joona says, then stomps on the shotgun, shattering it.

The man is coughing hard, trying to get his breath back. Joona hears heavy footsteps echo on the stairs, and then Jim walks in, looking very pale, blood running down one cheek.

"Shit, he knocked me out," Jim mutters, then stops in the doorway when he sees Nathan's body.

84

SAGA IS STEPPING OVER THE DEAD WOMAN'S BODY WHEN she hears a shotgun blast from the kitchen. She aims her pistol at the door and moves silently along the hall. The barrel quivers slightly as the shotgun goes off a second time.

Saga waits a few seconds, then goes back into Axel's room, sees the body of the boy in the bed, and confirms that her colleague is dead before she returns to Mimmi's room.

Silence.

The girl has opened the window and climbed out. She only has socks on her feet. Her footprints lead in a wide arc around the house through the snow.

Saga takes out her radio and calls Joona. When he tells her that Nathan is dead, she just feels like crying.

But she also realizes that this family's insane rage means that Jurek has been here.

And if Jurek has been here, they may know something about Pellerina and Valeria.

Saga quickly tells Joona that the young boy, Ingrid, and the mother are dead, and that she's about to go after the daughter.

"Get going, find her," he says.

It's snowing heavily again now, and her footprints will soon be covered.

Saga climbs up and sits on the windowsill, then shuffles out onto the tin roof. She braces herself with her hands, and jumps.

She lands softly on the snow and takes a step forward to stop herself from falling.

The girl has a five-minute head start, at most, and her tracks are still visible.

Saga runs around the house. She can feel the snow melting in her shoes and pant legs.

The snow has blown into large drifts behind the garage. She keeps moving, pistol in hand. It's darker there, as if the forest was casting a shadow across the yard.

The playhouse is rust-red with white trim, white windows with net curtains, and a black roof.

The original footprints are still just about visible through the freshly fallen snow, but the new prints are perfectly clear.

All the footprints lead straight to the playhouse door with its stained-glass window.

Saga stands beside the door and knocks.

"Mimmi? Come out now."

She knocks again, waits a few seconds, and pushes the handle.

She tries pushing and pulling, but the door's locked.

"Mimmi, can you open the door? I just want to talk to you. I think you can help me."

Saga thinks she can hear a noise. It sounds like something being dragged across the floor, something heavy.

"I need to come in," she says.

She breaks the little window in the door with her pistol, then sweeps the barrel around the edges to get rid of the worst of the remaining shards.

The inside of the playhouse is pitch-black.

A rancid smell hits her as she tries to reach in with her arm. Her sleeve rides up a bit before coming to a stop.

The opening is too small.

Saga takes her jacket and shirt off, dropping them on the ground.

She's just wearing a white tank top now, her sports bra visible through the thin cotton. Her slim athletic arms are covered in bruises and scratches. The cold feels sharp against her bare skin, and every snowflake that lands on her burns like a stray spark from a sparkler.

She tries to look through the hole in the door.

There's no movement inside.

Holding her pistol in her right hand, she carefully puts her arm through, and the girl starts to scream so loudly that her voice breaks. Saga tries to reach the lock, but she needs to push her hand in even lower.

The girl stops screaming abruptly.

Saga leans her body against the door, cutting her armpit, and finally reaches the handle on the inside. The key is still in the lock.

She tries to turn it with stiff, frozen fingers. She hears the shuffling sound again, but forces herself to go on.

Finally, the lock clicks, and Saga carefully pulls her arm back, pushes the handle down to open the door, and moves out of the way.

Nothing but silence.

It's too dark for her to see anyone inside.

"Mimmi, I'm coming in now," Saga says.

She crouches down, and has to put one hand on the floor to get through the low door.

The room smells like wet clothes and must.

Saga bumps into a piece of furniture in the darkness. She sees that it's a toy stove with some pinecones in a small pan.

"We need to talk," she says quietly.

A bulky figure moves in one corner. The girl is sitting on the floor, wrapped in blankets, covering her ears.

When Saga gets used to the darkness, she can make out the girl's pale face. In her eyes is a look of abject terror.

JOONA DRAGS THE FATHER INTO THE DINING ROOM AND handcuffs him to one leg of the heavy table. Then he tears down part of the screen and lays it over Nathan's body.

Nathan's been his friend and colleague since Joona started working at the National Crime Unit. He can't count the number of times he's gone to see Nathan over the years, just to sit down and collect his thoughts in his friend's company.

Joona notices that a thin arc of blood has already seeped through the fabric around Nathan's head.

Jim is sitting on one of the high chairs at the dining table. He's pale, his face is shiny with sweat, and he's unbuttoned the collar of his uniform.

"Ambulances and more police are on their way," Joona says to Jim. "But we need to help Saga look for the girl; we can't let her get away."

"What?"

"Do you think you can handle that?"

"I just need . . . I think I heard Bauer right," he says. "Is Ingrid dead? Did they kill her? Is that true?"

"I'm sorry," Joona says. "I'm so sorry."

"No, but . . . We were warned. You tried to stop us from coming with you," he says, rubbing his face hard with one hand. "What the hell is wrong with these people? We were just trying to help them, and they—"

"I know," Joona interrupts calmly.

"I just don't get it," Jim mutters. He looks at Joona as though he can't remember who he is. "I'll go after the girl," he says, swaying slightly as he gets up from the chair.

"Remember, she's only a child," Joona says.

Jim doesn't answer. He walks out into the hall, pulling his flashlight from his belt as he goes. The front door opens and slams closed again. The remains of the fabric screen sway in the air.

Joona is certain that Valeria and Pellerina are buried here somewhere. A dog handler is on the way. If they're still alive, then there really isn't any time to lose. The temperature has fallen to thirteen degrees Fahrenheit in the past twenty-four hours.

Joona looks out at the snow-covered landscape, then turns back toward the man. He's lying with his cheek against the floor. His blond mustache is dark with blood, and one of his eyes is badly swollen.

"You'll be taken into custody soon," Joona says. "But if you help me now, I might be able to help you."

"You don't understand," the man slurs.

"I know that Valeria de Castro and Pellerina Bauer are here somewhere."

"It was self-defense, survival. . . ."

"Tommy," Joona says, crouching down to look the man in the eye, "the reason I didn't shoot you is that I need answers. . . . I know you've met Jurek Walter. You have to tell me what he made you do."

85

SAGA HAS PULLED HER JACKET BACK ON INSIDE THE PLAY-house. She offered her sweater to Mimmi, but got no answer.

It's obvious that the girl has hidden here many times. She has blankets and a sleeping bag, and the floor is littered with empty cookie boxes, soda cans, and candy wrappers.

"So—why do you hide in here?"

"Don't know," the girl says blankly.

"Because you can't handle what's happening in the house?"

Mimmi shrugs her shoulders almost imperceptibly.

"We're here because we're looking for a woman and a girl, named Valeria and Pellerina."

"Oh."

Saga takes out her cell phone and shows her a few pictures. Mimmi looks at them very briefly, then lowers her eyes. Her face looks like it's sculpted out of ice in the cold glare of the screen.

"Do you recognize them?" she asks.

"No," the girl replies, and turns her face away.

"Take another look."

"I don't want to."

When Saga turns off her phone, the playhouse is plunged into darkness again.

"Whatever you and your family have been doing here, it's over now. Things are going to be tough for a while, and there will be lots of police, but you can still help. Let's go back to the house."

"I can't," she says in a shaky voice.

"I understand. I saw your little brother," Saga says.

Mimmi starts to cry just as a beam of light reaches the playhouse. Saga crawls over to the window.

It's Jim, approaching the playhouse with a flashlight in his hand.

The beam bounces on the snow with each step he takes. He's following their footprints.

"Bauer? Are you in there?"

"We're in here," she calls back.

There are heavy footsteps outside, and then the door opens and Jim crawls into the playhouse, breathing heavily. He puts the flashlight down on the doll's bed. The beam shines through the bars, filling the small space. The furnishings are old and water-stained; the pink wallpaper is peeling off the walls; there are spiderwebs on the broken ceiling lamp, and the windowsill is covered with dead flies.

"I was told to come look for you," he mumbles, knocking the stove over as he sits down on the floor.

The playhouse creaks as he turns and makes his way over to the girl. His breathing is shaky, and snot is dripping from his nose.

"It was you, wasn't it? You killed my partner," he says in an anguished voice.

Suddenly he's holding his pistol to the girl's head.

"Jim, take your finger off the trigger," Saga says quickly.

"Did you have to kill Ingrid?" he asks, on the verge of tears.

"Calm down, Jim," Saga says firmly. "Take your finger off the trigger and put the gun down."

The pistol wavers in front of the girl's face. Jim's forehead is covered in sweat, and his eyes are wide open.

"How does it feel now?" he asks in an agitated voice, jabbing the barrel and making her head rock.

"Don't do it," Saga says. "I know you're upset, but it wasn't—"

"How does it feel?" he yells.

"Good," the girl replies, looking him in the eye.

The pistol trembles in his hand again.

"Listen, Jim, Mimmi didn't kill Ingrid," Saga says.

"But . . ."

"It was her mom," Saga says. "We didn't know she was there. She was hiding."

"Her mom?"

"She was hiding in the boy's room."

"What the hell is wrong with you people?" he says weakly, lowering his pistol.

Saga takes the pistol out of his hand, puts the safety on, and removes the bullet from the chamber.

"Go make sure the ambulances find us," she says.

He crawls out, hitting his head on the door frame, and closes the door behind him.

"I'm sorry he threatened you. Sometimes people do terrible things when someone close to them dies."

Mimmi nods weakly and looks at her.

"I know you can help me," Saga says.

"You don't understand—I can't."

"Look at these pictures again," Saga says, pulling up the images of Valeria and Pellerina on her phone.

"I know who they are," she snarls, batting the phone away. "They did it, don't you get that? They burned him—they killed him. . . . Are they just going to get away with that? It isn't right, they ruined everything. . . ."

Saga puts one arm around her shoulders. Mimmi tells her about the man from the Russian security service in a low voice. She doesn't remember his name, but he had tracked the woman and the child all the way through Ukraine and Poland to Sweden. They're both seriously mentally ill. They met at the Serbsky Institute, and then somehow escaped. They have a secret pact. They pick a family and kill all the members, one after another.

"They always start with the youngest child," she whispers.

"Where are they now? Do you know?"

She takes a deep, shaky breath and explains that the man from the Russian security service is going to get them out of Sweden and make sure they face justice in Russia.

"In Sweden, they'd just get medical treatment, and then they'd be released. They'd come here and kill us. . . . In Russia, they'll be sent to Penal Colony Fifty-six for the rest of their lives."

Saga pulls up a picture of Jurek on her phone.

"Is this the man?"

Mimmi lowers her eyes and nods.

"Do you know where Valeria and Pellerina are now?"

"No," she says faintly.

"I have to find them. They didn't kill anyone. . . ."

"My little brother—they killed him. They burned his face, then they broke his arms and . . ."

She starts to sob loudly.

"Mimmi, did you see that happen? With your own eyes?"

The girl just keeps crying.

"You never saw who killed your brother, did you?"

Mimmi calms down slightly, but her breathing is still ragged.

"He told us all about it," she sniffs. "Every detail. He was so sorry he hadn't gotten here in time to save Axel."

"This man doesn't work for the Russian security service. He killed your brother, and somewhere Valeria and Pellerina are lying buried in coffins. . . . That's what he does."

The girl gets to her knees and throws up. She pauses for breath, then throws up again. She sits down heavily, leans back against the wall, and wipes her mouth on her sleeve.

"Show me," Saga says.

JOONA IS STANDING BY THE DINING-ROOM WINDOW AGAIN, looking out at the playhouse. The light from Jim's flashlight is shining through the open door and three windows.

The footprints have disappeared completely now.

He can see the large dining-room table and the man on the floor reflected in the glass. He's lying on his side with his hands over his head. Joona has told him that they'll have tracking dogs at the house soon, but the man is still refusing to say anything, although Joona suspects that he's starting to realize his mistake.

The light inside the playhouse suddenly changes, and Saga crawls out with the flashlight. She turns and helps the girl out.

They walk back toward the house through the deep snow.

In spite of the poor light and the clouds of breath obscuring their faces, Joona can tell that something has changed.

He meets them in the entryway, then follows them downstairs to a den with brown leather furniture and a pool table.

The ceiling is low, and there's a faint smell of a cellar.

The girl tries to push the pool table aside, and Joona goes over to help her.

No one says anything.

Slowly they roll the table aside until it hits the wall. A picture frame rattles, and one of the balls bounces off the table's side cushion.

Joona and Mimmi pull the large rug in the opposite direction.

A jagged rectangle, approximately one by two meters in size, has been cut into the floorboards. Joona takes out his knife, nudges one edge up, and lifts the panel.

The beams and insulation under the house rise with the boards.

He takes a firmer grip and scratches his lower arm as he drags the panel out of the way.

The girl has sunk onto the floor by the pool table. She covers her ears with her hands.

Joona goes over to the opening and feels ice-cold air flowing up through it.

"Oh God," he whispers.

"Hurry up," Saga whimpers.

In the ground beneath the house are two unpainted coffins.

86

JOONA IS WAITING FOR NEWS IN THE EMERGENCY ROOM OF Karolinska Hospital in Huddinge. He's pacing restlessly up and down the hallway.

His hair is a mess, his shirt and pants are crinkled, and his face reveals worry and fatigue. He's washed the worst of the blood and dirt off himself.

Fragments of the chaotic scene in the basement keep overwhelming him.

The images are horrific.

Nathan's brutal death, the two coffins under the house, the stench of the bodies, the fear in the paramedics' eyes, and the screams of the teenage girl as she was led away by an officer.

For something like the fortieth time, Joona stops at the windows in the black doors at the end of the hallway. He looks at the two uniformed police officers standing guard outside the wing, then turns and starts to walk back the other way.

Security is tight—sixteen officers are guarding the wing—but Joona knows that it won't be over until they catch Jurek.

He thinks back to Saga's panicked reaction.

She was holding the flashlight with both hands, but she couldn't stand still, so shadows from the flashlight's beam kept shaking and lurching aggressively up the walls.

She was like a caged animal—trapped with an unbearable anguish.

Joona keeps pacing.

He can't stop thinking about it.

The clasps on the coffins made a loud snapping sound when he pulled them loose, and he had to tear at the straps to get them off, scratching his back on the rough edge of the sawn floorboards in the process. The harsh light cut through the dust his shoes had churned up from the dry ground.

He grabbed the lid of the first coffin with both hands and wrenched it aside.

Valeria was inside, covered with a gray blanket. She looked like a corpse wrapped in a winding-sheet.

Her face was gray and dirty, and her lips were cracked. Her eyes were closed, and she didn't react until the harsh light hit her face, when she started fumbling for the lid with her hands.

"No more," she cried, trying to get up.

"Valeria, it's me, Joona," he said. "It's all right, we're here now."

Her whole body was shaking. She couldn't believe it was him. She kept flailing her arms, hitting him in the mouth.

He helped her out, and the blanket slid off as she struggled over the edge of the coffin. She was blinking in the light, dazed and confused. She almost fell, then started to crawl toward the other coffin.

"Pellerina," she cried as she tried to force the lid open.

She was too weak. Her hands were swollen; her nails were broken, and her fingertips were caked with blood.

"Open the coffin!" Saga cried. "You have to get it open!"

Joona stops and leans against the wall with both hands. Two nurses hurry past in pale-blue scrubs.

He looks down at the strips of tape on the floor that indicate where carts and beds should be parked, but all he can see is the basement in the house: him pulling Valeria away from the second coffin and passing her up to the first paramedics to reach the scene, wearing yellow jackets with wide reflective strips, wet boots.

One of the paramedics started to cry.

The stretcher hit the side of the staircase, knocking flakes of paint to the floor.

Saga dropped the flashlight. It hit the edge of the floorboards and landed on the dry soil next to Valeria's coffin and rolled under the house.

Joona cut the straps on the other coffin, dropped his knife, and heaved the lid off.

Saga screamed until her voice broke. Someone tried to hold her back, but she pulled free and fell on her knees at the edge of the roughly sawed hole, whispering her sister's name.

Pellerina was lying in the coffin in a pair of baggy pants and a padded blue jacket. Her pale face was completely motionless, and she didn't react to the light of the paramedics' flashlights.

Her little round mouth had sunk into her face, and her cheek-bones were very pronounced.

Joona gently lifted Pellerina's body out of the coffin, holding her to his chest like a sleeping child, one hand behind her neck and her head against his cheek. He couldn't hear a heartbeat, couldn't feel a pulse.

"No, no, no," Saga said, sobbing.

Another stretcher arrived just as Joona detected faint breath from Pellerina's mouth.

"I think she's alive. Hurry up, she's alive!" he cried. "Take her, she must have hypothermia. . . ."

He lurched forward and held the girl up to the two paramedics, who laid her down gently on the stretcher. Saga stroked her cheek and kept telling her that everything was going to be all right.

Joona continues pacing back and forth along the hospital wing. He runs his hand through his hair, then sits down on one of the chairs. It creaks when he leans back to rest his head against the wall.

Just as he's getting up again, the door opens and a doctor in short-sleeved white scrubs comes out.

"Joona Linna?" she says.

"Is she conscious?"

"I tried to tell her that she should rest, but she was adamant about seeing you."

"How is she?"

"Extremely weak, but stable."

When she was brought in, Valeria was suffering from sepsis, acute dehydration, malnourishment, and severe hypothermia. Her body temperature was less than ninety degrees in the ambulance, but they've managed to bring that back up to normal levels in the past five hours. Her hands and toes were frostbitten, and at first they thought amputation would be necessary, but now that looks unlikely.

Joona thanks the doctor, taps gently on the door, and goes in.

Valeria is lying in a hospital bed with the rails on both sides raised. Her face is pale and thin. She's connected to a pulse oximeter, an EKG, and a blood-pressure monitor. Oxygen is being fed through her nose, and she has cannulas on the inside of both elbows.

"Valeria," he says softly.

He walks over and touches her hand. She opens her eyes and looks at him wearily.

"Thanks for finding me . . . you damn cop," she says, and smiles.

"They say you're going to be fine."

"I'm already fine."

She purses her lips, and he bends over and kisses her. They look at each other for a moment, then become serious again.

"They won't tell me anything about Pellerina," she says quietly.

"Me, neither . . . She barely had a pulse when we found her."

Valeria's eyelids are heavy, and she lets them close. Her dark curls spread across the pillow, and almost reach the thin pine headboard set into the chrome frame of the bed.

"What happened in that house?" she asks, opening her eyes again. "I mean, why were they doing that to us?"

"Don't worry about that now. You need to rest. I'll sit here with you."

Valeria moistens her dry lips. "But I need to know," she says. "I know that they were angry with us. They thought it was our fault their son died."

"It sounds like Jurek said something to them, but I don't know the details. Saga was the one who questioned the daughter," Joona says, pulling a chair over to her bed.

He has just told her that Nathan and a colleague from the Södertälje Police were killed in the operation when Saga comes into the room. She's obviously been crying. Her eyes are red and swollen.

"Pellerina's been sedated," she tells them in a subdued voice. "Her condition's critical. They've raised her body temperature, but they're having trouble with her heart, it's beating too fast...."

Her voice cracks, and she swallows hard. "They had to use a defibrillator to slow it down.... What if she never wakes up?" she whispers after a pause. "Then that coffin will be the last thing she ever experienced—darkness, loneliness."

"We talked the whole time," Valeria says, before breaking into a cough.

"Did you?" Saga asks, staring at her despairingly.

"She wasn't scared. I swear, she wasn't," Valeria continues. "She was cold and thirsty ... but we were lying next to each other, and every time she said my name I'd talk to her.... She was positive you were going to rescue her, and you did."

"She doesn't know I was there," Saga whispers.

"I think she knows," Valeria says.

"I should get back to her," Saga says quietly, and blows her nose.

"Of course," Joona says.

"Wait—why were they doing that to us?" Valeria asks.

"Jurek destroyed that family," Saga says. "They didn't do anything to him, but he needed that location, and he needed their loyalty for a few weeks ... so he murdered the youngest child and blamed you and Pellerina."

"It's so horrible," Valeria whispers. She coughs again weakly. "Someone needs to stop him."

"Yes," Joona replies.

"Not you—you've done more than enough already," she says quickly.

"Valeria, I'll stay here until you recover," Joona says. "But this isn't over. Jurek isn't finished, he'll be coming back for you. There's no need to be afraid now. There are sixteen police officers in the hospital, and that will keep him away.... But we can't get complacent."

"What are you planning?" Saga asks.

"I'm going to keep looking into the constellation. . . . It's a gamble, but the star that represents Pollux's heart—it's located on a small island in Lake Mälaren."

"You can't do this on your own," Saga says heavily. "I would go with you, you know that, but I have to stay with Pellerina. I have to be here when she wakes up."

"I can handle it."

"Listen to her," Valeria says, her voice agitated.

"Joona, you can't do this alone," Saga repeats. "It's too dangerous, you know that. You have to talk to Carlos."

"There's no point."

"A small team," Saga pleads.

"No," Joona says.

"How about Rinus Advocaat—can't you call him? He could be here in a few hours," Saga says.

Joona's face stiffens, and he puts one hand on the chrome bed frame.

"How did you know about Rinus?" he asks quietly.

"You talked about him after Disa's death," Saga says. "You were almost dead yourself. I could tell that you trusted him. Can't you ask him for help?"

"No," Joona replies. Saga has never seen his eyes this dark.

"Oh, no . . ." Saga says, fear creeping into her voice. "Joona? Tell me it isn't true."

"How bad is it?" he asks gruffly.

"When Jurek took Pellerina, I panicked. I tried to reach you, I had no other choice."

"Saga . . ." Joona says, getting up heavily.

"I was panicking," she says, almost inaudibly. "I thought you could tell me where Jurek's brother's remains were."

"What did you do?" Joona asks.

She rubs her eyes to get rid of the tears.

"It's probably nothing. I thought that, if you were going to hide, then you'd need help. . . . Nils would do anything for you, but he isn't tough, not in that way . . . which is why I thought of Rinus.

So I called him at home in Amsterdam, and spoke to a guy named Patrik. . . . He said Rinus was at work, and I gave him my number. . . . No one ever got back to me."

"Is there any way Jurek could have had access to your phone?"

"Sorry," Saga whispers.

"He's going to take my daughter," Joona says, heading for the door.

87

LUMI IS SYSTEMATICALLY SCANNING ZONE 1 USING THE night goggles. She lingers on the bushes and garden furniture, then moves on to the abandoned main house.

Everything is strangely quiet tonight.

She looks at the boarded-up door and the warped sheets of plywood over the windows.

She lowers the sight to get a broader view and looks out. She can't let her concentration slip.

The temperature has stayed below freezing for the past few days, and the sky is unusually clear.

Without the night goggles, the old house is invisible in the darkness. Every once in a while, she can see truck headlights on the highway shining through the bushes and trees.

Gray light hovers over the nearest village, Maarheeze, and in the distance the lights of Weert form a colorless aurora in the night sky.

Lumi raises the night goggles again and looks toward the workshop, scanning the overgrown piece of machinery in the ditch. She's always thought it looked like a huge hair-curler. It's actually the rotating cylinder from the front of a combine harvester.

Slowly, she lets her eyes follow the pitted gravel lane leading to the workshop, all the way around the meadow, to the barrier where she said goodbye to her dad at dawn in the mist.

As she studies the narrow road leading to Rijksweg, she starts to panic. She's sent her dad off on a mission from which he might never return, straight to the person he wanted to hide from.

That first day she was alone in the workshop with Rinus had been tense and quiet. They did what they had to do, followed their routines, but they still had time on their hands.

They started to keep each other company, getting coffee for one another, making small talk, and eventually talking properly.

Rinus, understanding that she felt guilty about the fight with her dad, told her about the time he first heard about Jurek Walter, many years ago.

"Joona called me on a secure line, and I told him about this place. I know he wanted to come here with you and your mom, but in the end he made a different decision. . . . You must have been, what, four years old when you left Sweden?"

"Three," she replied.

"But you're alive, and you have a life."

She nodded in the darkness, then stared at the distant green-house through the binoculars. "I have a life now. . . . I grew up with my mom in Helsinki; I used to be very shy," she said. "But now I live in Paris and have lots of friends. . . . I have a really handsome boyfriend—I never thought that would happen. I mean, I always thought, you know, who's going to want me?"

"The young are very careless with their youth," Rinus sighed.

"Maybe."

"Does your dad know you have a boyfriend?"

"I've mentioned it."

"Good." He nodded.

Lumi is still thinking about that first conversation with Rinus when she moves her chair and the night goggles to Zone 3. She's moving calmly, without any urgency. The whole process has become routine.

She looks out into the darkness. All she can see through the hatch are the red lights on the cell tower, and the distant glow of Eindhoven, about twenty kilometers away.

Near Central Station is the youth hostel where Joona has rented a room for her, in case she has to flee.

Just as Lumi is about to raise the night goggles again, Rinus comes in with two cans of Coke and a bag of warm popcorn. His shift hasn't started yet, but he usually shows up an hour or so early, so they have time to chat.

"Did you get any sleep?"

"One eye at a time," he jokes, handing her one of the cans.

"Thanks."

She puts it down on the floor next to the rifle, then checks the patch of gravel and the run-down barbed-wire fence in front of the meadow closest to the workshop.

Rinus eats his popcorn in front of the monitor showing the cameras that are focused on the inside of the garage and the workshop's immediate vicinity.

She follows her usual routine, scanning the sector in sections, moving from the meadow to the clump of trees where the secret tunnel emerges.

"I was thinking about what you said this morning, how you haven't really opened up to your dad yet," Rinus says. "I never did with mine. . . . His name was Sjra. You only find that name down here. . . . He never even went north of the Waal River. We were very Catholic and . . . I don't know, Dad meant well, but the church was like a prison to me."

"What about your mom?"

"She's visited me and Patrik in Amsterdam a couple of times, but I don't think she's ever really understood that he's the love of my life, even though I've told her we're getting married."

Saga moves the night goggles to the large shovel lying at the edge of the trees.

"Before I met Laurent, I was seeing an older man. He was married, ran a gallery," she tells him.

"I tried that, too," Rinus says, putting the popcorn down on the floor. "Well, he didn't run a gallery, but he was older. . . ."

"Father complex." She smiles.

"I was really flattered at first, impressed by everything he said . . . but it didn't work out. He kept belittling me for my opinions."

Lumi lets out a sympathetic sigh. "I broke up with the gallery owner because he wanted to set me up in an apartment he rented . . . so I'd be available as his lover whenever it suited him."

"Laurent sounds like an improvement," Rinus says.

"Yes, he is. . . . He's got a few things he could work on, but he's pretty okay."

Rinus takes over at two o'clock, and moves the chair to Zone 5. Lumi passes him the night goggles and the rifle, then stands behind him with the can of Coke in her hand.

"How are you keeping up with your classes while you're away?" he asks.

"I don't know. I'm supposed to be working on a graphics project about 'dysfunctional integration,'" she replies.

"What's that?" Rinus asks.

"No idea." She smiles. "That's probably what I'm supposed to be finding out."

"Well, dysfunctional integration makes me think of families— everyone's sort of stuck with each other no matter what."

"That's seems too easy."

"What about love . . . or sex?" he suggests.

"That's good, Rinus!" Lumi says, smiling.

"A flash of creative genius." He laughs, fanning himself with his hand.

She laughs, too, then looks at the time and says she'll bring him his meal once she finishes exercising. Her room is warm, and she turns the thermostat on the radiator down slightly. She grabs her gym clothes.

When she walks back, she hears the floor in the hallway creak behind her. She stops and turns around, thinking she's dropped something.

All she can see is the closed door to the last bedroom and the blocked emergency exit with the words "Stairway to Heaven."

She walks past the kitchen again, through the door at the top of the stairs, and goes down to the ground floor.

When she passes the storeroom where they keep food and weapons, she hears the electrical box ticking quietly next to the closet.

On one of their first days here, she pushed through the clothes in the closet to check the escape route. She heaved the heavy steel beam aside, opened the door, and felt the cool air from the tunnel rush up and hit her face.

She puts her bag down on the wooden bench in the changing room and slips her gym clothes on.

As she lifts one foot onto the bench to tie her shoelace, she sees a loose wooden slat lift up a few centimeters at the other end. Out of sheer habit, she thinks about how she could pull it off and use it as a weapon if need be.

Lumi cycles for an hour at a relatively fast pace, then does push-ups and sit-ups on the cold floor. When she's finished, she takes off her sweaty clothes in the changing room, then goes into the bathroom.

She locks the door. The room is cold, and she gets goose bumps.

Every time she showers, she checks the bathroom cabinet, taking out the pistol and making sure that it's loaded. The sights on it are a little too close together for her: ideally, the gap between them should be a little bigger—especially in a situation like this, when speed is more important than accuracy.

She puts the gun back, closes the mirrored door, and looks at her tired reflection.

The ceiling light flickers.

There's a thin layer of dust on top of its white glass dome.

Holding the white shower curtain back with one hand, Lumi turns the water on.

The first drops form gray rings on the white polyester, and a roaring sound fills the bathroom. She waits to get in until the steam billows out and the mirror starts to fog.

88

LUMI STEPS INTO THE SHOWER AND PULLS THE CURTAIN shut behind her.

She's thinking about Laurent, and the way he would sit on her bed naked, cigarette between his lips, strumming his guitar.

The water cascades over her head, and her muscles relax.

Lumi hears a scraping sound through the walls, and pushes the curtain aside to check the lock on the door.

Cooler air hits her.

There are small pearls of condensation on the sink and toilet.

She soaps her armpits, breasts, and thighs.

The lather runs down her stomach and legs and vanishes into the drain in the floor. The white shower curtain becomes slightly translucent when it's wet.

The wooden unit beneath the basin looks like a dark shadow.

Like someone crouching down.

Lumi looks down at the floor and can't help thinking about her dad. She's worried because he hasn't been in touch yet.

She tilts her head back, closes her eyes, and lets the water wash over her face.

Through the gentle rumble of the water, she imagines she can hear voices, men screaming in pain.

She wipes the water from her eyes, spits, and looks at the trembling shower curtain again, at the shadow beneath the basin.

It's only the bathroom cabinet.

Just as she's reaching for the shampoo, the lamp flickers and becomes weaker, before everything suddenly goes dark.

Lumi's heart is pounding.

She turns the shower off, pushes the curtain aside, and listens.

All she can hear is the drops of water hitting the floor.

She dries herself in the darkness, then gets the pistol out of the cabinet. She cautiously opens the door.

The hinges creak softly as it swings open.

It's just as dark out there.

She quickly gets dressed, keeping the pistol close.

She crosses the floor without a sound, crouches down, opens the door, and looks out.

The entire ground floor is pitch-black.

She thinks she can hear footsteps upstairs.

She puts one hand on the wall and follows it to the fuse box.

The circuit breakers are all set correctly.

In theory, it's impossible to cut off the electricity unless someone is digging outside and manages to hit the cable by chance.

She turns around. Gray light is bouncing off the walls.

It's coming from upstairs.

She hears footsteps.

A flickering light reaches the ground floor.

She quickly moves back, presses up against the wall, and raises the pistol. There's no way she can get to the escape route without being seen.

Her sweater is damp and cold against her back from her wet hair.

It's Rinus, with a flashlight in one hand and pistol in the other.

"I'm here," she says in the darkness, lowering the barrel of the pistol toward the floor.

"Lumi?"

His voice is wary, but he doesn't sound alarmed.

"I checked the fuse box," she says. "None of them have blown."

They go upstairs to the surveillance room. The monitor is dead.

As Rinus moves between the various zones, Lumi opens a wooden crate and swaps her pistol for a G36 Kurz, a good, short-barreled assault rifle that's easy to handle in confined spaces. She quickly inserts a magazine, then tucks two more into her pockets.

"Okay, it looks like there's a total power outage south of here," Rinus says, lowering the binoculars. "Maarheeze and Weert are both dark."

"I was a little scared," Lumi confesses, going over to him. "I was in the shower when everything went out."

"I want us to remain on high alert," he says.

"Okay," she says, moving over to Zone 5.

She can see the neighboring farm and the old bus through the night goggles. There are no lights in any of the windows. Everything is dark.

She rapidly checks the zone's meadows, ditches, and fences before moving on.

She slowly scans the gravel lane from the workshop, following it around the meadow and up to the closed gate.

Suddenly she stops, almost instinctively.

She saw a movement.

Her eyes registered it, and she reacted before her brain had processed the information. She scans back along the empty lane and starts again.

She slows down.

There. A couple hundred meters from the gate. There's something in the ditch.

The weeds are moving.

She breathes out when a black cat jumps out and runs across the lane.

"The power should be back on soon," Rinus says behind her.

"Let's hope so," she replies.

The alarm system has switched over to its backup power source. It'll last for about forty-eight hours, but the security cameras have been knocked out, and the hydraulic door can't function.

Lumi raises the night goggles again and scans Zone 1.

Dry leaves blow across the yard.

Just as she's about to check the main road, she stops.

Something's caught her eye.

The gate is open.

"Rinus," she says, and a shiver runs down her spine.

"A car," she goes on. "It's gone through the gate with its lights off."

She can't see the driver's face. Rinus rushes over and takes the night goggles from her.

"Jurek Walter," he says curtly.

"We can't be sure of that."

"Lumi, it's happening. Make sure you've got your bag," he says, quickly pulling on a protective vest.

89

THEY BOTH HEAR THE CAR APPROACHING THE WORKSHOP. Its headlights are off. Somehow Jurek found their hiding place. He must have sabotaged the substation on the outskirts of Weert to cut off their electricity.

Lumi blackens her face and wipes her hands on a cloth. She pulls on her waterproof camouflage jacket and changes into a pair of sturdy sneakers. Rinus is busy by the ammunition boxes. He's lit up in the flashlight's beam. They've been through this plan countless times. Lumi knows she can just grab her bag and escape through the tunnel, but for some reason Jurek wants them to see him coming. Maybe he's not even in the car. Maybe he's out there somewhere, watching them with a thermal camera, waiting for Lumi to run.

Rinus grabs a plastic container full of magazines, containing different combinations of tracer, armor-piercing, and regular ammunition, and carries it over to one of the windows.

The magazines are transparent, so you can see the ammunition inside, but Rinus also has his own system, so he can identify them with his fingertips in total darkness.

The car is slowly approaching through the yard, at an angle that would require Lumi or Rinus to open the hatch completely and lean out to be able to fire at it.

"How many people do you think are inside?" Lumi asks.

"I'm guessing two," he says.

Rinus drags a wooden crate across the floor. "The only thing that would be hard to handle is if he tries to burn the building," he says, opening the crate. "But your dad didn't think that was likely. Jurek wants to take you alive."

Rinus takes out three packs of plastic explosives, puts two in his green canvas bag, then cuts the third in half, through the wrapper, and wipes his knife on his pants.

The explosive gives off a faint smell of ammonia.

He pulls four Russian fuses with sturdy detonators from a smaller box.

"I don't think he'll try to force the door downstairs. He would need explosives or antitank rifles, and I don't think he'd be able to get them in the Netherlands."

"You think he has a ladder?"

"I don't know, but he has something planned," Rinus says, turning the flashlight off again. "If I was going to break in here, I'd choose the emergency exit . . . and I'd assume it was guarded and mined."

"Yes."

Rinus isn't planning to mine the door itself—he's going to position the explosives a bit down the hall. Moving quickly, he feels his way through the darkness. He runs over to Lumi's room and puts the bag down on the floor.

He looks at the sealed emergency exit at the end of the hall, estimating the number of steps.

He attaches an entire pack of explosives with duct tape behind the door frame to Lumi's room, approximately one meter off the floor.

The charge is completely invisible from the hallway, but it's powerful enough to blow up half of the second floor.

He presses the fuse into the gray mass, then takes down the picture from the opposite wall, ties a length of thin nylon thread to the screw, rehangs the picture, and stretches the thread across the floor back to the explosive. He removes the safety, then slowly backs away.

You can see the glint of the nylon thread if you have a flashlight trained on it, but otherwise it's invisible. You'd have to move very slowly, inching your way forward with the beam in front of you to catch a glimpse of it.

By the time you feel the thread against you, it's already too late. A tiny bit of pressure is enough to pull the pin out and trigger the detonator.

Rinus sets up a similar trap immediately outside the door to Joona's room.

He retreats to the kitchen and quickly constructs a fake trap by stretching a thread just above the floor.

Someone will waste time disarming that.

Next he closes the creaking door to the hallway, tapes half a pack of explosives at eye level, pushes the detonator in, runs the thread from the pin to the door handle, and then pulls the fuse.

He goes back to the surveillance room. Jurek is very experienced, but it would take a bomb squad a long time to disarm those traps.

"He's driving right to the workshop," Lumi says quietly. She can hear the loose gravel clattering against the chassis of the car.

She moves sideways to be able to see the car. It slows down and stops in front of the main doors. It's still impossible to hit from any of the hatches.

"It stopped," she says.

They can only see part of the rear bumper and the trunk.

"What's he doing?"

"I can't tell. I don't know if he's still inside."

Rinus switches to a magazine marked in tape with a red cross. Every tenth bullet in it carries phosphorus, which will leave a trail of light in the darkness.

The car is idling.

The loose garage door is creaking in the wind.

Lumi scans the scene outside again. The bare branches over by the barbed-wire fence are trembling.

The car engine starts to rev.

A bird takes off and flies away.

The cloud of exhaust fumes drifts off on the wind toward the meadows.

The car reverses one meter, then stops. The driver is still revving the engine.

He wants us to see this, she thinks.

Suddenly he puts the car in gear and accelerates so hard that gravel flies up behind the wheels. There's a loud crash as the car drives straight through the double doors, followed by a clanging thud and the sound of breaking glass when it hits the reinforced wall and stops.

The engine falls silent.

One of the garage doors breaks off its hinges and falls to the ground.

Lumi hurries across the floor and looks through one of the internal hatches. The garage is dark and silent. She can smell metal and gas.

"Stay back," Rinus says, going over to the next hatch.

Without a sound, Rinus pushes the barrel of his assault rifle through the hole and angles it downward, then waits several seconds before leaning forward to look through the sights.

The image is blurred and grainy, as if he's looking through murky water.

He can see the car. The front end is crumpled, the windshield smashed. Tiny, sparkling glass shards are scattered across the ground.

He can make out the rounded shape of a head in the driver's seat.

He puts his finger on the trigger, but he can't fire at it from this angle.

"What's happening?" Lumi says beside him.

"I don't know."

He moves to the farthest hatch, pushes the barrel through, waits, then looks through the sights. The car's front right quarter-panel has broken off and is lying on the garage floor. One windshield wiper is moving sluggishly back and forth even though the glass is gone.

Rinus puts his finger on the trigger again and accidentally knocks the barrel against the side of the hatch. A metallic sound rings out.

Slowly, he moves the barrel to face the driver's seat, where he sees a hand resting on the steering wheel.

He follows the row of white buttons on the bloodstained shirt toward the collar, where he sees a gold necklace.

And then he sees the face.

It's Patrik.

He's injured, but still alive. Blood is running from his nose, down over his mouth. His glasses have fallen off, and he's blinking slowly.

Rinus is absolutely certain he didn't tell Patrik where he was going. He just said he had to go away for work. He never mentioned that he was going into hiding.

But Patrik has known about the workshop for years. He was alarmed when the far-right populists were gaining ground in the Netherlands. He was afraid that, as a gay Jewish man, he would be targeted. When things were at their worst, Rinus took him to the workshop in an effort to make him feel safer, to show him that there was a plan if they ever needed it.

90

RINUS'S HEART IS POUNDING. THE SIGHTS TREMBLE ON THE rifle and the seconds tick past. Patrik's mouth is slightly open, the way it usually is when he's asleep.

With his finger on the trigger, Rinus starts to look for Jurek, scanning the inside of the car before looking around it.

The darkness beneath the car looks oddly fluid.

The floor looks wet.

Suddenly the image flares white, and Rinus instinctively jerks his face back.

The glare lingers on his retinas in the darkness.

Rinus looks down into the garage again without the sights and sees a dancing glow beside the car.

It flits up against the wall.

Something's burning.

Rinus quickly switches to another hatch and looks down. A strip of burning cloth is hanging out of the car's gas tank.

"Patrik!" he yells through the hatch. "You have to get out of the car!"

He runs back to the first hatch. In the flickering light, he sees Patrik open his eyes wearily.

"Patrik!" he cries. "The car's going to explode! Get out of the garage! You have to get out of—"

The explosion happens in two hard bursts, and the garage fills with fire. Rinus staggers backward.

Flames shoot out through every embrasure.

There's a loud clattering sound from the garage as car parts rain down across the floor. The fire roars.

"Was Patrik still in the car?" Lumi asks, her voice numb.

Rinus nods and looks at her. His eyes are lifeless. He shuts the embrasures, one by one.

Lumi hurries to the last zone and opens the hatch. In two places outside the workshop she can see vivid yellow flames, and pitch-black columns of smoke.

"He's burning tires," Lumi says.

She pulls on her lightweight backpack. She knows that Jurek is trying to divert their attention and distract any thermal cameras.

He's going to try to break in soon, she thinks, moving to the next zone.

What's he waiting for?

The large combine-harvester drum is no longer lying in the ditch. The dead grass has been torn away, and there are deep tracks running across the yard and around the building.

Heavy thuds echo from the bedroom hallway.

Rinus hangs several hand grenades from his belt.

There's a creak, then several seconds of silence before they hear more loud clunks, and the alarm linked to the emergency exit goes off.

"He's inside, isn't he?" Lumi asks, even though she already knows the answer.

Adrenaline kicks in, and her mind becomes clear. Jurek leaned the combine-harvester drum against the wall like a ladder to get in.

"Come with me," she says.

Rinus turns away and switches the alarm off. Silence descends for a moment. Then they hear a tinkling sound from the kitchen. Jurek has dismantled the first two traps and made it past the fake one in a matter of seconds.

"Thanks for everything," she whispers.

He has his back to her. He nods to himself, then turns and meets her gaze, but cannot bring himself to smile.

Lumi brushes the curtain aside and spots the explosive that's been fixed to the door. Then she hurries down the stairs.

As soon as she's gone, Rinus sets up one last trap behind the curtain, then takes up position.

He hears a scraping sound, before the door to the hallway opens with a soft creak.

There's no explosion.

Jurek must have nudged the door open very slightly, stuck a thin knife blade through the gap, and cut the thread.

Rinus can't understand how he's been able to identify and disarm the traps so quickly. It's as if he knew exactly where the explosives had been placed.

Rinus looks through the night scope of the assault rifle and sees slight movement in the curtain, then the glint of a knife blade. It slips up the gap between the fabric and the wall and cuts the thread to his last trap.

Rinus fires nine bullets through the curtain in a downward diagonal pattern.

The barrel flares, and he feels the familiar recoil of the weapon in his shoulder. The empty shell casings clatter to the floor.

Rinus then takes aim at the explosive and fires the tenth shot.

The blazing phosphorus charge leaves a dark trail through the darkness.

The explosive detonates instantly.

He tries to take cover, but the detonation is instantaneous.

The pressure wave hits Rinus's chest, and the back of his head slams into the wall.

The entire section of wall surrounding the curtain disintegrates, the floorboards are ripped up, and debris flies through the room. The door to the hallway and the railing on the stairs are gone.

Rinus gets up on one knee. Splinters and plaster rain down on him as he empties the rest of the magazine in three seconds. He fires through what's left of the wall and the jagged opening to the kitchen.

He quickly rolls sideways, releases the magazine, and inserts a fresh one, but it's too late.

A thin man is running toward him along one wall.

Rinus draws his knife and stands up in the same movement, then swipes at the man, from below and off to one side.

But the man deflects his arm and sticks a narrow blade into his side, just below the strap of his bulletproof vest.

It slides beneath his ribs, up toward his liver.

Rinus ignores the pain. He changes the direction of his knife, aiming at Jurek's neck, but the man takes a step back and pulls out a pin.

A detonator explodes almost without a sound inside Rinus.

His legs buckle, and he hits the floor hard, blood gushing out of the small hole in his side.

Only now does he realize what's happened.

It wasn't an ordinary knife.

Jurek must have taken the Russian detonator and attached it to some sort of blade or spike when he disarmed one of the traps.

Rinus raises his head slightly and sees Jurek standing in the window, holding the night goggles.

The pain in his side is like a horrible cramp. The floor is wet with blood.

He lowers his head again, panting from exertion, and loosens a hand grenade from his belt to blow them both up.

But it's already too late.

Jurek is heading toward the stairs. If he knows about the escape route, he'll be able to see Lumi running across the fields.

91

LUMI FOLDS UP THE SHOULDER SUPPORT OF HER ASSAULT rifle, closes the door to the closet behind her, and removes the bar across the steel door.

Just as she is about to go into the small hallway, she hears automatic fire, then a loud explosion.

She carefully closes and locks the door behind her.

More automatic fire ticks into the walls, followed by silence.

Lumi's hand is shaking as she turns her flashlight on. She hurries down the narrow concrete stairs to another steel door.

She has to shove her shoulder against it to get it to move. It swings open with a creak, and she shines her flashlight into a cramped passageway with earthen walls. The wooden planks in the roof are held up by thick posts, and small drifts of soil and stones are lying on the loose planks on the floor of the tunnel.

The light sways as she shines it toward the entrance to a large concrete pipe.

Rinus described the escape route as "a tubular section" 250 meters long, but she didn't realize he was literally talking about a buried pipe.

An underground passageway that needs to work only once.

It's a very simple solution.

It looks like an old mine shaft, and seems just as dangerous.

Lumi lets the steel door swing shut, then hurries across the uneven planks, crouches down, and goes into the tunnel.

Her backpack scrapes against the roof as she runs, bent almost double.

She counts her steps, moving as quickly as she can.

The flashlight shines on the joints between the sections of pipe, which spread out ahead of her like a sequence of thin rings.

The barrel of the rifle knocks against the side of the tunnel.

She stumbles over an uneven joint, falls forward, and braces herself with her hands, breaking the glass in the flashlight. When she gets up again, she feels a sharp pain in one knee, but limps on.

Warm blood is trickling down her shin.

The flashlight is still working, but the beam is no longer as focused.

She forces herself to run again.

Jurek could be dead.

Rinus is very experienced. She's seen him assemble weapons in a matter of seconds.

It doesn't seem that anyone would be able to beat him in close combat, but she still has to assume that she's fleeing for her life.

She hears steps behind her, and terror seizes her heart. It's probably just the echo of her own movements, but even so she stops and turns the flashlight off with trembling hands. She points the assault rifle behind her and looks through the night scope, but there's no ambient light down here for the sight to enhance.

She blinks away the sweat running into her eyes.

The only sound she can hear is her own breathing.

She tries to switch the flashlight back on.

It clicks, but doesn't light up.

She shakes it gently, but nothing happens.

She stands there, eyes wide open, staring into total darkness.

Very carefully, she removes the last of the broken glass and presses the small bulb in slightly.

It works.

She crouches down again and continues through the pipe.

She's breathing too shallowly, and the air feels thin.

As she runs, she multiplies the number of steps and the length of her stride, and when she figures out that she shouldn't have more than forty meters left, she stops and shines the flashlight ahead of her.

The beam is blurred, but she can still see that the end of the tunnel is full of earth, right up to the top. This end of the tunnel seems to have collapsed, sealing the pipe under a mountain of dirt.

She calms her breathing. She puts the flashlight and assault rifle down, crawls up the pile of dirt, and starts digging. She heaves the soil behind her, trying not to panic.

Her back is wet with sweat, and her heart is pounding in her chest.

The soil isn't densely packed, which is a good sign. If the ground above her had fully collapsed, it would be impossible to dig through with her bare hands.

Going back isn't an option.

She cuts her fingertips on a sharp rock but doesn't stop digging. Gasping for breath, she moves backward, heaves the soil and stones farther into the pipe, digs farther into the mound of dirt, until she eventually reaches the top of the heap.

She shines the flashlight along the tunnel ahead and sees that one of the supports has given way, letting in an avalanche of earth.

The plank in the roof is bowed, but it hasn't fully collapsed.

Lumi shoves the assault rifle and bag through the opening before squeezing in after them.

Dry soil trickles down over her neck and back.

As carefully as she can, she crawls into a small room with concrete walls.

The soil from the collapsed section of the pipe has spread halfway across the floor.

She climbs a ladder that's fixed to the wall to reach the steel hatch in the roof. With her bruised and bleeding fingers, she loosens the rusty fastenings, pulls the cross-strut out, and pushes up with one hand.

The hatch is stuck.

She undoes the waist strap of the backpack and uses it to strap herself to the ladder so she can use both hands. When she's let go of the ladder, she puts her hands and feet flat against the hatch and uses them to push.

The frost on the hatch crunches as it opens.

She takes a deep breath, concentrates, and pushes hard again. The ladder creaks alarmingly, and her muscles tremble, but slowly the hatch starts to move. Soil falls onto her face as the grass and moss above give way.

Lumi switches the flashlight off and crawls out into the cold air. She closes the hatch and brushes grass and leaves over it with her hand, then shuffles backward into a clump of trees.

She looks up at the night sky and locates the North Star to get her bearings, then runs across the dark field at a crouch. After five hundred meters, she takes cover in a ditch and looks back for the first time.

The tires are still burning in the yard, casting an eerie glow over the metal walls. Other than that, everything looks peaceful and still. She adjusts the assault rifle to its three-round-burst setting, then scans the field and clump of trees through the night scope before she starts to run again.

Some birds take off close to her, and she instinctively throws herself to the ground and crawls sideways into a deeper ditch.

After a few seconds, she checks the workshop through the scope and sees the combine-harvester drum leaning against the wall.

The ground seems like it's swaying in the glow of the burning tires.

She lowers the gun and looks at the building. Wind is blowing the flames around, obstructing her view. But when it dies down, she thinks she can see a thin figure.

She quickly raises the rifle again and looks through the sights, but now all she can see are the flames and the smoke obscuring the façade of the building.

She turns around and runs across the field along a dike, then climbs over an electric fence and crosses a meadow.

She passes the dark greenhouse from Zone 1 at a distance.

Lumi follows the lane to the main road and starts to walk parallel to it.

She keeps the assault rifle hidden from passing cars.

She pulls some dry grass from the side of the road and wipes her face without stopping. The sharp pain in her knee has faded to a dull ache.

Her dad was right.

Jurek did find them.

She knows that, but her brain is still having trouble accepting it.

Dawn is breaking by the time she reaches Eindhoven.

Trash and leaves are lying in drifts beside a noise barrier. The ground shakes as a truck drives past.

She limps through a small patch of woodland that borders a neighborhood of brown brick houses with white woodwork.

The streets are still empty, but the city is slowly waking up.

An almost empty bus pulls away from a stop.

Lumi wipes the blood from her hand on her pants, then starts to dismantle the rifle as she walks.

She drops the magazine down one drain, the bolt down another, and throws the rest of the gun in a rubble dumpster.

She crosses a road and enters downtown Eindhoven, where she steps into a doorway and shrugs off the backpack. She looks quickly through the plastic folder that holds her passport, hotel key, and cash, then takes out the pistol and checks that it's fully loaded before tucking it inside her jacket.

A garbageman jumps down from his truck and stands next to the idling vehicle, staring at her.

She runs away before he has time to say anything.

She strides through the city center toward the train station, passing a row of closed shops and a murky-looking canal. Once there, she walks past the bike racks to the hostel's entrance.

Lumi walks through the garish yellow lobby.

She's filthy and smeared with blood. Her hair hangs in dirty clumps, and her eyes look intense against her dirt-streaked face.

A group of kids holding heart-shaped balloons fall silent when she enters the lobby. Lumi walks straight through the group toward the elevators, as if she hadn't even seen them.

92

AFTER HE LEFT THE HOSPITAL, JOONA FLEW STRAIGHT TO Antwerp, where he rented a black Mercedes-Benz and drove due east along the E34. It was early morning and still very dark. The highway was almost empty.

Jurek knows where Lumi was hiding.

There's still a long way to go before dawn.

Joona crossed a boundary when he shot Jurek's traumatized brother. He had no choice, but it still left a stain on his soul.

According to the postmortem report, the brother's remains were transferred to the Karolinska Institute's surgery department for use in research.

Joona stole the body to atone. He had it cremated and scattered the ashes in the same Garden of Remembrance where the two brothers' father's ashes had been scattered.

Presumably, Jurek has visited the garden and seen his brother's plaque next to his father's. He must know what had happened.

Jurek knew that Saga's inquiries would lead back to Joona.

Because Joona ran from the hospital and drove straight to the airport, he had no opportunity to grab a gun. He just hopes to get to Lumi before Jurek does, so he can take her to another contact in Berlin.

Joona's heart starts to pound. Maarheeze is in darkness. There's been a huge power outage. It seems to stretch all the way to Weert, and is probably affecting Rinus's bunker.

He leaves the highway and slows down as he drives along the narrow access road.

The house and fields lie in darkness.

He sees blue lights flashing across the pavement.

A white police van is parked across the road, which is cordoned off.

Joona turns and drives straight through the cordon tape, thundering along the narrow lane toward the main buildings.

He can see five police cars parked on the far side of the meadow, and two ambulances and a fire engine next to the workshop.

He parks without blocking the ambulances, gets out of the car, not bothering to shut the door, and runs across the meadow.

One of the garage doors is lying on the ground, and he can see debris from an explosion in the yard and tall grass.

The blue lights flash across the metal walls.

He's too late. The battle is over.

There are police everywhere, talking on their radios. They're trying to figure out the severity of the incident and establish an investigative team. One officer is worried that there could be more explosives and wants to wait for the bomb squad. A German shepherd is tugging anxiously at its leash, barking loudly.

Joona passes the melted remains of a burned tire and walks up to one of the uniformed officers. He shows his ID and tells him that Interpol has been called in. He pretends not to hear the officer telling him to wait, and walks under the cordon tape into the garage.

The reinforced walls are smeared with soot, and the fire has left a strong acrid smell.

The remains of a burned-out car are resting against the internal wall.

There's a disturbingly contorted body sitting in the driver's seat, charred.

Joona walks through the armored door, which has been sawed open.

He opens the fire-safety cabinet and grabs the ax that's hanging next to the extinguisher, then hurries toward the staircase.

If Jurek is still here, Joona needs to make sure that he's dead.

The door to the closet and the emergency escape route is closed.

He can hear voices above him.

The stairs are littered with plaster and splintered wood from an explosion, and the debris crunches beneath his feet.

The internal walls upstairs are almost nonexistent now, and the remaining fragments are perforated with bullet holes.

Two paramedics are lifting someone onto a stretcher. One leg is hanging limply over the edge, and Joona can see bloodstained pants and a military boot.

The ax swings in Joona's hand as he approaches the man on the stretcher.

The beam from the headlamp of one of the paramedics is aimed downward, and Joona catches a fleeting glimpse of Rinus's blood-smeared face.

Joona climbs over a blackened beam and puts the ax down against the wall, staggering slightly from a sudden headache.

There's a loud ringing in his ears.

Rinus has an oxygen mask over his mouth and nose. His eyes are staring up at the ceiling, and he seems to be trying to figure out what's going on.

"Lieutenant," Joona says, stopping beside the stretcher.

With a weak hand, Rinus pulls the mask aside and moistens his lips. One of the paramedics lifts his foot onto the stretcher and straps the belt across his thighs.

"He went after her," Rinus says almost inaudibly, before closing his eyes.

Joona rushes out through the garage, past the police officers who are waving the first ambulance through. He runs across the frost-covered meadow toward his car, a headache throbbing in his skull.

93

A CLOUD OF DUST FLIES UP FROM THE GROUND AS JOONA drives away from the warehouse.

There's a police car in the way.

Joona swerves and drives straight through the rosebushes and across the ditch. With a bang, the glove compartment flies open, scattering documents across the floor and passenger seat.

He swings up onto the rutted lane again and accelerates. The yellow grass whips the sides of the car.

He drives through the fresh cordon tape that a police officer is putting up.

He turns left when he reaches the police van, skidding across the narrow road and up onto the shoulder.

Dirt sprays up behind the car as the tires thunder across the uneven ground. The car lurches back onto the pavement and races along the road.

It will be light soon.

When Joona reaches Maarheeze, he heads down a hill. He's going so fast that the car slides across the highway and scrapes the concrete divider.

The driver's-side window shatters, and small cubes of glass fly into the car.

He accelerates again and turns left at the traffic circle.

Jurek is used to operating behind enemy lines. Lumi won't realize he's following her. She'll lead him right to the student hostel.

Joona pulls out onto the highway, veering into oncoming traffic to pass a truck, and puts his foot down as hard as he can.

The wind roars through the broken window.

He drives through a patch of forest and reaches Eindhoven.

The sky is slightly lighter over to the east now, and the city is shining in the last darkness.

Brown brick buildings flash past.

He's rapidly approaching a red light. One car has already stopped, and there's a bus about to cross from the right.

Joona honks his horn and passes the waiting car. He accelerates hard in front of the bus and hears it brake behind him.

He swerves into Vestdijk, and steers into the bus lane. Large modern buildings rush past. A delivery truck and two smaller cars are blocking the two lanes in front of him. They're going too slowly.

Joona's migraine explodes behind one eye. It's still only a precursor to the real thing, but the car lurches and almost drives into the oncoming traffic before he regains control.

Though he honks his horn, there's nowhere for the other vehicles to go.

Joona pulls into the bike lane and passes them on the inside, tearing a trash can loose from the sidewalk. He sees it fly across and shatter a shopwindow in the rearview mirror.

The car swerves out onto the road again, the wheels thundering over the curb.

He makes a sharp right on shrieking tires.

Maybe he's already too late.

Joona races over a pedestrian crossing and into the square in front of the station. Eindhoven's Central Station is tucked next to the student hostel.

It's still too early for most of the morning commuters. There aren't many people moving behind the glass doors of the station. A beggar is kneeling on a piece of cardboard next to a stack of free newspapers.

Joona pulls in beyond the row of waiting taxis and stops.

Glass cascades from his clothes as he gets out of the car and runs toward the hostel.

He automatically looks around for some sort of weapon.

A uniformed police officer is standing in the empty lobby of the station, by the yellow ticket machines. He's hunched over, eating a sandwich from a bag.

Joona changes direction and walks toward him. The policeman is middle-aged, with blond sideburns and almost white eyelashes. Pieces of lettuce keep dropping from the sandwich.

Joona darts behind two pillars and approaches the officer from behind. He reaches forward, unfastens the man's holster, and takes his pistol.

The police officer turns around, his mouth full of food. He has a pair of sunglasses sticking out of his breast pocket.

"Interpol—this is an emergency," Joona says, glancing over at the hostel.

He starts to walk away, but the police officer grabs his jacket. Joona turns around and pushes him away. The man's head hits the wall, and he drops his sandwich.

"Listen, lives are at stake here," Joona says.

The policeman pulls out his baton and raises it to strike. Joona manages to parry the blow but still gets hit in the cheek. He wraps his arm around the man's shoulder and jerks him backward, sending him sprawling to the floor. The officer tries to get up by leaning on one hand, but Joona stomps on one of his knees. The police officer lets out a cry of pain.

Joona grabs his radio, tosses it onto the roof of a currency-exchange kiosk, and runs over to the hostel.

He checks the magazine. It looks like it contains eight or nine bullets.

Joona can still hear the policeman yelling as he strides into the hostel.

It's early morning, but already there are around twenty teenagers hanging out in the lobby and lounge.

Joona keeps the pistol aimed at the floor.

Two of the elevators are broken, and the third is stuck on the eighth floor, where Lumi's room is.

Joona's headache is making his vision pulse. He yanks open the door to the stairs and runs up them.

His footsteps echo through the stairwell.

His pulse is thudding in his ears by the time he reaches the eighth floor. He turns a corner quickly, sending a display of brochures flying.

"*Wacht even.*"

A young man is standing in the way, gesturing for Joona to pick the brochures up. Joona shoves him out of the way. Another man, standing in one of the doorways, has been looking on. He protests noisily, but stops when Joona points the pistol at his face.

Joona can hear a faint ticking sound.

He runs along the corridor to Lumi's room.

The lock has been broken, and the room is empty.

The bed is untouched, and Lumi's bag is sitting on one of the chairs. The wastebasket has been knocked over.

Joona's heart is pounding so hard he can feel it in his throat.

He hurries out of the room, rushes around the corner, and finds himself staring at Jurek's pallid face.

Jurek has a rope over his shoulder, and is dragging a large, plastic-wrapped bundle into the elevator.

The glare from the wall lamp glints off his rigid prosthetic hand.

Joona raises the pistol, but Jurek is already gone.

He hears a ringing sound as the doors close. Joona runs over and presses the button, but the elevator is already on its way upward.

It stops at the top, on the twenty-eighth floor.

Joona runs back to the stairwell and starts to climb.

He knows that Jurek could break Lumi's neck at any moment. But that wouldn't be enough for him. It's not that simple for him.

Ever since Joona first caught Jurek, many years ago, there's been a special connection between them. Jurek has spent a large part of his life locked up and isolated. And every day he has thought about how to grind Joona into the dirt.

He was going to take everyone Joona loves and bury them all alive.

Joona would have to spend his life looking for them, unless, consumed by loneliness, he gave up and hanged himself.

That's how Jurek envisaged his revenge.

He would have been planning to take Lumi with him and bury her somewhere. That's what his instincts are telling him to do—that's how he operates.

But now that Joona has caught up with him, he's quickly changed his plan, just like he did last time, when he took Disa.

94

JOONA REACHES THE TOP FLOOR BUT KEEPS GOING, RUNNING
up the last, narrower flight of steps leading to the roof. He opens
the door, scans both directions with the pistol, then walks out into
the cold air.

The sun is rising above the wide horizon. The city spreads out
in all directions.

Most of the hostel's roof is hidden by a black shed housing the
top of the stairwell and the elevator shaft.

Joona stands with his back to the wall, still out of breath.

The roof is covered with a layer of polished stones, and a narrow
path made of planks has been laid out across it.

Joona looks around and takes a few steps.

There's no one in sight.

Some rusty bolts hold up an antenna with a red light at the top
of it. White bird excrement has trickled down the side of a ventilation unit.

Joona starts to think that he's been tricked, and he'll have to go
back down, when he suddenly sees tracks in the gravel beside the
path.

Something heavy has been dragged across the roof.

Joona starts to run along the side of the shed with the pistol
raised. He aims the gun around the corner and just catches a
glimpse of Jurek before he disappears around the next corner.

Jurek has wrapped Lumi in heavy-duty plastic and tied a thick
rope around the bundle, forming a loop that he can hold over his

shoulder so he can drag her behind him. Joona has no idea if she can breathe, or if she's even alive.

He runs after them.

The stones slide beneath his feet.

He gets back up onto the planks, and runs along the long side of the shed.

Up ahead, Jurek is dragging Lumi toward the edge of the roof between a ventilation unit and a large array of solar panels.

Joona doesn't know if Jurek is armed.

He can hear sirens down in the street.

Joona moves quickly sideways, trying to get a decent line of fire.

The early-morning sun is hitting the solar panels, and the reflection dazzles him.

Jurek vanishes like a shadow behind the glare.

Joona stops, holds his pistol in both hands, and aims at the slender silhouette through the flashes of light.

"Jurek," he shouts.

The sights tremble as he keeps moving sideways. He sees a shot through the reflections and fires as soon as he catches sight of Jurek again.

He squeezes the trigger three times, and hits Jurek in the back with all three shots. The sharp crack of the fire echoes over the rooftops. Jurek stumbles forward, turns around, and draws Lumi's pistol.

Joona fires three more times, right into his chest.

Jurek loses his grip on the gun, and it slips through the slats in the path; then he quickly turns and continues dragging Lumi toward the edge.

He must have picked up a bulletproof vest from Rinus's workshop.

Joona is gaining on them.

Jurek is behind the ventilation unit now. Five large fans are whirring behind thick mesh.

Joona sees him again, aims lower, and shoots him in the thigh. The bullet tears straight through the muscle. Blood sprays out in front of him, the drops sparkling in the sharp sunlight.

Joona moves closer with the pistol raised and his finger on the trigger. He can only see Jurek intermittently through the chimneys and air vents.

Lumi is not getting enough air. Joona can see she's suffocating. Her lips are blue, her eyes wide open. Her sweaty hair is stuck to her face inside the plastic.

Joona's migraine flares behind one eye, and he almost falls.

Jurek lifts Lumi up and limps toward the low edge of the roof.

This is his new plan.

Joona will be too late again.

Jurek wants him to plead and threaten, and then watch his daughter fall.

Joona gets past the ventilation unit, quickly takes aim, and shoots Jurek in his other leg. The bullet hits the back of his knee and exits through his kneecap.

Lumi lands hard on the round stones on the roof. Jurek staggers sideways and falls.

Joona runs forward, still aiming at Jurek. He pulls Lumi away from him and tears through the plastic covering her face.

He hears her gasping for breath and coughing, but he turns back to Jurek, presses the pistol against the back of his head, and squeezes the trigger.

The gun clicks, then clicks again.

Joona pulls the magazine out.

It's empty.

A helicopter is approaching, and he can hear more sirens now.

A small crowd has gathered down in the street in front of the hostel. They're all looking up, filming with their phones.

Joona turns back to Lumi, unties the rope around her, and tears the plastic away.

She's going to be okay.

Jurek is sitting up against one of the chimneys now. His prosthetic arm has come loose and is hanging from its straps.

He's pulling a long plank from the path.

Joona feels pure rage course through him. Pulling the rope behind him, he stops in front of Jurek and ties a noose.

Jurek looks at him with pale eyes, then lets go of the plank. His wrinkled face betrays no sign of pain or anger.

Joona widens the noose and sees that Jurek is slipping into shock from loss of blood.

"I'm already dead," Jurek says, still trying to fend off the rope with his hand.

Joona grabs the hand and twists, breaking the arm at the elbow. Jurek lets out a groan, then looks at him again and moistens his lips.

"If you look into the abyss, the abyss looks back at you," he says, making a pointless attempt to move his head away from the noose.

Joona manages to get it around his neck on the second attempt, and tightens the knot at the back of his neck, pulling it so taut that Jurek's breathing becomes a hiss.

"That's enough, Dad, stop it," Lumi pants behind him.

Joona walks over to the back of the solar panels and ties the end of the rope to one of the sturdy supports.

The whirring of the helicopter is getting closer.

Joona drags Jurek to the edge of the roof. The prosthesis drags behind him, then falls off altogether. Jurek tenses his neck, coughs, and tries to breathe.

"Dad, what are you doing?" Lumi asks in a frightened voice. "The police are on their way. He'll spend the rest of his life in prison, and . . ."

Joona drags Jurek to his feet. He's so groggy he can barely stand. Blood is pouring over his shoes from the gunshot wounds.

They can hear voices from the stairwell.

Jurek's broken arm is twitching.

Joona takes a step back and looks into Jurek's eyes.

There's an odd expression in them.

It's as if Jurek is looking for something in Joona's eyes, or trying to see himself reflected in his pupils.

Lumi has turned away, and is crying now.

Jurek staggers and whispers something just as Joona shoves him in the chest with both hands, knocking him over the edge.

Lumi screams.

The rope slips quickly across the smooth stones and over the edge of the roof. It makes a ringing sound as it hits the side of the building and pulls taut. A window below shatters, and fragments of glass fall on the crowd gathered on the pavement. The solar panel next to Joona sways and creaks.

Joona runs toward the stairwell, pushes aside the caretaker who tries to stop him, and hurries down the stairs to the twentieth floor. He hears the screaming before he even reaches the hallway. The door to one of the suites opens and a woman stumbles out, dressed in only jeans and a bra.

Joona walks past her into the room, then closes and locks the door behind him.

The window is broken, and fragments of glass are glinting on the gray carpet and bed.

Jurek is swinging gently in and out through the window.

He's dead—his spinal column has snapped.

Blood is running from the deep furrow cut by the noose.

Joona stands in front of Jurek and looks at the thin, wrinkled face and pale eyes.

The body swings back into the room again.

Joona feels an incredible fatigue wash over him.

Jurek Walter is dead.

He won't be coming back.

The body sways back and forth slowly. The blood from the gunshot wounds drips from his feet, leaving a thin trail across the carpet and window frame.

Joona isn't sure how long he's been standing there staring at Jurek when the lock on the door clicks behind his back.

Lumi walks in and tells him very gently that he has to leave.

"It's over, Dad," Lumi whispers.

"Yes," he replies.

Lumi puts her arm around his waist and leads him out of the room.

95

VALERIA IS DOZING IN HER BED IN THE INTENSIVE-CARE unit, thinking about the conversation she just had with Saga.

Pellerina's condition is deteriorating. Her heart has started racing again, and defib is no longer working.

Saga was pale, with dark rings under her eyes. She was so agitated that she could barely stand still and was constantly brushing hair away from her face. All she wanted to talk about were Valeria's conversations with Pellerina.

"It felt a little like we were holding hands," Valeria said to calm Saga down.

Saga nodded, but was clearly having trouble concentrating.

When Valeria didn't get any response from Pellerina, she was convinced they had moved Pellerina into the house. Clearly, she had actually lost consciousness by that point.

A nurse with braided hair and a silver eyebrow ring came in to give Valeria more morphine for the pain in her hands and feet.

Saga hurried back to the surgery department.

Now Valeria's pain is fading, and the room grows darker as her pupils contract. Everything looks fuzzy. The lights all grow into ragged circles, like big brass cogs.

The nurse is standing beside her bed, checking her temperature and blood pressure. Valeria can no longer make out her face, it's just a dark blur.

Her body feels warm, and pleasantly tingly.

When the nurse leans over and explains something to her, Valeria sees that the buttons on her scrubs now have a yellowish tint. Valeria is on the verge of asking a question when she forgets all about it.

Her eyelids are getting heavier.

The police officers outside her room have finally stopped talking about soccer.

WHEN VALERIA WAKES UP, SHE OPENS HER EYES, BUT STILL can't really see.

A different nurse is checking the EKG and blood levels. She has no idea how long she's been asleep.

She tries to focus on the drip regulator and the glistening drops running into the tube.

Everything slides away again, and she shuts her eyes as the nurse makes her comfortable. Valeria is almost asleep when the phone rings.

"My phone," she mumbles weakly, opening her eyes.

The nurse picks it up from the bedside table and passes it to her. She can't read the screen, but she answers anyway.

"Valeria," she says in a tired voice.

"It's me," Joona says. "How are you?"

"Joona?" she asks.

"How are you?"

"Fine, just a bit groggy from the drugs, but . . ."

"And Pellerina?"

"Not good . . . Her heart isn't beating properly, it's too fast. . . . It's terrible," she replies.

"Did you speak to Saga?"

The nurse calmly and methodically wipes the cannula with rubbing alcohol.

She can tell from Joona's voice that he's different, that something has happened.

"I'm afraid to ask," she says quietly.

"Lumi's fine," Joona says.

"Thank God."

"Yes."

Neither of them says anything. The nurse connects a syringe to the cannula and checks it.

"What happened?" Valeria asks, watching as blood gets sucked into the tube and mixes with the fluid in the syringe.

"Jurek's dead."

"Jurek Walter's dead?"

"Yes . . . it's over," Joona says.

"You finally stopped him."

"Yes."

The nurse puts something on the cart beside the bed, then leaves the room.

"You're not hurt, are you?" Valeria asks, closing her eyes again.

"No, but I'm going to be here for a while. I need to answer some questions."

"Are you going to end up in prison again?" she asks. She hears the door close softly.

"I'll be okay. I've got Interpol and the International Liaison Office back home behind me," he replies.

"You sound sad," Valeria says.

"I'm just worried about you, and Saga and Pellerina. . . . They haven't cut back on the security, have they?"

"This hospital's crawling with cops. There are two right outside the door, twenty-four hours a day. It feels like being back in prison."

"Valeria, you need protection."

"I'd feel better if you came home."

"Lumi's going back to Paris tomorrow."

"I'd like to go, too."

"I'll pick you up as soon as I'm done here."

"Just need to change into some better clothes."

"I love you," he says quietly.

"I've always loved you," she replies.

They end the call. Valeria smiles. Her eyes are burning with fatigue. She falls asleep with the phone in her hand, thinking about Joona coming back.

When she wakes up again, the morphine has faded, and she feels a little nauseated.

The police officers outside her door are talking soccer again.

She's lying on her back, staring up at the ceiling.

Her vision has come back and she can see clearly.

One of the ceiling tiles has a damp gray patch on it that looks like a photograph of one of the moon's craters.

She's thirsty. She turns her head to look at the bedside table, but her eye gets caught on the tube leading into her left elbow.

A syringe full of clear liquid is still attached to the cannula.

She thinks back to the nurse who was with her when she was talking to Joona. The injection was prepared, but never finished: the nurse just left the room without a word.

There's a small, empty glass bottle on the metal trolley beside the bed. Valeria reaches out for it and turns it around in her hand.

"Ketalar 50 mg/ml," she reads on the label. A drug used to sedate people for operations.

She can't understand why they were going to sedate her. No one said anything to her about an operation.

While she was talking to Joona, she glanced at the nurse cleaning the cannula in her arm. She doesn't remember the face—everything was too blurry—but she did notice the beautiful pearl hanging from the nurse's earlobe.

Chalk-white, with a sort of creamy glow around it.

Valeria remembers feeling like a small child while the nurse was fussing over her.

The woman was at least six feet tall, she thinks, and shudders.

96

SAGA IS WAITING FOR THE NEW CARDIOLOGIST IN THE HEART Clinic's intensive-care unit. Her face is tight with anxiety and exhaustion. There's a crumpled paper cup on the table in front of her.

She brushes a stray lock of hair from her cheek with an agitated gesture, then leans forward so she can see down the hall.

"This is hopeless," she whispers to herself.

She stares blankly at the aquarium with its little shoals of neon tetras and thinks back to the time Joona came to her dad's house to beg her to flee with her family. She remembers feeling sorry for him, thinking that he'd lost it.

When Joona realized she wasn't going to hide, he warned her about meeting Jurek.

Saga gets up from the chair and walks out into the hallway.

She remembers feeling insulted by his warnings: she had spent more time with Jurek than Joona had.

She was ignoring the fact that Joona had lived with Jurek's presence for years, that he had been preparing for the coming confrontation for a long time.

Joona's first piece of advice was to kill Jurek immediately, no matter what.

The second was that Jurek thinks and behaves like a twin. And to remember that, with his new accomplice, he could be in two places at the same time.

The last piece of advice concerned a hypothetical situation in which Jurek had taken a member of her family. If that happened, Joona said, "you need to remember that you can't make deals with him, because they'll never work in your favor. He won't let go, and with each one you make, you'll end up deeper in his trap."

If only she had heeded any of that advice, she'd still have her old life.

Saga knows she betrayed Joona. Not intentionally, but contacting Patrik was what led Jurek to Lumi's hiding place. It was almost as if Jurek had chosen her to do it, had made her a Judas figure.

Her thoughts are interrupted when a woman in her fifties with shoulder-length blond hair and no makeup comes over and introduces herself as Magdalena Herbstman. She's the current cardiologist responsible for Pellerina's care.

"I know that you're worried about your sister," she says, sitting down.

"The last doctor said that her heart's beating too fast due to the hypothermia," Saga says, clenching her jaw tightly.

Herbstman nods and frowns. "It's a lot to take in, but, yes, the cold temperature led to a serious disturbance in the rhythm in one chamber of her heart, so-called ventricular tachycardia, VT. . . . And when her heart is racing, it puts your sister's body under a lot of strain. At first, the tachycardia was working itself out—that's often what happens—but last night it got even faster and went on for longer, which is why we tried to stop it with defibrillation and medication."

"I thought that helped," Saga says, starting to bounce one of her legs nervously.

"It did at first . . . but the problem is so severe that she's ended up in what's known as an electrical storm, repeated sequences of tachycardia. We're keeping her sedated and are preparing for ablation."

"Ablation?" Saga asks, brushing the hair from her face.

"I'm going to insert a catheter into her heart, try to identify the area that's sending out the wrong impulses, and create some scar tissue there instead."

"What does that do?"

"I want to scorch off the tiny area that's causing the problem. If that works, her heart should start beating normally again."

"You mean she's going to be all right?"

"I always try to be honest. . . . Your sister's condition is critical, but I promise I will do the best I can," Herbstman says, standing up.

"I have to be with her," Saga says, getting up so abruptly that her chair slams into the wall. "I need to see what's happening. I'm going crazy sitting here waiting."

"You can sit with my clinical assistant."

"Thank you," Saga whispers, and follows the doctor down the hall.

Saga needs the cardiologist to realize that she and Pellerina are real people, not just patients passing through, not just part of her ordinary workday. Maybe she should tell her that her dad was a cardiologist, and worked at the Karolinska Institute in Solna. They may have known each other.

Saga is shown through a door into what looks like the control room in a recording studio, with a huge array of screens and computers. She can hear clattering sounds and muffled voices over a loudspeaker.

It all feels like a dream.

There are EKG readings on various screens, the contractions marked by a regular bleep.

She says hello to an older woman but doesn't catch her name. The woman's glasses are hanging around her neck on a gold chain.

Saga mumbles her own name, then walks slowly toward the glass wall.

There are at least five people in the brightly lit operating room. They're all wearing pale-blue scrubs, and masks over their mouths.

A small figure is lying motionless on the operating table.

Saga can't believe that's her younger sister.

The older woman says something and pulls out an office chair for Saga. The cardiologist has entered the operating room.

Saga stops in front of the glass wall.

There's a blue sheet covering Pellerina's hips, her upper body is bare, and she has an oxygen mask over her face.

Saga stares at her little sister. Two defibrillator pads are attached to her chest, diagonally, on either side of her heart.

Saga brushes the hair from her face.

She tells herself that if Pellerina gets better it will mean that she didn't get there too late. She will have managed to save her sister after all.

If Pellerina survives, then there is a point to it all.

The older woman taps something on one of the computers, then explains calmly that she's going to be keeping an eye on everything.

"You can sit down," she says. "I promise that I—"

She breaks off, presses the button on the microphone, and tells the team in the room that another electrical storm is on its way.

Saga looks at her sister; she's lying perfectly still, but on the EKG screens her heartbeat starts to race alarmingly.

There's a loud whining sound from the operating room as the defibrillator charges. The team back away just before it goes off.

Pellerina's body jerks violently, then lies still.

It looked like someone hit her in the back with a baseball bat.

Her heart starts to race again.

The alarm goes off.

There's another bang, and Pellerina's body jerks up.

Saga stumbles sideways and grabs the desk for support.

The defibrillator whines as it charges again.

Another bang.

Her sister's shoulders fly up, and her skin quivers.

The older woman speaks into the microphone, informing her colleagues in the operating room of the various readings.

Pellerina's heart is beating even faster.

The team backs away from her sister, and there's another bang.

Her body jerks upward.

Tears are streaming down Saga's cheeks.

Someone adjusts the blue sheet covering Pellerina's hips, then steps back moments before the next shock.

They defibrillate her sister eleven times to break the recurring VT episodes, and eventually her heart calms down and the readings return to normal.

"Dear God," Saga whispers, sinking down onto her chair. She wipes the tears from her face.

Everything that's happened, everything that's happening right now—it's all her fault, she's responsible for it.

She was the one who revealed Pellerina's hiding place to Jurek. She was confused and numb after their father's death, and she just wanted to get her sister and hide her away somewhere.

Saga stopped buzzing the apartment, realizing that what she was doing was too dangerous, but by then the damage had been done. She had already shown him the way.

SAGA IS BACK ON HER FEET, AND CAN FEEL HER LEGS SHAKING as she stands in front of the glass wall facing the brightly lit operating room, watching the cardiologist work calmly and methodically.

She has inserted a tube into Pellerina's right thigh, and is working through the veins to her heart in order to find the area where the impulses that make her heart race are triggered.

Using fluoroscopy, she can see the exact position of the tube on a large screen. The cardiologist and her assistant seem to agree on the location.

Saga knows that they need to hurry and finish before the next storm starts.

Everyone in the room is working in silence, concentrating.

They all know what they have to do.

The cardiologist is studying a three-dimensional image of Pellerina's heart. She slowly adjusts the catheter, then begins the ablation.

A piercing sound cuts through the room as the doctor burns away the tissue.

The catheter moves a tiny bit.

Saga keeps telling herself that Pellerina wasn't scared in her coffin, because Valeria was with her the whole time.

She wasn't scared of the dark then, and she isn't scared of the dark now.

The older woman says something into the microphone, sounding distressed.

Saga glances quickly at the EKG screens. The waves are getting closer together.

"Prepare for defibrillation," the assistant says loudly.

The cardiologist tries, right up to the last second, to burn away another area, while the ringing tone merges with the whine of the charging defibrillator.

The assistant reads out the measurements into the microphone.

The members of the team step back, and an instant later there's a bang.

Pellerina's chest jolts, and her head sways sideways.

Another storm has begun.

Saga realizes that Pellerina isn't going to be able to cope with this much longer.

The screens show that her heart is beating too quickly, but her sister is lying on the operating table perfectly still now, as if nothing were happening inside her.

There's another bang, then another.

Her heart is still racing.

The cardiologist is sweating. She says something in an agitated voice, then moves the tube and tries to ablate Pellerina's heart again.

The anesthesiologist's hands are shaking when she checks the oxygen supply.

They make another attempt with the defibrillator.

Another bang, but her heart doesn't slow down; then, suddenly, the line on the EKG screens goes flat.

The system sets off an alarm.

The team starts to massage Pellerina's heart. The cardiologist has stepped back slightly and pulled off her mask. She stares intently at the screen, then walks out.

Saga stands behind the glass wall, looking at the man whose hands are pressing her sister's chest in an even rhythm.

The door opens, and the cardiologist comes in. She walks over to Saga and says she needs to speak with her.

Saga doesn't answer, just pulls her arm away when the cardiologist tries to comfort her.

"I wanted to tell you in person. We weren't able to find the area causing your sister's ventricular tachycardia," she says. "We tried everything, but we weren't able to stop that last attack."

"Try again," Saga says.

"I'm sorry, but it's too late. We're going to have to stop all attempts at resuscitation."

The cardiologist walks out. The man stops massaging Pellerina's heart.

Saga puts both hands on the glass.

They remove the defibrillator paddles from Pellerina's body.

Saga feels like screaming.

She turns and heads for the door past the assistant. She doesn't hear what the woman says as she walks into the operating room.

The monitors are switched off, and the room falls silent as the tube is removed.

Someone pulls the pale-blue sheet up over Pellerina's chest.

Everything is too quiet.

The lights above the operating table are turned off. The lights were so bright before that at first it feels like it's gone completely dark, but the room is still perfectly light.

The members of the team drift off, like ripples in a pool of water.

Leaving Pellerina behind at the center of the rings.

The plastic covers of the lamps tick as they cool.

Saga approaches her dead sister as if in a trance. They can't stop, they can't give up.

The oxygen mask has left a pink mark on Pellerina's pale face.

You have to try again, Saga thinks.

Her legs threaten to buckle beneath her as she gets closer.

She grasps her sister's limp hand.

"I'm here now," she whispers.

The nurses clear the equipment away.

Saga has never felt so exhausted. She wants to lie down beside her sister, but the operating table is too narrow.

There are drops of blood on the plastic floor next to a cart full of hemostats, scissors, and scalpels.

The light reflects off the metal onto the ceiling.

Saga sways as she looks at her sister's little hand, then at her sunken mouth and pink eyelids.

It's all her fault. She thought that she had the situation under control, that she could deceive Jurek, but instead she killed her own father and led Jurek to Pellerina's hiding place.

It's her fault that Pellerina is dead now.

Saga leans over her sister, strokes her cheek, then straightens up and turns away.

She picks up a scalpel from the trolley and stumbles out of the operating room.

Two police officers are still on duty outside the door. She doesn't hear what they say to her.

The automatic doors at the end of the hall swing open for a group of nurses.

Saga turns right and goes into the bathroom, locks the door behind her, and walks over to the sink.

They're all dead—her mother, her father, her sister.

It's all her fault.

She presses the sharp blade of the scalpel to her left wrist and makes an incision. The blade sinks through the skin and taut veins, ligaments, and muscle, almost without resistance, right down to the bone.

When the scalpel cuts through the artery, the first jet of blood shoots up across the mirror and tiles. Tiny red dots splatter the toilet lid and cistern.

She gasps at the burning pain from the incision.

The blood is pumping out in strong pulses, hitting the edge of the sink before running down the drain.

Her heart starts to beat faster and faster to compensate for the loss in pressure.

She reaches out for the wall to keep her balance.

Her legs are about to give out.

She sits down on the toilet lid and holds her arm over the sink. Her fingers are ice-cold.

There's a blue plastic shoe-cover on the floor. Daylight reaches in through the crack under the door.

She's breathing faster now, and leans her head back against the wall, closing her eyes. She feels nothing but relief.

This is where she's been headed for years.

She hears a knock, but it's distant, as if it's coming from a different world.

Her pulse is roaring in her ears. It reminds her of a train racing over the track.

Her arm falls from the sink.

Saga opens her eyes and stares blankly at the white walls. She's forgotten where she is. She can't find the energy to raise her arm again. The blood runs over her hand and drips onto the floor.

She doesn't hear when the knocks on the door turn into thuds.

The cut stings badly.

She gasps for breath and closes her eyes again.

A huge angel is gliding across the floor of a ballroom. Its footsteps make no sound at all as it heads straight for her, hitting its head on the large chandelier and making it swing.

Its heavy wings are folded behind its back.

The crystal prisms tinkle; then the noise fades.

The angel stops in front of her and looks at her with a sad yet welcoming gaze.

EPILOGUE

IT'S THE MIDDLE OF MAY, AND THE EVENING IS SURPRISINGLY mild. The Beaver leaves the Grand Hotel and walks past Raoul Wallenberg Square. The water in Nybro Bay is almost still in the hazy light.

He goes into Riche and pushes his way through a group of teens. The music is too loud; the conversations are stupid.

The Beaver is wearing a crumpled linen suit and a pink shirt that keeps coming untucked, revealing his hairless stomach.

The look in his eyes is calm when he sits down on one of the tall bar stools.

"What an evening," he says to the woman sitting on the stool next to him.

"It's wonderful," she says politely before continuing her conversation with a friend.

When the bartender comes over, the Beaver orders five shots of Finlandia vodka.

He looks at the woman's hand resting beside her wineglass. She has neat fingernails and a smooth wedding ring.

A glint of light reflects off the bottle. The bartender lines up the five small glasses and fills them to the brim.

"Perfect," the Beaver says, and knocks back the first.

He looks at the small glass in his hand, turning it around in his fingers before putting it back down on the bar.

The Beaver is currently running a locksmith service in Årsta.

He's put in a bid on a chemical factory in Amiens, in northern France, and is building up a shipping company in Gothenburg.

As he feels the warmth of the alcohol reach his stomach, he thinks back to the time he paid Valeria de Castro a visit in the hospital back in the winter. The plan was to sedate her, then take her to a grave on an island in Lake Mälaren. Because she was tired from the effects of the morphine and didn't recognize him, he was able to prepare the anesthetic syringe without having to resort to violence. She was talking on the phone, and sounded like she was about to drift off to sleep.

The person she was talking to had just told her Jurek was dead.

It sounded like fact, but he remembers thinking that it wasn't necessarily true.

"You finally stopped him," she had said.

When he heard those words, he started to hear the mechanical ticking sound inside his head for a matter of seconds, no more. He saw a large clock face before him, its Roman numerals marked out in brown and gold.

Tick-tock, tick-tock.

The ornate minute hand moved forward one notch and was pointing at the number one as he saw his own face.

He was about to turn back toward Valeria, but his eye was caught by his own reflection in the mirror above the sink instead.

The clock went on ticking and was pointing at the number two before he saw her face.

He was going to die before Valeria, and he had to leave.

He had already left his signature on the mirror, to mock the police.

It was only a game, after all.

Two bearded men sit down next to the Beaver and order a Swedish craft beer. The slightly older one is evidently the other man's boss. They stand with their backs to the bar and talk about capital investments, trying to sound more worldly than they actually are.

The Beaver empties the second glass, then kicks his shoes off onto the floor.

"Please keep your shoes on," the younger man says.

"I'm sorry," the Beaver says. "I suffer from water retention, and my feet are swollen."

"Well, if that's the case . . ." The man grins.

The Beaver nods and carefully raises the third glass to his lips. He downs the burning liquid in one gulp, then puts the glass down.

You have to solve the whole puzzle for the police and hand them the last piece, he thinks. It's like asking a beetle to solve a quadratic equation.

"Nice earrings," the younger man says.

"Thanks," he replies. "I wear them as a tribute to my sister."

"I'm kidding."

"I know," the Beaver says. "Don't worry, it's fine."

The Beaver had walked out of the hospital, and thrown away his ID card, keys, and nurse's uniform when he emerged onto Katrinebergs Street.

Jurek Walter had saved his life, so he had accepted his harsh punishments when he made mistakes. He would take his shirt off himself, and hand Jurek the belt.

But now that Jurek is dead, the Beaver has erased every connection to him. He's destroyed his computers and phones, thrown away the research material and pictures, cleaned and dismantled the guns.

That part of his life is very nearly at an end, he thinks as he downs the last glass of vodka.

"Nearly," he whispers, as he crushes the glass in his hand.

There is just one thing left. A small color photograph that he keeps in his wallet. The crease across the middle looks like a streak of snow, right across Joona Linna's throat.

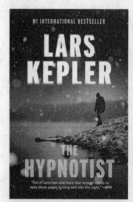 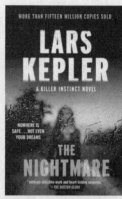 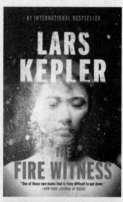
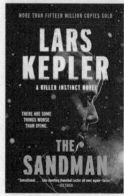  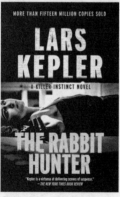